O9-BTO-004

"Pohl has fleshed out the future human civilization in great detail with seemingly minimal touches . . . Pohl throws us one new concept after another . . . In a final burst of extrapolative brilliance, Pohl answers all *necessary* questions about the Heechee, and portions out some outstanding cosmological speculations. This is one to press into the hands of skeptical unbelievers."—*Heavy Metal*

". . . an engrossing story, a different but worthy successor to *Gateway*."—*Publishers Weekly*

"Certainly very few books have ever held my attention in such an iron grip right up until the last paragraph, built so irresistably to such satisfying *series* of blockbuster punch lines, left me so breathless with admiration, achieved such truly cosmic scope."
—*Analog Science Fiction Magazine*

BEYOND
THE BLUE
EVENT HORIZON

Frederik Pohl

A Del Rey Book

BALLANTINE BOOKS • NEW YORK

CONTENTS

1

Wan

It was not easy to live, being young, being so completely alone. "Go to the gold, Wan, steal what you want, learn. Don't be afraid," the Dead Men told him. But how could he not be afraid? The silly but worrisome Old Ones used the gold passages. They might be found anywhere in them, most likely at the ends of them, where the gold skeins of symbols ran endlessly into the center of things. That is, exactly where the Dead Men kept coaxing him to go. Perhaps he had to go there, but he could not help being afraid.

Wan did not know what would happen if the Old Ones ever caught him. The Dead Men probably knew, but he could not make any sense out of their ramblings on the subject. Once long ago, when Wan was tiny—when his parents were still alive, it was that long ago—his father had been caught. He had been gone for a long time and then had come back to their green-lit home. He was shaking, and two-year-old Wan had seen that his father was afraid and had screamed and roared because that was so frightening to him.

Nevertheless he had to go to the gold, whether the grave old frog-jawed ones were there or not, because that was where the books were. The Dead Men were well enough. But they were tedious, and touchy, and often obsessed. The best sources of knowledge were books, and to get them Wan had to go where they were.

The books were in the passages that gleamed gold. There were other passages, green and red and blue, but there were no books there. Wan disliked the blue corridors, because they were cold and dead, but that was where the Dead Men were. The green was used up. He spent most of his time where the winking red cobwebs of light were spread against the walls and the hoppers still held food; he was sure to be untroubled there, but he was also alone. The gold was still in use, and therefore rewarding, and therefore also perilous. And now he was there, cursing fretfully to himself—but under his breath—because he was stuck. Bloody damn Dead Men! Why did he listen to their blathering?

He huddled, trembling, in the insufficient shelter of a berry bush, while two of the foolish Old Ones stood thoughtfully plucking berries from its opposite side and placing them precisely into their froggy mouths. It was unusual, really, that they should be so idle. Among the reasons Wan despised the Old Ones was that they were always busy, always fixing and carrying and chattering, as though driven. Yet here these two were, idle as Wan himself.

Both of them had scraggly beards, but one also had breasts. Wan recognized her as a female he had seen a dozen times before; she was the one who was most diligent in pasting colored bits of something—paper? plastic?—onto her sari, or sometimes onto her sallow, mottled skin. He did not think they would see him, but he was greatly relieved when, after a time, they turned together and moved away. They did not speak. Wan had almost never heard any of the grave old frog-jaws speak. He did not understand them when they did. Wan spoke six languages well—his father's Spanish, mother's English, the German, the Russian, the Cantonese and the Finnish of one or another of the Dead Men. But what the frog-jaws spoke he did not comprehend at all.

As soon as they had retreated down the golden corridor—quick, run, grab! Wan had three books and was gone, safely back in a red corridor. It might be that the Old Ones had seen him, or perhaps not. They did not react quickly. That was why he had been able to avoid them so long. A few days in the passages, and then he was gone. By the time they had become aware he was around, he wasn't; he was back in the ship, away.

He carried the books back to the ship on top of a pannier of food packets. The drive accumulators were nearly recharged. He could leave whenever he liked, but it was better to charge them all the way and he did not think there was any need to hurry. He spent most of an hour filling plastic bags with water for the tedious journey. What a pity there were no readers in the ship to make it less tedious! And then, wearying of the labor, he decided to say good-bye to the Dead Men. They might, or might not, respond, or even care. But he had no one else to talk to.

Wan was fifteen years old, tall, stringy, very dark by nature and darker still from the lights in the ship, where he spent so much of his time. He was strong and self-reliant. He had to be. There was always food in the hoppers, and other goods for the taking, when he dared. Once or twice a year, when they remembered, the Dead Men would catch him with their little mobile machine and take him to a cubicle in the blue passages for a boring day during which he was given a rather complete physical examination. Sometimes he had a tooth filled, usually he received some long-acting vitamin and mineral shots, and once they had fitted him with glasses. But he refused to wear them. They also reminded him, when he neglected it too long, to study and learn, both from them and from the storehouses of books. He did not need much reminding. He enjoyed learning. Apart from that, he was wholly on his own. If he wanted clothes, he went into the gold and stole them from the Old Ones. If he was bored, he invented something to do. A few days in the passages, a few weeks on the ship, a few more days in the other place, then back to repeat the process. Time passed. He had no one for company, had not had since he was four and his parents disappeared, and had almost forgotten what it was like to have a friend. He did not mind. His life seemed complete enough to him, since he had no other life to compare it with.

Sometimes he thought it would be nice to settle in one place or another, but this was only dreaming. It never reached the stage of intention. For more than eleven years he had been shuttling back and forth like this. The other place had things that civilization did not. It had the dreaming room, where he could lie flat and close his eyes and seem not to feel alone. But he could not live there, in spite of plenty of food and no dangers, because the single water accumulator produced only a trickle. Civilization had much that the outpost did not have: the Dead Men and the books, scary exploring and daring raids for clothes or trinkets, something *happening*. But he could not live there either, because the frog-jaws would surely catch him sooner or later. So he commuted.

The main lobby door to the place of the Dead Men did not open when Wan stepped on the treadle. He almost bumped his nose. Surprised, he stopped and then gingerly pushed against the door, then harder. It took all his strength to force it open. Wan had never had to open it by hand before, though now and then it had hesitated and made disturbing noises. That was an annoyance. Wan had experienced machines that broke down before; it was why the green corridors were no longer very useful. But that was only food and warmth, and there was plenty of that in the red, or even the gold. It was worrisome that anything should go wrong around the Dead Men, because if they broke down he had no others.

Still, all looked normal; the room with the consoles

was brightly fluoresced, the temperature was comfortable and he could hear the faint drone and rare click of the Dead Men behind their panels as they thought their lonely, demented thoughts and did whatever they did when he was not speaking to them. He sat in his chair, shifting his rump as always to accommodate to the ill-designed seat, and pulled the headset down over his ears.

"I am going to the outpost now," he said.

There was no answer. He repeated it in all of his languages, but no one seemed to want to talk. That was a disappointment. Sometimes two or three of them would be eager for company, maybe even more. Then they could all have a nice, long chat, and it would be as though he were not really alone at all. Almost as though he were part of a "family", a word he knew from the books and from what the Dead Men told him, but hardly remembered as a reality. That was good. Almost as good as when he was in the dreaming place, where for a while he could have the illusion of being part of a hundred families, a million families. Hosts of people! But that was more than he could handle for very long. And so, when he had to leave the outpost to return for water, and for the more tangible company of the Dead Men, he was never sorry. But he always wanted to come back to the cramped couch and the velvety metal blanket that covered him in it, and to the dreams.

It was waiting for him; but he decided to give the Dead Men another chance. Even when they were not eager for talk, sometimes they were interestable if addressed directly. He thought for a moment, and then dialed number fifty-seven.

A sad, distant voice in his ear was mumbling to itself: ". . . tried to tell him about the missing mass. Mass! The only mass on *his* mind was twenty kilos of boobs and ass! That floozy, Doris. One look at her and, oh, boy, forget about the mission, forget about me. . . ."

Frowning, Wan poised his finger to cancel. Fifty-seven was such a nuisance! He liked to listen to her when she made sense, because she sounded a little like the way he remembered his mother. But she always seemed to go from astrophysics and space travel and other interesting subjects directly to her own troubles. He spat at the point in the panels behind which he had elected to believe fifty-seven lived—a trick he had learned from the Old Ones—hoping she would say something interesting.

But she didn't seem to intend to. Number fifty-seven —when she was coherent she liked to be called Henrietta—was babbling on about high redshifts and Arnold's infidelities with Doris. Whoever they were. "We could have been heroes," she sobbed, "and a ten-million-dollar grant, maybe more, who knows what they'd pay for the drive? But they kept on sneaking off in the lander, and— Who are you?"

"I'm Wan," the boy said, smiling encouragingly even though he did not think she could see him. She seemed to be coming into one of her lucid times. Usually she didn't know he was speaking to her. "Please keep on talking."

There was a long silence, and then, "NGC 1199," she said. "Sagittarius A West."

Wan waited politely. Another long pause, and then she said, "*He* didn't care about proper motions. He made all his moves with Doris. Half his age! And the brain of a turnip. She should never have been on the mission in the first place—"

Wan wobbled his head like a frog-jawed Old One. "You are very boring," he said severely, and switched her off. He hesitated, then dialed the professor, number fourteen:

". . . although Eliot was still a Harvard undergraduate, his imagery was that of a fully mature man. And a genius at that. 'I should have been a pair of ragged claws.' The self-deprecation of mass man carried to its symbolic limit. How does he see himself? Not merely as a crustacean. Not *even* as a crustacean, only the very *abstraction* of a crustacean: claws. And ragged, at that. In the next line we see—"

Wan spat again at the panel as he disconnected; the whole face of the wall was stained with the marks of his displeasure. He liked when Doc recited poetry, not so much when he talked about it. With the craziest of the Dead Men, like fourteen and fifty-seven, you didn't have any choice about what happened. They rarely responded, and almost never in a way that seemed relevant, and you either listened to what they happened to be saying or you turned them off.

It was almost time for him to go, but he tried one more time: the only one with a three-digit number, his special friend, Tiny Jim. "Hello, Wan." The voice was sad and sweet. It tingled in his mind, like the sudden *frisson* of fear that he felt near the Old Ones. "It is you, Wan, isn't it?"

"That is a foolish question. Who else would it be?"

"One keeps on hoping, Wan." There was a pause, then Tiny Jim suddenly cackled, "Have I told you the one about the priest, the rabbi and the dervish who ran out of food on the planet made of pork?"

"I think you have, Tiny Jim, and anyway I don't want to hear any jokes now."

The invisible loudspeaker clicked and buzzed for a moment, and then the dead man said, "Same old thing, Wan? You want to talk about sex again?"

The boy kept his countenance impassive, but that familiar tingle inside his lower abdomen responded. "We might as well, Tiny Jim."

"You're a raunchy stud for your age, Wan," the Dead Man offered; and then, "Tell you about the time I almost got busted for a sex offense? It was hot as hell. I was going home on the late train to Roselle Park, and this girl came in, sat across the aisle from me, put her feet up, and began to fan herself with her skirt. Well, what would you do? I looked, you know. And she kept on doing it, and I kept looking, and finally around Highlands she complained to the conductor and he threw me off the train. Do you know what the funny thing was?"

Wan was rapt. "No, Tiny Jim," he breathed.

"The funny thing was I'd missed my regular train. I had time to kill in the city, so I went to a porn flick. Two hours of, my God, every combination you could think of. The only way I could've seen more was with a proctoscope, so why was I slouching out over the aisle to peek at her little white panties? But you know what was funnier than that?"

"No, Tiny Jim."

"She was right! I was staring, all right. I'd just been watching acres of crotches and boobs, but I couldn't take my eyes off hers! That wasn't the funniest thing, though. Do you want me to tell you the funniest thing of all?"

"Yes, please, Tiny Jim. I do."

"Why, she got off the train with me! And took me to her home, boy, and we just made out over and over, all night long. Never did catch her name. What do you say to that, Wan?"

"I say, is that true, Tiny Jim?"

Pause. "Aw. No. You take all the fun out of things."

Wan said severely, "I don't want a made-up story, Tiny Jim. I want to learn facts." Wan was angry, and thought of turning the Dead Man off to punish him, but was not sure whom he would be punishing. "I wish you would be nice, Tiny Jim," he coaxed.

"Well—" The bodiless mind clicked and whispered to itself for a moment, sorting through its conversational gambits. Then it said, "Do you want to know why mallard drakes rape their mates?"

"No!"

"I think you really do, though, Wan. It's interesting. You can't understand primate behavior unless you comprehend the whole spectrum of reproductive strategies. Even strange ones. Even the Acanthocephalan worms. They practice rape, too, and do you know what *Moniliformis dubius* does? They not only rape their females, they even rape competing males. With like plaster of Paris! So the poor Other Worm can't get it up!"

"I don't want to hear all this, Tiny Jim."

"But it's funny, Wan! That must be why they call him 'dubius'!" The Dead Man was chuckling mechanically, a-*heh*! A-*heh*!

"Stop it, Tiny Jim!" But Wan was not just angry any more. He was hooked. It was his favorite subject, as Tiny Jim's willingness to talk about it, at length and in variety, was what made him Wan's favorite among the Dead Men. Wan unwrapped a food packet and, munching, said, "What I really want to hear is how to make out, Tiny Jim, please?"

If the Dead Man had had a face it would have shown the strain to trying to keep from laughing, but he said kindly, " 'Kay, sonny. I know you keep hoping. Let's see, did I tell you to watch their eyes?"

"Yes, Tiny Jim. You said if their pupils dilate it means they are sexually aroused."

"Right. And I mentioned the existence of the sexually dimorphic structures in the brain?"

"I don't think I know what that means, exactly."

"Well, I don't, either, but it's anatomically so. They're different, Wan, inside *and* out."

"Please, Tiny Jim, keep telling me about the differences!" The Dead Man did, and Wan listened absorbedly. There was always time to go to the ship, and Tiny Jim was unusually coherent. All of the Dead Men had their own special subjects that they zeroed in to talk about, as though each had been frozen with one big thought in his mind. But even on the favored topics you could not always expect them to make sense. Wan pushed the mobile unit that they used to catch him—when it was working—out of the way and sprawled on the floor, chin in hands, while the Dead Man chattered and reminisced and explained courtship, and gifting, and making your move.

It was fascinating, even though he had heard it before. He listened until the Dead Man slowed down, hesitated, and stopped. Then the boy said, to confirm a theory:

"Teach me, Tiny Jim. I read a book in which a male and a female copulated. He hit her on the head and copulated her while she was unconscious. That appears to me an efficient way to 'love', Tiny Jim, but in other stories it takes much longer. Why is this?"

"That was not love, sonny. That was what I was

telling you about. Rape. Rape is a bad idea for people, even if it works for mallard ducks."

Wan nodded and urged him on: "Why, Tiny Jim?"

Pause. "I will demonstrate it for you mathematically, Wan," the Dead Man said at last. "Attractive sex objects may be defined as female, no more than five years younger than you are, no more than fifteen years older. These figures are normalized to your present age, and are also only approximate. Attractive sex objects may further be characterized by visual, olfactory, tactile, and aural qualities stimulating to you, in descending weighted order of significance plotted against probability of access. Do you understand me so far?"

"Not really."

Pause. "Well, that's all right for now. Now pay attention. On the basis of those four preliminary traits, some females will attract you. Up to the point of contact you will not know about other traits which may repel, harm or detumesce you. 5/28 of subjects will be menstruating. 3/87 will have gonorrhea, 2/95 syphilis. 1/17 will have excessive bodily hair, skin blemishes or other physical deformities concealed by clothing. Finally, 2/71 will conduct themselves offensively during intercourse, 1/16 will emit an unpleasant odor, 3/7 will resist rape so extensively as to diminish your enjoyment; these are subjective values quantified to match your known psychological profile. Cumulating these fractions, the odds are better than six to one that you will not receive maximum pleasure from rape."

"Then I must not copulate a woman without wooing?"

"That's right, boy. Not counting it's against the law."

Wan was thoughtfully silent for a moment, then remembered to ask, "Is all this true, Tiny Jim?"

Cackle of glee. "Got you that time, kid! Every word."

Wan pouted like a frog-jaw. "That was not very exciting, Tiny Jim. In fact, you have detumesced me."

"What do you expect, kid?" Tiny Jim said sullenly. "You told me not to make up any stories. Why are you being so unpleasant?"

"I am getting ready to leave. I do not have much time."

"You don't have anything else!" cackled Tiny Jim.

"And you have nothing to say that I want to hear," said Wan cruelly. He disconnected them all, and angrily he went to the ship and squeezed the launch control. It did not occur to him that he was being rude to the only friends he had in the universe. It had never occurred to him that their feelings mattered.

2

On the Way to the
Oort Cloud

On the twelve hundred and eighty-second day of our all-expense-paid joyride on the way to the Oort Cloud, the big excitement was the mail. Vera tinkled joyously and we all came to collect it. There were six letters for my horny little half-sister-in-law from famous movie stars—well, they're not all movie stars. They're just famous and good-looking jocks that she writes to, because she's only fourteen years old and needs some kind of male to dream about, and that write back to her, I think, because their press agents tell them it's going to be good publicity. A letter from the old country for Payter, my father-in-law. A long one, in German. They want him to come back to Dortmund and run for mayor or Bürgermeister or something. Assuming, of course, that he is still alive when he gets back, which is only an assumption for any of the four of us. But they don't give up. Two private letters to my wife, Lurvy, I assume from ex-boyfriends. And a letter to all of us from poor Trish Bover's widower, or maybe husband, depending on whether you considered Trish alive or dead:

> Have you seen any trace of Trish's ship?
> Hanson Bover

Short and sweet, because that's all he could afford, I guess. I told Vera to send him the same reply as always —"Sorry, no." I had plenty of time to take care of that correspondence, because there was nothing for Paul C. Hall, who is me.

There is usually not much for me, which is one of the reasons I play chess a lot. Payter tells me I'm lucky to be on the mission at all, and I suppose I wouldn't be if he hadn't put his own money into it, financing his whole family. Also his skills, but we've all done that. Payter is a food chemist. I'm a structural engineer. My wife, Dorema—it's better not to call her that, and we mostly call her "Lurvy"—is a pilot. Damn good one, too. Lurvy is younger than I am, but she was on Gateway for six years. Never scored, came back next to broke, but she learned a lot. Not just about piloting. Sometimes I look at Lurvy's arms with the five Out bangles, one for each of her Gateway missions; and her hands, hard and sure on the ship controls, warm and warming when we touch . . . I don't know much about what happened to her on Gateway. Perhaps I shouldn't.

And the other one is her little jailbait half-sister, Janine. Ah, Janine! Sometimes she was fourteen years old, and sometimes forty. When she was fourteen she wrote her gushy letters to her movie stars and played with her toys—a ragged, stuffed armadillo, a Heechee prayer fan (real) and a fire-pearl (fake) which her father had bought her to tempt her onto the trip. When she was forty what she mostly wanted to play with was me. And there we are. In each other's pockets for three and a half years. Trying not to need to commit murder.

We were not the only ones in space. Once in a great while we would get a message from our nearest neighbors, the Triton base or the exploring ship that had got itself lost. But Triton, with Neptune, was well ahead of us in its orbit—round-trip message time, three weeks. And the explorer had no power to waste on us, though they were now only fifty light-hours away. It was not like a friendly natter over the garden hedge.

So what I did, I played a lot of chess with our ship-board computer.

There's not an awful lot to do on the way to the Oort except play games, and besides it was a good way to stay noncombatant in The War Between Two Women that continually raged in our little ship. I can stand my father-in-law, if I have to. Mostly he keeps to himself, as much as he can in four hundred cubic meters. I can't always stand his two crazy daughters, even though I love them both.

All this would have been easier to take if we had had more room—I told myself that—but there is no way to go for a cooling-down walk around the block when you are in a spaceship. Once in a while a quick EVA to check the side-cargos, yes, and then I could look around—the sun still the brightest star in its constellation, but only just; Sirius ahead of us was brighter, and so was Alpha Centauri, off below the ecliptic and to the side. But that was only an hour at a time, and then back inside the ship. Not a luxury ship. A human-made antique of a spaceship that was never planned for more than a six-month mission and that we had to stay cooped up in for three and a half years. My God! We must have been crazy to sign up. What good is a couple million dollars when getting it drives you out of your head?

Our shipboard brain was a lot easier to get along with. When I played chess with her, hunched over the console with the big headset over my ears, I could shut out Lurvy and Janine. The brain's name was Vera, which was just my own conceit and had nothing to do with her, I mean its, gender. Or with her truthfulness, either, because I had instructed her she could joke with me sometimes. When Vera was downlinked with the big computers that were in orbit or back on Earth, she was very, very smart. But she couldn't carry on a conversa-tion that way, because of the 25-day round-trip communications time, and so when she wasn't in link she was very, very dumb—

"Pawn to king's rook four, Vera."

"Thank you . . ." Long pause, while she checked my parameters to make sure who she was talking to and what she was supposed to be doing, "Paul. Bishop takes knight."

I could beat the ass off Vera when we played chess, unless she cheated. How did she cheat? Well, after I had won maybe two hundred games from her she won one. And then I won about fifty, and then she won one, and another, and for the next twenty games we were about even and then she began to clobber me every time. Until I figured out what she was doing. She was transmitting position and plans to the big computers on Earth and then, when we recessed games, as we sometimes did, because Payter or one of the women would drag me away from the set, she would have time to get Downlink-Vera's criticism of her plans and suggestions to amend her strategies. The big machines would tell Vera what they thought my strategies might be, and how to counteract them; and when Downlink-Vera guessed right, Shipboard-Vera had me. I never bothered to make her stop. I just didn't recess games any more, and then after a while we were so far away that there just wasn't time for her to get help and I went back to beating her every game.

And the chess games were about the only games I won, those three and a half years. There was no way for me to win anything in the big one that kept going on between my wife, Lurvy, and her horny fourteen-year-old half-sister, Janine. Old Payter was a long time between begats, and Lurvy tried to be a mother to Janine, who tried to be an enemy to Lurvy. And succeeded. It wasn't all Janine's fault. Lurvy would take a few drinks —that was her way of relieving the boredom—and then she would discover that Janine had used her toothbrush, or that Janine had unwillingly done as she had been told and cleaned up the food-preparation area before it began to stink, but hadn't put the organics in the digester. Then they were off. From time to time they would go through ritualized performances of woman talk, punctuated by explosions—

"I really love those blue pants on you, Janine. Do you want me to tack that seam?"

"All *right*, so I'm getting *fat*, is that what you're saying? Well, it's better than drinking myself *stupid* all the time!"—and then back to blow-drying each other's hair. And I would go back to playing chess with Vera. It was the only safe thing to do. Every time I tried to intervene I achieved instant success by uniting them against me: "Fucking male chauvinist pig, why don't *you* scrub the kitchen floor?"

The funny thing was, I did love them both. In different ways, of course, though I had trouble getting that across to Janine.

We were told what we were getting into when we signed up for the mission. Besides the regular long-voyage psychiatric briefing, all four of us went through a dozen session hours on the problem during the pre-flight, and what the shrink said boiled down to "do the best you can." It appeared that during the refamilying process I would have to learn to parent. Payter was too old, even if he was the biological father. Lurvy was undomestic, as you would expect from a former Gateway pilot. It was up to me; the shrink was very clear about that. It just didn't say how.

So there I was at forty-one, umpty zillion kilometers from Earth, way past the orbit of Pluto, about fifteen degrees out of the plane of the ecliptic, trying not to make love to my half-sister-in-law, trying to make peace with my wife, trying to maintain the truce with my father-in-law. Those were the big things that I woke up with (every time I was allowed to go to sleep), just staying alive for another day. To get my mind off them, I would try to think about the two million dollars apiece we would get for completing the mission. When even that failed I would try to think about the long-range importance of our mission, not just to us, but to every human being alive. That was real enough. If it all worked out, we would be keeping most of the human race from dying of starvation.

That was obviously important. Sometimes it even *seemed* important. But it was the human race that had jammed us all into this smelly concentration-camp for what looked like forever; and there were times when— you know?—I kind of hoped they *would* starve.

Day 1283. I was just waking up when I heard Vera beeping and crackling to herself, the way she does when there's an action message coming in. I unzipped the restraining sheet and pushed myself out of our private, but old Payter was already hanging over the printer.

He swore creakily. "*Gott sei dammt!* We have a course changing." I caught hold of a rail and pushed myself over to see, but Janine, busily inspecting her cheekbones for pimples in the wall mirror, got there ahead of me. She ducked her head in front of Payter's, read the message, and slid herself away disdainfully. Payter worked his mouth for a minute and then said savagely, "This does not interest you?" Janine shrugged minutely without looking at him.

Lurvy was coming out of the private after me, zipping up her skivvies. "Leave her alone, Pa," she said. "Paul, go put some clothes on." It was better to do what she said, besides which she was right. The best way to stay out of trouble with Janine was to behave like a puritan. By the time I fished my shorts out of the tangle of sheets, Lurvy had already read the message. Reasonably enough; she was our pilot. She looked up, grinning. "Paul! We have to make a correction in about eleven hours, and maybe it's the last one! Back away," she ordered Payter, who was still hanging over the terminal, and pulled herself down to work Vera's calculator keys. She watched while the trajectories formed, pressed for a solution and then crowed: "Seventy-three hours eight minutes to touchdown!"

"I myself could have done that," her father complained.

"Don't be grouchy, Pa! Three days and we're there. Why, we ought to be able to see it in the scopes when we turn!"

Janine, back to picking at her cheekbones, commented over her shoulder, "We could have been seeing it for *months* if somebody hadn't busted the big scope."

"Janine!" Lurvy was marvelous at holding her temper in—when she was able to do it at all—and this time she managed to stay in control. She said in her voice of quiet reason, "Wouldn't you say this was an occasion for rejoicing, not for starting arguments? Of course you would, Janine. I suggest we all have a drink—you, too."

I stepped in quickly, belting my shorts—I knew the rest of *that* script. "Are you going to use the chemical rockets, Lurvy? Right, then Janine and I will have to go out and check the side-cargos. Why don't we have the drink when we come back?"

Lurvy smiled sunnily. "Good idea, dear. But perhaps Pa and I will have one short one now—then we'll join you for another round later, if you like."

"Suit up," I ordered Janine, preventing her from saying whatever inflammatory remark was in her mind. She obviously had decided to be placatory for the moment, because she did as she was told without comment. We checked each other's seals, let Lurvy and Payter double-check us, crowded one by one into the exit and swung out into space on our tethers. The first thing we both did was look toward home—not very satisfying; the sun was only a bright star and I couldn't see the Earth at all, though Janine usually claimed she could. The second thing was to look toward the Food Factory, but I couldn't see anything there. One star looks a lot like another one, especially down to the lower limits of brightness when there are fifty or sixty thousand of them in the sky.

Janine worked quickly and efficiently, tapping the bolts of the big ion-thrusters strapped to the side of our ship while I inspected for tightness in the steel straps. Janine was really not a bad kid. She was fourteen years old and sexually excitable, true, but it was not at all her fault that she had no satisfactory person to practice being a woman on. Except me and, even less satisfactorily, her father. Everything checked out, as of course we had been pretty sure it would. She was waiting by the stub of the big telescope's mounting by the time I

finished, and a measure of her good humor was that she
didn't even say anything about who let it crack loose
and float away in the crazy time. I let her go back in the
ship first. I took an extra couple of minutes to float out
there. Not because I particularly enjoyed the view.
Only because those minutes in space were about the
only time I had had in three and a half years to be
anything approaching alone.

We were still moving at better than three kilometers
a second, but of course you couldn't tell that with nothing around to compare. It felt a lot as though we
weren't moving at all. It had felt that way, a lot, for all
of the three and a half years. One of the stories we had
all been hearing for all that time from old Peter—he
pronounces it "Pay-ter"—was about his father, the S.S.
Werewolf. The werewolf couldn't have been more than
sixteen when The Big One ended. His special job was
transporting jet engines to a Luftwaffe squadron that
had just been fitted out with ME-210s. Payter says his
daddy went to his death apologizing for not getting the
engines up to the squadron in time to cream the Lancs
and the B-17s and change the outcome of the war. We
all thought that was pretty funny—anyway, the first
time we heard it. But that wasn't the real funny part.
The real funny part was how the old Nazi freighted
them. With a team. Not horses. Oxen. Not even pulling
a wagon—it was a sledge! The newest, up to the minute, state of the art jet turbines—and what it took to
get them operational was a tow-headed kid with a wil-
low switch, ankle deep in cowflop.

Hanging there, creeping through space, on a trip that
a Heechee ship could have done in a day—if we had
had one, and could have made it do what we wanted it
to—I felt a kind of a sympathy with Payter's old man.
It wasn't that different with us. All we were missing was
the cowflop.

Day 1284. The course change went very smoothly,
after we all struggled into our life-support systems and
wedged ourselves into our acceleration seats, neatly
fitted to our air and vital-signs packs. Considering the

tiny delta-V involved, it was hardly worth the effort. Not to mention that there wouldn't be much use in life-support systems if anything went wrong enough for us to need them, five thousand A.U.s from home. But we did it by the book, because that was the way we had been doing it for three and a half years.

And—after we had turned, and the chemical rockets had done their thing and stopped and let the ion-thrusters take over again, and after Vera had fumbled and clucked and hesitantly announced that it looked all right, as far as she could tell, of course pending confirmation some weeks later from Earth—we saw it! Lurvy was the first one out of her seat and at the visuals, and she snapped it into focus in a matter of seconds.

We hung around, staring at it. The Food Factory!

It jiggled annoyingly in the speculum, hard to keep in focus. Even an ion rocket contributes some vibration to a spaceship, and we were still a long way off. But it was there. It gleamed faintly blue in the darkness punctuated by stars, strangely shaped. It was the size of an office building and more oblong than anything else. But one end was rounded, and one side seemed to have a long, curved slice taken out of it. "Do you think it's been hit by something?" Lurvy asked apprehensively.

"Ah, not in the least," snapped her father. "It is how it was constructed! What do we know of Heechee design?"

"How do you know that?" Lurvy asked, but her father didn't answer that; didn't have to, we all knew that he had no way to know, was only speaking out of hope, because if it was damaged we were in trouble. Our bonuses were good just for going out there, but our hopes for real payoff, the only kind of payoff that would pay for seven round-trip years of misery, rested on the Food Factory being operable. Or at least study-able and copyable. "Paul!" Lurvy said suddenly. "Look at the side that's just turning away—aren't those ships?"

I squinted, trying to make out what she saw. There were half a dozen bulges on the long, straight side of the artifact, three or four smallish ones, two quite large.

They looked like pictures I had seen of the Gateway asteroid, right enough, as far as I could tell. But— "You're the ex-prospector," I said. "What do you think?"

"I think they are. But, my God, did you see those two end ones? They were *huge*. I've been in Ones and Threes, and I've seen plenty of Fives. But nothing like that! They'd hold, I don't know, maybe fifty people! If we had ships like that, Paul— If we had ships like that—"

"If, if," snarled her father. "If we had such ships, and if we could make them go where we wanted, yes, the world would be ours! Let us hope they still work. Let us hope any part of it works!"

"It will, Father," caroled a sweet voice from behind us, and we turned to see Janine, propped with one knee under the digester hose, holding out a squeeze bottle of our best home-made genuine recycled grain neutral spirits. "I'd say this *really* calls for a celebration." She smiled.

Lurvy looked at her thoughtfully, but her control was in good shape and she only said, "Why, that's a nice idea, Janine. Pass it around."

Janine took a ladylike small swig and handed it to her father. "I thought you and Lurvy might like a nightcap," she said, after clearing her throat—she had just graduated to drinking the hard stuff on her fourteenth birthday, still did not like it, insisted on it only because it was an adult prerogative.

"Good idea," Payter nodded. "I have been up now for, what is it, yes, nearly twenty hours. We will all need our rest when we touch down," he added, handing the bottle to my wife, who squeezed two ounces into her well-practiced throat and said:

"I'm not really sleepy yet. You know what I'd like to do? I'd like to play Trish Bover's tape again."

"Oh, God, Lurvy! We've all seen it a zillion times!"

"I know, Janine. You don't have to watch if you don't want to, but I kept wondering if one of those ships was Trish's and—Well, I just want to look at it again."

Janine's lips thinned, but the genes were strong and her control was as good as her sister's when she wanted it to be—that was one of the things we were measured on, before they signed us for the mission. "I'll dial it up," she said, pushing herself over to Vera's keyboard. Payter shook his head and retired to his own private, sliding the accordion-pleated barrier into place to shut us out, and the rest of us gathered around the console. Because it was tape we could get visual as well as sound, and in about ten seconds it crackled on and we could see poor, angry Trish Bover talking into the camera and saying the last words anybody would ever hear from her.

Tragedy can only be tragic just so long, and we'd heard it all for three and a half years. Every once in a while we'd play the tape, and look at the scenes she had picked up with her hand-held camera. And look at them. *And* look at them, freeze-frame and blowup, not because we thought we'd get any more information out of them than Gateway Corporation's people already had, although you never knew. Just because we wanted to reassure ourselves it was all worth it. The real tragedy was that Trish didn't know what she had found.

"This is Mission Report Oh-Seventy-Four Dee Nineteen," she began, steadily enough. Her sad, silly face was even trying to smile. "I seem to be in trouble. I came out at a Heechee artifact kind of thing, and I docked, and now I can't get away. The lander rockets work. But the main board won't. And I don't want to stay here till I starve." Starve! After the boffins went over Trish's photos they identified what the "artifact" was—the CHON-Food Factory they had been looking for.

But whether it was worth it was still an open question, and Trish surely didn't think it was worth it. What she thought was that she was going to die there, and for nothing, not even going to cash in her awards for the mission. And then at the end, what she finally did, she tried to make it back in the lander.

She got into the lander and pointed it for the sun, and turned on the motors, and took a pill. Took a lot of pills; all she had. And then she turned the freezer up to max and got in and closed the door behind her. "Defrost me when you find me," she said, "and remember my award."

And maybe somebody would. When they found her. *If* they found her. Which would likely be in about ten thousand years. By the time her faint radio message was heard by anybody, on maybe its five hundredth automatic repetition, it was too late to matter to Trish; she never answered.

Vera finished playing the tape and quietly restowed it as the screen went dark. "If Trish had been a real pilot instead of one of those Gateway go-go prospectors, jump in and push the button and let the ship do its thing," said Lurvy, not for the first time, "she would have known better. She would have used what little delta-V she had in the lander to kill some angular momentum instead of wasting it by pointing straight in."

"Thank you, expert rocket pilot," I said, not for the first time either. "So she could've counted on being inside the asteroids a whole lot sooner, right? Maybe in as little as six or seven thousand years."

Lurvy shrugged. "I'm going to bed," she said, taking a last squeeze from the bottle. "You, Paul?"

"Aw, give me a break, will you?" Janine cut in. "I wanted Paul to help me go over ignition procedures for the ion-thrusters."

Lurvy's guard went up at once. "You sure that's what you want him to go over? Don't pout, Janine. You know you've gone over it plenty already, and anyway it's Paul's job."

"And what if Paul's out of action?" Janine demanded. "How do we know we won't hit the crazy time just as we're doing it?"

Well, nobody could know that, and as a matter of fact I had been forming the opinion that we would. It came in cycles of about a hundred and thirty days, give or take a dozen. We were pushing it close. I said, "Actually, I'm a little tired, Janine. I promise we'll do it tomorrow." Or whenever one of the others was awake at the same time—the important thing was not to be alone with Janine. In a ship with the total cubage of a motel room, you'd be surprised how hard that is to arrange. Not hard. Practically impossible.

But I really wasn't tired, and when Lurvy was tucked alongside me and out of it, her breathing too quiet to be called anything like a snore, but diagnostic of sleep all the same, I stretched against the sheets, wide awake, counting up our blessings. I needed to do that at least once a day. When I could find any to count.

This time I found a good one. Four thousand A.U. plus is a long trip—and that's as the crow flies. Or, actually, as the photon fires, because of course there aren't a lot of crows in near-interstellar space. Call it half a trillion kilometers, near enough. And we were spiraling out, which meant most of a revolution around the sun before we got there. Our track wasn't just 25 light-days, it was more like 60. And, even power-on the whole way, we weren't coming up to anything like the speed of light. Three and a half years . . . and all the way we were thinking, Jeez, suppose someone figures out the Heechee drive before we get there? It wouldn't have helped us a bit. It would've been a lot more than three and a half years before they got around to doing all the things they wanted to do when that happened. And guess where on that list the job of coming after us would have been?

So the good thing I found to dwell on was that at least we weren't going to find the trip was for nothing, because we were almost there!

All that remained was to strap the big ion-thrusters onto it . . . see if it worked . . . start the slow return trip, shoving the thing back down toward the Earth . . . and, somehow, survive till we got there. Call it, oh, another four years—

I went back to cherishing the fact that we were almost there.

The idea of mining comets for food wasn't new, it went back to Krafft Ehricke in the 1950s anyway, only what he suggested was that people colonize them. It made sense. Bring along a little iron and trace elements

—the iron to build a place to live in, the trace elements to turn CHON-chow into quiche lorraine or hamburgers—and you can live indefinitely on the food around you. Because that's what comets are made of. A little bit of dust, a few rocks, and a hell of a lot of frozen gases. And what are the gases? Oxygen. Nitrogen. Hydrogen. Carbon dioxide. Water. Methane. Ammonia. The same four elements over and over again. CHON. Carbon, hydrogen, oxygen, nitrogen, and what does CHON spell?

Wrong. What comets are made of is the same thing you are made of, and what C-H-O-N spells is "food."

The Oort cloud was made up of millions of megaton-sized servings of chow. Back on Earth there were ten or twelve billion hungry people looking toward it and licking their lips.

There was still a lot of argument about what comets were doing there, out in the cloud. It was still arguable about whether they even came in families. Öpik a hundred years ago said more than half the comets ever sighted fit into well-defined groups, so there, and so did his followers ever since. Whipple said bullshit, there's not a group you can identify that has more than three comets in it. And so did *his* followers. Then Oort came along to try to make sense of it. His idea was that there was this great shell of comets all the hell around the solar system, and every once in a while the sun would reach out and pluck one out, and it would come loping in to perihelion. Then we would have Halley's comet, or the one that was supposed to have been the Star of Bethlehem, or whatever. Then a bunch of the guys began kicking that around, asking why exactly that should happen. It turned out it couldn't—not if you assume Maxwellian distribution for the Oort cloud. In fact, if you assume normal distribution, you also have to assume that there isn't any Oort cloud in the first place. You can't get the observed nearly parabolic orbits out of an Oort cloud; so said R. A. Lyttleton. But then somebody else said, well, who says the distribution can't be non-Maxwellian? And so it proved. It's all lumpy. There are clusters of comets, and great volumes of space with almost none.

And while no doubt the Heechee had set their machine to graze in rich comet pastures, that had been a lot of hundreds of thousands of years ago, and it was now in a kind of cometary desert. If it worked, it had little left to work on. (Maybe it had eaten them all up?)

I fell asleep wondering what CHON-food would taste like. It couldn't be a lot worse than what we had been eating for three and a half years, which was mainly recycled us.

Day 1285. Janine almost got to me today. I was playing chess with Vera, everybody asleep, happy enough, when her hands came around the big earpieces and covered my eyes. "Cut it out, Janine," I said. When I turned around she was pouting.

"I just wanted to use Vera," she said.

"For what? Another hot love letter to one of your movie stars?"

"You treat me like a child," she said. For a wonder, she was fully dressed; her face shone, her hair was damp and pulled down straight to the back of her neck. She looked like your model serious-minded young teenager. "What I *wanted*," she said, "was to go over thruster alignments with Vera. Since you won't help me."

One of the reasons Janine was along with us was that she was smart—we all were; had to be to be accepted for the mission. And one of the things she was smart at was getting at me. "All right," I said, "you're right, what can I say? Vera? Recess the game and give us the program for providing propulsion for the Food Factory."

"Certainly," she said, ". . . Paul." And the board disappeared, and in its place she built up a holo of the Food Factory. She had updated her specs from the telescopic views we had obtained, and so it was shown complete with its dust cloud and the glob of dirty snowball adhering to one side. "Cancel the cloud, Vera," I ordered, and the blur disappeared and the Food Factory showed up like an engineering drawing. "Okay, Janine. What's the first step?"

"We dock," she said at once. "We hope the lander facsimile fits, and we dock it. If we can't dock we link up with braces to some point on the surface; either way, our ship becomes a rigid part of the structure, so we can use our thrust for attitude control."

"Next?"

"We all dismount the number-one thruster and brace it to the aft section of the factory—there." She pointed out the place on the holo. "We slave it to the board here, and as soon as it is installed we activate."

"Guidance?"

"Vera will give us coordinates—oops, sorry, Paul." She had been drifting out of orientation with me and Vera, and she caught my shoulder with her hand to pull herself back. She kept her hand there. "Then we repeat the process with the other five. By the time we have all six going we have a delta-V of two meters per second per second, running off the ^{239}Pu generator. Then we start spreading the mirror foils—"

"No."

"Oh, sure, we inspect all the moorings to see that they're holding under thrust first; well, I take that for granted. Then we start with solar power, and when we've got it all spread we should be up to maybe two and a quarter meters—"

"At first, Janine. The closer we get in, the more power we get. All right. Now let's go through the hardware. You're bracing our ship to the Heechee-metal hull; how do you go about it?"

And she told me, and kept on telling me; and by gosh she knew it all. The only thing was her hand on my shoulder became a hand under my arm, and it moved across my chest, and began to roam; and all the time she was giving me the specs for coldwelding and how to get collimation for the thrusters, her face serious and concerned, and her hand stroking my belly. Fourteen years old. But she didn't look fourteen, or feel fourteen, or smell fourteen—she'd been into Lurvy's quarter of an ounce of remaining Chanel. What saved me was Vera; good thing, everything considered, because I was losing interest in saving myself. The holo froze while Janine was adding an extra strut to one of the thrusters, and Vera said, "Action message coming in. Shall I read it out for you . . . Paul?"

"Go ahead." Janine withdrew her hand slightly as the holo winked away, and the screen produced the message:

> *We've been requested to ask you for a favor. The next outbreak of the 130-day syndrome is estimated to occur within the next two months. HEW thinks that a full-coverage visual of all of you describing the Food Factory and emphasizing how well things are going and how important it is will significantly reduce tensions and consequent damage. Please follow the accompanying script. Request compliance soonest possible so that we may tape and schedule broadcast for maximum effect.*

"Shall I give you the script?" Vera asked.

"Go ahead—hard copy," I added.

"Very well . . . Paul." The screen turned pale and empty, and she began to squirt out typed sheets of paper. I picked them up to read while I sent Janine off to wake up her sister and father. She didn't object. She loved doing television for the folks back home, it always meant fan letters from famous people for the brave young astronette.

The script was what you would expect. I programmed Vera to roll it for us line by line, and we could have read it in ten minutes. That was not to be. Janine insisted her sister had to do her hair, and even Lurvy decided she had to make up and Payter wanted his beard trimmed. By me. So, all in all, counting four rehearsals, we blew six hours, not counting a month's power, on the TV broadcast. We all gathered before the camera, looking domestic and dedicated, and explained what we were going to be doing to an audience that wouldn't be seeing it for a month, by which time we would already be there. But if it would do them any good, it was worth it. We had been through eight or nine attacks of the 130-day fever since we took off from Earth. Each time it had its own syndrome, satyriasis or depression, lethargy or light-hearted joy. I had been outside when one of them hit—that was how the big telescope got broken—and it had been about an even bet whether I would ever make it back inside the ship. I simply didn't care. I was hallucinating loneliness and anger, being chased by apelike creatures and wishing I were dead. And back on Earth, with billions of people, nearly all of them affected to one degree or another, in one or another way, each time it hit it was pure hell. It had been building up for ten years—eight since it was first identified as a recurring scourge—and no one knew what caused it.

But everybody wanted it stopped.

Day 1288. Docking day! Payter was at the controls, wouldn't trust Vera on a thing like that, while Lurvy was strapped in over his head to call off course corrections. We came to relative rest just outside the thin cloud of particles and gas, no more than a kilometer from the Food Factory itself.

From where Janine and I were sitting in our lifesupport gear it was hard to see what was going on outside. Past Payter's head and Lurvy's gesticulating arms we could catch glimpses of the enormous old machine, but only glimpses. No more than a glimmer of blue-lit metal and now and then a docking pit or the shape of one of the old ships—

"Hellfire! I'm drifting away!"

"No, you aren't, Payter. The goddam thing's got a little acceleration!"

—and maybe a star. We didn't really need the lifesupport; Payter was nudging us gently as he would a jellyfish in a tank. I wanted to ask where the acceleration came from, or why; but the two pilots were busy, and besides I did not suppose they knew the answer.

"That's got it. Now bring her in to that center dock-ing pit, middle of that row of three."

"Why that one?"

"Why not? Because I say so!"

And we edged in for a minute or two, and came to relative rest again. And we matched and locked. The Heechee capsule at the forward end mated neatly with the ancient pit.

Lurvy reached down and killed the board, and we all looked at each other. We were there.

Or, to put it another way, we were halfway. Halfway home.

Day 1290. It was no surprise that the Heechee had breathed an atmosphere we could survive in. The sur-prise was that any of it was left in this place, after all the tens or hundreds of thousands of years since anyone breathed any of it. And that was not the only surprise. The others came later, and were scarier and worse.

It was not just the atmosphere that had survived. The whole ship had survived—in working condition! We knew it as soon as we were inside and the samplers had shown us we could take off our helmets. The blue-gleaming metal walls were warm to the touch, and we could feel a faint, steady vibration. The temperature was around twelve—cool, but no worse than some Earthside homes I've been in. Do you want to guess what the first words were spoken by human beings in-side the Food Factory? They came from Payter, and they were:

"Ten million dollars! Jesus, maybe even a hundred!"

And if he hadn't said it, one or another of us would. Our bonus was going to be astronomical. Trish's report hadn't said whether the Food Factory was operational or not—for all we knew, it could have been a riddled hulk, empty of anything that made it worthwhile. But here we had a complete and major Heechee artifact, in working condition! There was simply nothing like it to judge against. The tunnels on Venus, the old ships, even Gateway itself had been carefully emptied of nearly all their contents half a million years before.

This place was *furnished*! Warm, livable, thrumming, soaked with weak microwave radiation, it was alive. It did not seem old at all.

We had little chance to explore; the sooner we got the thing moving in toward Earth, the sooner we would cash in on its promise. We allowed ourselves an hour to roam around in the breathable air, poking into chambers filled with great gray and blue metal shapes, slithering down corridors, eating as we wandered, telling each other over the pocket communicators (and relayed through Vera to Earth) what we found. Then work. We suited up again and began the job of derigging the side-cargos.

And that was where we ran into the first trouble.

The Food Factory was not in free orbit. It was accelerating. Some sort of thrust was driving it. It was not great, less than one percent of a G.

But the electric rocket assemblies weighed more than ten tons each.

Even at one percent of perceived weight, that meant over a hundred kilograms of weight, not counting ten tons worth of inertia. As we began to unship the first one it pulled itself free at one end and began to fall away. Payter was there to catch it, but it was more than he could hold for long; I pulled myself over and grabbed the side-cargo with one hand, the brace it had been fastened to with the other, and we managed to keep it in place until Janine could secure a cable over it.

Then we retired inside the ship to think things over.

We were already exhausted. After three-plus years in confined quarters, we were not used to hard work. Vera's bio-assay unit reported we were accumulating fatigue poisons. We bickered and worried at each other for a while, then Payter and Lurvy went to sleep while Janine and I schemed out a rigging that would let us secure each side-cargo before it was released and swing it around the Food Factory on three long cables, belayed by smaller guiding cables so that it would not smash into the hull at the far end of its travel and pound itself into scrap. We had allowed ten hours to move a rocket into position. It took three days for the first one. By the time we had it secured we were stark, staring wrecks, our heartbeats pounding, our muscles one solid ache. We took a full sleep shift and a few hours of loafing around the interior of the Food Factory before we went back to securing the rocket so that it could be started. Payter was the most energetic of us; he went prowling as far as he could go down half a dozen corridors. "All come to dead ends," he reported when he came back. "Looks like the part we can reach is only about a tenth of the object—'less we cut holes through the walls."

"Not now," I said.

"Not ever!" said Lurvy strongly. "All we do is get this thing back. Anybody wants to start cutting it up, it will be after we've collected our money!" She rubbed her biceps, arms folded across her chest, and added regretfully, "And we might as well get started on securing the rocket."

It took us another two days to do that, but finally we had it in place. The welding fluxes they had given us to secure steel to Heechee metal actually worked. As far as we could tell from static inspection, it was solid. We retired into the ship and commanded Vera to give it a ten percent thrust.

At once we felt a tiny lurch. It was working. We all grinned at each other, and I reached into my private hold-all for the bottle of champagne I had been saving for this occasion—

Another lurch.

Click, click, click, click—one after another our grins snapped off. There should have been only one felt acceleration.

Lurvy jumped to the cyber board. "Vera! Report delta-V!"

The screen lighted up with a diagram of forces: the Food Factory imaged in the middle, force arrows showing in two directions. One was our thruster, doing its job of pushing against the hull. The other was not.

"Additional thrust now affecting course . . . Lurvy," Vera reported. "Vector result now same in direction and magnitude as previous delta-V."

Our rocket was pushing against the Food Factory. But it wasn't doing much good. The factory was pushing back.

Day 1298. So we did what we obviously had to do. We turned everything off and screamed for help.

We slept, and ate, and wandered around the factory for what seemed like forever, wishing the 25-day delay did not exist. Vera wasn't much help. "Transmit full telemetry," she said, and, "Stand by for further directives." Well, we were doing that already.

After a day or two I pulled the champagne out anyway, and we all drank up. At .01G the carbonation had more muscle than gravity did, and actually I had to hold my thumb over the bottle and my palm over each glass to squirt and catch the spraying champagne. But after a fashion we toasted. "Not so bad," said Payter when he had chug-a-lugged his wine. "At least we've got a couple million each."

"If we ever live to collect it," snarled Janine.

"Don't be such a downer, Janine. We knew when we started out that the mission might bum out." And so we had; the ship was designed so that we could start back on our basic fuel, then rerig the photon-thrusters to get us home—in another four years or so.

"And then what, Lurvy? I'll be an eighteen-year-old virgin! And a failure."

"Oh, God. Janine, go explore for a while, won't you? I'm tired of the sight of you."

And so were all of us, of each other. We were more tired of each other, and less tolerant, than we had been all the way out in the cramped quarters of the ship. Now that we had more space to lose each other in, as much as a quarter-kilometer of it at farthest stretch, we were more abrasive on each other than ever. Every twenty hours or so Vera's small, dull brain would stumble through her contingency programs and come up with some new experiment: test thrusts at one percent of power, at thirty percent of power, even at full power. And we would get together long enough to suit up and carry them out. But they were always the same.

No matter how hard we pushed against the Food Factory, the artifact sensed it, and pushed back at exactly the right magnitude and in exactly the right direction to keep its steady acceleration to whatever goal it had in mind. The only useful thing Vera came up with was a theory: the factory had used up the comet it was working on and was moving on to a new one. But that was only intellectually interesting. It did not do a practical thing to help. So we wandered around, mostly alone, carrying the cameras into every room and corridor we could reach. What we saw they saw, and what they saw was transmitted on the time-sharing beam to Earth, and none of it offered much help.

We found where Trish Bover had entered the factory easily enough—Payter did that, and called us all to look, and we gathered silently to inspect the remnants of a long-decayed lunch, the discarded pantyhose and the graffiti she had scratched on the walls:

TRISH BOVER WAS HERE

and

GOD HELP ME!

"Maybe God will," said Lurvy after a while, "but I don't see how anybody else can."

"She must have been here longer than I thought," Payter said. "There's junk scattered all around in some of the rooms."

"What kind of junk?"

"Old spoiled food, mostly. Down toward the other landing face, you know where the lights are?" I did, and Janine and I went to see. It was her idea to keep me company, and not an idea I had been enthusiastic about at first. But maybe the 12°C. temperature and the lack of anything like a bed tempered her interest, or maybe she was too depressed and disappointed to be very interested in her ambition to lose her virginity. We found the discarded food easily enough. It didn't look like Gateway rations to me. It seemed to come in packets; a couple of them were unopened, three biggish ones, the size of a slice of bread, wrapped in bright red something or other—it felt like silk. Two smaller ones, one green, one the same red as the others but mottled with pink dots. We opened one experimentally. It stank of rotten fish and was obviously no longer edible. But it had been.

I left Janine there to go back to find the others. They opened the little green one. It did not smell spoiled, but was hard as rock. Payter sniffed it, then licked it, then broke off a crumb against the wall and chewed it thoughtfully. "No taste at all," he reported, then looked up at us, looked startled, then grinned. "You waiting for me to drop dead?" he inquired. "I don't think so. You chew on it awhile, it gets soft. Like stale crackers, maybe."

Lurvy frowned. "If it really was food—" She stopped and thought. "If it really was food, and Trish left it there, why didn't she just stay here? Or why didn't she mention it?"

"She was scared silly," I suggested.

"Sure she was. But she did tape a report. She didn't say a word about food. The Gateway techs were the ones who decided this was a Food Factory, remember? And all they had to go on was the wrecked one they found around Phyllis's World."

"Maybe she just forgot."

"I don't think she forgot," said Lurvy slowly, but she didn't say any more than that. There wasn't anything more to be said. But for the next day or two we did not do much solitary exploring.

Day 1311. Vera received the information about the food packages in silence. After a while she displayed an instruction to submit the contents of the packages to chemical- and bio-assay. We had already done that on our own, and if she drew conclusions she did not say what they were.

For that matter, neither did we. On the occasions when we were all awake together what we mostly talked about was what we would do if Base could not

figure out a way for us to move the Food Factory. Vera
had already suggested that we install the other five side-
cargos, turn them all on full-power at once and see if
the factory could out-muscle six thrusters. Vera's suggestions were not orders, and Lurvy spoke for all of us
when she said, "If we turn them on full and they don't
work, the next step is to turn them on to over rated
capacity. They could get damaged. And we could get
stuck."

"What do we do if we hear from Earth and they
make it an order?" I asked.

Payter cut in ahead of her. "We bargain," he said,
nodding sagely. "They want us to take extra risks, they
give us extra pay."

"Are you going to do the bargaining, Pa?"

"You bet I am. And listen. Suppose it don't work.
Suppose we have to go back. You know what we do
then?" He nodded to us again. "We load up the ship
with everything we can carry. We find little machines
that we can take out, you know? Maybe we see if they
work. We stuff that ship with everything it can hold,
throw away everything we can spare. Leave most of the
side-cargos here and load on big machines outside, you
see? We could come back with, God, I don't know,
another twenty, thirty million dollars worth of artifacts."

"Like prayer fans!" Janine cried, clapping her hands.
There were piles of them in the room where Payter had
found the food. There were other things there, too, a
sort of metal-mesh couch, tulip-shaped things that
looked like candleholders on the walls. But hundreds of
prayer fans. By my quick guess, at a thousand dollars
each, there was half a million dollars worth of prayer
fans in that room alone, delivered to the curio markets
in Chicago and Rome . . . if we lived to deliver them.
Not counting all the other things I could think of, that I
was inventorying in my mind. I wasn't the only one.

"Prayer fans are the least of it," Lurvy said thoughtfully. "But that's not in our contract, Pa."

"Contract! So what are they going to do with us,

shoot us? Cheat us? After we give up eight years of our lives? No. They'll give us the bonuses."

The more we thought about it, the better that sounded. I went to sleep thinking about which of the gadgets and what-you-call-'ems I'd seen could be carried back, and what among them seemed the most valuable, and had my first pleasant dreams since we had tested the thruster—

And woke up with Janine's urgent whisper in my ear. "Pop? Paul? Lurvy? Can you hear me?"

I swam up to a sitting position and looked around. She wasn't speaking in my ear; it was my radio. Lurvy was awake beside me, and Payter came hurrying around a corner to join us, their radios going too. I said, "We hear you, Janine. What—"

"Shut up!" the whisper came, hissing out with white sound as though her lips were pressed against the microphone. "Don't answer me, just listen. There's someone here."

We stared at each other. Lurvy whispered, "Where are you?"

"I said shut up! I'm out at the far docking area, you know? Where we found that food. I was looking for something we could bring back with us, like Pop said, only— Well, I saw something on the floor. Like an apple, only it wasn't—kind of reddish brown on the outside and green on the inside, and it smelled like— I don't know what it smelled like. Strawberries. And it wasn't any hundred thousand years old, either. It was fresh. And I heard—wait a minute."

We did not dare answer, just listened to her breathing for a moment. When she spoke again her whisper sounded scared. "It's coming this way. It's between me and you, and I'm stuck. I—keep thinking it's a Heechee, and it's going to be—"

Her voice stopped. We heard her gasp; then, out loud, "Don't you come any closer!"

I had heard enough. "Let's go," I said, jumping toward the corridor. Payter and Lurvy were right behind me as we hurried in long, swimming leaps down the blue-walled tunnel. When we got near the docks we stopped, looking around irresolutely.

Before we could make a decision on which way to search, Janine's voice came again. It was neither whisper nor terrified cry. "He—he stopped when I told him," she said unbelievingly. "And I don't think he's a Heechee. He looks like just an ordinary person to me— well, kind of scruffy. He's just standing there staring at me, kind of sniffing the air."

"Janine!" I shouted into the radio. "We're at the docks—which way from here?"

Pause. Then, strangely, a kind of shocked giggle. "Just keep coming straight," she said shakily. "Come on quick. You—you wouldn't believe what he's doing now!"

3

Wan in Love

The trip to the outpost seemed longer than usual to Wan, because he was troubled in his mind. He missed the companionship of the Dead Men. He missed even more what he had never had. A female. The notion of Wan in love was a fantasy for him, but it was a fantasy he wanted to make real. So many of the books helped it along, *Romeo and Juliet* and *Anna Karenina* and the old romantic Chinese classics.

What drove the fantasies out of his mind at last was the sight of the outpost as he drew near. The board lighted up to signal the beginning of docking maneuvers, the flow lines on the screen melted away, and the shape of the outpost snapped into vision. But it was not the same shape as always. There was a new ship in one of the docking hatches, and a strange jagged structure strapped to one side of the hull.

What could such things mean? When the docking

was complete Wan poked his head through the hatch and stared around, sniffing and listening.

After a time he concluded that no one was near. He did not remove his books or other possessions from the ship. He resolved to stay ready to flee at a moment's notice, but he decided to explore. Once before, long ago, some other person had been at the outpost, and he believed it had been a female. Tiny Jim had helped him identify the garment then. Perhaps he should ask Tiny Jim for advice now? Munching on a fruitberry, he handed himself easily along the rails toward the dreaming room, where the pleasure couch lay surrounded by the book machines.

And stopped.

Had that been a sound? A laugh, or a cry, from far away?

He threw the berryfruit away and stood for a moment, all his senses tensely extended. The sound was not repeated. But there was something—a smell, very faint, quite pleasant, quite strange. It was not unlike the smell in the garment he had found, and carried around for many days until the last vestige of scent was gone from it and he put it back where it was found.

Had that person come back?

Wan began to shake. A person! It had been a dozen years since he had smelled or touched a person! And then only his parents. But it might not be a person, it could be something else. He launched himself toward the dock where that other person had been, craftily avoiding the main passages, hurling himself down narrower, less direct ways where he did not think any stranger was likely to go. Wan knew every inch of the outpost, at least as far within it as it was possible to travel without coming to the dead-end locked walls that he did not know how to open. It took him only a few minutes to reach the place where he had carefully rearranged the debris left by the outpost's one visitor.

Everything was there. But not, he saw, as he had left it. Some things had been picked up and dropped again. Wan knew he had not done that. Apart from the discipline he had always imposed upon himself, of leaving the outpost exactly as he had found it, so that no one could ever know he was there, this time he had been especially careful to arrange the litter precisely as it had been left. Someone else was on the outpost.

And he was many minutes away from his ship.

Cautiously but quickly he returned to the docks on the other side, pausing at every intersection to look and smell and listen. He reached his ship and hovered at the hatch, indecisively. Run or explore?

But the smell was stronger now, and irresistible.

Step by step he ventured down one of the long, dead-end corridors, ready to retreat instantly.

A voice! Whispering, almost inaudible. But it was there. He peered around a doorway, and his heart pounded. A person! Huddled against a wall, with a metal object at its lips, staring at him in terror. The person cried out at him: "Don't you come any closer!" But he could not have if he had wanted to; he was frozen. It was not merely a person. It was a *female* person! The diagnostic signs were clear, as Tiny Jim had explained them to him: two swellings at the chest, a swelling around the hips and a narrowing at the waist, a smooth brow with no bulges over the eye sockets— yes, female! And young. And dressed in something that revealed bare legs and, oh, bare arms; smooth hair tied behind the head in a long tail, great eyes staring at him.

Wan responded as he had learned to respond. He fell gently to his knees, opened his garment and touched his sex. It had been several days since he had masturbated, and with no such stimulus as this; he was erect at once and shuddering with excitement.

He hardly noticed the noises behind him as three other persons came racing up. It was not until he was finished that he stood up, adjusted his clothing and smiled politely to them where they were ranged around the young female, talking excitedly and almost hysterically among themselves. "Hello," he said. "I am Wan." When they did not respond, he repeated the greeting in Spanish and Cantonese, and would have gone on to his

other languages except that the second female person
stepped forward and said:

"Hello, Wan. I'm Dorema Herter-Hall—they call me
'Lurvy'. We're very glad to see you."

In all of Wan's fifteen years there had never been
twelve hours as exciting, as frightening and as heart-
stoppingly thrilling, as these. So many questions! So
much to say and to hear. So shuddery-pleasant to touch
these other persons, and to smell their smells and feel
their presence. They knew so incredibly little, and so
astonishingly much—did not know how to get food
from the lockers, had not used the dreaming couch, had
never seen an Old One or talked with a Dead Man.
And yet they knew of spaceships and cities, of walking
under an open sky ("sky"? it took a long time for Wan
to grasp what they were talking about) and of Making
Love. He could see that the younger female was willing
to show him more of that, but the older one did not
wish her to; how strange. The older male did not seem
to make love with anyone; even stranger. But it was all
strange, and he was expiring of the delights and terrors
of so much strangeness. After they had talked for a
long time, and he had shown them some of the tricks of
the outpost, and they had shown him some of the wonders of their ship (a thing like a Dead Man, but which
had never been alive; pictures of people on Earth; a
flush toilet)—after all these wonders, the Lurvy person
had commanded that they all rest. He had at once
started toward the dreaming couch, but she had invited
him to stay near them and he could not say no, though
all through the sleep he woke from time to time, trembling and sniffing and staring around in the dim blue
light.

So much excitement was bad for him. When they
were all awake again he found himself still shaking, his
body aching as though he had not slept at all. No matter.
The questions and the chatter began again at once:

"And who are the Dead Men?"

"I don't know. Let us ask them? Perhaps—sometimes they call themselves 'prospectors'. From a place called 'Gateway'."

"And this place they are in, is it a Heechee artifact?"

"Heechee?" He thought; he had heard the word, long ago, but he did not know what it meant. "Do you mean the Old Ones?"

"What do the Old Ones look like?" And he could not say in words, so they gave him a sketch pad again and he tried to draw the big waggling jaws, the frowsty beards, and as each sketch was finished they snatched it up and held it before the machine they called "Vera".

"This machine is like a Dead Man," he offered, and they flew in with questions again:

"Do you mean the Dead Men are computers?"

"What is a 'computer'?"

And then the questions would go the other way for a while, as they explained to him the meaning of "computer", and presidential elections, and the 130-day fever. And all the while they were roaming the ship, as he explained to them what he knew of it. Wan was becoming very tired. He had had little experience of fatigue, because in his timeless life when he was sleepy he slept and did not get up until he was rested. He did not enjoy the feeling, or the scratchiness in his throat, or the headache. But he was too excited to stop, especially when they told him about the female person named Trish Bover. "She was here? Here in the outpost? And she did not stay?"

"No, Wan. She didn't know you would come. She thought if she stayed she would die." What a terrible pity! Although, Wan calculated, he had only been ten years old when she came, he could have been a companion for her. And she for him. He would have fed her and cared for her and taken her with him to see the Old Ones and the Dead Men, and been very happy.

"Then where did she go?" he asked.

For some reason, that question troubled them. They looked at each other. Lurvy said after a moment, "She got in her ship, Wan."

"She went back to Earth?"

"No. Not yet. It is a very long trip for the kind of ship she had. Longer than she would live."

The younger man, Paul, the one who coupled with Lurvy, took over. "She is still traveling, Wan. We don't know where exactly. We are not even sure she is alive. She froze herself."

"Then she is dead?"

"Well—she is probably not alive. But if she is found, maybe she can be revived. She's in the freezing compartment of her ship, at minus-forty degrees. Her body will not decay for some time, I think. She thought. At any rate, she thought it was the best chance she had."

"I could have given her a better one," Wan said dejectedly. Then he brightened. There was the other female, Janine, who was not frozen. Wishing to impress her, he said, "That is a gosh number."

"What is? What kind of a number?"

"A gosh number, Janine. Tiny Jim talks about them. When you say 'minus-forty' you don't have to say whether it is in Celsius or Fahrenheit, because they are the same." He tittered at the joke.

They were looking at each other again. Wan could see that something was wrong, but he was feeling stranger, dizzier, more fatigued at every second. He thought perhaps they had not understood the joke, so he said, "Let us ask Tiny Jim. He can be reached just down this passage, where the dreaming couch is."

"Reached? How?" demanded the old man, Payter.

Wan did not answer; he was not feeling well enough to trust what he said, and, besides, it was easier to show them. He turned abruptly away and hauled himself toward the dreaming chamber. By the time they followed he had already keyed the book in and called for number one hundred twelve. "Tiny Jim?" he tried; then, over his shoulder, "Sometimes he doesn't want to talk. Please be patient." But he was lucky this time, and the Dead Man's voice responded quite quickly.

"Wan? Is that you?"

"Of course it is me, Tiny Jim. I want to hear about gosh numbers."

"Very well, Wan. Gosh numbers are numbers which represent more than one quantity, so that when you perceive the coincidence you say, 'Gosh.' Some gosh numbers are trivial. Some are perhaps of transcendental importance. Some religious persons count gosh numbers as a proof of the existence of God. As to whether or not God exists, I can give you only a broad outline of—"

"No, Tiny Jim. Please stick to gosh numbers now."

"Yes, Wan. I will now give you a list of a few of the simplest gosh numbers. Point-five degrees. Minus-forty degrees. One thirty-seven. Two thousand and twenty-five. Ten to the 39th. Please write one paragraph on each of these, identifying the characteristics which make them gosh numbers and—"

"Cancel, cancel," Wan squeaked, his voice rising higher because it smarted so. "This is not a class."

"Ph, well," said the Dead Man gloomily, "all right. Point-five degrees is the angular diameter of both the sun and the Moon as seen from Earth. Gosh! How strange that they should be the same, but also how useful, because it is partly because of this coincidence that Earth has eclipses. Minus-forty degrees is the temperature which is the same in both Fahrenheit and Celsius scales. Gosh. Two thousand twenty-five is the sum of the cubes of the integers, one cubed plus two cubed plus three cubed and so on up to nine cubed, all added together. It is also the square of their sum. Gosh. Ten to the thirty-ninth is a measure of the weakness of the gravitational force as compared with the electromagnetic. It is also the age of the universe expressed as a dimensionless number. It is also the square root of the number of particles in the observable universe, that is, that part of the universe relative to Earth in which Hubble's constant is less than point-five. Also—well, never mind, but gosh! Gosh, gosh, gosh. On these goshes P.A.M. Dirac constructed his Large Numbers Hypothesis, from which he deduced that the force of gravity must be weakening as the age of the universe increased. Now, there is a gosh for you!"

"You left out one thirty-seven," the boy accused.

The Dead Man cackled. "Good for you, Wan! I wanted to see if you were listening. One thirty-seven is Eddington's fine structure constant, of course, and turns up over and over in nuclear physics. But it is more than that. Suppose you take the inverse, that is one over one thirty-seven, and express it as a decimal. The first three digits are Double Ought Seven, James Bond's identification as a killer. There is the lethality of the universe for you! The first eight digits are Clarke's Palindrome, point oh seven two nine nine two seven oh. There is its symmetry. Deadly, and two-faced, that is the fine structure constant! Or," he mused, "perhaps I should say, there is its inverse. Which would imply that the universe itself is the inverse of that? Namely kind and uneven? Help me, Wan. I am not sure how to inter-pret this symbol."

"Oh, cancel, cancel," said Wan angrily. "Cancel and out." He was feeling irritable and shaky, as well as more ill than he had ever been, even when the Dead Men had given him shots. "He goes on like that," he apologized to the others. "That's why I don't usually speak to him from here."

"He doesn't look well," said Lurvy worriedly to her husband, and then to Wan, "Do you feel all right?" He shook his head, because he did not know how to an-swer.

Paul said, "You ought to rest. But—what did you mean, 'from here.' Where is, uh, Tiny Jim?"

"Oh, he is in the main station," said Wan weakly, sneezing.

"You mean—" Paul swallowed hard. "But you said it was forty-five days away by ship. That must be a very long way."

The old man, Payter, cried: "Radio? Are you talking to him by radio? *Faster-than-light* radio?"

Wan shrugged. Paul had been right; he needed to rest, and there was the couch, which had always been the exact proper place to make him feel good and rested.

"Tell me, boy!" shouted the old man. "If you have a working FTL radio— The bonus—"

"I am very tired," said Wan hoarsely. "I must sleep." He felt himself falling. He evaded their clutching arms, dove between them and plunged into the couch, its comforting webbing closing around him.

4

Robin Broadhead, Inc.

Essie and I were water-skiing on the Tappan Sea when my neck radio buzzed to tell me that a stranger had turned up on the Food Factory. I ordered the boat to turn immediately and take us back to the long stretch of waterfront property owned by Robin Broadhead, Inc. before I told Essie what it was. "A *boy*, Robin?" she shouted over the noise of the hydrogen motor and the wind. "Where in hell a boy comes to Food Factory?"

"That's what we have to find out," I yelled back. The boat skillfully snaked us in to shallow water and waited while we jumped out and ran up the grass. When it recognized that we were gone, it purred down the shoreline to put itself away.

Wet as we were, we ran directly to the brain room. We had begun to get opticals already, and the holo tank showed a skinny, scraggly youth wearing a sort of divided kilt and a dirty tunic. He did not seem threatening in any way, but he sure as hell had no right to be there. "Voice," I ordered, and the moving lips began to speak—queer, shrill, high-pitched, but good enough English to understand:

"—from the main station, yes. It is about seven seven-days—weeks, I mean. I come here often."

"For God's sake, *how*?" I could not see the speaker, but it was male and had no accent: Paul Hall.

"In a ship, to be sure. Do you not have a ship? The Dead Men speak only of traveling in ships, I do not know any other way."

"Incredible," said Essie over my shoulder. She backed away, not taking her eyes off the tank, and came back with a terrycloth robe to throw over my shoulders and one for herself. "What do you suppose is 'main station'?"

"I wish to God I knew. Harriet?"

The voices from the tank grew fainter, and my secretary's voice said, "Yes, Mr. Broadhead?"

"When did he get there?"

"About seventeen point four minutes ago, Mr. Broadhead. Plus transit time from the Food Factory, of course. He was discovered by Janine Herter. She did not appear to have had a camera with her, so we received only voice until one of the other members of the party arrived." As soon as she stopped speaking the voice from the figure in the tank came up again; Harriet is a very good program, one of Essie's best.

"—sorry if I behaved improperly," the boy was saying. Pause. Then, old Peter Herter:

"Never mind that, by God. Are there other people on this main station?"

The boy pursed his lips. "That," he said philosophically, "would depend, would it not, on how one defines 'person'? In the sense of a living organism of our species, no. The closest is the Dead Men."

A woman's voice—Dorema Herter-Hall. "Are you hungry? Do you need anything?"

"No, why should I?"

"Harriet? What's that about behaving improperly?" I asked.

Harriet's voice came hesitantly. "He, uh, he brought himself to orgasm, Mr. Broadhead. Right in front of Janine Herter."

I couldn't help it, I broke out laughing. "Essie," I said to my wife, "I think you made her a little too ladylike." But that wasn't what I was laughing at. It was the plain incongruity of the thing. I had guessed—anything. Anything but this: a Heechee, a space pirate, Martians—God knows what, but not a horny teen-aged boy.

There was a scrabble of steel claws from behind and something jumped on my shoulder. "Down, Squiffy," I snapped.

Essie said, "Just let him nuzzle neck for a minute. He'll go away."

"He isn't dainty in his personal habits," I snarled. "Can't we get rid of him?"

"Na, na, galubka," she said soothingly, patting the top of my head as she got up. "Want Full Medical, don't you? Squiffy comes along." She kissed me and wandered out of the room, leaving me to think about the thing that, to my somewhat surprise, was making all sorts of tiny but discomforting stirrings inside me. To see a Heechee! Well, we hadn't—but what if we did?

When the first Venus explorers discovered the traces the Heechee had left, glowing blue-lined empty tunnels, spindle-shaped caves, it was a shock. A few artifacts, another shock—what were they? There were the scrolls of metal somebody named "prayer fans" (but did the Heechee pray, and if so to whom?) There were the glowing little beads called "fire pearls", but they weren't pearls, and they weren't burning. Then someone found the Gateway asteroid, and the biggest shock of all, because on it were a couple of hundred working space-ships. Only you couldn't direct them. You could get in and go, and that was it . . . and what you found when you got there was shock, shock, shock, shock.

I knew. I had had the shocks, on my three silly missions—No. Two silly missions. And then one terribly unsilly one. It had made me rich and deprived me of somebody I loved, and what is silly about either of those things?

And ever since then the Heechee, dead half a million years, not even a written word left to tell what they were up to, had permeated every part of our world. It was all questions, and not very many answers. We didn't even know what they called themselves— certainly not "Heechee", because that was just a name the explorers made up for them. We had no idea what these remote and godlike creatures called themselves. But we didn't know what God called Himself, either. Jehovah, Jupiter, Baal, Allah—those were names people made up. Who knew by what name He was known to His buddies?

I was trying to let myself feel what I might have felt if the stranger in the Food Factory had actually been Heechee when the toilet flushed, Essie came out and Squiffy made a dash for the bowl. There are indignities to having Full Medical coverage, and a mobile bio-assay unit is one of them.

"You are wasting my program time!" Essie scolded, and I realized that Harriet had been sitting patiently in the tank, waiting to be told to get on with her information about the other claims on my attention. The report from the Food Factory was all being taped and stored in any case, so Essie went to her own office to deal with her own priorities, I told Harriet to start the cook on lunch, and then I let her do her secretarial duties.

"You have an appointment to testify before the Senate Ways and Means Committee tomorrow morning, Mr. Broadhead."

"I know. I'll be there."

"You're due for your next checkup this weekend. Shall I confirm the appointment?"

That's one of the penalties of Full Medical, and besides Essie insists—she's twenty years younger than I, and reminds me of it. "All right, let's get it over with."

"You are being sued by one Hanson Bover, and Morton wants to talk to you about it. Your consolidated statement for the quarter came in and is on your desk file—except for the food mine holdings, which will not be complete until tomorrow. And there are a number of minor messages—most of which I have already dealt with—for your review at your convenience."

"Thank you. That's all for now." The tank went transparent and I leaned back in my chair to think.

I didn't need to see the consolidated statement—I already pretty well knew what it would say. The real estate investments were performing nicely; the little bit I had left in sea farming was moving toward a record profit year. Everything was solid, except for the food mines. The last 130-day fever had cost us. I couldn't blame the guys in Cody, they weren't any more responsible than I was when the fever hit. But they had somehow let the thermal drilling get out of control, and five thousand acres of our shale were burning away underground. It had taken three months to get the mine back in operation at all, and we still didn't know what it was going to cost. No wonder their quarterly statement was late.

But that was only an annoyance, not a disaster. I was too well diversified to be killed by any one sector going bad. I wouldn't have been in the food mines except for Morton's advice; the extraction allowance made it a really good thing, tax-wise. (But I'd sold most of my sea-farming holdings to buy in.) Then Morton figured out that I still needed a tax shelter, so we started The Broadhead Institute for Extra-Solar Research. The Institute owns all my stock, but I vote it, and I vote it for what I want to do. I got us into the coownership with the Gateway Corporation that financed probes to four detected but unvisited Heechee-metal sources in or near the solar system, and one of them had been the Food Factory. As soon as they made contact we spun off a separate exploitation company to deal with it—and now it was looking really interesting.

"Harriet? Let me have the direct from the Food Factory again," I said. The holo sprang up, the boy still talking excitedly in his shrill, squeaky voice. I tried to catch the thread of what he was saying—something about a Dead Man (only it wasn't a man, because its name was Henrietta) speaking to him (so it wasn't dead?) about a Gateway mission she had been on (when? why hadn't I heard of her?). It was all perplexing, so I had a better idea. "Albert Einstein, please," I said, and the holo swirled to show the sweet old lined face peering at me.

"Yes, Robin?" said my science program, reaching for his pipe and tobacco as he almost always does when we talk.

"I'd like some best-guess estimates from you on the Food Factory and the boy that turned up there."

"Sure thing, Robin," he said, tamping the tobacco with his thumb. "The boy's name is Wan. He appears to be between fourteen and nineteen years of age, probably toward the young end of the spread, and I would guess that he is fully genetically human."

"Where does he come from?"

"Ah, that is conjectural, Robin. He speaks of a 'main station', presumably another Heechee artifact in some ways resembling Gateway, Gateway Two and the Food Factory itself, but without any self-evident function. There do not appear to be any other living humans there. He speaks of 'Dead Men', who appear to be some sort of computer program like myself, although it is not clear whether they may not in fact be quite different in origin. He also mentions living creatures he calls 'the Old Ones' or 'the frog-jaws'. He has little contact with them, in fact avoids it, and it is not clear where they come from."

I took a deep breath. "Heechee?"

"I don't know, Robin. I cannot even guess. By Occam's Razor one would conjecture that living non-humans occupying a Heechee artifact might well be Heechee—but there is no direct evidence. We have no idea what Heechee look like, you know."

I did know. It was a sobering thought that we might soon find out.

"Anything else? Can you tell me what's happening with the tests to bring the factory back?"

"Sure thing, Robin," he said, striking a match to the pipe. "But I'm afraid there's no good news. The object appears to be course-programmed and under full control. Whatever we do to it it counteracts."

It had been a close decision whether to leave the Food Factory out in the Oort cloud and somehow try to ship food back to Earth, or bring the thing itself in. Now it looked as though we had no choice. "Is there— do you think it's under Heechee control?"

"There is no way to be sure as yet. Narrowly, I would conjecture not. It appears to be an automatic response. However," he said, puffing on his pipe, "there is something encouraging. May I show you some visuals from the factory?"

"Please do," I said, but actually he hadn't waited; Albert is a courteous program, but also a smart one. He disappeared and I was looking at a scene of the boy, Wan, showing Peter Herter how to open what seemed to be a hatch in the wall of a passage. Out of it he was pulling floppy soft packages of something in bright red wrappings.

"Our assumption as to the nature of the artifact seems to be validated, Robin. Those are edible and, according to Wan, they are continually replenished. He has been living on them for most of his life and, as you see, appears to be in excellent health, basically—I am afraid he is catching a cold just now."

I looked at the clock over his shoulder—he always keeps it at the right time for my sake. "That's all for now, then. Keep me posted if anything that affects your conclusions turns up."

"Sure thing, Robin," he said, disappearing.

I started to get up. Talking of food reminded me that lunch should be about ready, and I was not only hungry, I had plans for an afterlunch break. I tied the robe around me—and then remembered the message about the lawsuit. Lawsuits are nothing special in any rich man's life, but if Morton wanted to talk to me I probably ought to listen.

He responded at once, sitting at his desk, leaning forward earnestly. "We're being sued, Robin," he said. "The Food Factory Exploitation Corp., the Gateway Corp., plus Paul Hall, Dorema Herter-Hall and Peter

Herter, both in *propria persona* and as guardian for codefendant Janine Herter. Plus the Foundation and you personally."

"I seem to have a lot of company, at least. Do I have to worry?"

Pause. Thoughtfully, "I think you might, a little. The suit is from Hanson Bover. Trish's husband, or widower, depending on how you look at it." Morton was shimmering a little. It's a defect in his program, and Essie keeps wanting to fix it—but it doesn't affect his legal ability and I kind of like it. "He has got himself declared conservator of Trish Bover's assets, and on the basis of her first landing on the Food Factory he wants a full mission-completed share of whatever comes out of it."

That wasn't too funny. Even if we couldn't move the damn thing, with the new developments that bonus might be quite a lot. "How can he do that? She signed the standard contract, didn't she? So all we have to do is produce the contract. She didn't come back, therefore she doesn't get a share."

"That's the way to go if we wind up in court, yes, Robin. But there are one or two rather ambiguous precedents. Maybe not even ambiguous—her lawyer thinks they're good, even if they are a little old. The most important one was a guy who signed a fifty-thousand-dollar contract to do a tightrope walk over Niagara Falls. No performance, no pay. He fell off halfway. The courts held that he had given the performance, so they had to pay up."

"That's crazy, Morton!"

"That's the case law, Robin. But I only said you might have to worry a little. I think *probably* we're all right, I'm just not *sure* we're all right. We have to file an appearance within two days. Then we'll see how it goes."

"All right. Shimmer away, Morton," I said, and got up, because by now I was absolutely sure it was time for lunch. In fact, Essie was just coming through the door, and, to my disappointment, she was fully dressed.

Essie is a beautiful woman, and one of the joys of

being married to her for five years is that every year she looks better to me than the year before. She put her arm around my neck as we walked toward the dining porch and turned her head to look at me. "What's matter, Robin?" she asked.

"Nothing's the matter, dear S. Ya.," I said. "Only I was planning to invite you to shower with me after lunch."

"You are randy old goat, old man," she said severely. "What is wrong with showering after dark, when we will then naturally and inevitably go to bed?"

"By dark I have to be in Washington. And tomorrow you're off to Tucson for your conference, and this weekend I have to go for my medical. It doesn't matter, though."

She sat down at the table. "You are also pitifully bad liar," she observed. "Eat quickly, old man. One cannot take too many showers, after all."

I said, "Do you know, Essie, that you are a thoroughly sensual creature? It's one of your finest traits."

The quarterly statement on my food mines holdings was on my desk file in my Washington suite before breakfast. It was even worse than I had expected; at least two million dollars had burned up under the Wyoming hills, and another fifty thousand or so more was smoldering away every day until they got the fire all out. If they ever did. It did not mean I was in trouble, but it might mean that a certain amount of easy credit would no longer be easy. And not only did I know it, but by the time I got to the Senate hearing room it appeared that all of Washington knew it too. I testified quickly, along the same lines I had testified before, and when I was through Senator Praggler recessed the hearing and took me out to brunch. "I can't figure you out, Robin," he said. "Didn't your fire change your mind about anything?"

"No, why should it? I'm talking about the long pull."

He shook his head. "Here's somebody with a sizeable position in food mine stocks—you—begging for higher taxes on the mines! Doesn't make sense."

I explained it to him all over again. Taken as a whole, the food mines could easily afford to allocate, say, ten percent of their gross to restoring the Rockies after scooping out the shale. But no company could afford to do it on its own. If we did it, we'd just lose any competitive position, we'd be undersold by everybody else. "So if you put through the amendment, Tim," I said, "we'll all be *forced* to do it. Food prices will go up, yes—but not a lot. My accountants say no more than eight or nine dollars a year, per person. And we'll have an almost unspoiled countryside again."

He laughed. "You're a weird one. With all your do-gooding—and with your money, not to mention those things—" he nodded at the Out bangles I still wore on my arm, three of them, signifying three missions that had each scared the hell out of me when I earned them as a Gateway prospector, "why don't you run for the Senate?"

"Don't want to, Tim. Besides, if I ran from New York I'd be running against you or Sheila, and I don't want to do that. I don't spend enough time in Hawaii to make a dent. And I'm not going to move back to Wyoming."

He patted me on the shoulder. "Just this once," he said, "I'm going to use a little old-fashioned political muscle. I'll try to get your amendment through for you, Robin, though God knows what your competitors are going to do to try to stop it."

After I left him I dawdled back to the hotel. There was no particular reason to hurry back to New York, with Essie in Tucson, so I decided to spend the rest of the day in my hotel suite in Washington—a bad decision, as it turned out, but I didn't know that then. I was thinking about whether I minded being called a "do-gooder" or not. My old psychoanalyst had helped me along to a point where I didn't mind taking credit for things I thought deserved credit, but most of what I did I did for me. The revegetation amendment wouldn't cost me a dime; we'd make it up in raising prices, as I had explained. The money I put into space might pay off in dollar profits—probably would, I figured—but anyway it was going there because space was where my money had come from. And besides, I had some unfinished business out there. Somewhere. I sat by my window on the penthouse floor of the hotel, forty-five stories up, looking toward the Capitol and the Washington Monument, and wondered if my unfinished business was still alive. I hoped so. Even if she was hating me still.

Thinking about my unfinished business made me think of Essie, by now arriving in Tucson, and that gave me a twinge of worry. We were about due for another attack of the 130-day fever. I hadn't thought about that early enough. I didn't like the idea of her being three thousand kilometers away, in case it was a bad one. And, although I am not a jealous person, even if it was a mild, but lecherous and orgiastic one, as they seemed to be becoming more and more frequently, I really preferred that she be lecherous and orgiastic with me.

Why not? I called Harriet and had her make me reservations on an afternoon flight to Tucson. I could conduct my business as well from there as anywhere else, if not quite as comfortably. And then I started conducting some of it. Albert first. There was nothing significantly new, he said, except that the boy seemed to be developing a bad cold. "We've instructed the Herter-Hall party to administer standard antibiotics and symptom-suppressants," he told me, "but they will not receive the message for some weeks, of course."

"Serious?"

He frowned, puffing at his pipe. "Wan has never been exposed to most viruses and bacteria," he said, "so I can't make any definite statement. But, no, I would hope not. In any case, the expedition has medical supplies and equipment capable of dealing with most pathologies."

"Do you know anything more about him?"

"A great deal, but not anything that changes my previous estimates, Robin." Puff, puff. "His mother was Hispanic and his father American-Anglo, and they were both Gateway prospectors. Or so it would seem. So, apparently, in some way, were the personalities he refers to as the 'Dead Men,' although it is still unclear just what those are."

"Albert," I said, "look up some old Gateway missions, at least ten years back. See if you can find one that had an American and a Hispanic woman on it—and didn't come back."

"Sure thing, Bob." Some day I must tell him to change to a snappier vocabulary, but actually he works very well as he is. He said almost at once, "There is no such mission. However, there was a launch which contained a pregnant Hispanic woman, still unreported. Shall I display the specs?"

"Sure thing, Albert," I said, but he is not programmed to pick up that sort of nuance. The specs didn't tell much. I hadn't known the woman; she was before my time. But she had taken a One out after surviving a mission in which her husband and the other three crew members had been killed in a Five. And had never been heard of again. The mission was a simple go-out-and-see-what-you-get. What she had got had been a baby, in some strange place.

"That doesn't account for Wan's father, does it?"

"No, Robin, but perhaps he was on another mission. If we assume that the Dead Men are in some way related to unreturned missions, there must have been several."

I said, "Are you suggesting that the Dead Men are actual prospectors?"

"Sure thing, Robin."

"But how? You mean their brains might have been preserved?"

"Doubt it, Robin," he said, rekindling his pipe thoughtfully. "There's insufficient data, but I'd say whole-brain storage is no more than a point-one probability."

"Then what are the other points?"

"Perhaps a readout of the chemical storage of memory—not a high probability, perhaps put it at point-three. Which is still the highest probability we've got. Voluntary interface on the part of the subjects—for instance, if they talked all their memories onto tape somehow—really low. Point-zero zero one, tops. Direct mental link—what you might call telepathy of some sort—about the same. Means unknown, point-five plus. Of course, Robin," he added hurriedly, "you realize that all of these estimates are based on insufficient data and on inadequate hypotheses."

"I suppose you'd do better if you could talk to the Dead Men direct."

"Sure thing, Bob. And I am about to request such a hookup through the Herter-Hall shipboard computer, but it needs careful programming beforehand. It is not a very good computer, Robin." He hesitated. "Uh, Robin? There is one other interesting thing."

"What's that?"

"As you know, several large ships were docked at the Food Factory when it was discovered. It has been under frequent observation since, and the number of ships remained the same—not counting the Herter-Hall ship and the one in which Wan arrived two days ago, of course. But it is not certain they are the same ships."

"What?"

"It isn't certain, Robin," he emphasized. "One Heechee ship looks very much like another. But careful scan of the approach photos seems to show a different orientation on the part of at least one of the large ones. Possibly all three. As though the ships that were there had left, and new ones had docked."

A cold feeling went up and down my spine. "Albert," I said, finding it hard to get the words out, "do you know what that suggests to me?"

"Sure thing, Robin," he said solemnly. "it suggests that the Food Factory is still in operation. That it is converting the cometary gases to CHON-food. And sending them somewhere."

I swallowed hard, but Albert was still talking. "Also," he said, "there is quite a lot of ionizing radiation in the environment. I have to admit I don't know where it comes from."

"Is that dangerous to the Herter-Halls?"

"No, Robin, I would say not. No more than, say,

piezovision broadcasts are to you. It is not the risk, it is that I am puzzled about the source."

"Can't you ask the Herter-Halls to check?"

"Sure thing, Robin. I already have. But it'll take fifty days to get the answer."

I dismissed him and leaned back in my chair to think about the Heechee and their queer ways. . . .

And then it hit.

My desk chairs are all built to maximum comfort and stability, but this time I almost tipped it over. In a split second, I was in pain. Not just in pain; I was dizzy, disoriented, even hallucinating. My head felt as though it were about to burst, and my lungs seared like flame. I had never felt so sick, in both mind and body, and at the same time I found myself fantasizing incredible feats of sexual athletics.

I tried to get up, and couldn't. I flopped back in the chair, absolutely helpless. "Harriet!" I croaked. "Get a doctor!"

It took her a full three seconds to respond, and then her image wavered worse than Morton. "Mr. Broadhead," she said, looking queerly worried, "I cannot account for it, but the circuits are all busy. I— I— I—" It was not just her voice repeating, her head and body looked like a short loop of video tape, over and over shaping the same beginning of a word and snapping back to begin it again.

I fell off the chair onto the floor, and my last coherent thought was:

The fever.

It was back. Worse than I had ever felt it before. Worse, perhaps, than I could live through, and so bad, so painful, so terrifyingly, psychotically strange that I was not sure I wanted to.

5

Janine

The difference between the ages of ten and fourteen is immense. After three and a half years in a photon-powered spaceship en route to the Oort cloud, Janine was no longer the child who had left. She had not stopped being a child. She had just reached that early maturation plateau wherein the individual recognizes that it still has a great deal of growing to do. Janine was not in a hurry to become an adult. She was simply working at getting the job done. Every day. All the time. With whatever tools came to hand.

When she left the others, on the day when she met Wan, she was not particularly searching for anything. She simply wanted to be alone. Not for any really private purpose. Not even because, or not only because, she was tired of her family. What she wanted was something of her own, an experience not shared, an evaluation not helped by always-present grownups;

she wanted the look and touch and smell of the strangeness of the Food Factory, and she wanted it to be hers.

So she pushed herself at random along the passages, sucking from time to time at a squeeze bottle of coffee. Or what seemed to be "coffee" to her. It was a habit Janine had learned from her father, although, if you had asked her, she would have denied that she had learned any.

All of her senses thirsted for inputs. The Food Factory was the most fabulously exciting, delightfully scary thing that had ever happened to her. More than the launch from Earth when she was a mere child. More than the stained shorts that had announced she had become a woman. More than anything. Even the bare walls of the passages were exciting, because they were Heechee metal, a zillion years old, and still glowing with the gentle blue light their makers had built into them. (What sort of eyes had seen by that light when it was new?) She patted herself gently from chamber to chamber, only the balls of her feet ever touching the floor. In this room were walls of rubbery shelves (what had they held?), in that squatted a huge truncated sphere, top and bottom sliced off, mirror chrome in appearance, queerly powdery to the touch—what was it *for*? Some of the things she could guess at. The thing that looked like a table certainly was a table. (The lip around it was no doubt there to keep things from skittering off it in the Food Factory's gentle gravity.) Some of the objects had been identified for them by Vera, accessing the information stores of Heechee artifacts cataloged by the big data sources back on Earth. The cubicles with cobwebby green tracings on the walls were thought to have been for sleeping accommodations; but who was to know if dumb Vera was right? No matter. The objects themselves were thrilling. So was the presence of space to move around in. Even to get lost in. For until they reached the Food Factory, Janine had never, ever, not once in her life, had the chance to get lost. The idea made her itch with scary pleasure. Especially as the quite adult part of her fourteen-year-old brain was always aware that, no matter how lost she got, the Food Factory simply was not large enough for her to stay lost.

So it was a safe thrill. Or seemed so.

Until she found herself trapped by the farside docks, as something—Heechee? Space monster? Crazed old castaway with a knife?—came shambling out of the hidden passages toward her.

And then it was none of those things, it was Wan.

Of course, she didn't know his name. "Don't you come any closer!" she whimpered, heart in mouth, radio in hand, forearms hugged across her new breasts. He didn't. He stopped. He stared at her, eyes popping, mouth open, tongue almost hanging out. He was tall, skinny. His face was triangular, with a long, beaked nose. He was wearing what looked like a skirt and what looked like a tank-top, both dirty. He smelled male. He was shaking as he sniffed the air, and he was *young*. Surely he was not much older than Janine herself and the only person less than triple her age she had seen in years; and when he let himself drop gently to his knees and began to do what Janine had never seen any other person do she moaned while she giggled—amusement, relief, shock, hysteria. The shock was not at what he was doing. The shock came from *meeting a boy*. In her sleep Janine had dreamed wildly, but never of this.

For the next few days Janine could not bear to let Wan out of her sight. She felt herself to be his mother, his playmate, his teacher, his wife. "No, Wan! Sip it slowly, it's hot!" "Wan, do you mean to say you've been all alone since you were *three?*" "You have really beautiful eyes, Wan." She didn't mind that he was not sophisticated enough to respond by telling her that she had beautiful eyes, too, because she could definitely tell that she fascinated him in all her parts.

The others could tell that, too, of course. Janine did not mind. Wan had plenty of senses-sharp, eyes-bright, obsessed adoration to share around. He slept even less than she. She appreciated that, at first, because it meant there was more of Wan to share, but then she could see that he was becoming exhausted. Even ill. When he began to sweat and tremble, in the room with the glittering silver-blue cocoon, she was the one who cried, "Lurvy! I think he's going to be sick!" When he lurched toward the couch she flew to his side, fingers stretched to test his dry and burning forehead. The closing cover of the cocoon almost trapped her arm, gouging a long, deep slash from wrist to knuckles on her hand. "Paul," she shouted, drawing back, "we've got to—"

And then the 130-day madness hit them all. Worst of any time. Different from any time. Between one heartbeat and the next Janine was *sick*.

Janine had never been sick. Now and then a bruise, a cramp, a sniffle. Nothing more. For most of her life she had been under Full Medical and sickness simply did not occur. She did not comprehend what was happening to her. Her body raged with fever and pain. She hallucinated monstrous strange figures, in some of whom she recognized her caricatured family; others were simply terrifying and strange. She even saw herself—hugely bosomed and grossly hipped, but herself—and in her belly rumbled a frenzy to thrust and thrust into all the seen and imagined cavities of that fantasy something that, even in fantasy, she did not have. None of this was clear. Nothing was clear. The agonies and the insanities came in waves. Between them, for a second or two now and then, she caught glimpses of reality. The steely blue glow from the walls. Lurvy, crouched and whimpering beside her. Her father, vomiting in the passage. The chrome and blue cocoon, with Wan writhing and babbling inside the mesh. It was not reason or will that made her claw at the lid and, on the hundredth, or thousandth, try get it open; but she did it, at last, and dragged him whimpering and shaking out.

The hallucinations stopped at once.

Not quite as quickly, the pain, the nausea and the terror. But they stopped. They were all shuddering and reeling still, all but the boy, who was unconscious and breathing in a way that terrified Janine, great, hoarse, snoring gasps. "Help, Lurvy!" she screamed. "He's dying!" Her sister was already beside her, thumb on the boy's pulse, shaking her head to clear it as she peered dizzily at his eyes.

"Dehydrated. Fever. Come on," she cried, struggling with Wan's arms. "Help me get him back to the ship. He needs saline, antibiotics, a febrifuge, maybe some gamma globulin—"

It took them nearly twenty minutes to tow Wan to the ship, and Janine was in terror that he would die at every bounding, slow-motion step. Lurvy raced ahead the last hundred meters, and by the time Paul and Janine had struggled him through the airlock she had already unsealed the medic kit and was shouting orders. "Put him down. Make him swallow this. Take a blood sample and check virus and antibody titers. Send a priority to base, tell them we need medical instructions— if he lives long enough to get them!"

Paul helped them get Wan's clothes off and the boy wrapped in one of Payter's blankets. Then he sent the message. But he knew, they all knew, that the problem of whether Wan lived or died would not be solved from Earth. Not with a round-trip time of seven weeks before they could get an answer. Payter was swearing over the bio-assay mobile unit. Lurvy and Janine were working on the boy. Paul, without saying a word to anyone, struggled into his EVA suit and exited into space, where he spent an exhausting hour and a half redirecting the transmitter dishes—the main one to the bright double star that was the planet Neptune and its moon, the other to the point in space occupied by the Garfeld mission. Then, clinging to the hull, he radio-commanded Vera to repeat the SOS to each of them at max power. They might be monitoring. They might not. When Vera signaled that the messages were sent he reoriented the big dish to Earth. It took them three hours, first to last, and whether either of them would receive his message was doubtful. It was no less doubtful that either would have much help to offer. The Garfeld ship was smaller and less well equipped than their own, and the people at the Triton base were short-timers. But if either did they could hope for a message of aid—or at least sympathy—a lot faster than from Earth.

In an hour Wan's fever began to recede. In twelve the twitchings and babblings diminished and he slept normally. But he was still very sick.

Mother and playmate, teacher and at-least-fantasy wife, now Janine became Wan's nurse as well. After the first round of medication, she would not even let Lurvy give him his shots. She went without sleep to sponge his brow. When he soiled himself in his coma she cleaned him fastidiously. She had no concentration left for anything else. The amused or concerned looks and words from her family left her untouched, until she brushed Wan's unkempt hair off his face, and Paul made a patronizing comment. Janine heard the jealousy in the tone and flared, "Paul, you're *sickening*! Wan *needs* me to take care of him!"

"And you do enjoy it, don't you?" he snapped. He was really angry. Of course, that sparked more anger in Janine; but her father put in, gently enough, "Let the girl be a girl, Paul. Were you not yourself once young? Come, let us examine this *Träumeplatz* again—"

Janine surprised herself by letting the peacemaker succeed; it had been a marvelous chance of a furious spat, but that was not where her interests lay. She took time for a tight, small grin about Paul's jealousy, because that was a new service stripe to sew on her sleeve, and then back to Wan.

As he mended he became even more interesting. From time to time he woke, and spoke to her. When he was asleep she studied him. Face so dark, body olive; but from waist to thigh he had the palest skin, the color of bread dough, taut over his sharp bones. Scant body hair. None on his face except a soft, almost invisible strand or two—more lip-lashes than mustache.

Janine knew that Lurvy and her father made a joke of her, and that Paul was actually jealous of the attentions he had avoided so long. It made a nice change. She had status. For the first time in her life, what she was doing was the most significant activity of the group. The others came to her to sue for permission to question Wan, and when she thought he was tiring they accepted her command to stop.

Besides, Wan fascinated her. She mapped him against all her previous experience of Men, to his advantage. Even against her pen-pals, Wan was better looking than the ice-skater, smarter than the actors, almost as tall as the basketball player. And against all of them, especially against the only two males she had been within tens of millions of kilometers of in years, Wan was so marvelously *young*. And Paul and her father, not. The backs of old Peter's hands bore irregular blotches of caramel-colored pigment, which was gross. But at least the old man kept himself neat. Even dainty, in the continental way—even clipped the hairs that grew inside his ears with tiny silver scissors, because Janine had caught him at it. While Paul— In one of her skirmishes with Lurvy, Janine had snarled, *"That's what you go to bed with? An ape with hairy ears? I'd puke."*

So she fed Wan, and read to him, and drowsed over him while he slept. She shampooed his hair, and trimmed it to a soup-bowl mop, allowing Lurvy to help her get it even, and blow-dried it smooth. She washed his clothes and, spurning Lurvy for this, patched them and even cut down some of Paul's to fit him. He accepted it all, every bit, and enjoyed it as much as she.

As he grew stronger, he no longer needed her as much, and she was less able to protect him from the questions of the others. But they were protective, too. Even old Peter. The computer, Vera, burrowed into its medical programs and prepared a long list of tests to be performed on the boy. "Assassin!" raged Peter. "Has it no understanding of a young man who has been so close to death that it wishes to finish it?" It was not entirely consideration. Peter had questions of his own, and he had been asking them when Janine would allow it, sulking and fidgeting when she would not. "That bed of yours, Wan, tell me again what you feel when you are in it? As though you are somehow a part of millions of people? And also they of you, isn't that so?" But when Janine accused him of interfering with Wan's recovery, the old man desisted. Though never for long.

Then Wan was well enough for Janine to allow herself a full night's sleep in her own private, and when she woke her sister was at Vera's console. Wan was holding to the back of her chair, grinning and frowning at the unfamiliar machine, and Lurvy was reading off to him his medical report. "Your vital signs are normal, your weight is picking up, your antibody levels are in the normal range—I think you're going to be all right now, Wan."

"So now," cried her father, "at last we can talk? About this faster-than-light radio, the machines, the place he comes from, the dreaming room?" Janine hurled herself into the group.

"Leave him alone!" she snarled. But Wan shook his head.

"Let them ask what they like, Janine," he said in his shrill, breathy voice.

"Now?"

"Yes, now!" stormed her father. "Now, this minute! Paul, come you here and tell this boy what we must know."

They had planned this, Janine realized, the three of them; but Wan did not object, and she could not pretend he was unfit for questioning any longer. She marched over and sat beside him. If she could not prevent this interrogation, at least she would be there to protect him. She gave formal permission, coldly: "Go ahead, Paul. Say what you want to say, but don't tire him out."

Paul looked at her ironically, but spoke to Wan. "For more than a dozen years," he said, "every hundred and thirty days or so, the whole Earth has gone crazy. It looks like it's your fault, Wan."

The boy frowned, but said nothing. His public defender spoke for him. "Why are you picking on him?" she demanded.

"No one is 'picking', Janine. But what we experienced was the fever. It can't be a coincidence. When Wan gets into that contraption he broadcasts to the world." Paul shook his head. "Dear lad, do you have any idea of how much trouble you've caused? Ever since you began coming here, your dreams have been shared by millions of people. Billions! Sometimes you were peaceful, and your dreams were peaceful, and that wasn't so bad. Sometimes you weren't. I don't want you to blame yourself," he added kindly, forestalling Janine, "but thousands and thousands of people have died. And the property damage—Wan, you just can't imagine."

Wan shrilled defensively, "I have never harmed anyone!" He was unable to take in just what he was accused of, but there was no doubt in his mind that Paul was accusing. Lurvy put her hand on his arm.

"I wish it were so, Wan," she said. "The important thing is, you mustn't do that again."

"No more dreaming in the couch?"

"No, Wan." He looked to Janine for guidance, then shrugged.

"But that is not all," Paul put in. "You have to help us. Tell us everything you know. About the couch. About the Dead Men. About the faster-than-light radio, the food—"

"Why should I?" Wan demanded.

Patiently, Paul coaxed: "Because in that way you can make up for the fever. I don't think you understand how important you are, Wan. The knowledge in your head might mean saving people from starvation. Millions of lives, Wan."

Wan frowned over that concept for a moment, but "millions" was meaningless to him as applying to human beings—he had not yet adjusted to "five". "You make me angry," he scolded.

"I don't mean to, Wan."

"It is not what you mean to, it is what you do. You have just told me that," the boy grumbled spitefully. "All right. What do you want?"

"We want you to tell us everything you know," Paul said promptly. "Oh, not all at once. But as you remember. And we want you to go through this whole Food Factory with us and explain everything in it—as far as you can, I mean."

"This place? There is nothing here but the dreaming room, and you won't let me use that!"

"It is all new to us, Wan."

"It is nothing! The water does not run, there is no library, the Dead Men are hard to talk to, nothing grows! At home I have everything, and much of it is working, so you can see for yourself."

"You make it sound like heaven, Wan."

"See for yourself! If I can't dream, there is no reason to stay here!"

Paul looked at the others, perplexed. "Could we do that?"

"Of course! My ship will take us there—not all of you, no," Wan corrected himself. "But some. We can leave the old man here. There is no woman for him, anyway, so there is no pairing to destroy. Or even," he added cunningly, "only Janine and I can go. Then there will be more room in the ship. We can bring you back machines, books, treasures—"

"Forget that, Wan," Janine said wisely. "They'll never let us do that."

"Not so fast, my girl," her father said. "That is not for you to decide. What the boy is saying is interesting. If he can open the gates of heaven for us, who are we to stand outside in the cold?"

Janine studied her father, but his expression was bland. "You don't mean you'd let Wan and me go there alone?"

"That," he said, "is not the question. The question is, how can we most rapidly complete this God-bedamned mission and return to our reward. There is no other."

"Well," said Lurvy after a moment, "we don't have to decide that right now. Heaven will wait for us, for all our lives."

Her father said, "That is true, yes. But, expressed concretely, some of us have less lives to wait than others."

Every day new messages came in from Earth. Infuriatingly, these related only to a remote past, before

Wan, irrelevant to everything they were doing or planning now: Submit chemical analyses of this. X-ray that. Measure these other things. By now the slow packets of photons that transmitted the word of their reaching the Food Factory had arrived at Downlink-Vera on Earth, and perhaps replies were already on their way. But they would not arrive for weeks. The base at Triton had a smarter computer than Vera, and Paul and Lurvy argued for transmitting all their data there for interpretation and advice. Old Peter rejected the idea with fury. "Those wanderers, gypsies? Why should we give them what costs us so much to get!"

"But nobody's questioning us, Pa," Lurvy coaxed. "It's all ours. The contracts spell it all out."

"No!"

So they fed all that Wan told them into Shipboard-Vera, and Vera's small, slow intelligence painfully sorted the bits into patterns. Even into graphics. The external appearance of the place Wan had come from —it was probably not a very good likeness, because it was apparent that Wan had not had the curiosity to study it very closely. The corridors. The machines. The Heechee themselves; and each time Wan offered corrections:

"Ah, no. They both have beards, males and females. Even when they are quite young. And the breasts on the females are—" He held his hands just below his rib cage, to show how low they swung. "And you do not give them the right smell."

"Holos don't smell at all, Wan," said Paul.

"Yes, exactly! But they do, you see. In rut, they smell very much."

And Vera mumbled and whined over the new data, and shakily drew in the new revisions. After hours of this, what had been a game for Wan turned into drudgery. When he began saying, "Yes, it is perfect, that is exactly how the Dead Men's room looks," they all understood that he was merely agreeing with anything that would stop the boredom for a while, and gave him a rest. Then Janine would take him for a wander through the corridors, sound and vision pickups strapped to her shoulder, in case he said something of value or pointed out a treasure, and they spoke of other things. His knowledge was as astonishing as his ignorance. Both were unpredictable.

It was not only Wan that needed study. Every hour Lurvy or old Peter would come up with a new idea for diverting the Food Factory from its programmed drive, so that they could try to accomplish their original purpose. None worked. Every day more messages came in from Earth. They were still not relevant. They were not even very interesting; Janine let a score of letters from her pen-pals stay in Vera's memory without bothering to retrieve them, since the messages she was getting from Wan filled her needs. Sometimes the communications were odd. For Lurvy, the announcement that her college had named her its Woman of the Year. For old Peter, a formal petition from the city he had been born in. He read it and burst into laughter. "Dortmund still wishes me to run for Bürgermeister! What nonsense!"

"Why, that's really nice," Lurvy said agreeably. "It's quite a compliment."

"It is quite nothing," he corrected her severely. "Bürgermeister! With what we have I could be elected president of the Federal Republic, or even——" He fell silent, and then said gloomily, "If, to be sure, I ever see the Federal Republic again." He paused, looking over their heads. His lips worked silently for a moment, and then he said: "Perhaps we should go back now."

"Aw, Pop," Janine began. And stopped, because the old man turned on her the look of an alpha wolf on a cub. There was a sudden tension among them, until Paul cleared his throat and said:

"Well, that's certainly one of our options. Of course, there's a legal question of contract——"

Peter shook his head. "I have thought of that. They owe us so much already! Simply for stopping the fever, if they pay us only one percent of the damage we save it is millions. Billions. And if they won't pay——" He hesitated, and then said, "No, there is no question that they won't pay. We simply must speak to them. Report that we have stopped the fever, that we cannot move the

Food Factory, that we are coming home. By the time a return message can arrive we will be weeks on our way."

"And what about Wan?" Janine demanded.

"He will come with us, to be sure. He will be among his own kind again, and that is surely what is best for him."

"Don't you think we ought to let Wan decide that? And what happened to sending a bunch of us to investigate his heaven?"

"That was a dream," her father said coldly. "Reality is that we cannot do everything. Let someone else explore his heaven, there is plenty for all; and we will be back in our homes, enjoying riches and fame. It is not just a matter of the contract," he went on, almost pleadingly. "We are saviors! There will be lecture tours and endorsements for the advertising! We will be persons of great power!"

"No, Pop," Janine said, "listen to me. You've all been talking about our duty to help the world—feed people, bring them new things to make their lives better. Well, aren't we going to do our duty?"

He turned on her furiously. "Little minx, what do you know about duty? Without me you would be in some gutter in Chicago, waiting for the welfare check! We must think of ourselves as well!"

She would have replied, but Wan's wide-eyed, frightened stare made her stop. "I *hate* this!" she announced. "Wan and I are going to go for a walk to get away from the lot of you!"

"He is not really a bad person," she told Wan, once they were beyond the sound of the others. Quarreling voices had followed them and Wan, who had little experience of disagreements, was obviously upset.

Wan did not reply directly. He pointed to a bulge in the glowing blue wall. "This is a place for water," he said, "but it is a dead one. There are dozens of them, but almost all dead."

Out of duty, Janine inspected it, pointing her shoulder-held camera at it as she slid the rounded cover back and forth. There was a protuberance like a nose at the top of it, and what must be a drain at the bottom; it was almost large enough to get into, but bone dry. "You said one of them still works, but the water isn't drinkable?"

"Yes, Janine. Would you like me to show it to you?"

"Well, I guess so." She added, "Really, don't let them get to you. They just get excited."

"Yes, Janine." But he was not in a talkative mood.

She said, "When I was little he used to tell me stories. Mostly they were scary, but sometimes not. He told me about *Schwarze Peter,* who, as far as I can figure out, was something like Santa Claus. He said if I was a good little girl *Schwarze Peter* would bring me a doll at Christmas, but if I wasn't he'd bring me a lump of coal. Or worse. That's what I used to call him, *Schwarze Peter.* But he never gave me a lump of coal." He was listening intently as they moved down the glowing corridor, but he did not respond. "Then my mother died," she said, "and Paul and Lurvy got married and I went to live with them for a while. But Pop wasn't so bad, really. He came to see me as often as he could—I guess. Wan! Do you understand what I'm saying to you?"

"No," he said. "What's Santa Claus?"

"Oh, Wan!"

So she explained Santa Claus to him, and Christmas, and then had to explain winter and snow and gift-giving. His face smoothed, and he began to smile; and curiously, as Wan's mood improved Janine's grew worse. Trying to make Wan understand the world she lived in made her confront the world ahead. Almost, she thought, it would be better to do what Peter proposed, pack it all in, go back to their real lives. All the alternatives were frightening. Where they were was frightening, if she let herself feel it—in some kind of an artifact that was doggedly plowing its way through space to some unknown destination. What if it arrived? What would they confront? Or if they went back with Wan, what would be there? Heechee? Heechee! *There* was fear! Janine had lived all her young life with the Heechee just outside it—terrifying if real, less real than mythical. Like *Schwarze Peter* or Santa Claus. Like

God. All myths and deities are tolerable enough to believe in; but what if they become real?

She knew that her family were as fearful as she, though she could not tell that from anything they said —they were setting an example of courage to her. She could only guess. She guessed that Paul and her sister were afraid but had made up their minds to gamble against that fear for the sake of what might come of it. Her own fear was of a very special kind—less fear of what might happen than of how badly she might behave while it was happening to her. What her father felt was obvious to everyone. He was angry and afraid, and what he was afraid of was dying before he cashed in on his courage.

And what did Wan feel? He seemed so uncomplicated as he showed her about his domain, like one child guiding another through his toy chest. Janine knew better. If she had learned anything in her fourteen years, it was that nobody was uncomplicated. Wan's complications were merely not the same as her own, as she saw at once when he showed her the water fixture that worked. He had not been able to drink the water, but he had used it for a toilet. Janine, brought up in the great conspiracy of the Western world to pretend that excretion does not happen, would never have brought Wan to see this place of stains and smells, but he was wholly unembarrassed. She could not even make him embarrassed. "I had to go somewhere," he said sullenly, when she reproached him for not using the ship's sanitary like everybody else.

"Yes, but if you did it the right way Vera would have known you were sick, don't you see? She's always analyzing our, uh, the bathroom stuff."

"There ought to be some other way."

"Well, there is." There was the mobile bio-assay unit, which took tiny samples from each of them—which had, in fact, been put to work on Wan, once the necessity was perceived. But Vera was not a very smart computer, and had not thought to program her mobile unit to sample Wan until told to do so, a little late. "What's the matter?"

He was acting uncomfortable. "When the Dead Men give me a medical check they stick things in me. I don't like that."

"It's for your own good, Wan," she said severely. "Hey! That's an idea. Let's go talk to the Dead Men."

And there was Janine's own complicatedness. She didn't really want to talk to the Dead Men. She just wanted to get away from the embarrassing place they were in; but by the time they had propelled themselves to the place where the Dead Men were, which was also the place where Wan's dreaming couch was, Janine had decided to want something else. "Wan," she said, "I want to try the couch."

He tilted his head back and narrowed his eyes, appraising her over his long nose. "Lurvy told me not to do that any more," he stated.

"I know she did. How do I get in?"

"First you tell me I must do what you all say," he complained, "then you all tell me to do different things. It is very confusing."

She had already stepped into the cocoon and stretched out. "Do I just pull the top down over me?"

"Oh," he said, shrugging, "if you've made up your mind—yes. It snaps shut, there, where your hand is, but when you want to come out you just push."

She reached for the webby top and pulled it toward her, looking up at his petulant, concerned face. "Does it—hurt?"

"Hurt? No! What an idea!"

"Well, what does it feel like?"

"Janine," he said severely, "you are very childish. Why do you ask questions when you can see for yourself?" And he pushed down on the shimmery wire covering, and the catch midway down the side rustled and locked. "It is best if you go to sleep," he called down to her, through the shining blue network of wire.

"But I'm not sleepy," she objected reasonably. "I'm not anything. I don't feel a thing. . . ."

And then she did.

It was not what she had expected out of her own experience of the fever; there was no obsessive interference with her own personality, no point source of feelings. There was only a warm and saturating glow. She was surrounded. She was an atom in a soup of sensation. The other atoms had no shape or individuality. They were not tangible or hard-edged. She could still see Wan, peering worriedly down at her through the wire when she opened her eyes, and these other—souls?—were not at all as real or as immediate. But she could feel them, as she had never felt another presence. Around her. Beside her. Within her. They were warm. They were comforting.

When Wan at last wrenched open the metal wire and pulled at her arm, she lay there staring at him. She did not have the strength to rise, or the desire. He had to help her up, and she leaned on his shoulder as they started back.

They were less than halfway back to the Herter-Hall ship when the other members of the family interrupted them, and they were furious. "Stupid little brat!" Paul raged. "You ever do anything like that again and I'll paddle your pink little ass for you!"

"She won't!" her father said grimly. "I will see to that, right now; and as to you, little miss, I will see to you later."

They had all become so quarrelsome! No one paddled Janine's bottom for trying out the dreaming couch. No one punished her at all. They all punished each other, instead, and did it all the time. The truce that had held for three and a half years, because each of them enforced it for himself, the alternative being mutual murder, dissolved. Paul and the old man did not speak for two days, because Peter had dismantled the couch without consultation. Lurvy and her father spat and shouted at each other because she had programmed too much salt in their meal, and then again, when it was his turn, because he had programmed too little. And as to Lurvy and Paul—they no longer slept together; they hardly spoke; they would surely not have stayed married, if there had been a divorce court within 5,000 A.U.

But if there had been a source of authority of any kind within 5,000 A.U., at least the disputes could have been resolved. Someone could have made their decisions. Should they return? Should they try to overpower the Food Factory's guidance? Should they go with Wan to explore the other place—and if so, who should go and who should remain behind? They could not agree on grand plans. They could not even agree on the decisions of every hour, to take a machine apart and risk its destruction, or to leave it alone and give up the hope of some wonderful discovery that could change everything. They could not agree on who should talk to the Dead Men by radio, or what to ask them. Wan showed them, willingly enough, how to try to tempt the Dead Men into conversation, and they put Vera's sound system in linkage with the "radio". But Vera could not handle much give and take; and when the Dead Men did not understand her questions, or did not want to participate, or were simply too insane to be of any use, Vera was beaten.

All this was awful for Janine, but worst of all was Wan himself. The squabbling made him confused and indignant. He stopped following her around. And after one sleep, when she sat up and looked around for him, he was gone.

Fortunately for Janine's pride, everyone else was gone, too—Paul and Lurvy outside the ship to reorient the antennae; her father asleep, so that she had time to deal with her jealousy. Let him be a pig! she thought. It was stupid of him not to realize that she had many friends, while he had only her; but he would find out! She was busy writing long letters to her neglected correspondents when she heard Paul and her sister returning; and when she told them that Wan had been gone for at least an hour she was unprepared for their reaction. "Pa!" Lurvy cried, rattling at the curtain of her father's private. "Wake up! Wan's gone!"

As the old man came blinking out, Janine said disagreeably, "Now, what's the matter with all of you?"

"You don't understand, do you?" Paul asked coldly. "What if he's taken the ship?"

It was a possibility that had never occurred to Janine, and it was like a blow in the face. "He wouldn't!"

"Would he not?" snarled her father. "And how do you know that, little minx? And if he does, what of us?" He finished zipping his coverall and stood up, glowering at them. "I have told you all," he said—but looking at Lurvy and Paul, so that Janine understood she was not a part of their "all"—"I have told you that we must find a definite solution. If we are to go with him in his ship, we must do it. If not, we cannot take the risk that he will take it into his foolish little mind to go back without warning. That is assuredly certain."

"And how do we do that?" Lurvy demanded. "You're preposterous, Pa. We can't guard the ship day and night."

"And your sister cannot guard the boy, yes," the old man nodded. "So we must either immobilize the ship, or immobilize the boy."

Janine flew at him. "You monsters!" she choked. "You've been planning this all out when we weren't around!" Her sister caught and held her.

"Calm down, Janine," she ordered. "Yes, it's true we've talked about it—we had to! But nothing's settled, certainly not that we will hurt Wan."

"Then settle it!" Janine flared. "I vote we go with Wan!"

"If he hasn't gone already, by himself," Paul put in.

"He hasn't!"

Lurvy said practically, "If he has, it's too late for us to do anything about it. Outside of that, I'm with Janine. We go! What do you say, Paul?"

He hesitated. "I—guess so," he conceded. "Peter?"

The old man said with dignity, "If you are all agreed, then what does it matter how I vote? There is only the question remaining who is to go and who is to stay. I propose—"

Lurvy stopped him. "Pa," she said, "I know what you are going to say, but it won't work. We need to leave at least one person here, to keep in contact with Earth. Janine's too young. It can't be me, because I'm the best pilot and this is a chance to learn something about piloting a Heechee ship. I don't want to go without Paul, and that leaves you."

They took Vera apart, component by component, and redistributed her around the Food Factory. Fast memory, inputs, and displays went into the dreaming chamber, slow memory lining the passageway outside, transmission still in their old ship. Peter helped, silent and taciturn; the meaning of what they were doing was that further communications of interest would come from the exploring party, via the radio system of the Dead Men. Peter was helping to write himself off, and knew it. There was plenty of food in the ship, Wan told them; but Paul would not be satisfied with the automatic replenishment of God knew what product of the Food Factory, and he made them carry aboard rations of their own, as much as they could stow. Whereupon Wan insisted that they stock up with water, and so they depleted the recycling stocks in the ship to fill his plastic bags and loaded them, too. Wan's ship had no beds. None were needed, Wan pointed out, because the acceleration cocoons were enough to protect them during maneuvers, and to keep them from floating around while they slept in the rest of the voyage—suggestion vetoed by both Lurvy and Paul, who dismantled the sleeping pouches from their private and reinstalled them in the ship. Personal possessions: Janine wanted her secret stash of perfume and books, Lurvy her personal locked bag, Paul his cards for solitaire. It was long and hard work, though they discovered they could ease it by sailing the plastic waterbags and the softer, solider other stores along the corridors in a game of slow-motion catch; but at last it was done. Peter sat sourly propped against a corridor wall, watching the others mill about, and tried to think of what had been forgotten. To Janine it seemed as though they were already treating him as though he were absent, if not dead, and she said, "Pop? Don't take it so hard. We'll all be back as soon as we can."

He nodded. "Which comes to," he said, "let me see,

forty-nine days each way, plus as long as you decide to stay in this place." But then he pushed himself up, and allowed Lurvy and Janine to kiss him. Almost cheerfully, he said, "Bon voyage. Are you sure you have forgotten nothing?"

Lurvy looked around, considering. "I think not—unless you think we should tell your friends we are coming, Wan?"

"The Dead Men?" he shrilled, grinning. "They will not know. They are not alive, you know, they have no sense of time."

"Then why do you like them so much?" Janine demanded.

Wan caught the note of jealousy and scowled at her. "They are my friends," he said. "They cannot be taken seriously all the time, and they often lie. But they do not ever make me feel afraid of them."

Lurvy caught her breath. "Oh, Wan," she said, touching him. "I know we haven't been as nice as we might. We've all been under a great strain. We're really better people than we must seem to you."

Old Peter had had enough. "Go you now," he snarled. "Prove this to him, do not stand talking forever. And then come back and prove it to me!"

6
After the Fever

Less than two hours—the fever had never been so short before. Nor had it ever been as intense. The most susceptible one percent of the population had simply been out of it for four hours, and nearly everyone had been severely affected.

I was one of the lucky ones, because after the fever I was only stuck in my room, with nothing more than a bump on the head from falling over. I wasn't trapped in a wrecked bus, crashed out of a jet-liner, struck by a runaway car, or bleeding to death on an operating table while surgeons and nurses writhed helplessly on the floor. All I had was one hour, fifty-one minutes and forty-four seconds of delirious misery, and that diluted because it was shared with eleven billion other people.

Of course, everybody in all those eleven billion was trying to get in touch with everybody else, all at once, and so communications were jammed for fair. Harriet formed herself in the tank to tell me that at least twenty-five calls were coming in for me—my science program, my legal program, three or four accountancy programs from my holdings, and quite a few real, live people. None of them, she told me apologetically when I asked, was Essie; the circuits to Tucson were out entirely at the moment, and I couldn't place a call from my end either. None of the machines had been affected by the madness. They never were. The only time something went wrong with them was when some live person had injected himself into the circuit, for maintenance or re-design. But, as statistically that was happening a million times a minute, somewhere in the world, with some machine or another, it was not surprising that some things took a little while to get going again.

First order of business was business; I had to pick up the pieces. I gave Harriet a hierarchy of priorities, and she began feeding me reports. Quick bulletin from the food mines: no significant damage. Real estate: some minor incidents of fire and flooding, nothing that mattered. Someone had left a barrier open in the fish factories and six hundred million fingerlings swam out to lose themselves in the open sea; but I was only a minority stockholder in them anyway. Taken all in all, I had come out of the fever smelling of roses, I thought, or anyway a lot better than a lot of others. The fever had struck the Indian subcontinent after midnight of a day that already had seen one of the worst hurricanes the Bay of Bengal had produced in fifty years. The death toll was immense. Rescue efforts had simply stopped for two hours. Tens, maybe even hundreds, of millions of people had been simply unable to drag themselves to high ground, and southern Bangladesh was a swamp of corpses. Add in a refinery explosion in California, a train wreck in Wales, and a few as yet un-catalogued disasters—the computers did not yet have an estimate of deaths, but the news reports were calling it the worst ever.

By the time I had taken all the urgent-urgent calls the elevators were running again. I wasn't a captive any more. Looking out the window, I could see the Washington streets were normal enough. My trip to Tucson, on the other hand, was well bollixed. Since half the jets in the air had been on automatic pilot for two hours, seriously depleting their fuel, they had been landing where they could, and the lines had equipment in all sorts of wrong places. The schedules were scrambled. Harriet booked me the best she could, but the first space she could confirm was not until noon the next day. I couldn't even call Essie, because the circuits were still jammed. That was only an annoyance, not a problem. If I really wanted to get through, there were priorities at my disposal—the rich have their perks. But the rich have their pleasures, too, and I decided it would be fun to surprise Essie by dropping in on her.

And meanwhile I had time to spare.

And all this time my science program had been bursting with things to tell me. That was the dessert after the spinach and liver. I had put it off until I had a chance for a good, long natter; and that time had arrived. "Harriet," I said, "put him on." And Albert Einstein took form in the tank, leaning forward and twitching with excitement. "What is it, Al," I asked, "something good?"

"Sure thing, Robin! We've found out where the fever comes from—it's the Food Factory!"

It was my own fault. If I had let Albert tell me what was on his mind at once, I wouldn't have been just about the last person on Earth to find out that I owned the place all the trouble came from. That was the first thing that hit me, and I was thinking about possible liability and sniffing for advantages all the time he was explaining the evidence to me. First and conclusive, of course, was the on-the-spot pickup from the Food Factory itself. But we should have known all along. "If I had only timed the onsets carefully," Albert berated himself, "we could have located the source years ago. And there were plenty of other clues, consistent with their photonic nature."

"Their what nature?"

"They are electromagnetic, Robin," he explained. He tamped tobacco into his pipe and reached for a match.

"You realize, of course, that this is established by transmission time—we received whatever signal caused the madness at the same time as the transmission showing it happening."

"Wait a minute. If the Heechee have faster-than-light radio, why isn't this the same?"

"Ah, Robin! If we only knew that!" he twinkled, lighting his pipe. "I can only conjecture—" puff, puff, "that this particular effect is not compatible with their other mode of transmission, but the reasons for that I cannot even speculate on at this time. And, of course," he went on, "there are certain questions raised at once to which we do not as yet have any answers."

"Of course," I said, but I didn't ask him what they were. I was on the track of something else. "Albert? Display the ships and stations you drew information from in space."

"Sure thing, Robin." The flyaway hair and the seamed, cheerful face melted away, and at once the holographic tank filled with a representation of circumsolar space. Nine planets. A girdle of dust that was the asteroid belt, and a powdery shell far out that was the Oort cloud. And about forty points of colored light. The representation was in logarithmic scale, to get it all in, and the size of the planets and artifacts immensely enlarged. Albert's voice explained, "The four green ships are ours, Robin. The eleven blue objects are Heechee installations; the round ones are only detected, the star-shaped ones have been visited and are mostly manned. All the others are ships that belong to other commercial interests, or to governments."

I studied the plot. Not very many of the sparks were anywhere near the green ship and blue star that marked the Food Factory. "Albert? If somebody had to get another ship out to the Food Factory, which one could get there fastest?"

He appeared in the lower corner of the projection, frowning and sucking his pipe stem. A golden point near Saturn's rings began to flash on and off. "There's a Brazilian cruiser just departing Tethys that could make it in eighteen months," he said. "I have displayed only the ships that were involved in my radio-location. There are several others—" new lights winked on in a scatter around the tank, "that could do better, provided they have adequate fuel and supplies. But none in less than a year."

I sighed. "Turn it off, Albert," I said. "The thing is, we're into something I didn't expect."

"What's that, Robin?" he asked, filling the tank again and folding his hands over his belly in a comfortable way.

"That cocoon. I don't know how to handle it. I don't even see the point of it. What's it for, Albert? Have you got any conjectures?"

"Sure thing, Robin," he said, nodding cheerfully. "My best conjectures are a pretty low order of probability, but that's just because there are so many unknowns. Let's put it this way. Suppose you were a Heechee—something like an anthropologist, say—interested in keeping an eye on a developing civilization. Evolution takes a long time, so you don't want to just sit there and watch. What you'd like to do is get a quick estimate, maybe every thousand years or so, sort of a spot check. Well, given something like the cocoon, you could just send somebody over to the Food Factory every once in a while, maybe every thousand years or more; climb in the couch, get an instant feel for what was happening. It would take only minutes." He paused consideringly for a moment, before going on. "Then—but this is a speculation on top of a conjecture; I wouldn't even assign a probability rating to it at all—then, if you found anything interesting, you could explore further. You could even do something else. This is really far out, Robin. You might even *suggest* things. The cocoon transmits as well as receives, that's what the fevers came from. Perhaps it can also transmit concepts. We know that in human history many of the great inventions sprang up all over the world, apparently independently, maybe simultaneously. Are they Heechee suggestions, via the couch?"

He sat there, puffing his pipe and smiling at me, while I thought about that.

* * *

All the thinking in the world didn't make it good, clean fun. Thrilling, maybe. But nothing you could relax to. The world had changed in fundamental ways since the first astronauts discovered Heechee diggings on Venus, and the more we explored the bigger the changes got. A lost kid, playing with something he didn't understand, had plunged the whole human race into recurring madness for more than a decade. If we kept on playing with things we didn't understand, what were the Heechee going to give us for an encore?

To say nothing of the queasiness of Albert's suggestion that these creatures had been spying on us for hundreds of thousands of years—maybe even throwing us a crumb, now and then, to see what we would make of it.

I told Albert to bring me up to date on everything else he knew about what was going on on the Food Factory, and while he was running through the physical facts I called up Harriet. She appeared in one corner of the tank, looking questioning, and took my order for dinner while Albert kept right on with his show and tell. He was continuously monitoring all the transmissions even as he was reporting on them, and he showed me selected scenes of the boy, the Herter-Hall party, the interiors of the artifact. The damn thing was still determined to go its own way. Best course estimates suggested that it was moving toward a new cluster of comets, several million miles away—at present rates, it would get there in a few months. "Then what?" I demanded.

Albert shrugged apologetically. "Presumably it will then stay there until it has mined them of all the CHON ingredients, Robin."

"Then can we move it?"

"No evidence, Robin. But it's possible. Speaking of which, I have a theory about the controls of the Heechee ships. When one of them reaches an operating artifact—the Food Factory, Gateway, whatever—its controls unlock and it can then be redirected. At any rate, I think that may be what happened to Ms. Patricia

Bover—and that, too, has certain obvious implications," he twinkled.

I don't like to let a computer program think it's smarter than I am. "You mean that there may be a lot of stranded Gateway astronauts all over the Galaxy, because their controls unlocked and they didn't know how to get back?"

"Sure thing, Robin," he said approvingly. "That may account for what Wan calls the 'Dead Men'. We've received some conversations with them, by the way. Their responses are sometimes quite nonrational, and of course we're handicapped by not being able to interact. But it does appear that they are, or were, human beings."

"Are you telling me they were alive?"

"Sure thing, Robin, or at least in the sense that Enrico Caruso's voice on a tape was once the voice of a living Neapolitan tenor. Whether they are 'alive' now is a matter of definition. You might ask the same question—" puff, puff, "about me."

"Huh." I thought for a minute. "Why are they so crazy?"

"Imperfect transcription, I would say. But that is not the important thing." I waited until he drew on his pipe to get ready to tell me the important thing. "It seems rather sure, Robin, that the transcription occurred by some sort of chemical readout of the actual brains of the prospectors."

"You mean the Heechee killed them and poured their brains into a bottle?"

"Certainly not, Robin! First, I would hazard the opinion that the prospectors died naturally rather than being killed. That would degrade the chemistry of brain storage and contribute to the degradation of the information. And certainly not into a bottle! Into some sort of chemical analogs, perhaps. But the point is, how did this happen to be?"

I groaned. "Do you want me to abolish your program, Al? I could get all this quicker from straight visual synoptics."

"Sure thing you could, Robin, but not," he twinkled,

"perhaps, as entertainingly. At any rate, the question is, how did the Heechee happen to have equipment to read out a human brain? Think about it, Robin. It seems very improbable that the chemistry of the Heechee would be the same as the chemistry of a human being. Close, yes. We know that from general considerations, e.g., what they breathed and ate. Fundamentally their chemistry was not unlike ours. But peptides are quite complex molecules. It seems most unlikely that a compound which represents, e.g., the ability to play a Stradivarius well, or even toilet-training, would be the same in their chemistry as in ours." He started to relight his pipe, then caught my eye and added hurriedly, "So I conclude, Robin, that these machines were designed not for Heechee brains."

He startled me. "For humans, then? But why? How? How did they know? When—"

"Please, Robin. At your instructions, your wife has programmed me to make large deductions from small data. Therefore I cannot defend all that I say. But," he added, nodding sagely, "I have this opinion, yes."

"Jesus," I said. He did not seem to want to add anything to that, so I tucked it away and went on to the next worry. "What about the Old Ones? Are they human, do you think?"

He tapped his pipe out and reached for the tobacco pouch. "I would say not," he said at last.

I didn't ask him what the alternative was. I didn't want to hear it.

When Albert had run himself dry for the moment, I told Harriet to put my legal program on. I couldn't talk to him right away, though, because right then my dinner came up and the waiter was a human being. He wanted to ask me how I had got through the fever, so that he could tell me how he had, and that took time. But at last I sat down in front of the holo tank, sliced into my chicken steak and said, "Go ahead, Morton, what's the bad news?"

He said apologetically, "You know that Bover suit?"

"What Bover suit?"

"Trish Bover's husband. Or widower, depending on

how you look at it. We filed the appearance, only unfortunately the judge had a bad attack of the fever
and— Well. He is wrong in the law, Robin, but he
denied our request for time to set a hearing date and
entered summary judgment against."

I stopped chewing. "Can he do that?" I roared
through my mouthful of prime rare chicken.

"Well, yes, or at least he did it. But we'll get him on
appeal, only that makes it a little more complicated.
Her lawyer got a chance to argue, and he pointed out
that Trish did file a mission report. So there's some
question whether she actually completed the mission,
do you see? Meanwhile—"

Sometimes I think Morton is too humanly programmed; he does know how to draw out a discussion
so. "Meanwhile what, Morton?"

"Well, since the recent, ah, episode, there seems to
be another complication. Gateway Corp wants to go
slow until they figure out just where they are with this
fever business, so they've accepted service of an injunction. Neither you nor Food Factory Inc. is supposed to
proceed with exploitation of the factory."

I blew up. "Shit, Mort! You mean we can't *use* it
after we bring it all the way in from orbit?"

"I'm afraid I mean more than that," he apologized.
"You're enjoined to stop moving it. You're enjoined to
refrain from interfering with its normal activities in any
way, pending a declarative judgment. That's Bover's
action, on the grounds that if you prevent it from producing food by moving to a new comet cluster you're
endangering his interest. Now, we can get that vacated,
I'm sure. But by then Gateway Corp will have some
sort of action to stop doing *everything* until they get a
handle on the fever."

"Oh, God." I put down my fork. I wasn't hungry any
more. "The only good thing," I said, "is that's an order
they can't enforce."

"Because it will take so long to get a message to the
Herter-Hall party, yes, Robin," he nodded. "On the—"

He disappeared, *zit*. He slid diagonally away out of
the tank, and Harriet appeared. She looked terrible. I

have good programs for my computer help. But they don't always bring good news. "Robin!" she cried. "There's a message from Mesa General Hospital in Arizona—it's your wife!"

"Essie? *Essie?* Is she sick?"

"Oh, worse than that, Robin. Total somatic cessation. She was killed in a car crash. They've got her on life support, but— There's no prognosis, Robin. She isn't responding."

I didn't use my priorities. I didn't want to take the time. I went straight to the Washington office of the Gateway Corp, who went to the Secretary of Defense, who squeezed space for me out of a hospital plane leaving Bolling in twenty-five minutes, and I made it.

The flight was three hours, and I was in suspended animation all the way. There were no comm facilities for passengers in the plane. I didn't even want them. I just wanted to get there. When my mother died and left me it hurt, but I was poor and confused and used to hurting. When the love of my life, or at any rate the woman who seemed to come to be the love of my life after she was safely gone, also left me—without quite dying, because she was stuck in some awful astrophysical anomaly and far out of reach forever—that also hurt. But I was hurting all over anyway then. I wasn't used to happiness, hadn't formed the habit of it. There is a Carnot law to pain. It is measured not by absolutes but the difference between source and ambience, and my ambience had been too safe and too pleasurable for too long to equip me for this. I was in shock.

Mesa General was a low-rise, dug into the desert outside Tucson. All you could see as we came up to it were the solar installations on the "roof," but under them were six subterranean floors of hospital rooms, labs, and operating theaters. They were all full. Tucson is a commuting city, and the madness had struck at drive time.

When I finally got a floor nurse to stop and answer a question, what I heard was that Essie was still on the heart-lung, but might be taken off at any moment. It was a question of triage. The machines might better be used for other patients, whose chances were better than hers.

I am shamed to say how fast conceptions of fairness went out the window when it was my own wife who was on the machines. I hunted out a doctor's office—*he* wouldn't be using it for some time—kicked out the insurance adjustor who had borrowed his desk and got on the wires. I had two senators on the line at once before Harriet broke in with a report from our medical program. Essie's pulse had begun to respond. They now thought her chances were good enough to justify giving her the additional chance of staying on the machines for a while.

Of course, Full Medical helped. But the waiting room outside had all its benches full of people waiting for treatment, and I could see from the neck-bands that some of them were Full Medical too; the hospital was simply swamped.

I could not get in to see her. Intensive Care was *No Visitors*, and no visitors meant not even me; there was a Tucson city policeman at the door, forcing himself to stay awake after a very long, hard day and feeling mean. I fiddled with the absent doctor's desk set until I found a closed-circuit line that looked into Intensive Care, and I just left it on. I couldn't see how well Essie was doing. I couldn't even tell for sure which mummy she was. But I kept looking at it. Harriet called in from time to time to pass on little news items. She didn't bother with messages of sympathy and concern; there were plenty of those, but Essie had written me a Robinette Broadhead program to deal with social time-wasters, and Harriet gave callers an image and a worried smile and a thank you without bothering to cut me in to the circuit. Essie had been very good at that kind of programming—

Past tense. When I realized I was thinking of a past-tense Essie is when I felt really bad.

After an hour a Gray Lady found me and gave me bouillon and crackers, and a little later I spent forty-five minutes in line for the public men's room; and that was about all the diversion I had on the third floor of Mesa General until, at last, a candy-striper poked her head in the door and said, *"Señor Broad'ead? Por favor."* The cop was still at the door of Intensive Care, fanning himself with his sweaty Stetson to stay awake, but with the candy-striper leading me firmly by the hand he did not interfere.

Essie was under a positive-pressure bubble. There was a transparent patch just at her face, so that I could see a tube coming out of her nostril and a wad of bandaging over the left side of her face. Her eyes were closed. They had bundled her dirty-gold hair into a net. She was not conscious.

Two minutes was all they allowed, and that wasn't enough time for anything. Not enough even to figure out what all the lumpy, bulky objects under the translucent part of her bubble were all about. Not enough at all for Essie to sit up and talk to me or to change expression. Or even to have one.

In the hall outside, her doctor gave me sixty seconds. He was a short, pot-bellied old black man wearing blue-eyed contact lenses, and he looked at a piece of paper to see who it was he was talking to. "Oh, yes, Mr. Blackhead," he said. "Your wife is receiving the best of care, she is responding to treatment, there is some chance she will be conscious for a short time toward evening."

I didn't bother to correct him about the name and picked the three top questions on the list: "Will she be in pain? What happened to her? Is there anything she needs?—I mean *anything.*"

He sighed and rubbed his eyes. Evidently the contacts had been in too long. "Pain we can take care of, and she's already on Full Medical. I understand you are an important man, Mr. Brackett. But there is nothing for you to do. Tomorrow or the next day, maybe there'll be something she'll need. Today, no. Her whole left side was crushed when the bus folded in on her. She was bent almost double and stayed that way for six or seven hours, until somebody got to her."

I didn't know I had made a sound, but the doctor

heard something. A little sympathy came through the contact lenses as he peered up at me. "That was actually to her advantage, you know. It probably saved her life. Being squeezed was as good as compression pads, otherwise she would have bled to death." He blinked down at the scrap of paper in his hand. "Um. She's going to need, let me see, a new hip joint. Splints to replace two ribs. Eight, ten, fourteen—maybe twenty square inches of new skin, and there's considerable tissue loss to the left kidney. I think we'll want a transplant."

"If there's anything at all—"

"Nothing at all, Mr. Blackett," he said, folding up the paper. "Nothing now. Go away, please. Come back after six if you want to, and you may be able to talk to her for a minute. But right now we need the space you're taking up."

Harriet had already arranged for the hotel to move Essie's things out of her room and into a penthouse suite, and she had even ordered and had delivered toilet stuff and a couple of changes of clothing. I holed up there. I didn't want to go out. I didn't enjoy seeing the cheerful tipplers in the lobby bar, or the streets full of people who had got safely through the fever and wanted to tell each other what a close thing it had been for them.

I made myself eat. Then I made myself sleep. I succeeded in that much, but not in staying asleep very long. I took a long, hot whirly bath and played some music for background; it was actually quite a nice hotel. But when they went from Stravinsky to Carl Orff that lusty, horny Catullus poetry made me think about the last time I had played it with my lusty, horny, and, at the moment, seriously broken-up wife.

"Turn it off," I snapped and ever-vigilant Harriet stopped it in midshriek.

"Do you want to receive messages, Robin?" she inquired from the same audio speaker.

I dried myself carefully, and then said: "In a minute. I might as well." Dried, brushed, in clean clothes, I sat down in front of the hotel's comm system. They weren't quite nice enough to give their guests full holo, but Harriet looked familiar enough as she peered at me out of a flat-plate display. She reassured me about Essie. She was continuously monitoring, and everything was going well enough—not far enough, of course. But not badly. Essie's own real flesh-and-blood doctor was in the picture, and Harriet gave me a taped message from her. It translated to don't worry, Robin. Or, more accurately, don't worry *quite* as much as you think you ought to.

Harriet had a batch of action messages for me to deal with. I authorized another half-million dollars for fire-fighting in the food mines, instructed Morton to get a hearing time with the Gateway Corp for our man in Brasilia, told my broker what to sell to give me a little more liquidity as a hedge against unreported fever losses. Then I let the most interesting programs report in, finishing with Albert's latest synoptic from the Food Factory. I did all this, you understand, with great clarity and efficiency. I had accepted the fact that Essie's chances of survival were measurably improving all the time, so I didn't need to spare any energy for grief. And I had not, entirely, allowed myself to understand how many gobbets of flesh and bone had been gouged out of my love's lovely body, and that saved me all sorts of expenditures, for emotions I did not want to explore.

There was a time when I went through several long years of shrinkery, in the course of which I found out a lot of places inside my head that I didn't much like having there. That's okay. Once you take them out and look at them—well, they're pretty bad, but at least they're outside, now, not still inside and poisoning your system. My old psychiatric program, Sigfrid von Shrink, said it was like moving your bowels.

He was right, far as he went—one of the things I found unlikeable about Sigfrid was that he was infuriatingly reliably right, all too much of the time. What he didn't say was that you never got finished moving your bowels. I kept coming up with new excreta, and, you know, no matter how much of it you encounter, you never get to liking it.

I turned Harriet off, except for standby in case of something urgent, and watched some piezovision comedies for a while. I made myself a drink out of the suite's adequate wet bar, and then I made another. I wasn't watching the pv, and I wasn't enjoying the drink. What I was doing was encountering another great glob of fecal matter coming out of my head. My dearest beloved wife was lying all beaten and broken in Intensive Care, and I was thinking about somebody else.

I turned off the tap-dancers and called for Albert Einstein. He popped onto the plate, his white hair flying and his old pipe in his hand. "What can I do for you, Robin?" he beamed.

"I want you to talk to me about black holes," I said.

"Sure thing, Robin. But we've been over this a good many times, you know—"

"Fuck off, Albert! Just do it. And I don't mean in mathematics, I just want you to explain them as simply as you can." One of these days I would have to get Essie to rewrite Albert's program a little less idiosyncratically.

"Sure thing, Robin," he said, cheerfully ignoring my temper. He wrinkled his furry eyebrows. "Ah-ha," he said. "Uh-huh. Well, let's see."

"Is that a hard question for you?" I asked, more surprised than sarcastic.

"Of course not, Robin. I was just thinking how far back I should start. Well, let's start with light. You know that light is made up of particles called photons. It has mass, and it exerts pressure—"

"Not that far back, Albert, please."

"All right. But the way a black hole begins starts with a failure of light pressure. Take a big star—a blue Class-O, say. Ten times as massive as the sun. Burns up its nuclear fuel so fast that it only lives about a billion years. What keeps it from collapsing is the radiation pressure—call it the 'light pressure'—from the nuclear reaction of hydrogen fusing into helium inside it. But then it runs out of hydrogen. Pressure stops. It collapses. It does so very, very fast, Robin, maybe in only a matter of hours. And a star that used to be millions of kilometers in diameter is all of a sudden only thirty kilometers. Have you got that part, Robin?"

"I think so. Get on with it."

"Well," he said, lighting his pipe and taking a couple of puffs—I can't help wondering if he enjoys it!— "that's one of the ways black holes get started. The classical way, you might call it. Keep that in mind, and now go on to the next part: escape velocity."

"I know what escape velocity is."

"Sure thing, Robin," he nodded, "an old Gateway prospector like you. Well. When you were on Gateway, suppose you threw a rock straight up from the surface. It would probably come back, because even an asteroid has some gravity. But if you could throw it fast enough —maybe forty or fifty kilometers an hour—it wouldn't come back. It would reach escape velocity and just fly away forever. On the Moon, you'd have to throw it a lot faster still, say two or three kilometers a second. On the Earth, faster than that—better than eleven kilometers a second.

"Now," he said, reaching forward to tap coals out of his pipe and light it again, "if you—" tap, tap, "if you were on the surface of some object that had a very, *very* high surface gravity, the condition would be worse. Suppose the gravity were such that the escape velocity were up real high, say around three hundred and ten thousand kilometers a second. You couldn't throw a rock that fast. Even light doesn't quite go that fast! So even light—" puff, puff, "can't escape, because its velocity is ten thousand kilometers a second too slow. And, as we know, if light can't escape, then nothing can escape; that's Einstein. If I may be excused the vanity." He actually winked at me over his pipe. "So that's a black hole. It's black because it can't radiate at all."

I said, "What about a Heechee spaceship? They go faster than light."

Albert grinned ruefully. "Got me there, Robin, but we don't know *how* they go faster than light. Maybe a Heechee can get out of a black hole, who knows? But we don't have any evidence of one of them ever doing it."

I thought that over for a moment. "Yet," I said.

"Well, yes, Robin," he agreed. "The problem of going faster than light, and the problem of escaping from a black hole, are essentially the same problem." He paused. A long pause. Then, apologetically, "I guess that's about all we can profitably say on that subject, right now."

I got up and refreshed my drink, leaving him sitting there, patiently puffing his pipe. Sometimes it was hard to remember that there was really nothing there, nothing but a few interference patterns of collimated light, backed up by some tons of metal and plastic. "Albert," I said, "tell me something. You computers are supposed to be lightning-fast. Why is it that you take so long to answer sometimes? Just dramatic effect?"

"Well, Bob, sometimes it is," he said after a moment, "like that time. But I am not sure you understand how difficult it is for me to 'chat.' If you want information about, say, black holes, I have no trouble producing it for you. Six million bits a second, if you like. But to put it in terms you can understand, above all to put it in the form of conversation, involves more than accessing the storage. I have to do word-searches through literature and taped conversations. I have to map analogies and metaphors against your own mind-sets. I have to meet such strictures as are imposed by your defined normatives for my behavior, and by relevance to the tone of the particular chat. 'Tain't easy, Robin."

"You're smarter than you look, Albert," I said.

He tapped his pipe out and looked up at me under his shaggy white mop. "Would you mind, Bob, if I said so are you?"

I let him go, saying, "You're a good old machine, Albert." I stretched out on the jelly-bed couch, half asleep with my drink in my hand. At least he had taken my mind off Essie for a while, but there was a nagging question in my mind. Somewhere, sometime, I had said the same thing to some other program, and I couldn't remember when.

Harriet woke me up to say that there was an in-person call from our doctor—not the program, but the real live Wilma Liederman, M.D., who came to see us to make sure the machines were doing things right, every once in a while. "Robin," she said, "I think Essie's out of danger."

"That's—marvelous!" I said, wishing I had saved words like "marvelous" for when I really meant them, because they didn't do justice to the way I felt. Our program had already accessed the Mesa General circuits, of course. Wilma knew as much about her condition as the little black man I had talked to—and, of course, had pumped all of Essie's medical history back into the Mesa General store. Wilma offered to fly out herself if we wanted her to. I told her she was the doctor, not me, and she told me that she would get a Columbia classmate of hers in Tucson to look in on Essie instead.

"But don't go to see her tonight, Robin," she said. "Talk to her on the phone if you want to—I prescribe it—but don't tire her out. By tomorrow—well, I think she'll be stronger."

So I called Essie, and talked to her for three minutes —she was groggy, but she knew what was happening. And then I let myself go back to sleep, and just as I was dropping off I remembered that Albert had called me "Bob".

There was another program that I had been on friendly terms with, a long time ago, that sometimes called me "Robin" and sometimes "Bob" and even "Bobby". I hadn't talked to that particular program in quite a while, because I hadn't felt the need of it; but maybe I was beginning to.

Full Medical is—well, it's full medical. It's everything. If there's a way to keep you healthy, and especially to keep you alive, you've got it. And there are lots of ways. Full Medical runs to hundreds of thousands of dollars a year. Not too many people can afford it—something under one tenth of one percent even in the developed countries. But it buys a lot. Right after lunch the next day, it bought me Essie.

Wilma said it was all right, and so did everybody else. The city of Tucson had recovered enough for that sort of thing. The city had got over the emergency aspects of the fever. Its structures were back to business as usual, meaning that they once again had time to deliver what people paid for. So at noon a private ambulance trucked in bed, heart-lung machine, dialysis pack, and peripherals. At twelve-thirty a team of nurses moved into the suite across the hall, and at a quarter after two I rode up in the freight elevator with six cubic meters of hardware, in the heart of which was the heart of me, namely my wife.

Among the other things Full Medical bought were a trickle of pain-killers and mood-mediators, corticosteroids to speed healing and moderators to keep the corticosteroids from spoiling her cells, four hundred kilograms of plumbing under the framework of the bed to monitor all of what Essie did, and to intervene to help her do it when she couldn't. Just transferring her from the travel machine to the one in the master bedroom took an hour and a half, with Wilma's classmate supervising a team of internes and orderlies. They threw me out while that was going on, and I drank a couple of cups of coffee down in the hotel lobby, watching the teardrop-shaped elevators climb up and down the interior walls. When I figured I was allowed back I met the doctor from the hospital in the hall. He had managed to get a little sleep and he was wearing granny glasses instead of the contacts. "Don't tire her out," he said.

"I'm getting tired of hearing that."

He grinned and invited himself to share a third cup of coffee with me. He turned out to be quite a nice guy, as well as the best short basketball center Tempe had ever had, when he was an Arizona State undergraduate. There is something I like about a man of a hundred and sixty centimeters who goes out for the basketball team, and we parted friends. That was the most reassuring thing of all. He wouldn't have let that happen if he hadn't been pretty sure Essie was going to make it.

I did not then appreciate how much "making it" she was going to have to do.

She was still under the positive-pressure bubble, and that spared me from seeing quite how used up she looked. The day-duty nurse retreated to the sitting room, after telling me not to get Essie too tired, and we talked for a while. We didn't say anything, really. S. Ya. is not your talkative type person. She asked me what the news was from the Food Factory, and when I had given her a thirty-second synoptic on that she asked what the news was about the fever. By the time I had given her four or five thousand-word answers to her one-sentence questions it began to dawn on me that talking was really quite a strain and that I shouldn't tire her out.

But she was talking, and even talking coherently, and did not seem worried; and so I went back to my console and to work.

There was the usual raft of reports to get through and decisions to make. When that was done I listened to Albert's latest reports from the Food Factory for a while and then realized it was time for me to go to sleep.

I lay in bed for quite a while. I wasn't restless. I wasn't exhausted. I was just letting the tensions drain out of me. In the sitting room I could hear the night nurse moving around. On the other side, from Essie's room, came the constant faint sigh and hum and gurgle of the machines that were keeping my wife alive. The world had got well ahead of me. I was not taking it all in. I had not yet quite understood that forty-eight hours before, Essie had been dead. Kaput. Xed. No longer alive. If it hadn't been for Full Medical, and a lot of luck, I would along about now have been selecting the clothes to wear to her funeral.

And inside my head there was a small minority of cells of the brain that understood that fact and was thinking, well, you know, maybe, it just *might* have been tidier all around if she hadn't been brought back to life.

This had nothing to do with the fact that I *loved* Essie, loved her a lot, wished her nothing but well, had gone into shock when I heard she was hurt. The minority party in my brain spoke only for itself. Every time the question came up a thundering majority voted for loving Essie, whenever polled, however asked.

I have never been entirely sure what the word "love" means. Especially when applied to myself. Just before I fell asleep I thought for a moment of dialing Albert up and asking him to explain it. But I didn't. Albert was the wrong program to ask, and I didn't want to start up with the right one.

The synoptics kept coming in, and I watched the unfolding story of the Food Factory, and I felt like an anachronism. A couple of centuries ago the world-girdlers of England and Spain operated at a remove of a month or two from the action fronts. No cable, no satellites. Their orders went out on sailing ships, and replies came back when they could. I wished I could share their skills. The fifty days of round-trip time between us and the Herter-Halls seemed like forever. Here was I at Ghent, and there were they, Andy Jackson pounding the pee out of the British weeks after the war was over at New Orleans. Of course, I had sent out instant orders on how they were to conduct themselves. What questions they were to ask of the boy, Wan. What attempts they were to make to divert the Food Factory from its course. And five thousand astronomical units away, they were doing what occurred to them to do, and by the time my orders arrived all the questions would be moot.

As Essie mended, so did my spirits. Her heart pumped by itself. Her lungs kept her in air. They took the positive-pressure bubble off her and I could touch her and kiss her cheek, and she was taking an interest in what went on. Had been all along; when I said it was too bad she'd missed her conference she grinned up at me. "All on tape, dear Robin; have been playing it back when you were busy."

"But you couldn't give your own paper—"

"You think? Why not? I wrote 'Robinette Broadhead' program for you, did you not know I also wrote one for me? Conference moved in full holographics and S. Ya. Lavorovna-Broadhead projection gave complete text. To considerable approval. Even handled questions," she boasted, "by borrowing your Albert program in drag."

Well, she's an astonishing person, as I have always known. The trouble is that I expect her to be astonishing, and when I talked to her doctor he brought me down. He was on the hop, between the suite and Mesa General, and I asked him if I could bring her home. He hesitated, peering up at me through the blue contacts. "Yes, probably," he said. "But I'm not sure you understand how serious her injuries are, Mr. Broadhead. All that's happening now is that she's building up some reserves of strength. She's going to need them."

"Well, I know that, Doc. There'll have to be another operation—"

"No. Not one, Mr. Broadhead. I think your wife will spend most of the next couple of months in surgery and convalescence. And I don't want you assuming that the results are a foregone conclusion," he lectured. "There's a risk to every procedure, and she's up against some hairy ones. Cherish her, Mr. Broadhead. We reanimated her after one cardiac arrest. I don't guarantee it'll happen every time."

So I went in to see Essie in somewhat chastened mood to get on with the cherishing.

The nurse was standing by her bed, and both of them were watching Essie's tapes of the computer conference on her flat-plate viewer. Since Essie's plate was slaved to the big full-holographic interactive one I had had moved into my room, there was a little yellow attention light in the corner, meant for me. Harriet had something she wanted to tell me about. It could wait; when the light began to pulse and brighten and turn to red was when it got important, and at the moment Essie was at the top of my priorities. "You can leave us for a while, Alma," Essie said. The nurse looked at me and shrugged why-not, so I took the chair next to the bed and reached for Essie's hand.

"It's nice to be able to touch you again," I said.

Essie has a coarse, deep chuckle. I was glad to hear it. "Touch more in a couple weeks," she said. "Meanwhile, no rule against kissing."

So, of course, I kissed her—hard enough so that something must have registered on her telltales, because the day nurse popped her head in the door to see what was going on. She didn't stop us, though. We stopped ourselves. Essie reached up with her right hand —the left was still in its cast, covering God knew what —and pushed her streaky dark-blonde hair away from her eyes. "Very nice," she judged. "Do you want to see what Harriet has to say?"

"Not particularly."

"Untrue," she said. "You have been talking to Dr. Ben, I see, and he has told you to be sweet to me. But you always are, Robin, only not everybody would notice." She grinned at me and turned her head to the plate. "Harriet!" she called. "Robin is here."

I had not until that moment known that my secretary program would respond to my wife's commands as well as my own. But I hadn't known she could borrow my science program, either. Especially without my knowing about it. When Harriet's cheerful and concerned face filled the screen I told her, "If it's business I'll take it later—unless it can't wait?"

"Oh, no, nothing like that," Harriet said. "But Albert's desperate to talk to you. He's got some good stuff from the Food Factory."

"I'll take it in the other room," I started, but Essie put her free hand on mine.

"No. Here, Robin. I'm interested, too."

So I told Harriet to go ahead, and Albert's voice came on. But not Albert's face. "Take a look at this," Albert said, and the screen filled with a sort of American Gothic family portrait. A man and a woman—not really—a male and a female, standing side by side.

They had faces and arms and legs, and the female had
breasts. Both had skungy beards and long hair pulled
into braids, and they were wearing wrap-around garments like saris, with dots of color brightening the drab
cloth.

I caught my breath. The pictures had taken me by
surprise.

Albert appeared in the lower corner of the plate.
"These are not 'real,' Robin," he said. "They are simply compositions generated by the shipboard computer
from Wan's description. The boy says they are pretty
accurate, though."

I swallowed and glanced at Essie. I had to control
my breathing before I could ask, "Are these—are these
what the Heechee look like?"

He frowned and chewed on his pipe stem. The figures on the screen rotated solemnly, as though they
were doing a slow folk-dance, so that we could see all
sides. "There are some anomalies, Robin. For example,
there is the famous question of the Heechee ass. We
have some Heechee furniture, e.g., the seats before the
control panels in their ships. From these it was deduced
that the Heechee bottom was not as the human bottom,
because there seems to be room for a large pendulant
structure, perhaps a divided body like a wasp's, hanging
below the pelvis and between the legs. There is nothing
of this sort in the computer-generated image. But—
Occam's Razor, Robin."

"If I just give you time, you'll explain that," I commented.

"Sure thing, Robin, but it's a law of logic that I think
you know. In the absence of evidence, it is best to take
the simplest theory. We know of only two intelligent
races in the history of the universe. These people do not
seem to belong to ours—the shape of the skull, and
particularly the jaw, is different; there is a triangular
arcade, more like an ape's than a human being's, and
the teeth are quite anomalous. Therefore it is probable
that they belong to the other."

"Is somewhat scary," Essie offered softly. And it
was. Especially to me, since you might say that it was

my responsibility. I was the one who had ordered the Herter-Hall bunch to go out and look around, and if they found the Heechee in the process. . . .

I was not ready to think of what that might mean.

"What about the Dead Men? Do you have anything on them?"

"Sure thing, Robin," he said, nodding his dustmop head. "Look at this."

The pictures winked away, and text rolled up the screen:

MISSION REPORT

Vessel 5-2, Voyage O8D31. Crew A. Meacham, D. Filgren, H. Meacham.

Mission was science experiment, crew limited to allow instrumentation and computational equipment. Maximum life-support time estimated 800 days. Vessel still unreported day 1200, presumed lost.

"It was only a fifty thousand dollar bonus—not much, but it was one of the earliest from Gateway," Albert said over the text. "The one called 'H. Meacham' appears to be the 'Dead Man' Wan calls Henrietta. She was a sort of A.B.D. astrophysicist—you know, Robin, 'All But Dissertation'. She blew that. When she tried to defend it they said it was more psychology than physics, so she went to Gateway. The pilot's first name was Doris, which checks, and the other person was Henrietta's husband, Arnold."

"So you've identified one of them? They were really real?"

"Sure thing, Robin—point nine nine sure, anyway. These Dead Men are sometimes nonrational," he complained, reappearing on the plate. "And of course we have had no opportunity for direct interrogation. The shipboard computer is not really up to this kind of task. But, apart from the confirmation of names, the mission seems appropriate. It was an astrophysical investigation, and Henrietta's conversation includes repeated references to astrophysical subjects. Once you subtract the sexual ones, I mean," he twinkled, scratching his cheek with his pipestem. "For example. 'Sagittarius A West'—a radio source at the center of the Galaxy. 'NGC 1199'. A giant elliptical galaxy, part of a large cluster. 'Average radial velocity of globular clusters'— in our own galaxy, that comes to about 50 kilometers per second. 'High-redshift OSOs'—"

"You don't have to list them all," I said hastily. "Do you know what they all mean? I mean, if you were talking about all those things, what would you be talking about?"

Pause—but a short one; he was not accessing all the literature on the subject, he had already done that. "Cosmology," he said. "Specifically, I think I would be talking about the classic Hoyle-Öpik-Gamow controversy; that is, whether the universe is closed, or open ended, or cyclical. Whether it is in a steady state, or began with a big bang."

He paused again, but this time it was to let me think. I did, but not to much effect. "There doesn't seem to be much nourishment in that," I said.

"Perhaps not, Robin. It does sort of tie in with your questions about black holes, though."

Well, damn your calculating heart, I thought, but did not say. He looked innocent as a lamb, puffing away on his old pipe, calm and serious. "That'll be all for now," I ordered, and kept my eyes on the blank screen long after he had disappeared, in case Essie was going to ask me about why I had been inquiring about black holes.

Well, she didn't. She just lay back, looking at the mirrors on the ceiling. After a while she said, "Dear Robin, know what I wish?"

I was ready for it. "What, Essie?"

"Wish I could scratch."

All I could manage to say was, "Oh." I felt deflated —no; plugged up. I was all ready to defend myself— with all gentle care, of course, because of Essie's condition. And I didn't have to. I picked up her hand. "I was worried about you," I offered.

"Yes, so was I," she said practically. "Tell me, Robin. Is true that the fevers are from some sort of Heechee mind-ray?"

"Something like that, I suppose. Albert says it's electromagnetic, but that's all I know." I stroked the veins on the back of her hand, and she moved restlessly. But only from the neck up.

"I am apprehensive about Heechee, Robin," she said.

"That's very sensible. Even temperate. Me, I'm scared shitless." And, as a matter of fact I was; in fact, I was trembling. The little yellow light winked on at the corner of the screen.

"Somebody wants to talk to you, Robin."

"They can wait. I'm talking to the woman I love right now."

"Thank you. Robin? If you are scared of Heechee as I am, how is it that you go right ahead?"

"Well, honey, what choice do I have? There's fifty days of dead time. What we just heard is ancient history, twenty-five days old. If I told them to break off and go home right now, it would be twenty-five days before they heard it."

"Surely, yes. But if you could stop, would you?" I didn't answer. I was feeling very strange—a little frightened, a lot unlike myself. "What if Heechee don't like us, Robin?" she asked.

And what a good question that was! I had been asking it of myself ever since the first day I considered getting into a Gateway prospecting ship and setting out to explore for myself. What if we meet the Heechee and they don't like us? What if they squash us like flies, torture us, enslave us, experiment on us—what if they simply ignore us? With my eyes on the yellow dot, which was beginning to pulse slowly, I said, mothering her, "Well, there's not much chance that they will actually do us any harm—"

"I do not need soothing, Robin!" She was distinctly edgy, and so was I. Something must have been showing up on her monitors, because the day nurse looked in again, hovered indecisively in the doorway, and went away.

I said, "Essie, the stakes are too big. Remember last year in Calcutta?" We had gone to one of her seminars, and had cut it short because we couldn't bear the sight of the abject city of two hundred million paupers.

Her eyes were on me, and she was frowning. "Yes, I know, starvation. There has always been starvation, Robin."

"Not like this! Not like what it will be before very long, if something doesn't happen to prevent it! The world is bursting at the seams. Albert says—" I hesitated. I didn't actually want to tell her what Albert said. Siberia was already out of food production, its fragile land looking like the Gobi because of overpressure. The topsoil in the American Midwest was down to scant inches, and even the food mines were straining to keep up with demand. What Albert said was that we had maybe ten years.

The signal light had gone to red and was winking rapidly, but I didn't want to interrupt myself. "Essie," I said, "if we can make the Food Factory work, we can bring CHON-food to all the starving people, and that means no more starvation *ever*. That's only the beginning. If we can figure out how to build Heechee ships for ourselves, and make them go where we like—then we can colonize new planets. Lots of them. More than *that*. With Heechee technology we can take all the asteroids in the solar system and turn them into Gateways. Build space habitats. Terraform planets. We can make a paradise for a million times the population of the Earth, for the next million years!"

I stopped, because I realized I was babbling. I felt sad and delirious, worried and—lustful; and from the expression on Essie's face she was feeling something strange too. "Those are very good reasons, Robin," she began, and that was as far as she got. The signal light was bright ruby red and vibrating like a pulsar; and then it winked away and Albert Einstein's worried face appeared on the screen. I had never known him to appear without being invited before.

"Robin," he cried, "there is another emanation of the fever!"

I stood up shaking. "But it isn't time," I objected stupidly.

"It has happened, Robin, and it is rather strange. It peaked, let me see, just under one hundred seconds ago. I believe— Yes," he nodded, seeming to listen to an inaudible voice, "it is dying away."

And, as a matter of fact, I was already feeling less strange. No attack had ever been so short, and no other had quite felt like that. Apparently somebody else was experimenting with the couch.

"Albert," I said, "send a priority message to the Food Factory. Desist immediately, repeat immediately, from any further use of the couch for any purpose. Dismantle it if possible without irreversible damage. You will forfeit all pay and bonuses if there is any further breach of this directive. Got it?"

"It's already on its way, Robin," he said, and disappeared.

Essie and I looked at each other for a moment. "But you did not tell them to abandon the expedition and come back," she said at last.

I shrugged. "It doesn't change anything," I said.

"No," she agreed. "And you have given me some really very good reasons, Robin. But are they your reasons?"

I didn't answer.

I knew what Essie thought were my reasons for pushing on into the exploration of Heechee space, regardless of fevers or costs or risks. She thought my reasons had a name, and the name was Gelle-Klara Moynlin. And I sometimes was not sure she was wrong.

7

Heechee Heaven

Wherever Lurvy moved in the ship, she was always conscious of the mottled gray pattern in the viewplate. It showed nothing she could recognize, but it was a nothing she had seen before, for months on end.

While they were traveling faster than light on the way to Heechee Heaven they were alone. The universe was empty around them, except for that pebbly, shifting gray. They were the universe. Even on the long climb to the Food Factory it had not been this solitary. At least there were stars. Even planets. In tau space, or whatever crazy kind of space Heechee ships drove through or tunneled under or sidestepped around, there was nothing. Last times Lurvy had been in that much emptiness had been in her Gateway missions, and they were not sweet memories at all.

This ship was far the biggest she had ever seen. Gateway's largest held five people. This could have housed twenty or more. It contained eight separate compartments. Three were cargo, filled automatically (Wan explained) with the output of the Food Factory while the ship was docked there. Two seemed to be staterooms, but not for human beings. If the "bunks" that rolled out from the walls were bunks indeed, they were too tiny for human adults. One of the rooms Wan identified as his own, which he invited Janine to share. When Lurvy vetoed the notion he gave in sulkily, and so they roomed in segregated style, boys in one chamber, girls in the other. The largest room, located in the mathematical center of the ship, was shaped like a cylinder with tapered ends. It had neither floor nor ceiling, except that three seats were fixed to the surface facing the controls. As the surface was curved, the seats leaned toward each other. They were simple enough, of the design Lurvy had lived with for months at a time: Two flat metal slabs, joined together in a Vee. "On Gateway ships we stretched webbing across them," Lurvy offered.

"What is 'webbing'?" asked Wan; and, when it was explained, said, "What a good idea. I will do that next trip. I can steal some material from the Old Ones."

As in all Heechee ships, the controls themselves were nearly automatic. There were a dozen knurled wheels in a row, with colored lights for each wheel. As the wheels were turned (not that anyone would ever turn them while in flight; that was well established suicide), the lights changed color and intensity, and developed bands of light and dark like spectrum lines. They represented course settings. Not even Wan could read them, much less Lurvy or the others. But since Lurvy's time on Gateway, at great expense in prospectors' lives, the big brains had accumulated a considerable store of data. Some colors meant a good chance of something worthwhile. Some referred to the length of the trip the course director was set for. Some—many—were filed away as no-nos, because every ship that had entered faster-than-light space with those settings had stayed there. Or somewhere. Had, at least, never returned to Gateway. Out of habit and orders, Lurvy photographed every fluctuation of control lights and viewscreen, even when the screen showed nothing she could recognize as worth photographing. An hour after the group left the Food Factory, the star patterns began to shrink together to a winking point of brightness. They had reached the speed of light. And then even the point was gone. The screen took on the appearance of gray mud that raindrops had spattered, and stayed that way.

To Wan, of course, the ship was only his familiar schoolbus, used for commuting back and forth since he was old enough to squeeze the launch teat. Paul had never been in a real Heechee ship before, and was subdued for days. Neither had Janine, but one more marvel was nothing unusual in her fourteen-year-old life. For Lurvy, something else. It was a bigger version of the ships in which she had earned her Out bangles— and precious little else—and therefore frightening.

She could not help it. She could not convince herself that this trip, at least, was a regular shuttle run. She had learned too much fear blundering into the unknown as a Gateway pilot. She pushed herself around its vast —comparatively vast—space (nearly a hundred and fifty cubic meters!), and worried. It was not only the muddy viewscreen that kept her attention. There was the shiny golden lozenge, bigger than a man, that was thought to contain the FTL drive machinery and was known to explode totally if opened. There was the crystal, glassy spiral that got hot (no one had ever known why) from time to time, and lit up with tiny hot flecks of radiance at the beginning and end of each trip, and at one other very important time.

It was that time that Lurvy was watching for. And when, exactly twenty-four days, five hours and fifty-six minutes after they left the Food Factory, the golden coil flickered and began to light, she could not help a great sigh of relief.

"What's the matter?" Wan shrilled suspiciously.

"Just that we're halfway now," she said, noting the time in her log. "That's the turnaround point. That's what you look for in a Gateway ship. If you reach the halfway point with only a quarter of your life-support gone you know you won't run out and starve on the way home."

Wan pouted. "Don't you trust me, Lurvy? We will not starve."

"It feels good to know for sure," she grinned, and then lost the grin, because she was thinking about what was at the end of the trip.

So they rubbed along together, the best way they could, getting on each other's nerves a thousand times apiece a day. Paul taught Wan to play chess, to keep his mind off Janine. Wan patiently—more often impatiently—rehearsed again and again everything he could tell them about Heechee Heaven and its occupants.

They slept as much as they could. In the restraining net next to Paul, Wan's teen-aged juices bubbled and flowed. He tossed and turned in the random, tiny accelerations of the ship, wishing he were alone so that he could do those things that appeared to be prohibited when one was not alone—or wishing he were not alone, but with Janine, so that he could do those even better things Tiny Jim and Henrietta had described to him. He had asked Henrietta any number of times what the female role was in this conjugation. To this she always responded, even when she would not talk about anything else; but almost never in a way that was helpful to Wan. However her sentences began, they almost always ended by returning tearfully to the subject of her terrible betrayals by her husband and that floozy, Doris.

He did not know, even, in just what physical ways the female departed from the male. Pictures and words did not do it. Toward the end of the trip curiosity overpowered acculturation, and he begged Janine or Lurvy, either one, to let him see for himself. Even without touching. "Why, you filthy beast," said Janine diagnostically. She was not angry. She was smiling. "Bide your time, boy, you'll get your chances."

But Lurvy was not amused, and when Wan had gone disconsolately away she and her sister had, for them, a long talk. As long as Janine would tolerate. "Lurvy, dear," she said at last, "I *know*. I know I'm only fifteen —well, almost—and Wan's not much older. I know that I don't want to get pregnant four years away from a doctor, and with all kinds of things coming up that we don't know how we'll deal with—I know all that. You think I'm just your snotty kid sister. Well, I am. But I'm your *smart* snotty kid sister. When you say something worth listening to I listen. So piss off, dear Lurvy." Smiling comfortably, she pushed herself away after Wan, and then stopped and returned to kiss Lurvy. "You and Pop," she said. "You both drive me straight up the wall. But I love you both a lot—and Paul, too."

It was not altogether Wan's fault, Lurvy knew. They were all smelling extremely high. Among all their sweats and secretions were pheromones enough to make a monk horny, much less an impressionable virgin kid. And that was not at all Wan's fault, in fact exactly the reverse. If he had not insisted, they would not have lugged so much water aboard; if they had not, they would be even filthier and sweatier than their rationed sponge baths left them. They had, when you came right down to it, left the Food Factory far too impulsively. Payter had been right.

Astonishingly, Lurvy realized that she actually missed the old man. In the ship they were wholly cut off from communication of any kind. What was he doing? Was he still well? They had had to take the mobile bioassay unit—they had only one, and four people needed it more than one. But that was not really true, either, because away from the shipboard computer it was balled into a shiny, motionless mass, and would stay that way until they established radio contact with Vera from Heechee Heaven—and meanwhile, what was happening to her father?

The curious thing was that Lurvy loved the old man, and thought that he loved her back. He had given every sign of it but verbal ones. It was his money and ambition that had put them all on the flight to the Food Factory in the first place, buying them participants' shares by scraping the bottom of the money, if not of the ambition. It had been his money that had paid for her going to Gateway in the first place, and when the gamble went sour he had not reproached her. Or not directly, and not much.

After six weeks in Wan's ship, Lurvy began to feel adjusted to it. She even felt fairly comfortable, not counting the smells and irritations and worries; at least, as long as she didn't think too much about the trips that had earned her her five Out bangles from Gateway. There was very little good to remember in any of them.

Lurvy's first trip had been a washout. Fourteen months of round-trip travel to come out circling a planet that had been flamed clean in a nova eruption. Maybe something had been there once. Nothing was there when Lurvy arrived, stark solitary and already talking to herself in her one-person ship. That had cured her of single flights, and the next was in a Three. No better. None of them any better. She became famous in Gateway, an object of curiosity—strong contender for the record of most flights taken and fewest profits returned. It was not an honor she liked, but it was never as bad until the last flight of all.

That was disaster.

Before they even reached their destination she had awakened out of an edgy, restless sleep to horror. The woman she had made her special friend was floating bloodily next to her, the other woman also dead not far away, and the two men who made up the rest of the Five's crew engaged in screaming, mutilating hand-to-hand battle.

The rules of the Gateway Corporation provided that any payments resulting from a voyage were to be divided equally among the survivors. Her shipmate Stratos Kristianides had made up his mind to be the only survivor.

In actuality, he didn't survive. He lost the battle to her other shipmate, and lover, Hector Possanbee. The winner, with Lurvy, went on to find—again—nothing. Smoldering red gas giant. Pitiful little binary Class-M companion star. And no way of reaching the only detectable planet, a huge methane-covered Jupiter of a thing, without dying in the attempt.

Lurvy had come back to Earth after that with her tail

between her legs, and no second chance in sight. Payter had given her that opportunity, and she did not think there would be another. The hundred and some thousand dollars it had cost him to pay her way to Gateway had put a very big dent in the money he had accumulated over his sixty or seventy years—she didn't really know how many years—of life. She had failed him. Not just him. And she accepted, out of his kindness and forbearance to hate her, the fact that he really did love his daughter—and kind, pointless Paul and silly young Janine, too. In some way, Payter loved them all.

And was getting very little out of it, Lurvy judged.

She rubbed her Out bangles moodily. They had been very expensive to obtain.

She was not easy in her mind about her father, or about what lay ahead.

Making love to Paul helped pass the time—when they could convince themselves that they didn't have to supervise the younger ones for a quarter of an hour or so. It was not the same for Lurvy as making love to Hector, the man who had survived the last Gateway flight with her, the man who had asked her to marry him. The man who asked her to ship out with him again and to build a life together. Short, broad, always active, always alert, a dynamo in bed, kind and patient when she was sick or irritable or scared—there were a hundred reasons why she should have married Hector. And only one, really, why she did not. When she was wrenched out of that terrible sleep she had found Hector and Stratos battling. While she watched, Stratos died.

Hector had explained to her that Stratos had gone out of control to try to slay them all; but she had been asleep when the slaughter started. One of the men had obviously tried to murder his shipmates.

But she had never known for sure which one.

He proposed to her when things were bleakest and grimiest, a day before they reached Gateway on the sorry return trip. "We are really most delightfully good together, Dorema," he said, arms about her, consolingly. "Just us and no one else. I think I could not have borne this with the others around. Next time we will be more fortunate! So let's get married, please?"

She burrowed her chin into his hard, warm, cocoa-colored shoulder. "I'll have to think, dear," she said, feeling the hand that had killed Stratos kneading the back of her neck.

So Lurvy was not unhappy when the trip was over and Janine called her out of her private room, all thrilled and excited; the great glassy spiral was filling with hot specks of darting golden light, the ship was lurching tentatively in one direction and another; the mottled gray mud was gone from the viewscreen and there were stars. More than stars. There was an object that glowed blue in patches amid featureless gray. It was lemon-shaped and spun slowly, and Lurvy could form no idea of its size until she perceived that the surface of the object was not featureless. There were tiny projections jutting out here and there, and she recognized the tiniest of them as Gateway-type ships, Ones and Threes, and there a Five; the lemon had to be more than a kilometer long! Wan, grinning with pride, settled himself in the central pilot seat (they had stuffed it with extra clothing, a device that had never occurred to Wan), and grasped the lander control levers. It was all Lurvy could do to keep her hands off. But Wan had been performing this particular maneuver all his life. With coarse competence he banged and slammed the ship into a downward spiral that matched the slow spin of the blue-eyed gray lemon, intersected one of the waiting pits, docked, locked, and looked up for applause. They were on Heechee Heaven.

The Food Factory had been the size of a skyscraper, but this was a world. Perhaps, like Gateway, it had once been an asteroid; but, if so, it had been so tooled and sculpted that there was no trace of original structure. It was cubic kilometers of mass. It was a rotating mountain. So much to explore! So much to learn!

And so much to fear. They skulked, or strutted, through the old halls, and Lurvy realized she was clinging to her husband's hand. And Paul was clinging back. She forced herself to observe and comment. The sides of the walls were veined with luminous tracing of scarlet; the overhead was the familiar blue Heechee-metal glow. On the floor—and it was really a floor; they had weight here, though not more than a tenth of Earth-normal—diamond-shaped mounds contained what looked like soil and grew plants. "Berryfruit," said Wan proudly over his shoulder, shrugging toward a waist-high bush with fuzzed objects hanging among its emerald leaves. "We can stop and eat some if you like."

"Not right now," said Lurvy. A dozen paces farther along the corridor was another planted lozenge, this one with slate-green tendrils and soft, squashed cauliflower-shaped buds. "What's that?"

He paused and looked at her. It was clear he thought it was a silly question. "They are not good to eat," he shrilled scornfully. "Try the berryfruit. They are quite tasty."

So the party paused, where two of the red-lined corridors came together and one of them changed to blue. They peeled brown-green furry skins from the berryfruit and nibbled at the juicy insides—first tentatively, then with pleasure—while Wan explained the geography of Heechee Heaven. These were the red sections, and they were the best to be in. There was food here, and good places to sleep; and the ship was here, and here the Old Ones never came. But didn't they sometimes wander out of their usual places to pick the berryfruit? Yes, of course they did! But never (his voice rising half an octave) *here*. It had never happened. Over there the blue. His voice sank, in volume as well as pitch. The Old Ones came there quite often, or to some parts of the blue. But it was all *dead*. If it were not that the Dead Men's room was in the blue he would never go there. And Lurvy, peering down the corridor he pointed to, felt a chill of incredible age. It had the look of a Stonehenge or Gizeh or Angkor Wat. Even the ceilings were dimmer, and the plantings there were sparse and puny. The green, he went on, was all very well, but it was not working properly. The water jets did not function. The plantings died. And the gold—

His pleasure faded when he talked about the gold.

That was where the Old Ones lived. If it were not for needing books, and sometimes clothes, he would never go to the gold, though the Dead Men were always urging him to. He did not want to see the Old Ones.

Paul cleared his throat to say: "But I think we have to do that, Wan."

"Why?" the boy shrilled. "They are not interesting!"

Lurvy put her hand on his arm. "What's the matter, Wan?" she asked kindly, observing his expression. What Wan felt always showed on his face. He had never had the need to develop the skills of dissembling.

"He looks scared," Paul commented.

"He is not scared!" Wan retorted. "You do not understand this place! It is not interesting to go to the gold!"

"Wan, dear," Lurvy said, "the thing is, it's worth taking chances to find out more about the Heechee. I don't know if I can explain what it means to us, but the least part of it is that we would get money for it. A *lot* of money."

"He doesn't know what money is," Paul interrupted impatiently. "Wan. Pay attention. We are going to do this. Tell us how the four of us can safely explore the gold corridors."

"The four of us can not! One person can. *I* can," he boasted. He was angry now, and showed it. Paul! Wan's feelings about him were mixed, but most of the mixture were unfavorable. Speaking to Wan, Paul shaped his words so carefully—so contemptuously. As though he did not think Wan were smart enough to understand. When Wan and Janine were together, Paul was always near. If Paul was a sample of human males, Wan was not proud to be one. "I have gone to the gold many times," he boasted, "for books, or for berryfruit, or just to watch the silly things they do. They are so funny! But they are not entirely stupid, you know. *I* can go there safely. One person can. Perhaps two people can, but if we all go they will surely see us."

"And then?" Lurvy asked.

Wan shrugged defensively. He didn't really know the answer to that, only that it had frightened his father.

"They are not interesting," he repeated, contradicting himself.

Janine licked her fingers and tossed the empty berry-fruit skins to the base of the bush. "You people," she sighed, "are unreal. Wan? Where do these Old Ones come?"

"To the edge of the gold, always. Sometimes into the blue or the green."

"Well, if they like these berryfruits, and if you know a place where they come to pick them, why don't we just leave a camera there? We can see them. They can't see us."

Wan shrilled triumphantly, "Of course! You see, Lurvy, it is not necessary to go there! Janine is right, only—" he hesitated—"Janine? What is a camera?"

As they went, Lurvy had to nerve herself to pass every intersection, could not help staring down each corridor. But they heard nothing, and saw nothing that moved. It was as quiet as the Food Factory when they first set foot in it, and just as queer. Queerer. The traceries of light on every wall, the patches of growing things—above all, the terrifying thought that there were Heechee alive somewhere near. When they had dropped off a camera by a berryfruit bush in a space where green, blue, and gold came together, Wan hustled them away, directly to the room where the Dead Men lived. That was first priority: to get to the radio that would once again put them in touch with the rest of the world. Even if the rest of the world was only old Payter, fidgeting resentfully around the Food Factory. If they could not do that much, Lurvy reasoned, they had no business being here at all, and they should return to the ship and head for home; it was no good exploring if they could not report what they found!

So Wan, courage returning in direct proportion to his increasing distance from the Old Ones, marched them through a stretch of green, up several levels in blue, to a wide blue door. "Let us see if it is working right," he said importantly, and stepped on a ridge of metal before the door. The door hesitated, sighed and then creakily opened for them, and, satisfied, Wan led them inside.

This place at least seemed human. If strange. It even smelled human, no doubt because Wan had spent so much time there over his short life. Lurvy took one of the minicameras from Paul and settled it on her shoulder. The little machine hissed tape past its lens, recording an octagonal chamber with three of the forked Heechee seats, two of them broken, and a stained wall bearing the Heechee version of instrumentation—ridges of colored lights. There was a tiny sound of clicks and hums, barely perceptible, behind the wall. Wan waved at it. "In there," he said, "is where the Dead Men live. If 'live' is the right word for what they do." He tittered.

Lurvy pointed the camera at the seats and the knurled knobs before them, then at a domed, clawed object under the smeared wall. It stood chest high, and it was mounted on soft, squashed cylinders to roll on. "What's that, Wan?"

"It is what the Dead Men catch me with sometimes," he muttered. "They don't use it very often. It is very old. When it breaks, it takes forever to mend itself."

Paul eyed the machine warily, and moved away from it. "Turn on your friends, Wan," he ordered.

"Of course. It is not very difficult," Wan boasted. "Watch me carefully, and you will see how to do it." He sat himself with careless ease on the one unbroken seat, and frowned at the controls. "I will bring you Tiny Jim," he decided, and thumbed the controls before him. The lights on the stained wall flickered and flowed, and Wan said, "Wake up, Tiny Jim. There is someone here for you to meet."

Silence.

Wan scowled, glanced over his shoulder at the others and then ordered: "Tiny Jim! Speak to me at once!" He pursed his lips and spat a gobbet at the wall. Lurvy recognized the source of the stains, but said nothing.

A weary voice over their heads said, "Hello, Wan."

"That is better," Wan shrilled, grinning at the others. "Now, Tiny Jim! Tell my friends something interesting, or I will spit on you again."

"I wish you would be more respectful," sighed the voice, "but very well. Let me see. On the ninth planet of the star Saiph there is an old civilization. Their rulers are a class of shit-handlers, who exercise power by removing the excrement only from the homes of those citizens who are honest, industrious, clever, and unfailing in the payment of their taxes. On their principal holiday, which they call the Feast of St. Gautama, the youngest maiden in each family bathes herself in sunflower oil, takes a hazelnut between her teeth, and ritually—"

"Tiny Jim," Wan interrupted, "is this a true story?"

Pause. "Metaphorically it is," Tiny Jim said sullenly.

"You are very foolish," Wan reproved the Dead Man, "and I am shamed before my friends. Pay attention. Here are Dorema Herter-Hall, who you will call Lurvy, and her sister Janine Herter. And Paul. Say hello to them."

Long pause. "Are there other living human beings here?" the voice asked doubtfully.

"I have just told you there are!"

Another long pause. Then, "Good-bye, Wan," the voice said sadly, and would not speak again, no matter how loudly Wan commanded or how furiously he spat at the wall.

"Christ," grumbled Paul. "Is he always like that?"

"No, not always," Wan shrilled. "But sometimes he is worse. Shall I try one of the others for you?"

"Are they any better?"

"Well, no," Wan admitted. "Tiny Jim is the best."

Paul closed his eyes in despair, and opened them again to glare at Lurvy. "How simply bloody wonderful," he said. "Do you know what I'm beginning to think? I'm beginning to think your father was right. We should have stayed on the Food Factory."

Lurvy took a deep breath. "Well, we didn't," she pointed out. "We're here. Let's give it forty-eight hours, and then— And then we'll make up our minds."

Long before the forty-eight hours were up they had made up their minds to stay. At least for a while. There was simply too much in Heechee Heaven to abandon it.

The big factor in the decision was reaching Payter on the FTL radio. No one had thought to ask Wan if his ability to call Heechee Heaven from the Food Factory implied that he could call in the other direction. It turned out he could not. He had never had a reason to try, because there had never been anyone there to answer the phone. Lurvy drafted Janine to help her carry food and a few essentials out of the ship, fighting depression and worry all the way, and returned to find Paul proud and Wan jubilant. They had made contact. "How is he?" Lurvy demanded at once.

"Oh, you mean your father? He's all right," Paul said. "He sounded grouchy, come to think of it—cabin fever, I suppose. There were about a million messages. He patched them through as a burst transmission and I've got them on tape—but it'll take us a week to play them all." He rummaged through the stuff Janine and Lurvy had brought until he found the tools he had demanded. He was patching together a digitalized picture transmitter, to make use of the voice-only FTL circuits. "We can only transmit single frames," he said, eyes on the picture-tape machine. "But if we're going to be here for very long, maybe I can work out a burst-transmission system from here. Meanwhile, we've got voice and —oh, yeah. The old man said to kiss you for him."

"Then I guess we're going to stay for a while," said Janine.

"Then I guess we'd better bring more stuff out of the ship," her sister agreed. "Wan? Where should we sleep?"

So while Paul worked on the communications, Wan and the two women hustled the necessities of life to a cluster of chambers in the red-walled corridors. Wan was proud to show them off. There were wall bunks larger than the ones the ship had offered—large enough, actually, for even Paul to sleep in, if he didn't mind bending his knees. There was a place for toilet facilities, not quite of human design. Or not of very recent human design. The facilities were simply lustrous metal slits in the floor, like the squat-toilets of Eastern Europe. There was even a place to bathe. It was something between a wading pool and a tub, with something between a shower head and a small water-fall coming out of the wall behind it. When you got inside tepid water poured out. After that they all began to smell much better. Wan, in particular, bathed ostentatiously often, sometimes beginning to undress to bathe again before the last drops of unsopped water had dried on the back of his neck from the bath before. Tiny Jim had told him that bathing was a custom among polite people. Besides, he had perceived that Janine did it regularly. Lurvy watched them both, remembered how much trouble it had been to get Janine to bathe on the long flight up from Earth, and did not comment.

As pilot, therefore captain, Lurvy constituted herself head of the expedition. She assigned Paul to establish and maintain communication with her father on the Food Factory, with Wan's help in dealing with the Dead Men. She assigned Janine, with her own help and Wan's, to housekeeping tasks like washing their clothes in the tepid tub. She assigned Wan, with anyone who could be spared, to roam the safe parts of Heechee Heaven, photographing and recording for transmission to Payter and Earth. Usually Wan's companion was Janine. When someone else could be spared, the two young people were chaperoned, but that was seldom.

Janine did not seem to mind either way. She had not finished with the preliminary thrill of Wan's companionship and was in no hurry to move to a further stage —except when they touched. Or when she caught him staring at her. Or when she saw the knotted bulge in his ragged kilt. Even then, her fantasies and reveries were almost as good as that next stage, at least for now. She played with the Dead Men, and munched on berryfruit, brown-skinned and green-fleshed, and did her chores, and waited to grow up a little more.

There were not many objections to Lurvy's rule, since she had taken care to assign tasks that the draftees were willing to do anyhow, which left for herself such drudgery as going through the backed-up commands and persuasions from Payter, and far-off Earth.

The communication was a long way from satisfactory. Lurvy had not appreciated Shipboard-Vera until she had to get along without her. She could not command priority messages first, or have the computer sort them out by theme. There was no computer she could use, except the overtaxed one in her own head. The messages came in higgledy-piggledy, and when she replied, or transmitted reports for downlink relay to Earth, she had no confidence at all that they were getting where they were supposed to go.

The Dead Men seemed to be basically read-only memories, interactive but limited. And their circuits had been further scrambled in the makeshift attempt to use them for communication to the Food Factory, a task for which they had never been designed. (But what had they really been designed for? And by whom?) Wan blustered and bluffed, in his pose as expert, and then miserably confessed that they were not doing what they were supposed to do any more. Sometimes he would dial Tiny Jim and get Henrietta, and sometimes a former-English Lit professor named Willard; and once he got a voice he had never heard before, shaking and whispering on the near side of inaudibility, muttering on the far side of madness. "Go to the gold," whimpered Henrietta, fretful as ever, and without pause Tiny Jim's thick tenor would override: "They'll kill you! They don't like castaways!"

That was frightening. Especially as Wan assured them that Tiny Jim had always been the most sensible of the Dead Men. It puzzled Lurvy that she was not more terrified than she was, but there had been so many alarms and terrors that she had become used to them. Her circuits were scrambled, too.

And the messages! In one five-minute burst of clear transmission Paul had recorded fourteen hours of them. Commands from downlink: "Report all control settings shuttle ship. Attempt secure tissue samples Heechee/ Old Ones. Freeze and store berry fruit leaves, fruits, stems. Exercise extreme caution." Half a dozen separate communications from her father; he was lonesome; he didn't feel well; he was not receiving proper medical attention because they had taken the mobile bio-assay unit away; he was being barraged by peremptory orders from Earth. Information messages from Earth: their first reports had been received, analyzed and interpreted for them, and now there were suggestions for follow-up programs beyond counting. They should interrogate Henrietta about her references to cosmological phenomena—Shipboard-Vera was making a hash of it, and Downlink-Vera could not communicate in real time, and old Payter did not know enough astrophysics to ask the right questions, so it was up to them. They should interrogate all the Dead Men on their memories of Gateway and their missions—assuming they remembered anything. They should attempt to find out how living prospectors became stored computer programs. They should— They should do everything. All at once. And almost none of it was possible; tissue samples of the Heechee, forsooth! When an occasional message was clear and personal and undemanding, Lurvy treasured it.

And some of those were surprises. Besides the fan letters from Janine's pen-pals and the continuing plea for any information they might come across from Trish Bover's relict, there was one for Lurvy personally, from Robinette Broadhead:

"Dorema, I know you're being swamped. Your whole mission was important and hazardous to begin with, and now it turns out about a million times more so. All I expect from you is that you do the best you can. I don't have the authority to override Gateway Corp orders. I can't change your assigned objectives. But I want you to know I'm on your side. Find out all you can. Try not to get into a spot you can't retreat from. And I'll do everything I can to see that you get rewarded as fully and lavishly as you can hope for. I mean it, Lurvy. I give you my word."

It was a strange message, and oddly touching. It was also a surprise to Lurvy that Broadhead even knew her nickname. They had not exactly been intimates. When she and her family were interviewing for the Food Factory assignment they had met Broadhead several times. But the relationship had been of suppliant and monarch, and there was not much close interpersonal friendship involved. Nor had she particularly liked him. He was candid and amiable enough—high-rolling multimillionaire with an easy-going manner, but sharply on top of every dollar he spent and every development in every project he was involved in. She did not like being a client to a capricious Titan of finance.

And, to be fair, she had come to their meetings with a faint prejudice. She had heard about Robinette Broadhead long before he played any part in her own life. In Lurvy's own time on the Gateway asteroid and in its ships, she had once gone out in a three-person ship with an elderly woman who had once been shipmate with Gelle-Klara Moynlin. From the woman Lurvy had heard the story of Broadhead's last mission, the one that made him a multimillionaire. There was something questionable about it. Nine people had died on that mission. Broadhead was the only survivor. And one of the casualties had been Klara Moynlin, with whom (the old woman said) Broadhead had been in love. Maybe it was Lurvy's own experience with a mission in which most of the crew had died that colored her feelings. But they were there.

The curious thing about the Broadhead mission was that maybe "died" was not the right word for the casualties. This Klara and the rest had been trapped in a black hole, and perhaps they were still there, and perhaps still alive—prisoners of slowed-down time, maybe no more than a few hours older after all the years.

So what was the hidden agenda in Broadhead's message to Lurvy? Was he urging them on to try to find a way to penetrate Gelle-Klara Moynlin's prison? Did he know himself? Lurvy could not tell, but for the first time she thought of their employer as a human being. The thought was touching. It did not make Lurvy feel less afraid, but perhaps a little less alone. When she brought her latest batch of tapes to Paul, in the Dead Men's room, to record at high speed and transmit when he could, she tarried to put her arms around him and cling, which surprised him very much.

When Janine returned to the Dead Men's room from an exploration with Wan, something told her to move quietly. She looked in without being heard, and saw her sister and brother-in-law sitting comfortably against a wall, half listening to the maniac chatter of the Dead Men, half chatting desultorily with each other. She turned, put her finger to her lips and led Wan away. "I think they want to be alone," she explained. "Anyway, I'm tired. Let's take a break."

Wan shrugged. They found a convenient spot at an intersection of corridors a few dozen meters away and he settled himself pensively beside the girl. "Are they conjugating?" he asked.

"Cripes, Wan. You've only got the one thing on your mind all the time." But she was not annoyed, and let him move close to her, until one hand approached her breast. "Knock it off," she said mildly.

He withdrew his hand. "You are being very disturbed, Janine," he said, pouting.

"Oh, get off my back." But when he moved millimeters away, she let herself move a little closer again. She was quite content to have him want her and quite serene in believing that when anything happened, as "anything" sooner or later surely would, it would be when she wanted it to happen. Nearly two months with Wan had made her like him, and even trust him, and the rest could wait. She enjoyed his presence.

Even when he was grouchy. "You are not competing properly," he complained.

"Competing at what, for the Lord's sake?"

"You should talk to Tiny Jim," he said severely. "He will teach you better strategies in the reproduction race. He has fully explained the male role to me, so that I am sure I can compete successfully. Of course, yours is different. Basically, your best choice would be to allow me to copulate with you."

"Yes, you've said that. You know what, Wan? You talk too much."

He was silent for a moment, perplexed. He could not defend himself against that charge. He did not even know why it was a charge. In most of his life the only mode of interaction he had had was talk. He rehearsed all of Tiny Jim's teachings in his mind, and then his expression cleared. "I see. You want to kiss first," he said.

"No! I don't want to kiss 'first', and get your knee off my bladder."

He released her unwillingly. "Janine," he explained, "close contact is essential to 'love'. This is true of the lower orders as well as of us. Dogs sniff. Primates groom. Reptiles coil around each other. Even rose shoots nestle close to the mature plant, Tiny Jim says, although he does not believe that is a sexual manifestation. But you will lose the reproductive race if you are not careful, Janine."

She giggled. "To what? Old dead Henrietta?" But he was scowling and she took pity on him. She sat up and announced, kindly enough, "You've got some really wrong ideas, do you know that? The *last* thing I want, even if we ever do get around to your goddam conjugation, is to get caught in a place like this."

" 'Caught'?"

"Pregnant," she explained. "Winning the goddam reproductive race. Knocked up. Oh, Wan," she said, nuzzling the top of his head, "you just don't know where it's all at. I bet you and I are going to conjugate the hell out of each other, some time or other, and maybe we'll even get married, or something, and we'll just win that old reproductive race a whole bunch. But right now you're just a snotty-nosed kid, and so am I. You don't want to reproduce. You just want to make love."

"Well, that is true, yes, but Tiny Jim—"

"Will you shut up about Tiny Jim?" She stood up and regarded him for a moment, and said affectionately, "Tell you what. I'm going back to the Dead Men's room. Why don't you go read a book for a whi' to cool off?"

"You are silly!" he scolded. "I have no boo reader."

"Oh, for the Lord's sake! Then go somewhere and whack off until you feel better."

Wan looked up at her, then down at his freshly laundered kilt. No bulge was visible, but there was a pale, spreading spot of damp. He grinned. "I guess I don't need to any more," he said.

By the time they got back, Paul and Lurvy were no longer cozily nestling each other, but Janine could detect that they were more at peace than usual. What Lurvy could detect about Wan and Janine was less tangible. She looked at them thoughtfully, considered asking what they had been up to, decided against it. Paul was, in any event, more interested in what they had just discovered. He said, "Hey, kids, listen to this." He dialed Henrietta's number, waited until her weepy voice said a tentative hello and then asked: "Who are you?"

The voice strengthened. "I am a computer analog," it said firmly. "When I was alive I was Mrs. Arnold Meacham of mission Orbit Seventy-four, Day Nineteen. I have a bachelor of science and master's from Tulane and the Ph.D. from the University of Pennsylvania, and my special discipline is astrophysics. After twenty-two days we docked at an artifact and were subsequently captured by its occupants. At the time of my death I was thirty-eight years old, two years younger than—" the voice hesitated, "than Doris Filgren, our pilot, who—" it hesitated again, "who—who my husband seemed to—who had an affair with—who—" The voice was sobbing now, and Paul turned it off.

"Well, it doesn't last," he said, "but there it is. Poor dumb old Vera has sorted out some kind of a connection with reality for her. And not just for her. Do you want to know your mother's name, Wan?"

The boy was staring at him, pop-eyed. "My mother's ———ed.

————lse's. Tiny Jim, for instance. He was ——— pilot from Venus who got to Gate——— . His name is James Cornwell. Wil——— teacher. He embezzled money from ——— pay his way to Gateway—didn't get much joy out of it, of course. His first flight brought him here. The downlink computers wrote an interrogation program for Vera, and she's been working at it all along, and—what's the matter, Wan?"

The boy licked his lips. "My mother's name?" he repeated.

"Oh. Sorry," Paul apologized, reminded to be kind. It had not occurred to him that Wan's emotions would be involved. "Her name was Elfega Zamorra. But she doesn't seem to be one of the Dead Men, Wan. I don't know why. And your father—well, that's a funny thing. Your real father was dead before she came here. The man you talk about must have been somebody else, but I don't know who. Any idea why that is?" Wan shrugged. "I mean, why your mother or, I guess you'd call him, your step-father doesn't seem to be stored?" Wan spread his hands.

Lurvy moved closer to him. The poor kid! Responding to his distress, she put her arm around him and said, "I guess this is a shock to you, Wan. I'm sure we'll find out a lot more." She gestured at the mare's nest of recorders, encoders and processors that littered the once bare room. "Everything we find out gets transmitted back to Earth," she said. He looked up at her politely, but not entirely comprehendingly, as she tried to explain the vast complex of information-handling machinery on Earth, and how it systematically analyzed, compared, collated, and interpreted every scrap from Heechee Heaven and the Food Factory—not to mention every other bit of data, wherever derived. Until Janine intervened.

"Oh, leave him alone. He understands enough," she said wisely. "Just let him live with it for a while." She rummaged through the case of rations for one of the slate-green packages, and then said casually, "By the way. Why is that thing beeping at us?"

Paul listened, then sprang to his clutter of gadgets. The monitor slaved to their portable cameras was emitting a faint *Queep. Queep. Queep.* He spun it around so they could all see, swearing to himself.

It was the camera they had left by the berryfruit

bush, set patiently to record the unchanging scene and to sound an alarm whenever it detected movement.

It had. There was a face scowling out at them.

Lurvy felt a thrill of terror. "Heechee," she breathed.

But if so, the face showed no evidence of concealing a mind that could colonize a galaxy. It seemed to be down on all fours, peering worriedly at the camera, and behind it were four or five others like it. The face had no chin. The brow slanted down from a fuzzy scalp; there was more hair on the face than on the head. If the skull had had an occipital ridge, it would have looked like a gorilla. Taken all in all, it was not far from the shipboard computer's reconstruction of Wan's description, but on a cruder, more animal design. Yet they were not animals. As the face moved to one side Lurvy saw that the others, clustered around the berryfruit bush, wore what no animal had ever spontaneously worn. They were clothed. There were even evidences of fashion in what they wore, patches of color sewn to their tunics, what looked like tattoos on exposed skin, even a string of sharp-edged beads around the neck of one of the males. "I suppose," Lurvy said shakily, "that even the Heechee might degenerate in time. And they've had lots of time."

The view in the camera spun dizzily. "Damn him," Paul snapped. "He's not so degenerate he doesn't notice the camera. He's picked the damn thing up. Wan! Do you suppose they know we're here?"

The boy shrugged disinterestedly. "Of course they do. They always have, you know. They simply do not care."

Lurvy's heart caught. "What do you mean, Wan? How do you know they won't come after us?"

The view in the camera steadied; the Old One who had picked it up was handing it to another. Wan glanced at it and said, "I have told you, they almost never come into this part of the blue. Or ever, into the red; and there is no reason to go into the green. Nothing works there, not even the food chutes or the readers. Almost always, they stay in the gold. Unless they have eaten all the berryfruit there, and want more."

There was a mewling cry from the sound system of the monitor, and the view whirled again. It stopped momentarily on one of the female Old Ones, sucking a finger; then she reached out balefully for the camera. It spun and then went blank. "Paul! What did they do?" Lurvy demanded.

"Broke it, I suppose," he said, failing to get the picture back after manipulating the controls. "Question is, what do *we* do? Haven't we got enough here? Shouldn't we think about going back?"

And think about it Lurvy did. They all did. But however carefully they questioned Wan, the boy stubbornly insisted there was nothing to fear. The Old Ones had *never* troubled him in the corridors walled with red skeins of light. He had never seen them in the green—though, to be sure, he seldom went there himself. Rarely in the blue. And, yes, of course they knew there were people here—the Dead Men assured him the Old Ones had machines that listened, and sometimes watched, everywhere—when they were not broken, of course. They simply did not care very much. "If we don't go into the gold they will not trouble us," he said positively. "Except, of course, if they come out."

"Wan," Paul snarled, "I can't tell you how confident you make me feel."

But it developed that that was only the boy's way of saying that the odds were very good. "I go to the gold for excitement often," he boasted. "Also for books. I have never been caught, you know."

"And what if the Heechee come here for excitement, or books?" Paul demanded.

"Books! What would they do with books? For berryfruit, maybe. Sometimes they go with the machines—Tiny Jim says they are for repairing things that break. But not always. And the machines do not work very well, or very often. Besides, you can hear them far away!"

They all sat silent for a moment, looking at each other. Then Lurvy said, "Here's what I think. Let's give ourselves one week here. I don't think that's stretching our luck too much. We have, what is it, Paul?—five cameras left. We'll plant them around, slave them to the monitor here and leave them. If we take care, maybe we can conceal them so the Heechee won't find them. We'll explore all the red corridors, because they're safe, and as many of the blue and green as we can. Collect samples. Take pictures—I want to get a look at those repair machines. And when we've done as much of that as we can, we'll—we'll see how much time we have. And then we'll make a decision about going into the gold."

"But no more than one week. From now," Paul repeated. He was not insisting. He was only making sure he understood.

"No more," Lurvy agreed, and Janine and Wan nodded.

But forty-eight hours later they were in the gold, all the same.

They had decided to replace the broken camera, and so, all four of them together, they retraced their steps to the three-way intersection where the berryfruit bush rose, bare of ripe fruit. Wan was first, hand in hand with Janine, and she detached herself to swoop down on the wreck of the camera. "They really bashed it," she marveled. "You didn't tell us they were so strong, Wan. Look, is that blood?"

Paul snatched it from her hand, turning it over, frowning at the crust of black along one edge. "It looks like they were trying to get it open," he said. "I don't think I could do that with my bare hands. He must have slipped and cut himself."

"Oh, yes," shrilled Wan absently, "they are quite strong." His attention was not on the camera. He was peering down the long gold corridor, sniffing the air, listening more for distant sounds than to the others.

"You're making me nervous," Lurvy said. "Do you hear anything?"

He shrugged irritably. "You smell them before you hear them but, no, I do not smell anything. They are not very near. And I am not afraid! I come here often, to get books or to watch the funny things they do."

"I bet," said Janine, taking the old camera from Paul while he hunted a place to conceal the new one. There were not many places. Heechee decor was stark.

Wan bristled. "I have gone down that corridor as far as you can see!" he boasted. "Even the place where the books is is far down—do you see? Some of them are in the corridor."

Lurvy looked, but was not sure what Wan meant. A few dozen meters away was a heap of glittering trash, but no books. Paul, peeling tape from a sticky bracket to mount it as high as he could on the wall, said, "The way you carry on about those books of yours. I've seen them, you know, *Moby Dick* and *The Adventures of Don Quixote*. What would the Heechee be doing with them?"

Wan shrilled with dignity, "You are stupid, Paul. Those are only what the Dead Men gave me, they are not the real books. *Those* are the real books."

Janine looked at him curiously, then moved a few steps down the corridor. "They're not books," she called over her shoulder.

"Of course they are! I have told you they are!"

"No, they aren't. Come and look." Lurvy opened her mouth to call her back, hesitated, then followed. The corridor was empty, and Wan did not seem more than usually agitated. When she was halfway to the glittering scatter she recognized what she was looking at, and quickly joined Janine to pick one up.

"Wan," she said, "I've seen these before. They're Heechee prayer fans. There are hundreds of them on Earth."

"No, no!" He was getting angry. "Why do you say that I lie?"

"I'm not saying you lie, Wan." She unrolled the thing in her hands. It was like a tapering scroll of plastic; it opened easily in her hand, but as soon as she released it it closed again. It was the commonest artifact of Heechee culture, found by the scores in the abandoned tunnels on Venus, brought back by Gateway prospectors from every successful mission. No one had ever found what the Heechee did with them, and whether the name that they had been given was appropriate only the Heechee knew. "They're called 'prayer fans', Wan."

"No, no," he shrilled crossly, taking it away from her and marching into the chamber. "You do not pray with them. You read them. Like this." He started to put the scroll into one of the tulip-shaped fixtures on the wall, glanced at it, threw it down. "That is not a good one," he said, rummaging in the heaps of fans on the floor. "Wait. Yes. This is not good, either, but it is at least something one can recognize." He slipped it into the tulip. There was a quick tiny flutter of electronic whispers, and then the tulip and scroll disappeared. A lemon-shaped cloud of color enveloped them, and shaped itself to display a sewn book, opened at a page of vertical lines of ideographs. A tinny voice—a human voice!—began to declaim something in a staccato, highly tonal language.

Lurvy could not understand the words, but two years on Gateway had made her cosmopolitan. She gasped, "I—I think that's Japanese! And those look like haiku! Wan, what are the Heechee doing with books in Japanese?"

He said in a superior tone, "These are not really the Old Ones, Lurvy, they are only copies of other books. The good ones are all like that. Tiny Jim says that all the tapes and books of the Dead Men, all the Dead Men, even the ones that are no longer here, are stored in these. I read them all the time."

"My God," said Lurvy. "And how many times have I had one of those in my hands and not known what it was for?"

Paul shook his head wonderingly. He reached into the glowing image and pulled the fan out of its tulip. It came away easily; the picture vanished and voice stopped in mid-syllable, and he turned the scroll over in his hands. "That beats me," he said. "Every scientist in the world has had a go at these things. How come nobody ever figured out what they were?"

Wan shrugged. He was no longer angry; he was enjoying the triumph of showing these people how much more than they he knew. "Perhaps they are stupid too," he shrilled. Then, charitably, "Or perhaps they merely have only the ones that no one can understand—except perhaps the Old Ones, if they ever bothered to read them."

"Have you got one of those handy, Wan?" Lurvy asked.

He shrugged petulantly. "I never bother with those," he explained. "Still, if you do not believe me—" He rummaged around in the heaps, his expression making it clear that they were wasting time with things he had already explored and found without interest. "Yes. I think this is one of the worthless ones."

When he slipped it into the tulip, the hologram that sprang up was bright—and baffling. It was as hard to read as the play of colors on the controls of a Heechee spacecraft. Harder. Strange, oscillating lines that twined around each other, leaped apart in a spray of color, and then drew together again. If it was written language, it was as remote from any Western alphabet as cunei-form. More so. All Earthly languages had characteristics in common, if only that they were almost all repre-sented by symbols on a plane surface. This seemed meant to be perceived in three dimensions. And with it came a sort of interrupted mosquito-whine of sound, like telemetry which, by mistake, was being received on a pocket radio. All in all, it was unnerving.

"I did not think you would enjoy it," Wan observed spitefully.

"Turn it off, Wan," Lurvy said; and then, energeti-cally, "We want to take as many of these things as we can. Paul, take off your shirt. Load up as many as you can and take them back to the Dead Men's room. And take that old camera, too; give it to the bio-assay unit, and see if it can make anything out of the Heechee blood."

"And what are you going to do?" Paul asked. But he had already slipped off his blouse and was filling it with the glittery "books".

"We'll be right along. Go ahead, Paul. Wan? Can

you tell which are which—I mean, which are the ones you don't bother with?"

"Of course I can, Lurvy. They are very much older, sometimes a little chipped—you can see."

"All right. You two, take off your top clothes too—as much as you need to make a carrying-bag out of. Go ahead. We'll be modest some other time," she said, slipping out of her coverall. She stood in bra and panties, tying knots in the arms and legs of the garment. She could fit at least fifty or sixty of the fans in that, she calculated—with Wan's tunic and Janine's dress they could carry at least half of the objects away. And that would be enough. She would not be greedy. There were plenty more on the Food Factory, anyway—although probably they were the ones Wan had brought there, and thus only the ones he had found he could understand. "Are there readers on the Food Factory, Wan?"

"Of course," he said. "Why else would I bring books there?" He was sorting irritably through the fans, muttering to himself as he tossed the oldest, "useless" ones to Janine and Lurvy. "I am cold," he complained.

"We all are. I wish you'd worn a bra, Janine," she said, frowning at her sister.

Janine said indignantly, "I wasn't planning to take my clothes off. Wan's right. I'm cold, too."

"It's only for a little while. Hurry it up, Wan. You too, Janine, let's see how fast we can pick out the Heechee ones." They had her coverall nearly full, and Wan, scowling and dignified in his kilt, was beginning to stuff the fans into his. It would be possible, Lurvy calculated, to wrap a few dozen more in the kilt. After all, he had a breechcloth under it. But they were really doing very well. Paul had already taken at least thirty or forty. Her coverall seemed able to hold nearly seventy-five. And, in any event, they could always come back another time for the rest, if they chose.

Lurvy did not think she would choose to do that. Enough was enough. Whatever else they might do in Heechee Heaven, they had already acquired one price-less fact. The prayer fans were books! Knowing that that was so was half the battle; with that certainty before them, scientists would surely be able to unlock the secret of reading them. If they could not do it from scratch, there were the readers on the Food Factory; if worst came to worst they could read every fan before one of Vera's remotes, encode sound and image, and transmit the whole thing to Earth. Perhaps they could wrench a reading machine loose and bring it back with them. . . . And back they would go, Lurvy was suddenly sure. If they could not find a way to move the Food Factory, they would abandon it. No one could fault them. They had done enough. If there was a need for more, other parties could follow them, but meanwhile— Meanwhile they would have brought back richer gifts than any other human beings since the discovery of the Gateway asteroid itself! They would be rewarded accordingly, there was no question of that— she even had Robinette Broadhead's word. For the first time since they had left the Moon on the searing chemical flame of their takeoff rockets, Lurvy let herself think of herself not as someone who was striving for a prize, but as someone who had won. And how happy her father would be. . . .

"That's enough," she said, helping Janine grip the spilling sack of prayer fans. "Let's take them right to the ship."

Janine hugged the clumsy bundle to her small breasts and picked up a few more with a free hand. "You sound as if we're going home," she said.

"Maybe so," Lurvy grinned. "Of course, we'll have to have a conference and decide— Wan? What's the matter?"

He was at the door, his shirtful of fans under an arm. And he looked stricken. "We waited too long," he whispered, peering down the corridor. "There are Old Ones by the berryfruit."

"Oh, *no*." But it was true. Lurvy peered cautiously out into the corridor and there they were, staring up at the camera Paul had fixed to the wall. One reached up and effortlessly pulled it loose while she watched. "Wan? Is there another way home?"

"Yes, through the gold, but—" His nose was work-

ing. "I think there are some there, too. I can smell them
and, yes, I can hear them!" And that was true, too;
Lurvy could hear a faint sound of mellow, chirrupy
grunts, from where the corridor bent.

"We don't have a choice," she said. "There are only
two of them back the way we came. We'll take them by
surprise and just push our way through. Come on!" Still
carrying the tapes, she hustled the others ahead of her.
The Heechee might be strong, but Wan had said they
were slow. With any luck at all—

They had no luck at all. As they reached the opening
she saw that there were more than two, half a dozen
more, standing around and looking toward them in the
entrances to the other corridors. "Paul!" she shouted at
the camera. "We're caught! Get in the ship, and if we
don't get away—" And she could say no more, because
they were upon her; and, yes, they were strong!

They were hustled up through half a dozen levels,
their captors one to each arm, stolidly chirping at each
other, ignoring their struggles and their words. Wan did
not speak. He let them pull him as they would, all the
way up to a great open spindle-shaped volume, where
another dozen Old Ones waited and a huge blue-lit
machine sat silent behind them. Did the Heechee believe in sacrifice? Or perform experiments on captives?
Would they wind up as Dead Men themselves, rambling
and obsessed, ready for the next batch of visitors?
Lurvy looked upon all of these as interesting questions,
and had no answers for any of them. She was not yet
afraid. Her feelings had not caught up with the facts; it
was too recently that she had allowed herself to feel
triumph. The realization of defeat would have to wait.

The Old Ones chirruped to each other, gesticulating
toward the prisoners, the corridors, the great silent machine, like a battle tank without guns. Like a night-
mare. Lurvy could not understand any of it, even
though the situation was clear enough. After minutes of
jabber they were pushed into a cubicle, and found in
it—astonishingly!—quite familiar objects. Behind the
closed door Lurvy shuffled through them—clothing; a

chess set; long desiccated rations. In the toe of one shoe was a thick roll of Brazilian currency, more than a quarter of a million dollars of it, she guessed. They had not been the first captives here! But in none of the rubble was anything like a weapon. She turned to Wan, who was pale and shaking. "What will happen?" she demanded.

He waggled his head like an Old One. It was the only answer he could give. "My father—" he began, and had to swallow before he could go on. "They captured my father once and, yes, truly, they let him go again. But I do not think that is a rule, since my father told me I must never let myself be caught."

Janine said, "At least Paul got away. Maybe—maybe he can bring help. . . ." But she stopped there, and did not expect an answer. Any hopeful answer would have been fantasy, defined by the four years it would take another vessel like theirs to reach the Food Factory. If help came, it would not be soon. She began to sort through the old clothing. "At least we can get something on," she said. "Come on, Wan. Get yourself dressed."

Lurvy followed her example, and then stopped at a strange sound from her sister. It was almost a laugh! "What's so funny?" she snapped.

Janine pulled a sweater over her head before she answered. It was too big, but it was warm. "I was just thinking about the orders we got," she said. "To get Heechee tissue samples, you know? Well, the way it worked out—they got ours instead. All of them."

8

Schwarze Peter

When the shipboard computer's mail bell rang, Payter woke quickly and completely. It was an advantage of age that one slept shallowly and woke at once. There were not many advantages. He got up, rinsed his mouth, urinated into the sanitary, washed his hands, and took two food packets with him to the terminal. "Display the mail now," he ordered, munching on something that tasted like sour rye bread but was meant to be a sweet roll.

When he saw what the mail was, his good mood passed. Most of it was interminable mission orders. Six letters for Janine, one each for Paul and Dorema, and for himself only a petition addressed to *Schwarze Peter* and signed by eight hundred and thirty school-children of Dortmund, begging him to return and become their Bürgermeister. "Dumb head!" he scolded the computer. "Why do you wake me for this trash?" Vera did not answer, because he did not give her time to identify him and rummage through her slow magnetic bubbles to locate his name. Long before then, he was complaining, "Also this food is not fit for pigs! Attend to it at once!"

Poor Vera erased the attempt to interpret his first question and patiently attended to the second. "The recycling system is below optimal mass levels," she said, ". . . Mr. Herter. In addition, my processing routines have been subject to overload for some time. Many programs have been deferred."

"Do not defer the food question any more," he snarled, "or you will kill me, and there's an end to it." He gloomily commanded display of the mission orders while he forced himself to chew the remainder of his breakfast. The orders rolled for ten solid minutes. What marvelous ideas they had for him, back on Earth! And if only there were a hundred of him, perhaps they could do one one-hundredth of the tasks proposed. He allowed the end of it to run unwatched, while he carefully shaved his pink old face and brushed his sparse hair. And why was the recycling system depleted, so that it could not function properly? Because his daughters and their consorts had removed themselves and thus their useful by-products, as well as all the water Wan had stolen from the system. Stolen! Yes, there was no other word for it. Also they had taken the mobile bio-assay unit, so that there was only the sampler in the sanitary to monitor his health, and what could that tell of fever or arhythmic heart, if he should have either? Also they had taken all but one of the cameras, so that he must carry that one with him wherever he went. Also they had taken—

They had taken themselves, and *Schwarze Peter*, for the first time in his life, was wholly alone.

He was not only alone, he was powerless to change it. If his family came back, they would do so in their own good time and not before. Until then he was a reserve unit, a pillbox soldier, a standby program. He was given excessive tasks to do, but the real center of action was somewhere else.

In his long life Payter had taught himself to be patient, but he had never taught himself to enjoy it. It was maddening to be forced to wait! To wait fifty days for an answer from Earth to his perfectly reasonable proposals and questions. To wait almost as long for his family and that hooligan boy to get to where they were going (if they ever did) and report to him (if they should happen to choose to). Waiting was not so bad if one had enough of a life left to wait in. But how much, realistically, had he? Suppose he had a stroke. Suppose he developed a cancer. Suppose any part of the complicated interactions that kept his heart beating and his blood flowing and his bowels moving and his brain thinking broke down in any place. What then?

And some day they surely would, because Payter was old. He had lied about his age so many times that he was no longer sure of what it was. Not even his children knew; the stories he told about his grandfather's youth were really about his own. Age in itself did not matter. Full Medical could deal with anything, repair or replace, as long as it was not the brain itself that was damaged—and Payter's brain was in the best of shape, because had it not schemed and contrived to get him here?

But "here" there was no Full Medical, and age began to matter a great deal.

He was no longer a boy! But once he had been, and even then he had known that somehow, some day, he would possess exactly what he owned now: the key to heart's desire. Bürgermeister of Dortmund? That was nothing! Skinny young Peter, shortest and youngest in his unit of the Hitler Youth but their leader all the same, had promised himself he would have much more. He had even known that it would turn out to be something like this, some grand futuristic pattern would emerge, and he alone would be able to find the handle to wield it, like a weapon, like an axe, like a scythe, to punish or reap or remake the world. Well, here it was! And what was he doing with it? He was waiting. It had not been like that, in the boyhood stories by Juve and Gail and Dominik and the Frenchman, Verne. The people in them did not waste themselves so spinelessly.

But what, after all, was one to do?

So while he waited for that question to answer itself, he kept up his daily rounds. He ate four light meals a day, every other one of CHON-food, methodically dictating to Vera his impressions of taste and consistency. He ordered Vera to design a new mobile bio-assay out of what odds and ends of sensor instrumentation could be spared, and worked at building it as she found time to complete parts of the design. He worked out ten minutes each morning with the weights, half an hour every afternoon with bending and stretching. He methodically walked every pathway in the Food Factory, with his hand-held camera pointed into every cranny. He composed long letters of complaint to his masters on Earth, cagily arguing the merits of aborting the mission and returning to Earth as soon as he could summon the family back, and actually transmitted one or two of them. He wrote fierce and peremptory directives to his lawyer in Stuttgart, in code, arguing his position, demanding a revision to the contract. And most of all, he schemed. And about the *Träumeplatz* most of all.

It was seldom out of his thoughts, this dreaming place with its startling potential. When he was depressed and fretful, he thought how rightly it would serve Earth if he were to repair it and call Wan back to give them their fevers once again. When he was charged with force and determination he went to look at it, lid hanging from an ornamental projection on one wall, the joints and fasteners always with him in his coverall pouch. How easy it would be to bring in a cutting torch and lop it free, cram the ship full of that, and the communications system for the Dead Men, and whatever other goods and treasures he could find; and then cast loose in the rocket for Earth, start the long, slow downward spiral that would bring him—what would it bring him? God in heaven, what would it not! Fame! Power! Prosperity! All the things that were his due— yes, and his rightful property, too, if he only got back in time to enjoy them.

It made him ill to think about it. All the time the clock was ticking, ticking. Every minute he was one minute closer to the end of his life. Every second spent waiting was a second stolen from the happy time of greatness and luxury that he had earned. He forced himself to eat, sitting on the edge of his private and looking longingly at the ship's controls. "The food has not improved, Vera!" he called accusingly.

The confounded thing did not answer. "Vera! You must do something about the food!" It still did not answer, not for several seconds.

And then only, "One moment, please . . . Mr. Herter." It was enough to make one sick. In fact, he did feel somewhat sick, he realized. He gazed with hostility at the dish he had been doggedly forcing down, supposed to be a sort of schnitzel, or as close to it as Vera's limited recombinant capacities would allow, but tasting of whisky or sauerkraut, or both at once. He set it on the floor.

"I do not feel well," he announced.

Pause. Then, "One moment, please . . . Mr. Herter." Poor stupid Vera had just so much capacity. She was processing a burst of messages from Earth, endeavoring to carry on a conversation with the Dead Men by means of the faster-than-light radio, encoding and transmitting all of her own telemetry—all at once. She simply did not have time for his queasiness. But his accelerating unease would not be denied: a sudden rush of saliva under the tongue, a quick shuddering of the diaphragm. He barely made it to the sanitary, giving back, there, all he had taken. For the last time, he swore. He did not want to live so long as to see those God-bedamned organic compounds reworked for one more passage through his gut. When he was sure he had stopped vomiting he marched over to the console and pushed the override buttons. "All functions in standby except this," he ordered. "Monitor my bio-assay at once."

"Very well," she said at once, ". . . Mr. Herter." Silence for a moment, while the unit in the sanitary made what it could of what Peter had just deposited. "You are suffering from food poisoning," she reported, ". . . Mr. Herter."

"So! This I already know. What is to be done about it?"

Pause, while her tiny brain revolved the problem. "If you could add water to the system, the fermentation and recycling would be under better control," she said, ". . . Mr. Herter. At least one hundred liters. There has been considerable loss due to evaporation in the much larger volume of space now available, as well as the stocks withdrawn for the remainder of your party. My recommendation is that you replenish the system with available water as soon as possible."

"But that is not fit to drink for pigs even!"

"The solutes present problems," she acknowledged. "Therefore I recommend that at least half of any added water be distilled first. The system should be able to cope with the remainder of the solutes . . . Mr. Herter."

"God in Heaven! Am I to build a still out of nothing, and become a water-carrier too? And what of the bio-assay mobile unit, so that this will not happen again?"

Vera sorted through the questions for a moment. "Yes, I think that would be appropriate," she agreed. "If you wish, I will provide construction plans. Also . . . Mr. Herter, you may wish to consider relying more heavily on CHON-food for your diet, since you do not appear to have severe adverse reactions to it."

"Apart of course from the fact that it tastes like dog-biscuit," he sneered. "Very well. Complete the construction plans at once. Hard copy, making use of available materials, do you understand?"

"Yes . . . Mr. Herter." The computer was silent for a time, inventorying redundant parts and materials, devising linkages that would do the job. It was a formidable task for Vera's limited intelligence. Peter drew a cup of water and rinsed out his mouth, then grimly unwrapped one of the least unattractive CHON tablets and nibbled off a tentative corner. While he waited to see if he would throw up again he faced the possibility that he might in fact die here, and alone. He did not even have the option he had thought was his, of casting everything adrift and returning to Earth by himself—not, at least, unless he first added water as ordered, and did his best to insure that nothing else would go wrong.

And yet it was every day so increasingly tempting. . . .

To be sure, that would mean casting his daughters and his son-in-law adrift.

But would they ever return? Suppose they did not. Suppose that rude boy turned the wrong switch, or ran out of fuel. Or anything. Suppose, in short, they *died*. Must he then wither on the vine until he also was dead? And what benefit would that be to humanity, if he perished here, and the whole thing to do over again with a new crew . . . and himself, *Schwarze Peter*, done out of reward, done out of fame and power, done out of life itself?

Or—an idea struck him—was there another option? This be-damned Food Factory itself, so set on continuing its course. What if he could find the controls that directed it so? What if he could learn to change those directions, so that it could bring him back to Earth not in three years and more, but at once, in days? To be sure, that would doom his family, would it not? But perhaps not! Perhaps they would return, if they returned at all, to the Food Factory itself, wherever it might be. Even in close orbit around Earth! And how marvelously that would solve everyone's problems at once—

He threw the remainder of the packet into the sanitary, to add to the store of organics. *"Du bist verrückt, Peter!"* he snarled to himself. The flaw in that dream could not be ignored: he had sought with all his might, and the controls to the Food Factory were not to be found.

The frying-bacon sound of the hard-copy printer rescued him from his thoughts. He pulled the sheets out of the machine and frowned over them for a moment. So much work! Twenty hours, at least! And not merely time, but so much of it was hard physical labor! He would have to go out into space to reclaim piping from the struts that were meant to hold the auxiliary transmitters in place, cut them loose, bring them inside; and only then begin to weld them together and form them

into a spiral. Simply for the condensation section of the
still! He saw that he was beginning to shake—

He barely made it to the sanitary in time. "Vera!" he
croaked. "I must have medication for this!"

"At once . . . Mr. Herter. Yes. In the medical kit you
will find tablets marked—"

"Dumbhead! The medical kit is gone to Cuckoo-
land!"

"Oh, yes . . . Mr. Herter. One moment. Yes. I have
programmed appropriate pharmaceuticals for you. It
will take about twenty minutes for them to be prepared."

"In twenty minutes I could be dead," he snarled. But
there was no help for it, and so he sat and stewed for
twenty minutes, the pressures mounting. Illness, hunger, loneliness, overwork, resentment, fear. Anger!
That was what, in the end, they all fused into. Anger.
Many vectors. One vector sum. By the time Vera's dis-
pensary popped out his pills, it had submerged all the
others. He swallowed them greedily and retired to his
private to see what would happen.

Actually they did appear to work. He lay back while
the fires in his belly damped themselves, and fell imper-
ceptibly asleep.

When he woke he felt at least physically better. He
washed himself, brushed his teeth, brushed his thinning
yellow hair, and only then noticed the Christmas tree of
attention-demanding lights around Vera's console. On
the screen in bright red letters were the words:

URGENTLY REQUEST PERMISSION
TO RESUME NORMAL MODES.

He chuckled to himself. He had forgotten to cancel
the override. When he ordered the computer to get back
to business there was an instant explosion of bells and
signal lights, a cascade of hard copy out of the printer
and a voice. His elder daughter's voice, out of Vera's
taped storage: "Hello, Pop. Sorry we couldn't reach
you to tell you we arrived safely. We're going to explore now. Talk to you later."

* * *

Because Peter Herter loved his family, the joy of
their safe arrival flooded his heart and sustained him—
for hours. For almost two days. But joy does not flour-
ish in an existence of irritations and worries. He spoke
to Lurvy—twice; for no more than thirty seconds each
time. Vera simply could not handle more. Vera was
harder pressed than Peter himself, stripped and rearranged as she was, handling two-way traffic between
Heechee Heaven and the Earth, deferring top priority
action commands when even higher priorities demanded attention. The one voice link with the Heechee
place could not handle the volume it was given to carry,
and mere chitchat between father and daughter could
not be allowed.

That was not unjust, Peter conceded. Such marvels
they were finding! What was unjust was that he himself
was out of it. What was unjust was that among the
urgent and meaningful traffic, Vera found time to pass
on to him a hodgepodge of commands meant for himself. None reasonable. Some impossible to carry out.
Redeploy the thrusters. Inventory CHON-food. Submit
by return message complete analysis 2 cm by 3 cm by
12.5 cm packets in red and lavender wrappers. Do not
submit unnecessary analyses! Submit metallurgical
analysis "dreaming couch". Do not attempt physical
study "dreaming couch". Query Dead Men re Heechee
Drive. Query Dead Men re control panels. Query Dead
Men. How easy that was to command! How hard to
carry out, when they maundered and scolded and rambled and complained when he could hear them at all,
and when most often he was forbidden to take time on
the FTL voice circuit anyway. Some of the orders from
Earth contradicted others, and most of them came out
of order, with obsolete priority designations. And some
did not come at all. Poor Vera's storage circuits were
soon approaching overload, and she tried to rid herself
of unnecessary data by hard-printing it for him to,
somehow, attend to; but that made problems of its own,
because the recycling system that fed the printer rolls
was the same one that fed him, and the organics were

already depleted. So Peter had to open and dump CHON-food into the sanitary and then get busy on the still.

Even if Vera had had time for him, he had not much time for Vera. Struggle into EVA equipment. Cycle himself out on the hull of the Food Factory. Cut away tubing and bind it together. Sweat it back to the ship, always fighting the infuriating, dogged thrust of the Food Factory itself as it plunged toward somewhere or other. He could spare time only for an occasional glance at the pictures coming back from Heechee Heaven. Vera displayed them as they came in, one frame at a time; but then each one was whisked away to make storage space for the next one, and if Peter was not there to see they would go unseen. Even so, good heavens! The Dead Men, so featureless to look at. The corridors of Heechee Heaven. The Old Ones—Peter's heart almost stopped as he looked at the great broad face of an Old One on the screen. But he had time only for a look, and then the still was done and he must go on with the next task. Build himself a yoke for his shoulders. Seam together plastic sheeting (another drain on the recycler!) to make buckets. Squat impatiently by the one functioning—barely functioning—water source, holding the flexible disk around the spout and catching the foul-smelling dribble in the bags. Tote the water back, half into the still, the other half into the recycling tanks. Sleep when he could. Eat when he could force himself. Attend to his own personal priority messages when they trickled through, and when he was too exhausted for anything physical. Another message from Dortmund, three hundred municipal workers this time —stupid Vera, for letting such trash through! A coded communication from his lawyer, meaning half an hour to translate it. And then all it said was, "Am attempting secure more favorable terms. Can promise nothing. Meanwhile advise full compliance all directives." What a pig! Peter, swearing, sat before the console, slammed down the override key and dictated his reply:

"Full compliance with all stupid directives will kill me, and then what?" And he sent it in the clear; let

Broadhead and the Gateway Corp make what they would of it!

And perhaps the message was no lie. In all his stress and bustle, Peter had no time for aches and pains. He ate the CHON-food and, when new regular rations began to come out of the recycler, them, too. Even when they tasted foul—sometimes turpentine, sometimes mold—he was not sick. This was not ideal. Peter knew that he was operating on stress and adrenaline, and sometime there would be a price to pay. But he could see no way to avoid paying it when due.

And when at last he had the food processor working reasonably well once more, and had managed to catch up with what appeared the most peremptory of his own orders, he sat before Vera's console half-dozing, and then saw the greatest marvel of all. He scowled uncomprehendingly. What was that idiot boy doing with a prayer fan? Why in the next frame was he poking it into those foolish things that looked like flowerholders? And then the next frame began to build in the screen, and Peter gave a great shout. Suddenly a picture had appeared, some sort of book—Japanese or Chinese, by the look of it.

He was out of the ship and halfway to the *Traüme-platz* before his conscious mind quite articulated what some part of him had understood at once. The prayer fans! They contained information! He did not stop to wonder why the information had been in a Terrestrial language, or at least what looked like one. He had grasped the essential fact. He was determined to see for himself. Panting, he thrust himself into the room and scrabbled feverishly among the "fans". How was it done? Why in the name of God had he not waited to see more, to be sure of what he was doing? But there were the candleholders, or flowerpots, or whatever he had thought they were; he jammed the first prayer fan to hand into the nearest one. Nothing happened.

He tried six of them, narrow end first, wide end first, every way he could think of, before it occurred to him that perhaps not all of the reading machines were still working. And the second one he tried pulled the fan out of his hand and immediately sprang into light. He was looking at six dancers in black masks and bodystockings, and he was hearing a song he had not heard for many years.

It was a taped PV show! No. Not even that. It was older than that. Years older, not much more recent than the first years of the discovery of the Gateway asteroid; his second wife was still alive, and Janine not born yet, when that song was new. It had been simple old television, before the Heechee piezoelectric circuits had been incorporated into communications systems for human beings. It had perhaps been part of the library of some Gateway prospector, no doubt one of the Dead Men, and somehow it had been transcribed to a prayer fan.

What a cheat!

But then he realized that there were thousands of prayer fans, on Earth, in the tunnels of Venus, still on Gateway itself; wherever the Heechee had been they had left them. Whatever the source of this one, most of the others must have been left by the Heechee themselves! And that alone—dear God, that alone was worth more even than the Food Factory, for it was the key to all of the Heechee's knowledge! What a bonus there would be!

Exulting, Peter tried another fan (old movie), and another (slim volume of poetry, this time in English, by someone named Eliot), and another. How disgusting! If this was what Wan had got his notions of love from, some lascivious Gateway prospector carrying pornography with him to pass the time, no wonder his behavior was so foul! But he could not remain angry long, for he had too much to be glad about. He snatched it out of the reader, and then, in the quiet, heard the distant tiny sound of Vera's urgent-attention bell.

It had a frightening sound, even before he got back to the ship, even before he demanded the message and heard his son-in-law's voice, rasped with fear:

"Urgent override priority! For Peter Herter and immediate relay to Earth! Lurvy, Janine and Wan have been captured by the Heechee, and I think they are coming after me!"

The advantage of his new situation, and the only one, was that now that there were no more messages coming from Heechee Heaven Vera was better able to cope with her overload. Patiently Peter teased out of her all the pictures that had been transmitted before Paul's message had been taped, and saw the knot of Heechee at the end of the corridor, the blurred struggle, half a dozen quick glimpses of the ceiling of the corridor, something that might have been the back of Wan's head—then nothing. Or nothing that meant anything. Peter could not know that the camera had been jammed into the blouse of one of the Old Ones, but he could see that there was nothing to be seen: obscure shadowy shapes, perhaps a hint of texture.

Peter's mind was clear. But it was also empty. He did not allow himself to feel how empty his life had at once become. He carefully programmed Vera to go back over the voice messages and select the significant ones, and listened to what all of them had said. There was no hope in any of it. Not even when at last a new picture suddenly began to build on the screen, then another, then another. For half a dozen frames there was nothing that made sense, perhaps a fist over the lens, maybe a shot of a bare floor. Then, in one corner of the last frame, something that looked like—what? Like a *Sturmkampfwagen* from his earliest boyhood? But then it was gone, and the camera had once again been put where it showed nothing at all, and stayed that way through fifty frames.

What it noticeably did not show was any sign of either of his daughters, or of Wan. And as to Paul, the old man did not have a clue; after his last frantic message he was gone.

In some unwanted corner of his mind he found the realization that now he might be, probably was, the sole survivor of the mission, and so whatever bonus might come to all was now his alone.

He held the thought where he could look at it. But it meant nothing. He was now hopelessly alone, more alone than ever, as alone as Trish Bover frozen into her eternal ragged orbit that would go nowhere. Perhaps he could get back to Earth to claim his reward. Perhaps he could keep from dying. But how was he to keep from going insane?

It took Peter a long time to fall asleep. He was not afraid of sleeping. What he dreaded was waking up afterward, and when it came it was as bad as he had feared. In the first moment it was a day like any other day, and it was only after a peaceable moment of stretching and yawning that he remembered what had happened. "Peter Herter," he said to himself out loud, "you are alone in this very damned place, and you will die here, still alone." He noted that he was talking to himself. Already.

Through the habits of all those years he washed himself, cleaned his mouth, brushed his hair and then took time to snip off the loose ends around his ears and at the nape of his neck. It did not matter what he did, in any case. Having left his private, he opened two packets of CHON-food and ate them methodically before asking Vera if there were any messages from Heechee Heaven. "No," she said, ". . . Mr. Herter, but there are a number of downlink action relays."

"Later," he said. They did not matter. They would tell him to do things he had already done, perhaps. Or they would tell him to do things he had no intention of doing, perhaps to force himself outside, to rerig the thrusters, to try again. But the Food Factory would of course counter every thrust with an equal and opposite thrust of its own and continue its slow acceleration toward God, He knew what, for God, He knew why. In any event, nothing that came from Earth for the next fifty days would be relevant to the new realities.

And in less than fifty days—

In less than fifty days, what? "You talk as though you had a choice of options, Peter Herter!" he scolded himself.

Well, perhaps he had, he thought, if only he could perceive what they were. Meanwhile the best thing for him to do was to do what he had always done. To keep himself fastidiously neat. To do such tasks as were reasonable for him to do. To maintain his well established habits. He had learned through all those decades of life that the best time for him to move his bowels was some forty-five minutes after eating breakfast; it was now about that time; it was appropriate to do that. While he was squatting on the sanitary he felt a tiny, almost imperceptible lurch once more and scowled. It was an annoyance to have things happen when he did not know their cause, and it was an interruption in what he was doing, with his customary efficiency. Of course, one could not claim much personal credit for the functioning of sphincters that had been bought and transplanted from some hapless (or hungry) donor, or for a stomach inserted intact from another. Nevertheless, it pleased Peter that he functioned so well.

You are morbidly interested in your bowel movements, he told himself, but silently.

Also silently—it did not seem so bad to talk to oneself, as long as it was not aloud—he defended himself. It was not unjustified, he thought. It was only because the example of the bio-assay unit in the toilet was always before him. For three and a half years it had been monitoring every waste product of their bodies. Of course, so it must! How else to keep tabs on their health? And if it was proper for a machine to weigh and evaluate one's excrement, why not for the excrement's author?

He said aloud, grinning, *"Du bist verrückt, Peter Herter!"*

He nodded in agreement with himself as he cleaned himself and fastened his coverall, because he had summed it all up. Yes. He was crazy.

By the standards of ordinary men.

But what ordinary man had ever been in the present position of Peter Herter?

So when one had said that he was crazy, after all, one had said nothing that was relevant. What did the

standards of ordinary men signify as to *Schwarze Peter*?
It was only against extraordinary men that he could be
judged—and what a motley crew they were! Drug ad-
dicts and drunkards. Adulterers and traitors. Tycho
Brahe had a gutta-percha nose, and no one thought him
the less. The *Reichsführer* ate no meat. Great Frederick
himself spent many hours that could have been devoted
to the management of an empire in composing music
for tinkle-tankle chamber groups. He strolled across to
the computer and called, "Vera, what was that little
thump a few minutes ago?"

The computer paused to match the description
against her telemetry. "I cannot be sure . . . Mr. Herter.
But the moment of inertia is consistent with either the
launching or docking of one of the cargo ships that
have been observed."

He stood for a moment gripping the edge of the console seat. "Fool!" he shouted. "Why was I not told that
that was possible?"

"I'm sorry . . . Mr. Herter," she apologized. "The
analysis suggesting this possibility has been read out for
you as hard copy. Perhaps you overlooked it."

"Fool," he said again, but this time he was not sure
who he was talking to. The ships, of course! It had been
implicit all along that the production of the Food Factory had to go somewhere. And it had also been implicit that the ships had to return empty to be reloaded.
For what? Where?

That did not matter. What mattered was the perception that perhaps they would not always come empty.

And, following on that, the perception that one ship
at least, known to come to the Food Factory, was now
in Heechee Heaven. If it should come back, who or
what might be in it?

Peter rubbed his arm, which had begun to ache.
Pains or none, he could perhaps do something about
that! He had some weeks before that ship could possibly return. He could—what? Yes! He could barricade
that corridor. He could somehow move machines,
stores—anything that had mass—to block it, so that
when it did return, if it did, whoever was in it would be

stopped, or at least delayed. And the time to begin that
was now.

He delayed no further, but set off to find materials
for a barricade.

It was not hard to move even quite massive objects,
in the low thrust of the Food Factory. But it was tiring.
And his arms continued to ache. And in a little while, as
he was shoving a blue metal object like a short, fat
canoe down toward the dock, he became aware of a
strange sensation that seemed to come from the roots of
his teeth, almost like the beginning of a toothache; and
saliva began to flow from under his tongue.

Peter stopped and breathed deeply, forcing himself
to relax.

It did no good. He had known it would do no good. In
a few moments the pain in the chest began, first tentative, as though someone were pressing against him with a
sled runner along his breastbone, then painful, a hard,
bruising thrust, as though the runner were on top of
him and a hundred-kilo man standing on it.

He was too far from Vera to get medicine. He would
have to wait it out. If it was false angina, he would live.
If it was cardiac arrest, he would not. He sat patient and
still, waiting to see which it would be, while anger built
up and built up inside him. How unfair it was!

How unfair it all was! Five thousand astronomical
units away, serenely and untroubled, the people of the
world went about their business, neither knowing nor
caring that the person who could bring them so much—
who already had!—might be dying, alone and in pain.

Could they be grateful? Could they show respect,
appreciation, even common decency?

Perhaps he would give them a chance. If they responded with these things, yes, he would bring them
such gifts as they had never known. But if they were
wicked and disobedient—

Then *Schwarze Peter* would bring them such terrible
gifts that all the world would shudder and quake with
fear! In either case, they would never forget him . . . if
only he survived what was happening to him now.

9

Brasilia

The main thing was Essie. I sat by her bed every time she came out of surgery—fourteen times in six weeks—and every time her voice was a little weaker and she looked a little more gaunt. Everybody was after me all the time, the suit against me in Brasilia was going badly, reports poured in from the Food Factory, the fire in the food mines still would not go out. But Essie was up front. Harriet had her orders. Wherever I was, asleep or awake, if Essie asked for me she was put through at once. "Oh, yes, Mrs. Broadhead, Robin will be with you right away. No, you won't be disturbing him. He just woke up from a nap." Or he's just between appointments, or he's just coming up the lawn from the Tappan Sea, or anything that would not deter Essie from speaking to me right away. And then I would go into the darkened room, all sun-tanned and grinning and relaxed, and tell her how well she was looking. They had taken my billiard room and moved a whole

161

operating theater into it, and cleared the books out of the library next door to make it a bedroom for her. She was pretty comfortable there. Or said she was.

And actually, she didn't look bad at all. They had done the splints and the bone grafts, and plugged in two or three kilos of spare parts and tissues. They had even put the skin back, or I guess transplanted new skin from somebody else. Her face looked fine, except for a light bandage on one side, and she brushed her streaky blonde hair down over that. "So, stud," she would greet me. "How you hanging?"

"Just fine, just fine. A little horny," I would say, nuzzling her neck with my nose. "And you?"

"Just fine." So we reassured each other; and we weren't lying, you know. She was getting better every day, the doctors told me that. And I was getting—I don't know what I was getting. But I was all atremble with eagerness for every morning. Operating on five hours sleep a night. Never tired. Never felt better in my life.

But still she kept getting skinnier every time. The doctors told me what I must do, and I told Harriet and Harriet reprogrammed the cook. So we stopped having salads and bare broiled steaks. No coffee and juice breakfasts, but *tvoroznyikyi*, cream-cheese pancakes, and mugs of steaming cocoa. Caucasian lamb pilaff for lunch. Roast grouse in sour-cream sauce for dinner. "You're spoiling me, dear Robin," she accused, and I said:

"Only fattening you up. I can't stand skinny women."

"Yes, very well. But there is such a thing as being too ethnic. Is there nothing fattening that is not Russian?"

"Wait for dessert," I grinned. "Strawberry short-cake." And whipped with double Devonshire cream. As a matter of psychology, the nurse had persuaded me to start with small portions on large plates. Essie doggedly ate them all the way through, and as we gradually increased the size of the portions she gradually ate more each day. She didn't stop losing weight. But she slowed it down a lot, and by the end of six weeks the doctors

opined that her condition, cautiously, might be regarded as stable. Nearly.

When I told her the good news she was actually
standing up—tethered to the plumbing under her bed,
but able to walk about the room. "About time," she
said, reaching out to kiss me. "Now. You have been
spending too much time at home."

"It's a pleasure," I said.

"It is a kindness," she said soberly. "Is very dear to
me that you have always been here, Robin. But now
that I am almost well you must have affairs to attend
to."

"Not really. I get along fine with the comm facilities
in the brain room. Of course, it would be nice for the
two of us to go somewhere. I don't think you've ever
seen Brasilia. Maybe in a few weeks—"

"No. Not in few weeks. Not with me. If you have
need to go, please do it, Robin."

I hesitated. "Well, Morton thinks it might be useful."

She nodded briskly and called, "Harriet? Mr. Broadhead will be leaving for Brasilia tomorrow morning.
Make reservations et cetera."

"Certainly, Mrs. Broadhead," Harriet said from the
console at the head of Essie's bed. Her image sputtered
into blackness as quickly as it had appeared, and Essie
put her arms around me.

"I will see that you have complete communications
in Brasilia," she promised, "and Harriet will be instructed to keep you posted on my condition at all
times. Square count, Robin. If I need you, you will
know at once."

I said into her ear, "Well—"

She said into my shoulder, "Is no 'well'. Is settled,
and, Robin? I love you very much."

Albert tells me that every radio message I send is
actually a long, skinny string of photons, like a spear
thrown into space. A thirty-second burst communication is a column nine million kilometers long, each photon zipping along at the speed of light, in perfect step
all the way. But even that long, fast, skinny spear takes

forever to go 5,000 A.U. The fever that had wounded my wife had taken twenty-five days to get here. The orders to stop fooling with the couch had gone only a fraction of the way before they passed the second fever, the one the girl Janine had laid on us. Lightly, to be sure. Our message congratulating the Herter-Halls on arriving at the Food Factory, out somewhere past Pluto's orbit, had passed the one to tell us that most of them had gone skylarking off to Heechee Heaven. By now they were there; and our message telling them what to do about it was long since at the Food Factory for relay—for once two events had occurred at times close enough to have some meaning for each other.

But by the time we knew what meaning they had had, the event would again be twenty-five days in the past. What an annoyance! I wanted many things on the Food Factory, but what I wanted most of all at that moment was that faster-than-light radio. Astonishing that such a thing should be! But when I charged Albert with being caught flat-footed by it, he had smiled that gentle, humble smile and poked his pipestem at his ear and said, "Sure thing, Robin, if you mean the sort of surprise that one feels when an unlikely contingency turns out to be real. But it was always a contingency. Remember. The Heechee ships were able to navigate without error to moving targets. That suggests the possibility of communication at nearly instantaneous speeds over astronomical distances—ergo, a faster-than-light radio."

"Then why didn't you tell me about it?" I demanded.

He scratched one sneakered foot against the other sockless ankle. "It was only a possibility, Robin, estimated no more than point oh five. A sufficient condition, but not a necessary one. We simply didn't have enough evidence, until now."

I could have been chatting with Albert on the way down to Brasilia. But I was traveling commercial—the company aircraft aren't fast enough for those distances—and I like having Albert where I can see him when we talk, so I spent my time voice-only with company business and Morton. And of course with Harriet, who was under orders to check in once an hour, except when I was asleep, with a quick status report on Essie.

Even hypersonic, a ten-thousand-kilometer flight takes a while, and I had time for a lot of business. Morton wanted as much of it as he could get, mostly to try to talk me out of meeting with Bover. "You have to take him seriously, Robin," he whined through the plug in my ear. "Bover's represented by Anjelos, Carpenter and Gutmann, and they're high-powered people, with really good legal programs."

"Better than you?"

Hesitation. "Well—I hope not, Robin."

"Tell me something, Morton. If Bover didn't have much of a case to begin with, why are these high-powered people bothering with him?"

Although I couldn't see him, I knew that Morton would be assuming his defensive look, partly apologetic, partly you-laymen-wouldn't-understand. "It's not all that weak, Robin. And it hasn't gone well for us so far. And it's taking on some larger dimensions than we originally estimated. And I assume that they thought their connections would patch up the weak spots—I also assume that they're in for a son-of-a-bitching big contingency fee. You'd be better advised to patch up some of our own weak spots than take a chance with Bover, Robin. Your pal Senator Praggler is on this month's oversight committee. Go see him first."

"I'll go see him, but not first," I told Morton, and cut him off as we circled in for a landing. I could see the big Gateway Authority tower overshadowing the silly flat saucer over the House of Representatives, and off up the lake the bright reflections of tin roofs in the Free Town. I had cut it pretty close. My date with Trish Bover's widower (or husband, depending on how you looked at it) was in less than an hour, and I didn't really want to keep him waiting.

I didn't have to. I was already sitting at a table in the courtyard dining room of the Brasilia Palace hotel when he came in. Skinny. Tall. Balding. He sat down nervously, as if he were in a desperate hurry, or desperately eager to be somewhere else. But when I offered him lunch he took ten minutes to study the menu and wound up ordering all of it. Fresh hearts of palm salad, little fresh-water shrimp from the lake, all the way down to that wonderful raw pineapple flown up from Rio. "This is my favorite hotel in Brasilia," I informed him genially, hostfully, as he poured dressing on the hearts of palm. "Old. But good. I suppose you've seen all the sights?"

"I've lived here for eight years, Mr. Broadhead."

"Oh, I see." I hadn't known where the hell the son of a bitch lived, he was just a name and a nuisance. So much for travelog. I tried common interests. "I got a flash synoptic from the Food Factory on the way down here. The Herter-Hall party is doing well, finding out some marvelous things. Did you know that we've identified four of the Dead Men as actual Gateway prospectors?"

"I saw something about that on the PV, yes, Mr. Broadhead. It's quite exciting."

"More than that, Bover. It can change this whole world around—and make us all filthy rich, too." He nodded, his mouth full of salad. He kept on keeping his mouth full, too; I wasn't doing much good trying to draw him out. "All right," I said, "why don't we get down to business? I want you to drop that injunction."

He chewed and swallowed. With the next forkful of shrimp poised at his mouth he said, "I know you do, Mr. Broadhead," and refilled the mouth.

I took a long, slow sip of my wine and seltzer and said, with complete control of my voice and manner, "Mr. Bover, I don't think you understand what the issues are. I don't mean to put you down. I just can't believe you have all the facts. We're both going to lose if you keep that injunction in force." I went over the whole case with him, with care, exactly as Morton had spelled it out to me: Gateway Corp's intervention, eminent domain, the problem of complying with a court order when your compliance doesn't get to the people it affects until a month and a half after they've gone and done whatever they were going to do, the opportunity for a negotiated settlement. "What I'm trying to say," I said, "is that this is really big. Too big for us to be divided. They won't fuck around with us, Bover. They'll just go ahead and expropriate us."

He didn't stop chewing, just listened, and then when he had nothing more to chew he took a sip from his demitasse and said, "We really don't have anything to discuss, Mr. Broadhead."

"Of course we do!"

"Not unless we both think so," he pointed out, "and I don't. You're a little mistaken in some of the things you say. I don't have an injunction any more. I have a judgment."

"Which I can get reversed in a hot—"

"Yes, maybe you can. But not in a hot anything. The law will take its course, and it will take time. I won't make any deal. Trish paid for whatever comes out of this. Since she isn't around to protect her rights I guess I have to."

"But it's going to cost both of us!"

"That's as may be. As my lawyer says. He advised me against this meeting."

"Then why did you come?"

He looked at the remains of his lunch, then out at the fountains in the courtyard. Three returned Gateway prospectors were sitting on the edge of a reflecting pool with a slightly drunk Varig stewardess, singing and tossing crumbs of French pastry to the goldfish. They had struck it rich. "It makes a nice change for me, Mr. Broadhead," he said.

Out of the window of my suite, high up in the new Palace Tower, I could see the crown-of-thorns of the cathedral glinting in the sun. It was better than looking at my legal program on the full-service monitor, because he was eating me out. "You may have prejudiced our whole case, Robin. I don't think you understand how big this is getting."

"That's what I told Bover."

"No, really, Robin. Not just Robin Broadhead, Inc., not even just the Gateway Corporation. Government's getting into it. And not just the signatories to the Gateway Convention either. This may wind up a U.N. matter."

"Oh, come on, Morton! Can they do that?"

"Of course they can, Robin. Eminent domain. Your friend Bover isn't helping things any, either. He's petitioning for a conservator to take over your personal and corporate holdings in this matter, in order to administer the exploration properly."

The son of a bitch. He must have known that was happening while we were eating the lunch I bought him. "What's this word 'proper'? What have I done that was improper?"

"Short list, Robin?" He ticked off his fingers. "One, you exceeded your authority by giving the Herter-Hall party more freedom of action than was contemplated, which, two, led to their expedition to Heechee Heaven with all of its potential consequences and thus, three, brought about a situation of grave national peril. Strike that. Grave *human* peril."

"That's crap, Morton!"

"That's the way he put it in the petition," he nodded, "and, yes, we may persuade somebody it's crap. Sooner or later. But right now it's up to the Gateway Corp to act or not."

"Which means I better see the Senator." I got rid of Morton and called Harriet to ask about my appointment.

"I can give you the Senator's secretarial program now," she smiled, and faded to show a rather sketchy animation of a handsome young black girl. It was quite poor simulation, nothing like the programs Essie writes for me. But then Praggler was only a United States senator.

"Good afternoon," she greeted me. "The Senator asks me to say that he's in Rio de Janeiro on committee business this evening, but will be happy to see you whenever convenient tomorrow morning. Shall we say ten o'clock?"

"Let's say nine," I told her, somewhat relieved. I had been a little worried about Praggler's failure to get back to me right away. But now I perceived he had a good reason: the fleshpots of Ipanema. "Harriet?" When she came back I asked, "How's Mrs. Broadhead?"

"No change, Robin," she smiled. "She's awake and available now, if you'd like to speak to her."

"Bet your sweet little electronic tooshy I do," I told her. She nodded and drifted away. Harriet is a really good program; she doesn't always understand the words, but she can make a yes-no decision from the tone of my voice, and so when Essie appeared I said, "S. Ya. Lavorovna, you do nice work."

"To be sure, dear Robin," she agreed, preening herself. She stood up and turned slowly around. "As do our doctors, you will observe."

It took a moment for it to hit me. There were no life-support tubes! She wore flesh-form casts on her left side, but she was free of the machines! "My God, woman, what happened?"

"Perhaps healing has happened," she said serenely. "Although it is only an experiment. The doctors have just left, and I am to try this for six hours. Then they will examine me again."

"You look bloody marvelous." We chatted fill-in talk for a few minutes; she told me about the doctors, I told her about Brasilia, while I studied her as carefully as I could in a PV tank. She kept getting up and stretching, delighting in her freedom, until she worried me. "Are you sure you're supposed to do all that?"

"I have been told that I must not think of water skiing or dancing for a while. But perhaps not everything that is fun is prohibited."

"Essie, you lewd lady, is that a lustful look I see in your eye? Are you feeling well enough for that?"

"Quite well, yes. Well. Not *well*," she amplified, "but perhaps as though you and I had enjoyed a hard night's drinking a day or two ago. A little fragile. But I do not think I would be harmed by a gentle lover."

"I'll be back tomorrow morning."

"You will not be back tomorrow morning," she said firmly. "You will be back when you are entirely through with your business in Brasilia and not one moment before or else, my boy, you will not find any willing partner for your debauched intentions here."

I said good-bye in a rosy glow.

Which lasted all of twenty-five minutes, until I got around to double-checking with the doctor.

It took a little while, because she was just getting back to Columbia Medical when I called. "I'm sorry to be rushed, Mr. Broadhead," she apologized, shrugging out of her gray tweed suit-coat. "I've got to show students how to suture nerve tissue in about ten minutes."

"You usually call me Robin, Dr. Liederman," I said, cooling off quickly.

"Yes, I do—Robin. Don't get worried. I don't have bad news." While she was talking she was continuing to strip down, as far as brassiere level, before putting on a turtleneck and an operating-room gown. Wilma Liederman is a good-looking woman of a certain age, but I was not there to ogle her charms.

"But you don't have good news, either?"

"Not yet. You've talked to Essie, so you know we're trying her out without the machines. We have to know how far she can go on her own, and we won't know that for twenty-four hours. At least I hope we won't."

"Essie said six."

"Six hours to readouts, twenty-four to full workup. Unless she shows bad signs before that and has to go back on the machines right away." She was talking to me over her shoulder, scrubbing up at her little wash-stand. Holding her dripping hands in the air she came back closer to the comm set. "I don't want you worrying, Robin," she said. "All this is routine. She's got about a hundred transplants in her, and we have to find out if they've taken hold. I wouldn't let her go this far if I didn't think the chances were at least reasonable, Robin."

" 'Reasonable' doesn't sound real good to me, Wilma!"

"Better than reasonable, but don't push me. And don't worry, either. You're getting regular bulletins, and you can call my program any time you want more

—me too, if you have to. You want odds? Two to one everything's going to work. A hundred to one that if something fails it's something we can fix. Now I've got to transplant a complete lower genital for a young lady who wants to be sure she still has fun afterwards."

"I think I ought to get back there," I said.

"For what? There's nothing you can do but get in the way. Robin, I promise I won't let her die before you get back." In the background the P.A. system was chiming gently. "They're playing my song, Robin, talk to you later."

There are times when I sit at the center of the world, and when I know that I can reach out to any of the programs my good wife has written for me and pull back any fact, absorb any explanation or command any event.

There are also times when I sit with a full console and a head full of burning questions and learn nothing, because I do not know what to ask.

And there are times when I am so full of learning and being and doing that the moments zip past and the days are packed; and other times when I am floating in slack water beside a current, and the world is sliding speedily by. There was plenty to do. I didn't feel like doing it. Albert was bursting with news from Heechee Heaven and the Food Factory. I let him purge himself. But the synoptics plopped into my mind without raising a question or even a ripple; when he was through reporting about architectural deductions and interpretations of maunderings of the Dead Men I turned him off. It was intensely interesting, but for some reason I was not interested by it. I ordered Harriet to let my simulacrum deal with everything routine and tell everyone who was not urgent to call me another time. I stretched out on the three-meter watercouch looking out over the weird Brasilia skyline, and wished that it were that couch in the Food Factory, connected to someone I loved.

Wouldn't that be great? To be able to reach out to someone far away, as Wan had reached out to the whole Earth, and feel with them what they were feeling, let them feel the inside of you? What a wonderful thing for lovers!

And to that thought I reacted by calling up Morton on my console and telling him to look into the possibility of patenting that application of the couch.

It was not a very romantic response to a pretty romantic thought. The difficulty was that I was not quite sure which someone I wished I were connected to. My dear wife, so loved, so needful right now? Or someone a lot farther away and much harder to reach?

So I stagnated through the long Brazilian afternoon, with a soak in the pool, and a lounge in the setting sun, and a lavish dinner in my suite with a bottle of wine, and then I called Albert back to ask him what I really wanted to know. "Albert? Where, exactly, is Klara now?"

He paused, tamping tobacco into his pipe and frowning. "Gelle-Klara Moynlin," he said at last, "is in a black hole."

"Yes. And what does that mean?"

He said apologetically, "That's hard to say. I mean it's hard to put in simple terms, and also hard to say because I really don't know. Not enough data."

"Do your best."

"Sure thing, Robin. I would say that she is in the section of the exploration craft which remained in orbit, just under the event horizon of the singularity you encountered—which," he waved carelessly and a blackboard appeared behind him, "is of course just at the Schwarzschild radius."

He stood up, jamming the unlit pipe into the hip pocket of his baggy cotton slacks, picked up a piece of chalk and wrote:

$$\frac{2GM}{c^2}$$

"At that boundary, light can't go any farther. It is what you might think of as a standing wave-front where light has gone as far as it can go. You can't see into the black hole past it. Nothing can come up from behind it. The symbols, of course, stand for gravity and mass—and I don't have to tell an old faster-than-light person like you what c^2 is, do I? From the instrumentation you brought back, it would appear that this particular hole was maybe sixty kilometers in diameter, which would give it a mass of maybe ten times the sun. Am I telling you more than you want to know?"

"A little bit, Albert," I said, shifting uncomfortably on the watercouch. I wasn't really sure just what I was asking for.

"Perhaps what you want to know is whether she is dead, Robby," he said. "Oh, no. I don't think so. There's a lot of radiation around, and God knows what shear forces. But she hasn't had much time to be dead yet. Depends on her angular velocity. She might not yet even know you're gone. Time dilation, you see. That is a consequence of—"

"I understand about time dilation," I interrupted. And I did, because I was feeling almost as though I were living through some of it. "Is there any way we can find that out?"

" 'A black hole has no hair,' Robby," he quoted solemnly. "That's what we call the Carter-Werner-Robinson-Hawking Law, and what it means is that the only information you get out of a black hole is mass, charge and angular momentum. Nothing else."

"Unless you get inside it, the way she did."

"Well, yes, Robby," he admitted, sitting down and attending to his pipe. Long pause. Puff, puff. Then, "Robin?"

"Yes, Albert?"

He looked abashed, or as abashed as a holographic construct can. "I haven't been entirely fair with you," he said. "There is some information that comes out of black holes. But that gets us into quantum mechanics. And it doesn't do you any good, either. Not for your purposes."

I didn't really like having a computer program tell me what my "purposes" were. Especially since I wasn't all that sure myself. "Tell me about it!" I ordered.

"Well—we don't really know a lot. Goes back to Stephen Hawking's first principles. He pointed out that, in a sense, a black hole can be said to have a 'temperature'—which implies some kind of radiation. Some kinds of particles do escape. But not from the kinds of black holes that interest you, Robby."

"What kind do they escape from?"

"Well, mostly from the tiny ones. The ones with the mass of, say, Mount Everest. Submicroscopic ones. No bigger than a nuclear particle. They get real hot, a hundred billion Kelvin and up. The smaller they get, the faster the quantum tunneling goes on, the hotter they get—so they keep on getting smaller and hotter until they just blow up. Big ones, no. It goes the other way. The bigger they are, the more infall they get to replenish their mass, and the harder it is for a particle to tunnel out. One like Klara's has a temperature probably down around a hundred millionth of a Kelvin, which is really cold, Robin. And getting colder all the time."

"So you don't get out of one of those."

"Not any way I know about, no, Robin. Does that answer your questions?"

"For now," I said, dismissing him. And it did, all but one: Why was it that when he was talking to me about Klara he called me "Robby"?

Essie wrote good programs, but it seemed to me that they were beginning to overlap. I used to have a program that addressed me by childhood names from time to time. But it was a psychiatric program. I reminded myself to speak to Essie about straightening out her programming, because I certainly did not feel I had any need for the services of Sigfrid von Shrink now.

Senator Praggler's temporary office wasn't in the Gateway tower, but on the 26th floor of the legislators' office building. A courtesy from the Brazilian Congress to a colleague, and a flattering one, because it was only two stories below the top. In spite of the fact that I got up with the dawn, I got there a couple minutes late. I had spent the time wandering around the early-morning city, ducking under the overhead roadways, coming out in the parking lot. Strolling. I was still in a sort of temporary stasis of time.

But Praggler shook me out of it, all charged-up and beaming. "It's wonderful news, Robin!" he cried, pulling me into his office and ordering coffee. "Jesus! How stupid we've all been!"

For a moment I thought he meant that Bover had dropped his suit. That only showed how stupid I was still being; what he was talking about was a late flash from the Food Factory relay. The long-sought Heechee books had turned out to be the prayer fans that we had all seen for decades. "I thought you'd have known all about it," he apologized, when he had finished filling me in.

"I've been out walking," I said. It was pretty disconcerting for him to be telling me about something as big as that on my own project. But I recover fast. "Seems to me, Senator," I said, "that's a big plus for vacating that injunction."

He grinned. "You know, I could have guessed it would strike you that way. *Anything* would. Mind telling me how you figure that?"

"Well, it looks clear to me. What's the biggest purpose of the expedition? Knowledge about the Heechee. And now we find out that there's a lot of it lying around, just waiting for us to pick it up."

He frowned. "We don't know how to decode the damn things."

"We will. Now that we know what they are, we'll figure out a way to make them work. We've got the revelation. All we need is the engineering. We ought to—" I stopped myself in the middle of a sentence. I was going to say that it was a good idea to start buying up every prayer fan on the market, but that was too good an idea to give even a friend. I switched to, "We ought to get results pretty fast. The point is, the Herter-Hall expedition isn't our only iron in the fire any more, so any argument about national interests loses a lot of weight."

He accepted a cup of coffee from his secretary, the real-live one that didn't look a bit like his program, and then shrugged. "It's an argument. I'll tell it to the committee."

"I was hoping you'd do more than that, Senator."

"If you mean you want the whole thing dropped, Robin, I don't have that authority. I'm only here to oversee the committee. For one month. I can go home and raise hell in the Senate, and maybe I will, but that's the limit of it."

"And what's the committee going to do? Will they uphold Bover's claim?"

He hesitated. "I think it's worse than that. I think the sentiment's to expropriate you all. Then it's a Gateway Corporation matter, which means it sticks there until the signatories to the treaty unstick it. Of course, in the long run, you'll all get reimbursed—"

I slammed the cup back into its saucer. "Fuck the reimbursement! Do you think I'm in this for the money?"

Praggler is a pretty close friend. I know he likes me, and I even think he trusts me, but there wasn't any friendly look on his face when he said, "Sometime I wonder just why you are in it, Robin." He looked at me for a moment without expression. I knew he knew about me and Klara, and I also knew he'd been a guest at Essie's table at Tappan. "I'm sorry about your wife's illness," he said at last. "I hope she's all better real soon."

I stopped in his outer office to make a quick coded call to Harriet, to tell her to get my people started buying every prayer fan they could get their hands on. She had about a million messages, but I would only take one—and all that said was that Essie had passed a quiet night and would be seeing the doctors in about an hour. I didn't have time for the rest, because I had somewhere to go.

It is not easy to get a taxi in front of the Brazilian Congress; the doormen have their orders, and they know who rates priority. I had to climb up on the roadway and flag one down. Then, when I gave the driver the address, he made me repeat it twice, and then show it to him written down. It wasn't my bad Portuguese. He didn't really want to go to Free Town.

So we drove out past the old cathedral, under the immense Gateway tower, along the congested boulevard and out into the open planalto. Two kilometers of it. That was the green space, the *cordon sanitaire* the Brazilians defended around their capital city; but just beyond it was the shantytown. As soon as we entered it I rolled the window up. I grew up in the Wyoming food mines and I am used to twenty-four-hour stink, but this was a different stink. Not just the stench of oil. This was open-air toilets and rotting garbage—two million people without running water in their homes. The shanties had sprung up in the first place to give construction workers a place to live while they built the beautiful dream city. They were supposed to disappear when the city was finished. Shantytowns never disappear. They only become institutionalized.

The taxi-driver pushed his cab through nearly a kilometer of narrow alleys, muttering to himself, never faster than a crawl. Goats and people moved slowly out of our way. Little kids jabbered at me as they ran along beside us. I made him take me to the exact place, and get out and ask where Senhor Hanson Bover lived, but before he found out I saw Bover himself sitting on cinder-block steps attached to a rusty old mobile home. As soon as I paid him, the driver backed around and left, a lot faster than we had come, and by then he was swearing out loud.

Bover did not stand up as I came toward him. He was chewing on some kind of sweet roll, and didn't stop doing that, either. He just watched me.

By the standards of the barrio, he lived in a mansion. Those old trailers had two or three rooms inside, and he even had a little patch of something or other green growing alongside the step. The top of his head was bare and sunburned, and he was wearing dirty denim cut-offs and a tee-shirt printed with something in Portuguese that I didn't understand, but looked dirty too. He swallowed and said, "I would offer you lunch, Broadhead, but I'm just finishing eating it."

"I don't want lunch. I want to make a deal. I'll give you fifty per cent of my interest in the expedition plus a million dollars cash if you drop your suit."

He stroked the top of his head gingerly. It struck me strange that he got burned so fast, because I hadn't noticed sunburn the day before—but then I realized I hadn't noticed baldness, either. He had been wearing a toupee. All dressed up for his mingling with class society. No difference. I didn't like the man's manners, and I didn't like the growing cluster of audience around us, either. "Can we talk this over inside?" I asked.

He didn't answer. He just pushed the last bite of the roll into his mouth and chewed it while he looked at me.

That was enough of that. I squeezed past him and climbed the steps into the house.

The first thing that hit me was the stink—worse than outside, oh, a hundred times worse. Three walls of the room were taken up with stacks of cages, and breeding rabbits in every cage. What I smelled was rabbit shit, kilos of it. And not just from rabbits. There was a baby with a soiled diaper being nursed in the arms of a skinny young woman. No. A girl; she looked fifteen at the most. She stared up worriedly at me, but didn't stop nursing.

So this was the dedicated worshipper at his wife's shrine! I couldn't help it. I laughed out loud.

Coming inside had not been such a good idea. Bover followed me in, pulling the door shut, and the stink intensified. He was not impassive now, he was angry. "I see you don't approve of my living arrangements," he said.

I shrugged. "I didn't come here to talk about your sex life."

"No. Nor do you have any right to. You wouldn't understand."

I tried to keep the conversation where I wanted it to be. "Bover," I said, "I made you an offer which is better than you'll ever get in a court, and a lot more than you had any reason to hope for. Please accept it, so I can go ahead with what I'm doing."

He didn't answer me directly that time, either, just said something to the girl in Portuguese. She got up silently, wrapped a cloth around the baby's bottom, and went out on the steps, closing the door again behind her. Bover said, as though he hadn't heard me, "Trish has been gone for more than eight years, Mr. Broadhead. I still love her. But I've only got one life to live and I know what the odds are against ever sharing any of it with Trish again."

"If we can figure out how to run the Heechee ships properly we might be able to go out and find Trish," I said. I didn't pursue that; all it was doing was making him look at me with active hostility, as though he thought I were trying to con him. I said, "A million dollars, Bover. You can be out of this place tonight. Forever. With your lady and your baby and your rabbits, too. Full Medical for all of them. A future for the kid."

"I told you you wouldn't understand, Broadhead."

I checked myself and only said, "Then make me understand. Tell me what I don't know."

He picked a soiled baby dress and a couple of pins off the chair the girl had been sitting on. For a moment I thought he had relapsed into hospitality, but he sat there himself and said, "Broadhead, I've lived for eight years on welfare. Brazilian welfare. If we hadn't raised rabbits we wouldn't have had meat. If we didn't sell the skins I wouldn't have bus fare to meet you for lunch, or to go to my lawyer's office. A million dollars won't pay me for that, or for Trish."

I was still trying to keep my temper, but the stink was getting to me, and so was his attitude. I switched strategies. "Do you have any sympathy for your neighbors, Bover? Do you want to see them helped? We can end this kind of poverty forever, Bover, with Heechee technology. Plenty of food for everybody! Decent places to live!"

He said patiently, "You know as well as I do that the first things that come from Heechee technology—any technology—don't go to people in the barrio. They go to make rich people like you richer. Oh, maybe sooner or later it might all happen, but when? In time to make any difference to my neighbors?"

"Yes! If I can make it happen faster I will!"

He nodded judgmatically. "You say you will do that. I know *I* will, if I get control. Why should I trust you?"

"Because I give you my word, you stupid shit! Why do you think I'm cutting corners?"

He leaned back and looked up at me. "As to that," he said, "why, yes, I think I know why you're in such a hurry. It doesn't have much to do with my neighbors or me. My lawyers have researched you quite carefully, Broadhead, and I know all about your girl on Gateway."

I couldn't help it. I exploded. "If you know that much," I yelled, "then you know I want to get her out of where I put her! And I'll tell you this, Bover, I'm not going to let you and your jailbait whore keep me from trying!"

His face was suddenly as red as the top of his head. "And what does your wife think about what you're doing?" he asked nastily.

"Why don't you ask her yourself? If she lives long enough for you to hassle her. Fuck you, Bover, I'm going. How do I get a taxi?" He only grinned at me. Meanly. I brushed past the woman on the stoop and left without looking back.

By the time I got back to the hotel I knew what he was grinning about. It had been explained to me by two hours of waiting for a bus, in a square next to an open latrine. I won't even say what riding that bus was like. I've traveled in worse ways, but not since I left Gateway. There were knots of people in the hotel lobby, and they looked at me strangely as I walked across the floor. Of course, they all knew who I was. Everybody knew about the Herter-Halls, and my picture had been on the PV along with theirs. I had no doubt that I looked peculiar, sweated, and still furious.

My console was a fireworks display of attention signals when I slammed myself into my suite. The first thing I had to do was go to the bathroom, but over my shoulder, through the open door, I called: "Harriet! Hold all messages for a minute and give me Morton. One way. I don't want a response, I just want to give an order." Morton's little face appeared in the corner of the display, looking antsy but ready. "Morton, I just came from Bover. I said everything I could think of to him and it did no good, so I want you to get me private detectives. I want to search his record like it's never been searched before. The son of a bitch must have done something wrong. I want to blackmail him. If it's a ten-year-old parking ticket, I want to extradite him for it. Get busy on that." He nodded silently, but didn't go away, meaning that he was doing what I had said but wanted to say something himself, if only I would let him. Over him was the larger, waiting face of Harriet, counting out the minute's silence I had imposed on her. I came back into the room and said, "All right, Harriet, let's have it. Top priority first, one at a time."

"Yes, Robin, but—" She hesitated, making swift evaluations. "There are two immediate ones, Robin. First, Albert Einstein wishes to discuss with you the capture of the Herter-Hall party, apparently by the Heechee."

"Captured! Why the hell didn't you—" I stopped; obviously she couldn't have told me, because I was out of communication entirely for most of the afternoon. She didn't wait for me to figure that out but went on:

"However, I think you would prefer to receive Dr. Liederman's report first, Robin. I've been putting through a call, and she's ready to talk to you now, live."

That stopped me.

"Do it," I said, but I knew it couldn't be anything good, to make Wilma Liederman report live and in person. "What's the matter?" I asked as soon as she appeared.

She was wearing an evening dress, with an orchid on her shoulder, first time I had seen her like that since she came to our wedding. "Don't panic, Robin," she said, "but Essie's had a slight setback. She's on the life-support machines again."

"What?"

"It's not as bad as it sounds. She's awake, and coherent, feeling no pain, her condition is stable. We can keep her like that forever—"

"Get to the 'but'!"

"But she's rejecting the kidney, and the tissues around it aren't regenerating. She needs a whole new batch of transplants. She had uremic failure about two hours ago and now she's on full-time dialysis. That's not the worst part. She's had so many bits and pieces stuck in her from so many sources that her auto-immune system is all screwed up. We're going to have to scrounge to get a tissue match, and even so we're going to have to dope her with anti-immunes for a long time."

"Shit! That's right out of the Dark Ages!"

She nodded. "Usually we can get a four-four match, but not for Essie. Not this time. She's a rare-blood to begin with, you know. She's Russian, and her types are uncommon in this part of the world, so—"

"Get some from Leningrad, for Christ's sake!"

"So, I was about to say, I've checked tissue banks all over the world. We can come close. *Real* close. But in her present state there's still some risk."

I looked at her carefully, trying to figure out her tone. "Of having to do it over, you mean?" She shook her head gently. "You mean, of—of *dying*? I don't believe you! What the hell is Full Medical for?"

"Robin—she already has died of this, you know. We had to reanimate her. There's a limit to the shock she can survive."

"Then the hell with the operation! You said she's stable the way she is!"

Wilma looked at the hands clasped in her lap for a moment, then up at me. "She's the patient, Robin, not you."

"What's that supposed to mean?"

"It's her decision. She has already decided she doesn't want to be tied down to a life-support system forever. We're going to go in again tomorrow morning."

I sat there staring at the tank, long after Wilma Liederman had disappeared and my patient secretarial program had formed, silently waiting for orders. "Uh, Harriet," I said at last, "I want a flight back tonight."

"Yes, Robin," she said. "I've already booked you. There's no direct flight tonight, but there's one that you can transfer at Caracas, gets you in to New York about five AM. The surgery is not scheduled until eight."

"Thank you." She went back to silent waiting. Morton's silly face was still there in the tank, too, tiny and reproachful down in the lower right-hand corner. He did not speak, but every once in a while he cleared his throat or swallowed to let me know he was waiting. "Morton," I said, "didn't I tell you to get lost?"

"I can't do that, Robin. Not while I have an unresolved dilemma. You gave orders about Mr. Bover—"

"Damn right I did. If I can't handle him that way maybe I'll just get him killed."

"You don't have to bother," Morton said quickly. "There's a message from his lawyers for you. He has decided to accept your offer."

I goggled at him, wide-eyed and open-mouthed. "I don't understand it either, Robin, and neither do his lawyers," he said quickly. "They are quite upset. But there is a personal message for you, if it explains anything."

"What's that?"

"Quote, 'Maybe he does understand after all.' Close quote."

In a somewhat confusing life, and one that is rapidly becoming a long one, I've had a lot of confusing days, but that one was special. I ran a hot tub and soaked in it for half an hour, trying to make my mind empty. The effort didn't bring calm.

I had three hours before the Caracas plane left. I didn't know what to do with it. It was not that there wasn't plenty for me to do. Harriet kept trying to get my attention—Morton to firm up the contract with Bover, Albert to discuss the bioanalysis of the Heechee droppings somebody had collected, everybody to talk to me, about everything. I didn't want to do any of them. I was stuck in my dilated time, watching the world flash past. But it didn't flash, it crept. I didn't know what to do about it. It was nice that Bover thought I understood so well. I wondered what he would take to explain what I understood to me.

After a while I managed to work up enough energy to let Harriet put through some of the decision-needed calls for me, and I made what decisions seemed necessary; and a while after that, toying with a bowl of crackers and milk, I listened to a news summary. It was full of talk about the Herter-Hall capture, all of which I could get better from Albert than from the PV newscasters.

And at that point I remembered that Albert had wanted to talk to me, and for a moment I felt better. It gave me a point and purpose in living. I had someone to yell at. "Halfwit," I snapped at him as he materialized, "magnetic tapes are a century old. How come you can't read them?"

He looked at me calmly under his bushy white brows. "You're referring to the so-called 'prayer fans', aren't you, Robin? Of course we did try that, many times. We even suspected that there might be a synergy, and so we tried several kinds of magnetic fields at once, steady and oscillating, oscillating at different rates of speed. We even tried simultaneous microwave radiation, though, as it turned out, the wrong kind—"

I was still bemused, but not so much so that I didn't pick up on the implication. "You mean there's a *right* kind?"

"Sure thing, Robin," he grinned. "Once we got a good trace from the Herter-Hall instrumentation we just duplicated it. The same microwave radiation that's ambient in the Food Factory, a flux of a few microwatts of elliptically polarized million-Å microwave. And then we get the signal."

"Bloody marvelous, Albert! And what is it you got?"

"Uh, well," he said, reaching for his pipe, "actually not a lot, yet. It's hologram-stored and time-dependent, so what we get is a kind of choppy cloud of symbols.

And, of course, we can't read any of the symbols. It's Heechee language, you know. But now it's just straight cryptography, so to speak. All we need is a Rosetta stone."

"How long?"

He shrugged, and spread his hands, and twinkled.

I thought for a moment. "Well, stay with it. Another thing. I want you to read into my lawyer program the whole thing, the microwave frequencies, schematics, everything. There ought to be a patent in there somewhere, and I want it."

"Sure thing, Robin. Uh. Would you like to hear about the Dead Men?"

"What about the Dead Men?"

"Well," he said, "not all of them are human. There are some pretty strange little minds in those storage circuits, Robin. I think they might be what you call the Old Ones."

The back of my neck prickled. "Heechee?"

"No, no, Robin! Almost human. But not. They don't use language well, especially what seem to be the earliest of them, and I bet you can't even guess the computer-time bill you're going to get for analysis and mapping to make any sense of them at all."

"My God! Essie'll be thrilled when—"

I stopped. For a moment I had forgotten about Essie.

"Well," I said, "that's—interesting. What else is there to tell?"

But, really, I didn't care. I had used up my own last jolt of adrenaline, and there wasn't any more.

I let him tell me the rest of his budget of conversation, but most of it rolled right off me. Three members of the Herter-Hall party were known to be captured. The Heechee had brought them to a spindle-shaped place where some old machinery was lying about. The cameras were continuing to return frames of nothing very exciting. The Dead Men had gone haywire, were making no sense at all. Paul Hall's whereabouts were unknown; perhaps he was still at liberty. Perhaps he was still alive. The haywire link between the Dead Men's radio and the Food Factory was still functioning, but it was not clear how long it would last—even if it had anything to tell us. The organic chemistry of the Heechee was quite surprising, in that it was less unlike human biochemistry than one might guess. I let him talk until he ran down, not prompting him to continue, then turned back to the commercial PV. It had two rapid-fire comedians delivering bellylaugh lines to each other. Unfortunately, it was in Portuguese. It didn't matter. I still had an hour to kill, and I let it run. If nothing else, I could admire the pretty Carioca, fruit salad in her hair, whose scanty costume the comedians were tweaking off as they passed her back and forth, giggling.

Harriet's attention signal lighted up, bright red.

Before I could make up my mind to respond, the picture slid off the commercial PV channel and a man's voice said something stern in Portuguese. I couldn't understand a word of it, but I understood the picture that showed almost at once.

It was the Food Factory, taken out of stock, a shot from the Herter-Halls as they were approaching it to dock. And in the short sentence the announcer had spoken were two words that could have been "Peter Herter".

Could have been.

Were.

The picture didn't change, but a voice began, and it was old Herter's voice, angry and firm. "This message," it said, "is to be broadcast over all networks at once. It is a two-hour warning. In two hours I am going to cause a one-minute attack of the fever by entering the couch and projecting the necessary, uh, projections. I tell you all to take precautions. If you do not, it is your responsibility, not mine." It paused for a moment, then resumed. "Remember, you have two hours from a count which I will give you. No more. Shortly after that I will speak again to tell you the reason for this, and what I demand as my proper right if you do not wish this to happen many times. Two hours. Beginning . . . now."

And the voice stopped.

The announcer came back on, babbling in Portuguese, looking scared. It didn't matter that I couldn't understand what he was saying.

I had understood what Peter Herter had said, very well. He had repaired the dreaming couch and was going to use it. Not out of ignorance, like Wan. Not as a quick experiment, like the girl, Janine. He was going to use it as a weapon. He had a gun pointed at the heads of the entire human race.

And my first thought was: So much for the deal with Bover. Gateway Corp was sure to take over now, and I couldn't blame them.

10

The Oldest One

The Oldest One bestirred himself slowly, one organ at a time.

First came the piezophonic external receptors. Call them "ears". They were always "on", in the sense that sounds always reached them. Their tiny rag crystals were squeezed by vibrations in the air and, when the patterns of sound corresponded to the name the children of the Oldest One called him by, they passed a gate and went on to activate what corresponded to his peripheral nervous system.

At that point the Oldest One was not yet awake, but knew he was being wakened. His true ears, the inner ones that analyzed and interpreted sound, came to life. His cognitive circuits sampled the signals. The Oldest One heard the voices of his children and understood what they were saying. But only in an offhand and inattentive way, like a drowsy human aware of the buzzing of a fly. He had not yet "opened his eyes".

Some decision-making took place at that stage. If the interruption seemed worthwhile, the Oldest One woke further circuits. If not, not. A human sleeper may awaken enough to swat a fly. When the Oldest One was awakened for trivial reasons he had ways to "swat" his children. They did not wake him lightly. But if he decided to wake further, either to act or to punish the interruption to his sleep, the Oldest One then activated his major external optics, and with them a whole congeries of information-processing systems and short-term memories. He was then fully awake, like a man looking up at the ceiling after a nap.

The Oldest One's internal clocks told him that this nap had been rather short. Less than ten years. Unless there was a good reason for this awakening, someone would have to be swatted.

By then the Oldest One was fully aware of his surroundings, all of them. His internal telemetry was receiving status reports from all of its remote sensors, all through the ten million ton mass in which he and his children lived. A hundred inputs recirculated through his short-term memory: the words that had wakened him; the image of the three captives his children had just brought him; a breakdown in repair facilities in the 4700 Å sections; the fact that there was unusual activity among the stored intelligences; temperatures; inventories; moments of thrust. His long-term storage, though dormant, was accessible at need.

The wisest of his children was standing before him, with beads of sweat trickling through the sparse hairs on his cheeks and lip. The Oldest One perceived that this was a new leader, shorter and younger than the one he remembered from ten years before, but he wore the necklace of reading scrolls that symbolized the office as he waited for judgment. The Oldest One turned his major external lenses on him as a signal to speak. "We have captured intruders and brought them to you," the leader said, and added, trembling, "Have we done well?"

The Oldest One turned his attention to observe the captives. One was not an intruder, but the pup he had allowed to be born fifteen years before, now nearly grown. The other two, however, were strangers, and both female. That presented an option worth pondering. When the other intruders had presented themselves, he had failed to take advantage of the chance to establish new breeding stock until it was too late for any of the available specimens. And then they had stopped coming.

That was a chance the Oldest One had missed, and one which, on the basis of past terrifying experience, he should not have failed to take. The Oldest One was aware that for some thousands of years his judgments had not been always right, his opinions no longer confident. He was slowing down. He was subject to error. The Oldest One did not know what personal penalty he would have to pay for error and did not want to find out.

He began to make decisions. He reached into his long-term memory for precedents and prospects, and found that he had a satisfying number of alternatives. He activated mobility and handling effectors. His great metal body rose on its supports and moved past the leader, toward the chamber where the intruders were being kept. He heard the gasp from his children as he moved. All were startled. A few of the younger ones, who had never seen him move as adults, were terrified. "You have done well," he judged, and there was a long sigh of relief.

The Oldest One could not enter the chamber because of his size, but with long, soft-metal feelers he reached inside and touched the captives. It did not interest him that they screamed and struggled. His interest at that moment was only in their physical state. That was very satisfactory: two of them, including the male, were quite young, and therefore good for many years of use. In whatever fashion he might decide to use them. All seemed in good health.

As far as communicating with them went, there was the nuisance that their yells and imprecations were in one of those unpleasant languages their predecessors had used. The Oldest One did not understand one word. That was not a real problem, because he could always talk to them through the intervention of the stored intelligences of their predecessors. Even his own children, over the centuries, tended to evolve their language so that he could not have talked to them, either, if he had not stored one or two of them every dozen generations as translators—as nothing but translators, because the Oldest One's children regrettably did not seem to be much use for anything else. So such problems could be solved. Meanwhile the facts were favorable. Fact: The specimens were in good condition. Fact: They were clearly intelligent, tool-using, even technological. Fact: They were his to employ as he saw fit.

"Feed them. Keep them secure. Wait for further instructions," he commanded the children clustered behind him. He then turned down his external receptors so that he could consider just how to employ these intruders in the furtherance of the imperatives that were the central core of his very long life.

As a personality stored in a machine, the Oldest One's normal life expectancy was very great—perhaps as much as several thousand years—but not great enough to carry out his plans. He had extended it by diluting it. In standby mode he hardly aged at all. So he spent most of his time powered-down, motionless. He was not resting at such times, not even dreaming. He was merely abiding, while his children lived their lives and carried out his will and the astrophysical events outside crept sluggishly forward.

From time to time he woke at the urging of his internal clocks, to check and correct and revise. At other times his children woke him. They were instructed to do so at need, and very often (though not really very by any standard other than his own) the need arose.

Time was when the Oldest One was a flesh-and-blood creature, as much an animal as his present children or the captives they had brought him. That time had been very short indeed, less than a nap, from the moment when he was expelled from his mother's sweated and straining loins to the terrible time at its

end, lying helpless as strange needles poured sleep into
his veins and the whirling knives waited to trepan his
skull. He could remember that time quite clearly when
he chose. He could remember anything, in that short life
or in the long, long pseudolife that followed, provided
only that he could remember where to look for it in his
stored memories. And that he could not always remember. There was too much stored.

The Oldest One had no clear conception of how
many memories he had available to him, or of how
much time had passed, one way or another. Or even of
where things were. This place where he and his children
dwelt was "Here". That certain other place that figured
so largely in his thoughts was "There". Everything else
in the universe was merely "Everywhere else", and he
did not trouble to locate points as they related to one
another. Where did the intruders come from? From
somewhere or other. It did not matter exactly where.
Where was the food source that the boy visited? Some
other somewhere. Where had his people come from, in
the long ages before he himself had been born? It didn't
matter. The central Here had existed for a long, long
time—longer than one could comprehend, even for the
Oldest One himself. Here had sailed through space
since it was built and outfitted and launched; Here had
seen many births and deaths—nearly five million of
them—though at no one time did it hold more than a
few hundred living things, and seldom more than a few
score. Here had seen constant slow changes through all
that time. The newborns were larger, softer, fatter, and
more helpless as time went on. The adults were taller,
slower, less hairy. Here had often seen rapid changes,
as well. At such times the children were well advised to
wake the Oldest One.

Sometimes the changes were political, for Here had
held a thousand different social systems, one at a time.
There were spans of a generation or two, or even of
centuries, when the existing culture was sensate and
hedonistic, or puritanically stark; when one individual
became a despot or a divinity, or when none rose above

any other at all. There was never a democratic republic like those Earth had tried—Here was not big enough for representative government—and only once a racially stratified society. (It ended when the dun-furred lowers rose against the chocolate-furred uppers and wiped them out for good.) There had been many ideologies Here, and a various collection of moralities, but only one religion—at least, in the last many millennia. There was only room for one, when its living god rested among the children all the days of their lives, and awoke to smite or favor when it chose.

For many eons Here held no true people at all, only a collection of puzzled semisentients confronted with challenges that had been engineered to make them wise. The process worked. Only slowly. It took a hundred thousand years before the first of them comprehended even the concept of writing, nearly half a million more before one was found to be wise enough to be trusted with real work to do. That honor had gone to the Oldest One himself. It had not been welcome. No other had earned it since.

And that, too, was a failing, the Oldest One knew. Somehow he had failed. What had he done wrong?

Surely he had done his best! He had always, particularly in the first few centuries of his machine-bodied afterlife, been diligent and careful in supervising every act of the children. When they did wrong he punished. When they did well he praised. Always he cared for their needs.

But perhaps that was where he had gone wrong. There had been a time, long and long ago, when he had awakened with a terrible "pain" in the metal carapace he dwelt within. It was not the pain of flesh, but the sensors' report of unacceptable physical damage; but it was quite as alarming. His children were gathered around in terror, all shouting at once as they displayed to him the hacked-dead corpse of a young female. "She was insane!" they cried, quaking. "She tried to destroy you!"

The Oldest One's quick check of systems revealed

that the damage was trivial. It had been an explosive of some sort, and all it had cost him was a few effectors and some destruction of control nets, nothing that could not be repaired. He asked to know why she had done this. Their answers came only slowly, for they were terrified, but they came: "She wanted us to destroy you. She said you were damaging us, and that we could not grow without you. We beg forgiveness! We know we did wrong by not killing her sooner!"

"You did wrong," the Oldest One said justly, "but that was not the reason. If any such person appears among you again you are to awaken me at once. He may be restrained if it is necessary. But he may not be killed."

And then—was it a few centuries later? It seemed only the wink of an eye. And then there had been the time when they had not awakened him soon enough. For a dozen generations they had failed to observe the laws, and the reproductive budgets had not been met, and the total census of his living children was down to four individuals before they dared risk his displeasure by waking him. Well, they felt it. That had nearly been the end of all plans, because only one of the four was a female, and she near the end of child-bearing. He had used a dozen years of his life then, waking fretfully every few months, disciplining, teaching—worrying. With the help of biological lore stored deep in his oldest memories he had insured that the two babies the female managed to bear were also female. With stored sperm from the terrified males he kept the gene pool as diverse as he could. But it was a near thing. And some things had been forever lost. No other would-be assassin had ever risen against him. If only one would! No other like himself had ever appeared.

The Oldest One recognized that he had no real hope there would ever be another from his children. If it could happen, it would have. There had been time. Ten thousand generations of his children had been born and died since then, over a span of a quarter of a million years.

*   *   *

When the Oldest One moved again, all his children jumped too. They knew he would act. They did not know what the actions would be.

"The repair mechanisms in the 4700 Å corridors are to be replaced," he said. "Three artificers see to it." There was a stilled murmur of relief from the seventy-odd adults—punishment always came first, and if his first orders were not punishment then there would be none. This time. The three artificers the leader pointed to were less relieved, because that meant some days of very hard work in manhandling new machines to the green corridors and bringing back the old for repair; but it was their excuse to get away from the awful presence of the Oldest One. They seized it immediately.

"The male intruder and the older female are to be penned together," he said. If they were to breed they had best get on with it, and better to start with the older female. "Do any of you survive who have had experience with the rapporter?" Three of the children were pushed reluctantly forward. "One of you will educate the younger female," he instructed. "Do any survive who have had experience in preparing intruders for storage?"

"I prepared the last two," the leader said. "Also there are persons who assisted me still alive."

"See that the skills are maintained," the Oldest One ordered. "If one of you should die, he is to be prepared by the others, and new persons must be taught." That was a convenience. If the skills had been lost—and the lives of these creatures were so brief that many skills did get lost while he was powered down—it would have been necessary to set some of them to practicing brain surgery on others, to be ready in case he decided that these intruders, too, should go into storage. Continuing down his priority list, he gave additional instructions. Dead or spindly plantings should be replaced. All permitted areas of Here should be visited at least once a month. And, as the number of infants and young was only eleven, at least five babies should be born each year for the next ten years.

The Oldest One then powered down his external receptors, resumed his place at the central communications terminals and plugged himself in to his long-term memories. All about the central spindle his children were hastening to do his bidding as the leader parceled out assignments. Half a dozen left to dig up berryfruit bushes and airvines to replace the defective plants, others went to deal with the captives and attend to housekeeping chores, several young couples were sent to their quarters to breed. If they had had other plans, they were now deferred. At this particular awakening the Oldest One was not dissatisfied with his children, and whether they were dissatisfied with him did not occur to him to wonder.

His concerns were elsewhere.

With his externals reduced to the standby trickle of his resting mode, the Oldest One was not resting. He was assimilating these new factors into his reference store. There was change. Change was danger. Change was also opportunity, if approached right. Change might be used to advance his purposes, and could not be allowed to interfere with them. He had dealt with the immediate and the tactical. Now his attention went to the strategic and the ultimate.

He reached into his long-term memory. Some memories represented events very far away in space and in time, and were frightening even to the Oldest One. (How had he dared such temerity!) Some were quite near, and not frightening at all, for example those stored intruder intelligences the boy called "the Dead Men." There was nothing in them to be frightening. But, oh, how irritating they could be.

When the intruders first blundered Here, shattered castaways in their tiny ships, the Oldest One had had a moment of terror. They were unexplained. Who were they? Were they the lords he was trying to serve, come to reproach his presumption?

He quickly learned they were not. Were they, then, some other breed of servants to the lords, from whom he could learn new modes of service? They were not that either. They were wanderers. They had come Here by chance, in ancient, abandoned ships they did not truly know how to use. When their ships' course directors neutralized themselves, as they were meant to do on arriving Here, they were terrified.

They were not, as it turned out, even very interesting. He had used up many days of life with them as they appeared, first one, then another lone adventurer, then a group of three. In all there had been nearly twenty of them, in nine ships, not counting the child who had been born here, and none of them worth the concern they had caused him. The first few he had had his children sacrifice at once, in order to put their stored intelligence into the machine form that he could best deal with. The others he had given orders to preserve, even to allow to roam free, when it appeared they might be more interesting in an independent life in the unused areas of Here. He had given them everything he perceived they might need. He had even given some of. them immortality, as he himself had been made immortal—as fewer than one in a hundred thousand of his children ever were. It was a waste. Alive and capricious, or stored for eternity, they were more trouble than they were worth. They brought diseases to his children, and some of them had died. They caught diseases from the children, and some of the intruders died, too. And they did not store well. Properly programmed into his long-term memories, by the machine-directed techniques that had been used on him thousands of centuries ago and taught to his children ever since, they performed badly. Their time sense was deficient. Their response to interrogatories was erratic. Large sections of their memories were gone. Some of them could not be read at all. The fault was not in the techniques; they were defective to begin with.

When the Oldest One himself had been made immortal after the death of his flesh, he awoke as his exact self. All the knowledge and skills he had ever had were duplicated in the machine store. So with his children, when at random intervals he chose one to store. So even with his flesh ancestors, so far back that even his own immense age dwindled in comparison. So with those other stored memories that he did not like even to consult.

Not so with the intruders. There was something wrong with their chemistry. They recorded imperfectly and retrieved haphazardly, and there were times when he thought to erase them all. He had banished the little storage spheres and their readout systems to the remote periphery of Here, and his children never went near them. He had decided to preserve them at the last only out of thrift. A time might come when he would need them.

Perhaps that time was now.

With a sense of reluctant distaste, as a man might reach into a sewer to retrieve a dropped gem, the Oldest One opened the pathways that linked him to the stored intruder minds.

And recoiled.

Three of the children, hurrying Janine around the curvature of the spindle from her pen to the rapporter, saw the Oldest One's effectors quiver and external lenses flash open. They stumbled and stopped, waiting fearfully for what would come next.

Nothing came next. The effectors relaxed again. The lenses powered down to standby. After a moment, the children collected themselves and dragged Janine to the waiting metallic couch.

But inside the Oldest One's metal shell he had received his greatest shock in many awakenings. Someone had been interfering with his stored memories! It was not merely that they were mad. They had always been mad; worse, they were in some ways more sane now, or at least more lucid, as though something had been trying to reprogram them. There were inputs he had never given them. They contained memories he had never shared. These were not storage that had come to the surface from their past lives. They were new. They spoke of organized knowledge on a scale that dwarfed even his own. Spaceships and machines. Living intelligences by the tens of billions. Machine intelligences that were slow and even almost stupid, by his standards, but possessed incredible stores to draw on. It was no wonder that he had reacted physically, as a man shocked out of a reverie might start and twitch.

Somehow his stored intruders had made contact with the culture they had come from.

It was easy for the Oldest One to learn how that contact had been made. From Here to the food facility, by means of the long-unused communications net. Interpreted and processed on the food facility by a pathetically crude machine. Transmitted the long light-days to the planets that circled that nearest star, by means of the creeping electromagnetic impulses of light-speed radio. Contemptible! Until one considered how much information had been transmitted each way. The Oldest One was like a hydraulic engineer transfixed at the base of a hydroelectric dam, watching a thin needle of water spurt hundreds of meters into the air, out of an almost invisible pinhole. The quantity was trivial. But that so much poured through so tiny an opening bespoke the pressure of a vast body behind the dam.

And the leak went both ways.

The Oldest One acknowledged that he had been careless. In interrogating the stored intruders to find out what they knew, he had let them know much about himself. About Here. About the technology that guided it.

About his consecration, and about the lords his life was meant to serve.

At least the leak had been tiny, and the transmissions confused by the imperfections of the stored intelligences themselves. There was no part of that storage inaccessible to the Oldest One. He opened them up for study, and traced every bit. He did not "speak" to them. He allowed their minds to flow into his own. The Dead Men could not resist him, any more than a prepared frog on a dissecting table could resist a surgeon's scalpel.

When he was done, he withdrew to ponder.

Were his plans in jeopardy?

He activated his internal scanning systems, and a three-dimensional tank of the Galaxy sprang up in his "mind". It had no real existence. There was no vantage point from which any person could have seen it. He himself did not "see" it, he simply knew it was there. It was a sort of trompe-l'oeil. An optical illusion, except that it was not optical. On it, very far away, an object appeared, haloed in light. It had been many centuries since the Oldest One had allowed himself to observe that object. It was time to look at it again.

The Oldest One reached down into and activated long undisturbed memory stores.

It was not an easy experience. It was almost the equivalent of a session on the analyst's couch for a human, for he was uncovering thoughts, memories, guilts, worries, and uncertainties that his "conscious" mind—the reasoning and problem-solving circuits— had long since decided to lay away. Those memories were not gone. They had not become impotent. They still held "shame" and "fear" for him. Was he doing the right thing? Did he dare act on his own responsibility? The old circular arguments raced through his mind as they had done two hundred thousand years before, and were no closer to resolution. It was not possible for the Oldest One to fugue into hysteria or depression. His circuits did not allow it.

It was, however, possible for him to be terrified.

After a prolonged time he emerged from his introspection. He was still afraid. But he was committed. He had to act.

The children scattered in terror as the Oldest One woke once more.

His forward effectors quivered, straightened and pointed at a young female, caught in midpassage nearby. Any other would have done as well. "Come with me," he ordered.

She sobbed, but followed. Her mate took a step after her as they hurried toward a gold-lit corridor. But he had not been told to go with them, and so he stopped and looked sadly after. Ten minutes earlier they had been mating, in pleasure and obedience. Now he was not sure he would ever see her again.

The Oldest One's cruising pace was not a great deal faster than a rapid walk, but the little difference kept the weeping female trotting and panting to keep up. He glided on, past machines that had not been used even in his memories—wall aligners, landers huge as houses, a queer little six-screwed thing like a helicopter that had once, though even the Oldest One did not remember so far back, been used to stock Heechee Heaven with its angels. The gold skeins changed to radiant silver, the silver to purest white. A passage that none of the children had ever entered stood waiting open for them, the heavy door fanned wide as the Oldest One approached. By the time they reached a place where the female had never been, had not known existed, where the skeins in the wall ran in a riot of a dozen colors and strange patterns flickered in panels all around a great, dim chamber, she was out of breath. No rest. "Go there," the Oldest One commanded. "Adjust those wheels. Watch mine. Do as I do." At opposite sides of the chamber, too widely spaced for any one individual to operate them, were controls. Set on the floor at each was a sort of angled bench, very uncomfortable for the young female to sit on. In front of each bench, a sort of hummock of ridged wheels, ten of them in a row, with rainbow lights glinting faintly between them. The Oldest One ignored the bench and touched an effector to the nearest wheel, turning it slowly. The lights shivered and rippled. Green brightened to yellow, to pale orange, with a triple row of ochre lines in the middle of it. "Match my pattern!" The young female tried to obey. The wheel was terribly hard to turn, as though it had not been moved for a terribly long time. (It had not.) The colors merged and swirled, and it took forever for her to achieve the pattern of the controls before the Oldest One. He did not hurry or reprove her. He merely waited. He knew she was doing her best. By the time all ten wheels were showing the pattern he had chosen tears were gone and sweat was stinging her eyes and trickling through her sparse beard.

The colors were not a perfect match. Between the doubled, redundant, safed controls, the rosette of screens that should have displayed their course coordinates was blank. This was not surprising. The surprise might have been that, after eight hundred thousand years, the controls worked at all.

But they did work.

The Oldest One touched something under his own bank of controls and quickly, wonderfully, the lights developed a life of their own. They blurred and strengthened again, and now as the automatic fine-tuners took over the two patterns became identical. The rosette of screens sprang into life with a pattern of glowing dots and lines. The young female peered fearfully at the screens. She did not know that what she saw was a field of stars. She had never seen a star, or heard of one.

She felt what happened next.

So did everyone else Here. The intruders in their pens, the near hundred children all over the construct, the young female and the Oldest One himself all felt it, felt suddenly queasy as the eternal gravity died and was replaced by tweaks of pseudo-acceleration punctuating weightlessness.

After more than three-quarters of a million years of rolling slowly around Earth's very distant sun, the artifact pulled itself into a new orbit and surged away.

11

S. Ya. Lavorovna

At precisely five-fifteen AM a gentle green glow appeared in the bedside monitor of S. Ya. Lavorovna-Broadhead. It was not bright enough to disturb deep slumber, but she had been less than half asleep. "Very well," she called, "I am already awake, you do not have to continue this program. But give me a moment."

"*Da, gospozha,*" her secretary acknowledged, but the green glow remained. If S. Ya. did not show further signs of alertness the secretary would buzz gently in another minute, regardless of what she told it to do; that was what she had told it to do when she wrote the program.

In this case there was no need. Essie woke up quite clear in her mind. There was surgery again this morning, and Robin would not be here. Because old Peter Herter had given warning before he invaded the world's minds, there had been time to prepare. There had been almost no damage. Not real damage; but what made that possible was a frantic flurry of postponing and rearranging, and in the course of it Robin's flights had been inextricably confused.

Pity. Worse than that, even fear. But it was not as though he had not tried. Essie accepted that consolation from herself. It was good to know that he had tried.

"Am I allowed to eat?" she called.

"No, gospozha Broadhead. Nothing at all, not even a drink of water," her secretary responded at once. "Do you wish your messages?"

"Perhaps. What messages?" If they were of interest at all she would take them, she decided; anything to keep her mind off the surgery, and the indignities of catheters and tubes that bound her to this bed.

"There is a voice-only from your husband, gospozha, but if you wish I believe I can reach him direct. I have a location, if he is still there."

"Do so." Experimentally, Essie rose to sit on the edge of the bed while she was waiting for the connection to be completed, or, more likely, for her husband to be found in some transit lounge and called to the comm. She carefully kept the dozen tubes unkinked as she rose to her feet. Apart from feeling weak, she did not feel bad. Fearful. Thirsty. Even shaky. But there was no pain. Perhaps it would all have seemed more serious if it had hurt more, and perhaps that would have been good. These months of demeaning annoyance were only an irritation; there was enough of Anna Karenina in Essie to long to *suffer*. How trivializing the world had come to be! Her life was on the line, and all she felt was discomfort in her private parts.

"Gospozha Broadhead?"

"Yes?"

The visual program appeared, looking apologetic. "Your husband cannot be reached at present. He is en route from Mexico City to Dallas and has just taken off; all the aircraft's communications are at present required for navigation."

"Mexico City? Dallas?" The poor man! He would be

circumnavigating the Earth to get to her! "Then at least give me the recorded message," she ordered.

"Da, gospozha." Face and greenish glow shrank away, and out of the sound-circuits her husband's voice addressed her:

"Honey, I'm having a little trouble making connections. I got a charter to Merida, supposed to make connections to Miami, but I missed the flight. Now I'm hoping to make a connection to Dallas and— Anyway, I'm on my way." Pause. He sounded fretful, which was no surprise, and Essie could almost see him casting around for something cheerful to say. But it was all rambling. Something about the great news about prayer fans. Something about the Heechee who weren't Heechee, and—and just a babble. Poor creature! He was trying to be bright for her. She listened to the sound of his heart, rather than to his words, until he paused again, and then said, "Oh, hell, Essie. I wish I were there. I will be. Fast as I can. In the meantime— Take care of yourself. If you've got any spare time before you, uh, before Wilma gets going, I've told Albert to tape all the essential stuff for you. He's a good old program. . . ." Long pause. "I love you," he said, and was gone.

S. Ya. lay back on her gently humming bed, wondering what to do with the next (and perhaps last?) hour of her life. She missed her husband quite a lot, especially in view of the fact that in some ways she considered him quite a silly man. "Good old program"! How foolish of him to anthropomorphize computer programs! His Albert Einstein program was, she had no other word for it, *cute*. And it had been his idea to make the bio-assay unit look like a pet. And give it a name! "Squiffy." It was like giving a name to a cleaning machine or a shotgun. Foolish. Unless it were done by someone one cared for . . . in which case it was instead endearing.

But machines were machines. At the graduate institute at Akademogorsk young S. Ya. Lavorovna had learned very completely that machine intelligence was not "personal". You built them up, from adding machines to number-crunchers. You packed them full of data. You constructed for them a store of appropriate responses to stimuli and provided them with a hierarchical scale of appropriateness; and that was all there was to it. Now and then, to be sure, you were surprised by what came out of a program you had written. Of course you were; that was the nature of the exercise. None of that implied the existence of free will on the part of the machine, or of personal identity.

All the same, it was rather touching to watch him crack jokes with his programs. He was a touching man. He touched her in places where she was most open and vulnerable, because in some ways he was very like that only other man in her life who had ever really mattered to her, her father.

When Semya Yagrodna was a small girl her father had been the central person in the world—tall, skinny old man who played the ukelele and the mandolin and taught biology at the gymnasium. He was delighted to have a bright and inquiring child. It might have pleased him even more if her talents had seemed to go toward the life sciences rather than to physics and engineering, but he cherished her as she was. He taught her about the world when he could no longer teach her mathematics, because she had surpassed him. "You must be aware of what you will have to deal with," he explained to her. "Even here. Even now. Even when I was a young boy in Stalin's times, and the women's movements were promoting girls to lead machine-gun squads and run tractors. This is always the same, Semka. It is a fact of history that mathematics is for the young, and that girls excel equally with boys until the age of fifteen, perhaps, or at most twenty. And then, just when the boys are turning into Lobachewskis and Fermats, the girls stop. Why? For childbearing. For marriage. For heaven knows what. We will not let it happen to you, small dove. Study! Read! Learn! Comprehend! Every day, for as many hours as you must! And I will assist you in all the ways I can." And he did; and from the ages of eight to eighteen young Semya Yagrodna

Lavorovna came home from school every day, deposited one book bag in their apartment and picked up another, and trotted away to the old yellow building off the Nevsky Prospekt where her tutor lived. She had never dropped out of mathematics, and for this she had her father to thank. She had never learned to dance, either —or to try a thousand sorts of scent and makeup, or to date—not until she was away at Akademogorsk, and for that also she had her father to thank. Where the world tried to force her into a female role he defended her like a tiger. But at home, to be sure, there was a need to cook and sew, and to polish the rosewood chairs; and none of those things were done by *him*. Her father in physical appearance had not looked in the least like Robin Broadhead . . . but in other ways, so like!

Robin had asked her to marry him when they had known each other less than a year. It had taken her a full year beyond that to decide to say yes. She talked to everyone she knew about it. Her roommate. The dean of her department. Her former lover, who had married the girl next door. Stay away from this one, S. Ya., they all advised her. On the face of it the advice was sound, for who was he? A feckless millionaire, still mourning a woman he had loved and shatteringly lost, guilt-ridden, just out of years of intensive psychoanalysis—what a perfect description of the completely hopeless marriage risk! But— On the other hand— Nevertheless—

Nevertheless he touched her. They had gone to New Orleans for Mardi Gras in stinging cold weather, sitting most of the days inside the Cafe du Monde, never even seeing the parade. The rest of the time they stayed in their hotel, out of the sleet and the crowds, and made love, emerging only for fried sweet dough with clouds of powdered sugar, and sweet, milky, chicory-laced coffee in the mornings. Robin bestirred himself to be gallant. "Shall we go for a cruise on the river today? Visit an art gallery? Dance at a night club?" But she could see that he did not want to do any of these things, this man twice her age who wanted to marry her, sitting with his hands cupped around his coffee as though merely getting warm were formidable enough a task to contemplate for one day. And she made her decision.

She said, "I think instead we might get married, after all."

And so they had. Not that day, but as soon as they could. S. Ya. never regretted it; it was not a thing to regret. After the first few weeks she had not even worried about how it would turn out. He was not a jealous man or a mean one. If he was often absorbed in his work, well, so was she.

There was only this question of the woman, Gelle-Klara Moynlin, the lost love.

She might well be dead. Was as good as dead, in any case, because she was hopelessly out of human reach forever. It was well known that this was so, from the fundamental laws of physics . . . but there were times, Essie was sure, when her husband did not *believe* it to be so.

And then she wondered: If there was any possibility of a choice between them, how would Robin choose?

And what if the laws of physics, after all, turned out to permit an exception now and then?

There was the matter of the Heechee ships, and how could one apply known physical law to *them*? As with every other thinking person in the world, the questions raised by the Heechee had intrigued S. Ya. for a long time. The Gateway asteroid had been discovered while she was still a schoolgirl. The headlines announcing new findings had come every few weeks, all through her college years. Some of her classmates had taken the plunge and specialized in the theory of Heechee control systems. Two were on Gateway now. At least three had shipped out and never returned.

The Heechee ships were not uncontrollable. They could in fact be controlled precisely. The superficial mechanics of the process were known. Each ship possessed five main-drive verniers, and five auxiliaries. They located coordinates in space (how?), and, once set, the ship went there. Again, how? It then returned unerringly to its place of origin, or usually did, if it did not run out of fuel or encounter a mischance—a triumph of cybernetics that S. Ya. knew no human agency could reproduce. The difficulty was that until this very second no human being knew quite how to read the controls.

But what about the next second, or the one after that? With information pouring in, from the Food Factory and Heechee Heaven; with Dead Men talking; with at least one semicompetent human pilot, the boy, Wan— with all this, and especially with the flood of new knowledge that might be unlocked from the prayer fans. . . .

How long before some of the mysteries were solved? Perhaps not very long at all.

S. Ya. wished she could be a part of it all, as her classmates had become. As her husband had become. She wished even more that she did not suspect what part he most wanted to play. But the suspicion remained. If Robin could make a Heechee ship fly him to any destination he chose in all the universe, she thought she knew what that destination would be. .

Semya Yagrodna Lavorovna-Broadhead called to her secretary, "How much time do I have?"

The program appeared and said, "It is now five twenty-two. Dr. Liederman is expected at six forty-five. You will then be prepared for the procedure, which will occur at eight o'clock. You have a little more than an hour and a quarter. Perhaps you would like to rest?"

S. Ya. chuckled. It always amused her when her own programs offered her advice. She did not, however, feel any need to respond to it. "Have menus been prepared for today and tomorrow?" she asked.

"Nyet, gospozha."

That was both a relief and a disappointment. At least Robin had not prescribed more fattening foods for today—or perhaps his prescription had been overruled, because of the operation? "Select something," she ordered. The program was quite capable of preparing menus. It was only because of Robin himself that either of them ever gave a thought to such routine chores. But Robin was Robin, and there were times when cooking was a hobby for him, cutting onions paper-thin for a salad and standing to stir a stew for hours. Sometimes what he produced was awful, sometimes not; Essie was not critical, because she was not very interested in what she ate. And also because she was grateful that she felt no need to concern herself with such matters; in this respect, at least, Robin surpassed her father. "No, wait," she added, struck with a thought. "When Robin comes home he will be hungry. Serve him a snack—those crullers, and the New Orleans coffee. As at the Cafe du Monde."

"*Da, gospozha.*" How devious you are, thought Essie, smiling to herself. One hour and twelve minutes left.

It would do no harm to rest.

On the other hand, she was not sleepy.

She could, she thought, interrogate her medical program again. But she had no real wish to hear about the procedures she faced an additional time. Such large pieces to take from someone else's body for the sake of her own! The kidney, yes. One might well sell that and still have something left. As a student, Essie had known comrades who had done that, might even have done it herself if she had been just a shade poorer than she actually was. But, although she knew very little more of anatomy than her father had taught her at his knee, she knew enough to be sure that the person, or persons, who had given her all those other tissues would not have enough left to go on living with. It was a queasy feeling.

Almost as queasy as that other feeling that came with knowing that, even with Full Medical, from this particular invasion of her person by Wilma Liederman's knives she might not return.

Still an hour and eleven minutes.

Essie sat up once more. Whether she was to live or not, she was as dutiful a wife as she had been a daughter, and if Robin wished her to concern herself with prayer fans and Heechee she would. She addressed the computer terminal. "I wish the Albert Einstein program."

12

Sixty Billion Gigabits

When Essie Broadhead said, "I wish the Albert Einstein program," she set a large number of events in motion. Very few of these events were visible to the unaided senses. They did not take place in the macroscopic physical world, but in a universe composed largely of charges and pathways operating on the scale of the electron. The individual units were tiny. The total was not, being made up of some sixty billion gigabits of information.

At Akademogorsk, young S. Ya.'s professors had schooled her in the then current computer logics of ion optics and magnetic bubbles. She had learned to trick her computers into doing many marvelous things. They could find million-digit prime numbers or calculate the tides on a mud-flat for a thousand years. They could take a child's scribble of "House" and "Daddy" and refine it into an engineer's rendering of an architectural plan, and a tailor's dummy of a man. They could rotate the house, add a sunporch, sheath it in stucco or cover it with ivy. They could shave off a beard, add a wig, costume the man for yachting or golfing, for board-room or bar. These were marvelous programs for nine-teen-year-old Semka. She found them thrilling. But she had grown since then. By comparison with the pro-grams she was now writing, for her secretary, for "Al-bert Einstein" and for her many clients, those early ones were slow and stumbling caricatures. They did not have the advantage of circuits borrowed from Heechee technology, or of a circulating memory store of 6×10^{19} bits.

Of course, even Albert did not use all sixty billion gigabits all the time. For one thing, they were not all shared. Even the shared stores were occupied by tens of thousands of programs as subtle and complicated as Albert, and by tens of millions of duller ones. The program called "Albert Einstein" slipped through and among the thousands and the millions without inter-ference. Traffic signals warned him away from occupied circuits. Guideposts led him to subroutines and libraries needed to fulfill his functions. His path was never a straight line. It was a tree of branching decision points, a lightning-stroke of zigzag turns and reverses. It was not truly a "path", either; Albert never moved. He was never in a specific place to move from. It is at least arguable whether Albert "was" anything at all. He had no continuous existence. When Robin Broadhead was through with him and turned him off he ceased to be, and his subroutines picked up other tasks. When he was turned on again he recreated himself from whatever circuits were idle, according to the program S. Ya. had written. He was no more real than an equation, and no less so than God.

"I wish—" S. Ya. Lavorovna-Broadhead had said.

Before her voice was halfway through the first vowel the sound-activated gate in the monitor's receiver sum-moned up her secretarial program. The secretary did not appear. She read the first trace of the name that followed—

"—the Albert Einstein—"

—matched it against her command store, made a probabilistic assessment of the rest and issued an instruction. That was not all the secretary did. Before that she had recognized the voice of S. Ya. and confirmed that it was that of an authorized person—the person who had written her, in fact. She checked her store for undelivered messages, found several, and weighed their urgency. She made a quick sweep of Essie's telemetry readings to estimate her physical condition, retrieved the memory of her proximate surgery, balanced them against the messages and the present instruction, and decided the messages need not be delivered, and in fact could be handled by Essie's surrogate. All that took very little time and involved only a minor fraction of the secretary's full program. She did not need to remember, for instance, what she was supposed to look like or how her voice was supposed to sound. So she did not bother.

The secretary's instruction woke "Albert Einstein". He did not at first know that he was Albert Einstein. As he read his program he discovered several things about himself. First, that he was an interactive information-retrieval program, whereupon he searched for and found addresses for the principal categories of information he was supposed to supply. Second, that he was heuristic and normative, which obliged him to look for the rules, in the form of go and no-go gates, that determined his decision-making. Third, that he was the property of Robin—a.k.a. Robinette, Rob, Robby, Bob or Bobby—Stetley Broadhead and would be required to interact with him on a basis of "knowing" him. This impelled the Albert program to access the Robin Broadhead files, and rehearse their contents—by far the most time-consuming part of his task so far. When all this was done he discovered his name and the details of his appearance. He made a series of arbitrary choices of costume—pullover sweater, or stained gray sweatshirt; slippers or frayed tennis shoes with a toe poking out; socks or none—and appeared in the tank of the monitor in the guise of the real Albert Einstein, pipe in hand, mild eyes humorously inquiring, before the last echo of the command had died.

"—program."

He had had plenty of time. It had taken Essie nearly four-tenths of a second to speak his name.

As she had spoken in English, he greeted her, in the same language. "Good—" quick check of local time, "morning,—" fast assessment of Essie's mood and condition, "Mrs. Broadhead." If she had been dressed for the office he would have called her "Lavorovna."

Essie studied him appraisingly for several seconds, an infinity of time for Albert. He did not waste it. He was a shared-time program, and the parts of his capacity that were not in active use at any particular picosecond busied themselves at other tasks. Whatever task was going. While he waited, parts of him were excused to help other programs make a weather forecast for a sport-fishing vessel leaving Long Island Sound, teach the conjugation of French verbs to a little girl, animate a sexual doll for a wealthy, and quirky, old recluse, and tally gold prices received from the Peking exchange. There were almost always other tasks on line. When there were not, there were the waiting batch-process files of less urgent problems—nuclear particle path analysis, the refinement of asteroid orbits, the balancing of a million checkbooks—that any of the sixty billion gigabits might turn a hand to in an idle moment.

Albert was not the same as Robin's other programs —the lawyer, the doctor, the secretary, the psychoanalyst, or any of the surrogates who functioned for Robin Broadhead when Robin was busy or disinclined. Albert shared many memories with them. They freely accessed each other's files. Each had a specific universe of action, tasked for specific needs; but they could not carry out their tasks without awareness of each other.

Apart from that, they were each the personal property of Robin Broadhead, slaved to his will. So sophisticated was Albert that he could read contextual clues and deduce imperatives. He was not limited in his responses by what Robin said to him. He was able to read deeper questions from the totality of everything

Robin had ever said, to any of his programs. Albert could not betray a confidence of Robin's, or fail to recognize what was confidential. Generally.

There were exceptions. The person who had written Albert's program in the first place could easily write an overriding command, and had.

"Robin instructed you to prepare summaries for me," Essie told her creation. "Give them to me now." She watched critically and also admiringly as the program she had written nodded, scratched its ear with its pipestem and began to speak. Albert was quite a good program, she thought with pride. For a collection of electronic impulses living in rag stores—weakly crystalline dichalcogenides with the structure of a wet dishrag —Albert was a rather attractive person.

She adjusted her tubes and piping and leaned back against pillows to listen to what Albert had to say. It was all most exceedingly interesting. Even to her, even at this time when in—what was it?—in less than one hour ten minutes she would be sponged and stripped and shaved and basted for further invasions of her inner person. As all she demanded of the Albert program at this time was edited memories of conversations that had already occurred, she knew that he had dismissed large parts of himself to other work. But what was left, she observed critically, was quite solid. The transition from the interactive Albert waiting for her question to the remembered Albert talking to her husband was done smoothly and without jumps—if one did not look for such minor imperfections as that the pipe was suddenly alight, and the socks abruptly pulled up over the ankles. Satisfied, Essie paid attention to the content of what was going on. It was not just one conversation, she perceived. There were at least three. Robin must have been spending a lot of time talking to his science program in Brasilia, and while one part of her mind was listening to the exciting news from Heechee Heaven another part was smiling at herself. How amusing that she should be pleased at this evidence that he had not used his hotel suite for other purposes! (Or at least not exclusively, she amended.) He could not have been blamed if he had chosen a living companion instead. Even a female one. Under the circumstances, with a main lover in no condition to be very responsive, she would certainly have felt free to do the same. (Well, not *certainly*. There was enough early Soviet prudishness left in Essie for at least a doubt.) But she admitted to herself that she was pleased, and then made herself attend to the truly fascinating things that were being said. So much happening! So much to absorb!

First, the Heechee. The Heechee in Heechee Heaven were not Heechee! Or at least those Old Ones were not. It was proved by the bio-assay of the DNA, Albert was earnestly assuring her husband, punctuating his arguments with pipe thrusts. The bio-assay had produced not an answer but a puzzle, a basic chemistry that was neither human, nor yet inhuman enough to come from creatures evolved around some other star. "Also," said Albert, puffing, "there is the question of the Heechee seat. It does not fit a human being. But neither does it fit the Old Ones. So for whom was it designed? Alas, Robin. We do not know."

A quick flicker, the socks now gone, the pipe out and being filled, and Albert was talking about prayer fans. He had not, Albert apologized, unriddled the fans. The literature was vast but he had searched it all. There was no imaginable application of energy and no instrumentation that had not been applied to them. Yet they had stayed mute. "One can speculate," Albert said, striking a match to his pipe, "that all of the fans left for us by the Heechee are garbled, perhaps to tantalize us. I do not believe this. *Raffiniert ist der Herr Hietschie, aber Boshaft ist er nicht.*" In spite of everything, Essie laughed out loud. *Der Herr Hietschie* indeed! Had she written this sense of comedy into her program? She thought of interrupting him to command that he display this section of his instructions, but already that replay had ended and a slightly less rumpled Albert was talking about astrophysics. Here Essie almost closed her ears, for she quickly had enough of curious cosmologies. Was the universe open-ended or closed? She did not strongly care. Was some large quantity of mass "missing", in the sense that not enough could be observed to account for known gravitational effects? Very well, then let it stay missing. Essie felt no need to go looking for it. Someone's fantasy of storms of indetectible pions, and someone else—someone named Klube's—notion that mass might be created from nothing, interested her very little. But when the conversation switched to black holes, she paid close attention. She was not really concerned with the subject. She was concerned with Robin's concern for it.

And that, she told herself justly as Albert rambled on, was petty of her. Robin had kept no mean secrets. He had told her at once of the love of his life, the woman named Gelle-Klara Moynlin whom he had abandoned in a black hole—had told her, actually, far more than she wanted to know.

She said, "Stop."

Instantly the three-dimensional figure in the tank abandoned the word it had been speaking in midsyllable. It gazed politely at her, awaiting orders.

"Albert," she said carefully, "why did you tell me Robin was studying question of black holes?"

The figure coughed. "Why, Mrs. Broadhead," Albert said, "I have been playing a recording prepared especially for you."

"Not *this* time. Why did you volunteer this information *other* time?"

Albert's expression cleared and he said humbly, "That directive did not come from my program, gospozha."

"I thought not! You have been interacting with the psychoanalytic program!"

"Yes, gospozha, as you programmed me to do."

"And what was the purpose of this intervention from the Sigfrid von Shrink program?"

"I cannot say for sure—but," he added hastily, "perhaps I can offer a guess. Perhaps it is that the Sigfrid estimates your husband should be more open with you."

"That program is not charged with care of my mental health!"

"No, gospozha, not with yours, but with your husband's. Gospozha, if you wish more information, let me suggest that you consult that program, not me."

"I can do more than that!" she blazed. And so she could. She could speak three words—*Daite gorod Polymat*—and Albert, Harriet, Sigfrid von Shrink, every one of Robin's programs would be subsumed into the powerful program of her own, Polymath, the one she had used to write them in the first place, the over-riding program that contained every instruction they owned. And then let them try cunning evasions on her! Then let them see if they could maintain the confidentiality of their memories! Then—

"God," Essie said aloud, "am actually planning to teach lesson to my own programs!"

"Gospozha?"

She caught her breath. It was almost a laugh, nearly a sob. "No," she said, "cancel above. I find no fault with your programming, Albert, nor with shrink's. If shrink program judges Robin should release internal tensions, I cannot overrule and will not pry. Further," she corrected herself fairly.

The curious thing about Essie Lavorovna-Broadhead was that "fairness" meant something to her, even in dealing with her constructs. A program like Albert Einstein was large, complex, subtle, and powerful. Not even S. Ya. Lavorovna could write such a program alone; for that she needed Polymath. A program like Albert Einstein learned, and grew, and redefined its tasks as it went along. Not even its author could say why it gave one bit of information and not another. One could only observe that it was working, and judge it by how it carried out its orders. It was unfair to the program to "blame" it, and Essie could not be so unfair.

But, as she moved restlessly among her pillows (twenty-two minutes left!) it came to her that the world was not entirely fair to her. Not fair at all! It was not fair that all these fairytale wonders should be pouring in upon the world—not now. It was not fair that these perils and perplexities should manifest themselves, not now, not while she might not live to see how they came out. Could Peter Herter be dealt with? Would the others of his party be saved? Could the lessons of the prayer fans and the explorers make it possible to do all the things Robin promised, feed the world, make all men well and happy, allow the human race to explore the universe? All these questions, and before this day's sun had set she might be dead and never to know the answers! It was not fair, any of it. And least fair was that if she died of this operation she would never know, truly, which way Robin would have chosen, if somehow his lost love could be found again.

She became aware that time was passing. Albert sat patiently in the tank, moving only occasionally to suck his pipe or scratch under the hem of his floppy sweater —to remind her, that is, that he was still in standby mode.

Essie's thrifty cybernetician's soul was indignantly ordering her to use the program or turn it off—what a shocking waste of machine time! But she hesitated. There were questions still to ask.

At the door the nurse was looking in. "Good morning, Mrs. Broadhead," she said when she saw that Essie was wide awake.

"Is it time?" Essie asked, her voice suddenly unsteady.

"Oh, not for a few minutes yet. You can go on with your machine if you want to."

Essie shook her head. "Is no point," she said and dismissed the program. It was a decision lightly taken. It did not occur to her that some of the unasked questions might be consequential.

And when Albert Einstein was dismissed he did not allow himself to disintegrate at once.

"The whole of anything is never told," said Henry James. Albert knew "Henry James" only as an address, the information behind which he had never had occasion to seek. But he understood the meaning of that law. He could never tell the whole of anything even to

his master. He would fail in his programming if he
tried.

But what parts of the whole to select?

At its lowest structural level, Albert's program was
gated to pass items of a certain measured "importance"
and reject others. Simple enough. But the program was
redundant. Some items came to it through several gates,
sometimes as many as hundreds of gates; and when
some of the gates said "go" and others said "no go,"
what was a program to do? There were algorithms to
test importance, but at some levels of complexity the
algorithms taxed even the resources of sixty billion
gigabits—or of a universe full of bits; Meyer and Stock-
meyer had proved, long ago, that, regardless of computer power, problems existed which could not be
solved in the life of the universe. Albert's problems
were not quite that immense. But he could not find an
algorithm to decide for him, for instance, whether he
should bring up the puzzling implications of Mach's
Principle as applied to Heechee history. Worse. He was
a proprietary program. It would have been interesting
to pass on his conjectures on the subject to a pure
science research program. But that his basic programming did not permit.

So Albert held himself together for nearly a milli-
second, reconsidering his options. Should he, next time
Robin summoned him, volunteer his misgivings about
the potentially terrifying truth that lay behind Heechee
Heaven?

He reached no conclusion in all that long one thousandth of a second, and his parts were needed elsewhere.

So Albert allowed himself to come apart.

This part he poured into slow memory, that part into
ongoing problems as needed, until all of Albert Einstein
had soaked into the 6×10^{19} bits, like water into sand,
until not even a stain was left. Some of his routines
joined with others in a simulated war game, in
which Key West was invaded from Grand Cayman.
Some turned up to assist the traffic-controller program
at Dallas-Fort Worth, as Robin Broadhead's plane en-

tered its landing pattern. Much, much later, some of him helped to monitor Essie's vital functions as Dr. Wilma Liederman began to cut. One little bit, hours after, helped to solve the mystery of the prayer fans. And the simplest, crudest, tiniest part of all stayed on to supervise the program that prepared Cajun coffee and beignets for Robin when he arrived, and to see that the house was clean for him. Sixty billion gigabits can do much. They even do windows.

13

At the Halfway Point

To love someone is a grace. To marry someone is a contract. The part of me that loved Essie, was loving her wholeheartedly, sank in pain and terror when she relapsed, surged in fearful joy when she showed signs of recovering. I had plenty of occasion for both. Essie died twice in surgery before I could get home, and again, twelve days later, when they had to go in again. That last time they made her clinically dead on purpose. Stopped heart and breath, kept only the brain alive. And every time they reanimated her I was frightened to think she would live—because if she lived it meant she might die one more time, and I could not stand it. But slowly, painfully, she began to gain weight, and Wilma told me the tide had turned, as when the spiral begins to glow in a Heechee ship at the halfway point and you know you're going to live through the trip. I spent all that time, weeks and weeks of it, hanging around the house, so that when Essie could see me I would be there.

And all that time the part of me that had contracted to be married to her was resenting the bond, and wishing I were free.

How do you account for that? That was a good occasion for guilt, and guilt is a feeling that comes readily to me—as my old psychoanalytic program used to tell me all the time. And when I went in to see Essie, looking like a mummy of herself, the joy and worry filled my heart and the guilt and resentment clogged my tongue. I would have given my life to make her well. But that did not seem a practical strategy, or at least I could not see any way to make that deal, and the other guilty and hostile part of me wanted to be free to dwell on lost Klara, and whether somehow I might find her again.

But she mended, Essie did. She mended fast. The sunken bags of flesh under her eyes filled to be only bruises. The tubes came out of her nostrils. She ate like a pig. Before my very eyes she was filling out, the bust beginning to swell, the hips regaining their power to startle. "My compliments to the doctor," I told Wilma Liederman when I caught her on her way in to see her patient.

She said sourly, "Yes, she's doing fine."

"I don't like the way you said that," I told her. "What's the matter?"

She relented. "Nothing, really, Robin. All her tests are fine. She's in such a hurry, though!"

"That's good, isn't it?"

"Up to a point it is. And now," she added, "I have to get in to see my patient. Who will be up and about any day now and, maybe, back to normal in a week or two." What good news that was! And how reluctantly I received it.

I went through all those weeks with something hanging over me. Sometimes it seemed like doom, like old Peter Herter blackmailing the world and nothing the world could do to resist it, or like the Heechee stirring into anger as we invaded their complex and private worlds. Sometimes it seemed like golden gifts of opportunity, new technologies, new hopes, new wonders to explore and exploit. You would think that I would distinguish between hopes and worries, right? Wrong. Both scared the hell out of me. As good old Sigfrid used to tell me, I have a great talent not only for guilt but also for worry.

And when you came right down to it, I had some fairly real things to worry about. Not just Essie. When you reach a certain age you have, it seems to me, a right to expect some parts of your life to stay stable. Like what, for instance? Like money, for instance. I was used to a lot of it, and now here was my lawyer program telling me that I had to watch my pennies. "But I promised Hanson Bover a million cash," I said, "and I'm going to pay it. Sell some stock."

"I've *sold* stock, Robin!" He wasn't angry. He wasn't programmed to be able to be really angry, but he could be wretched and he was.

"So sell some more. What's the best to get rid of?"

"None of it is 'best,' Robin. The food mines're down because of the fire. The fish farms still haven't recovered from losing the fingerlings. A month or two from now—"

"A month or two from now isn't when I want the money. Sell." And when I signed him off and called Bover up to find out where to send his million, he actually seemed surprised.

"In view of Gateway Corp's action," he said, "I thought you'd call our arrangement off."

"A deal is a deal," I said. "We can let the legalities hang. They don't mean much while Gateway has preempted me."

He was suspicious immediately. What is it that I do that makes people suspicious of me when I am going miles out of my way to be fair? "Why do you want to hold off on the legalities?" he demanded, rubbing the top of his head agitatedly—was it sunburned again?

"I don't 'want' to," I said, "it just doesn't make any difference. As soon as you lift your injunction Gateway will drop theirs on me."

Alongside Bover's scowling face, my secretary program's appeared. She looked like a cartoon of the Good Angel whispering into Bover's ear, but actually what she was saying was for me: "Sixty seconds until Mr. Herter's reminder," she said.

I had forgotten that old Peter had given us another of his four-hour notices. I said to Bover, "It's time to button up for Peter Herter's next jab," and hung up—I didn't really care if he remembered, I only wanted to terminate the conversation. Not much buttoning up was involved. It was thoughtful—no, it was orderly—of old Peter to warn us each time, and then to perform so punctually. But it mattered more to airline pilots and automobilists than to stay-at-homes like me.

There was Essie, however. I looked in to make sure she was not actually being perfused or catheterized or fed. She wasn't. She was asleep—quite normally asleep, with her dark-gold hair spilling all around her, and gently snoring. And on the way back to my comfortable console chair I felt Peter in my mind.

I had become quite a connoisseur of invasions of the mind. It wasn't any special skill. The whole human race had, over a dozen years, ever since the fool kid, Wan, began his trips to the Food Factory. His were the worst, because they lasted so long and because he shared his dreams with us. Dreams have power; dreams are a kind of released insanity. By contrast, the one light touch we'd had from Janine Herter was nothing, and Peter Herter's precise two-minute doses no worse than a traffic light—you stop a minute, and wait impatiently until it is over, and then you go on your way. All I ever felt from Peter was the way he felt—sometimes the gut-griping of age, sometimes hunger or thirst, once the fading, angry sexual lust of an old man all by himself. As I sat down I remember telling myself that this time was nothing at all. More than anything else, it was like having a little dizzy spell, too much crouching in one position, when you stand up you have to pause a moment until it goes away. But it didn't go away. I felt the blurriness of seeing things with two sets of eyes at once, and the inarticulate anger and unhappiness of the old man—no words; just a sort of tone, as though someone were whispering what I could not quite hear.

It kept on not going away. The blurriness increased. I began to feel detached and almost delirious. That second vision, that is never sharp and clear, began to show things I had never seen before. Not real things. Fantasy things. Women with beaks like birds of prey. Great glittering metal monsters rolling across the inside of my eyelids. Fantasies. Dreams.

The two-minute measured dose of reminder had gone off track. The son of a bitch had fallen asleep in the cocoon.

Thank God for the insomnia of old men! It didn't last eight hours, not much more than one.

But they were sixty-odd unpleasant minutes. When I felt the unwanted dreams slide tracelessly out of my mind, and was sure they were gone, I ran to Essie's room. She was wide awake, leaning back against the pillows. "Am all right, Robin," she said at once. "Was an interesting dream. Nice change from my own."

"I'll kill the old bastard," I said.

Essie shook her head, grinning up at me. "Not practical," she said.

Well, maybe it wasn't. But as soon as I had satisfied myself that Essie was all right, I called for Albert Einstein: "I want advice. Is there anything that can be done to stop Peter Herter?"

He scratched his nose.

"You mean by direct action, I assume. No, Robin. Not by any means available now."

"I don't want to be told that! There must be something!"

"Sure thing, Robin," he said slowly, "but I think you're asking the wrong program. Indirect measures might work. As I understand it, you have some legal questions unresolved. If you could resolve them, you might be able to meet Herter's demands and stop him that way."

"I've tried that! It's the other way around, damn it! If I could get Herter to stop, then maybe I could get

Gateway Corp to give me back control. Meanwhile he's screwing up everybody's mind, and I want it stopped! Isn't there some kind of interference we could broadcast?"

Albert sucked his pipe. "I don't think so, Rob," he said at last. "I don't have a great deal to go on."

That startled me. "You don't remember what it feels like?"

"Robin," he said patiently, "I don't feel anything. It is important for you to remember that I am only a computer program. And not the right program, really, to discuss the exact nature of the signals from Mr. Herter—your psychoanalytic program might be more helpful. Analytically I know what happened—I have all the measurements of the radiation involved. Experientially, nothing. Machine intelligence is not affected. Every human being experienced something, I know because there are reports to say so. There is evidence that the larger-brained mammals—primates, dolphins, elephants—were also disturbed; and maybe other mammals were too, although the evidence is sketchy. But I have not experienced it directly. . . . As to broadcasting an interfering pattern, yes, perhaps that could be done. But what would be the effect, Robin? Bear in mind that the interfering signal would come from a nearby point, not one twenty-five light-days away; if Mr. Herter can cause some disorientation, what would a random signal do at close range?"

"It would be bad, I guess."

"Sure thing, Robin. Probably worse than you guess, but I could not say without experimentation. The subjects would have to be human beings, and such experiments I cannot undertake."

Over my shoulder Essie's voice said proudly, "Yes, you exactly cannot, as who would know better than I?"

She had come up behind me without a sound, barefoot in the thick rug. She wore a neck-to-ankle robe and her hair was done up in a turban. "Essie, what the hell are you doing out of bed?" I demanded.

"My bed has become excessively tedious," she said,

kneading my ear in her fingers, "especially occupied alone. Do you have plans for this evening, Robin? Because, if invited, I would like to share yours."

"But—" I said, and, "Essie—" I said, and what I wanted to say was either "You shouldn't be doing this yet!" or "Not in front of the computer!" She didn't give me a chance to decide which. She leaned down to press her cheek against mine, perhaps so that I might feel how round and full it had once again become.

"Robin," she said sunnily, "I am far more well than you believe. You may ask the doctor, if you wish. She will tell you how very rapidly I have healed." She turned her head to kiss me quickly and added, "I have some affairs of my own for the next few hours. Please continue chatting with your program until then. I am sure Albert has many interesting things to tell you, isn't that so, Albert?"

"Sure thing, Mrs. Broadhead," the program agreed, puffing cheerfully on his pipe.

"So, then. It's settled." She patted my cheek and turned away, and I have to say that as she walked back to her room she did not in the least look unwell. The robe was not tight, but it was shaped to her body, and the shape of her body was really fine. I could not believe that the wadding of bandage all along her left side was gone, but there was no sign of it.

Behind me, my science program coughed. I turned back, and he was puffing on his pipe, his eyes twinkling.

"Your wife is looking very well, Robin," he said, nodding judiciously.

"Sometimes, Albert," I said, "I don't know just how anthropomorphic you are. Well. What very interesting things do you want to tell me about?"

"Whatever you want to hear, Robin. Shall I continue on the subject of Peter Herter? There are some other possibilities, such as the abort mode. That is, setting aside for the moment the legal complications, it would be possible to command the shipboard computer, known as 'Vera', to explode the fuel tanks on the orbital craft."

"Hell it would! We'd destroy the greatest treasure we've ever found!"

"Sure thing, Robin, and it's even worse than that. The chance of an external explosion damaging the installation Mr. Herter is using is quite small. It might only anger him. Or strand him there, to do as he chooses, as long as he lives."

"Forget it! Don't you have anything *good* to tell me about?"

"As a matter of fact, Robin," he grinned, "I do. We've found our Rosetta stone." He shrank away to a dwindling spray of colored flecks and disappeared. As a luminous spindle-shaped mass of lavender color replaced him in the tank, he said, "That is the image of the beginning of a book."

"It's blank!"

"I haven't started it yet," he explained. The shape was taller than I, and about half as thick as it was tall. It began to shift before my eyes; the color thinned out until I could see through it clearly and then one, two, three dots began to appear inside it, points of bright red light that spun themselves out in a spiral. There was a sad chittering sound, like telemetry or like the amplified chirps of marmosets. Then the picture froze. The sound stopped. Albert's voice said:

"I have stopped it at this point, Robin. It is probable that sound is language, but we have not yet been able to isolate semantic units from it. However, the 'text' is clear. There are one hundred thirty-seven of those points of light. Now watch while I run a few more seconds of the book."

The spiral of 137 tiny stars doubled itself. Another coil of dots lifted itself from the original and floated to the top of the spindle, where it hung silently. The chitter of language began again and the original spiral expanded itself, while each of the dots began to trace a spiral of its own. When it was finished there was one large spiral, composed of 137 smaller spirals, each composed of 137 dots. Then the whole red pattern turned orange and it froze.

"Do you want to try to interpret that, Robin?" Albert's voice asked.

"Well, I can't count that high. But it looks like 137 times 137, right?"

"Sure thing, Robin. 137 squared, making 18,769 dots in all. Now watch."

Short green lines slashed the spiral into ten segments. One of the segments lifted itself off, dropped to the bottom of the spindle and turned red again. "That's not exactly a tenth of the number, Robin," said Sigfrid. "By counting you find that there are now 1840 dots at the bottom. I'll proceed." Once again, the central figure changed color, this time to yellow. "Notice the top figure." I looked closely, and saw that the first dot had turned orange, the third yellow. Then the central figure rotated itself on the vertical axis and spun out a three-D column of spirals, and Albert said, "We now have a total of 137 cubed dots in the central figure. From here on," he said kindly, "it gets a little tedious to watch. I'll run it through quickly." And he did, patterns of dots flying around and isolating themselves, colors changing through yellow to avocado, avocado to green, green to aqua, aqua to blue, and on through the spectrum, nearly twice. "Now, do you see what we have? Three numbers, Robin. 137 in the center. 1840 down at the bottom. 137 to the eighteenth power, which is roughly the same as 10 to the thirty-eighth, at the top. Or, in order, three dimensionless numbers: the fine structure constant, the ratio of the proton to the electron and the number of particles in the universe. Robin, you have just had a short course in particle theory from a Heechee teacher!"

I said, "My God."

Albert reappeared on the screen, beaming. "Exactly, Robin," he said.

"But Albert! Does that mean you can read all the prayer fans?"

His face fell. "Only the simple ones," he said regretfully. "This was actually the easiest. But from now on it's quite straightforward. We play every fan and tape it. We look for correspondences. We make semantic assumptions and test them in as many contexts as we can find—we'll do it, Robin. But it may take some time."

"I don't *want* to take time," I snarled.

"Sure thing, Robin, but first every fan must be located, and read, and taped, and coded for machine comparison, and then—"

"I don't want to hear," I said. "Just do it—what's the matter?"

His expression had changed. "It's a question of funding, Robin," he said apologetically. "There's a great deal of machine time involved here."

"Do it! As far as you can go. I'll have Morton sell some more stock. What else have you got?"

"Something nice, Robin," he grinned, shrinking in size until he was just a little face in the corner of the tank. Colors flowed in the center of the display and fused into a set of Heechee controls, displaying a pattern of color on five of the ten panels. The others were blank. "Know what that is, Robin? That's a composite of all the known Gateway flights that wound up at Heechee Heaven. All the patterns you see are identical in all seven known missions. The others vary, but it's a pretty good conjecture that they are not directly involved in course-setting."

"What are you saying, Albert?" I demanded. He had caught me by surprise. I found that I was beginning to shake. "Do you mean if we set ship controls for that pattern we could get to Heechee Heaven?"

"Point nine five yes, Robin," he nodded. "And I have identified three ships, two on Gateway and one on the Moon, that will accept that setting."

I put on a sweater and walked down to the water. I didn't want to hear any more.

The trickle pipes had been busy. I kicked my shoes off to feel the damp, pillowy grass and watched some boys, wind-trolling for perch, near the Nyack shore, and I thought: This is what I bought by risking my life on Gateway. What I paid for with Klara's.

And: Do I want to risk all this, and my life, again?

But it wasn't really a question of "want to". If one of those ships would go to Heechee Heaven and I could buy or steal a passage on it, I would go.

Then sanity saved me, and I realized I couldn't, after all. Not at my age. And not the way Gateway Corp was feeling about me. And, most of all, not in time. The Gateway asteroid orbits at right-angles to the ecliptic, just about. Getting there from Earth is a tedious long job; by Hohmann curves twenty months or more, under forced acceleration more than six. Six months from now those ships would have been there and back.

If they were coming back, of course.

The realization was almost as much of a relief as it was a sick, hungry sense of loss.

Sigfrid von Shrink never told me how to get rid of ambivalence (or guilt). He did tell me how to deal with them. The recipe is, mostly, just to let them happen. Sooner or later they burn themselves out. (He says.) At least, they don't have to be paralyzing. So while I was letting this ambivalence smolder itself into ash I was also strolling along the water, enjoying the pleasant under-the-bubble air and gazing proudly at the house I lived in and the wing where my very dear, and for some time wholly platonic, wife was, I hoped, getting herself good and rested. Whatever she was doing, she wasn't doing it alone. Twice a taxicart had brought someone over from the tube stop. Both of them had been women; and now another taxicart pulled up and let out a man, who gazed around quite unsurely while the taxi rolled itself around the circle and hurried off to its next call. I somehow doubted that he was for Essie; but I could think of no reason why he would be for me, or at least why he could not be dealt with by Harriet. So it was a surprise when the rifle-speaker under the eaves swiveled around to point at me and Harriet's voice said, "Robin? There's a Mr. Haagenbusch here. I think you ought to see him."

That was very unlike Harriet. But she was usually right, so I strolled up the lawn, rinsed my bare feet at the French windows and invited the man into my study. He was a pretty old specimen, pink-skin bald, with a dapper white pair of sideburns and a carefully American accent—not the kind people born in the United States usually have. "Thank you very much for seeing me, Mr. Broadhead," he said, and handed me a card that read:

Herr Doktor Advokat Wm. J. Haagenbusch

"I'm Pete Herter's lawyer," he said. "I flew this morning from Frankfort because I want to make a deal."

How very quaint of you, I thought; imagine coming in person to conduct business! But if Harriet wanted me to see this old flake she had probably talked it over with my legal program, so what I said was, "What kind of a deal?"

He was waiting for me to tell him to sit down. I did. I suspected he was also waiting for me to order coffee or cognac for two, as well, but I didn't particularly want to do that. He took off black kid gloves, looked at his pearly nails and said: "My client has asked for $250,000,000 paid into a special account plus immunity from prosecution of any kind. I received this message by code yesterday."

I laughed out loud. "Christ, Haagenbusch, why are you telling me? I haven't got that kind of money!"

"No, you don't," he agreed. "Outside of your investment in the Herter-Hall syndicate and some fish-farm stock, you don't have anything but a couple of places to live and some personal effects. I think you could raise six or seven million, not counting the Herter-Hall investment. God knows what that might be worth right now, everything considered."

I sat back and looked at him. "You know I got rid of my tourist stuff. So you checked me out. Only you forgot the food mines."

"No, I don't think so, Mr. Broadhead. My understanding is that that stock was sold this afternoon."

It was not altogether pleasant to find out that he knew more about my financial position than I did. So Morton had had to sell that out, too! I didn't have time to think about what that implied just then, because Haagenbusch stroked his sideburns and went on: "The situation is this, Mr. Broadhead. I have advised my client that a contract obtained under duress is not enforceable. He therefore no longer has any hope of attaining his purposes through an agreement with the Gateway Corporation, or even with your syndicate. So I have received new instructions: to secure immediate payment of the sum I have mentioned; to deposit it in untraceable bank accounts in his name; and to turn it over to him when, and if, he returns."

"Gateway won't like being blackmailed," I said. "Still, they may not have any choice."

"Indeed they do not," he agreed. "What is wrong with Mr. Herter's plan is that it won't work. I am sure they will pay over the money. I am also sure that my communications will be tapped and my offices bugged, and that the justice departments of every nation involved in the Gateway treaty will be preparing indictments for Mr. Herter when he returns. I do not want to be named in those indictments as an accomplice, Mr. Broadhead. I know what will happen. They'll find the money and take it back. They'll void Mr. Herter's previous contract on grounds of his own noncompliance. And they'll put him—him at least—in jail."

"You're in a tough situation, Mr. Haagenbusch," I said.

He chuckled dryly. His eyes were not amused. He stroked his sideburns for a moment and burst out: "You don't know! Every day, long orders in code! Demand this, guarantee that, I hold you personally responsible for this other! And then I send off a reply that takes twenty-five days to get there, by which time he has sent me fifty days of new orders and his thoughts are somewhere far beyond and he upbraids me and threatens me! He is not a well man, and he certainly is not a young one. I do not truly think that he will live to collect any of this blackmail— But he might."

"Why don't you quit?"

"I would if I could! But if I quit, then what? Then he has no one on his side at all. Then what would he do,

Mr. Broadhead? Also—" he shrugged, "he is a very old friend, Mr. Broadhead. He was at school with my father. No. I can't quit. Also I can't do what he asks. But perhaps you can. Not by handing over a quarter of a billion dollars, no, because you have never had that kind of money. But you can make him an equal partner with you. I think he would—no. I think he *might* accept that."

"But I've already—" I stopped. If Haagenbusch did not know I had already given half my holdings to Bover, I wasn't going to tell him. "Why wouldn't I void the contract too?" I asked.

He shrugged. "You might. But I think you would not. You are a symbol to him, Mr. Broadhead, and I believe he would trust you. You see, I think I know what it is he wants from all this. It is to live the way you do, for all that remains of his life."

He stood up. "I do not expect you to agree to this at once," he said. "I have perhaps twenty-four hours before I must reply to Mr. Herter. Please think about this, and I will speak to you in one day."

I shook his hand, and had Harriet order him a taxi-cart, and stood with him in the driveway until it rolled up and bore him briskly away into the early night.

When I came back into my own room Essie was standing by the window, looking out at the lights on the Tappan Sea. It was suddenly clear to me who her visitors had been this day. At least one had been her hairdresser; that tawny Niagara of hair hung true and even to her waist once more, and when she turned to smile at me it was the same Essie who had left for Arizona, all those long weeks before.

"You were so very long with that little man," she remarked. "You must be hungry." She watched me standing there for a moment, and laughed. I suppose that the questions in my mind were written on my face, because she answered them. "One, dinner is ready now. Something light, which we can eat at any time. Two, it is laid out in our room whenever you care to join me there. And, three, yes, Robin, I have Wilma's assurance that all of this is quite all right. Am much more well than you think, Robin dear."

"You surely look about as well as a person can get," I said, and must have been smiling because her pale, perfect eyebrows came down in a frown.

"Are you amused at spectacle of horny wife?" she demanded.

"Oh, no! No, it is not that at all," I said, putting my arms around her. "I was just wondering a moment ago why it was that anybody would want to live the way I do. Now I know."

Well. We made love tentatively and slowly, and then when I found out she wasn't going to break we did it again, rougher and rowdier. Then we ate most of the food that was waiting for us on the sideboard, and lounged around and hugged each other until we made love again. After that we just sort of drowsed for a while, spooned together, until Essie commented to the back of my neck, "Pretty impressive performance for old goat, Robin. Not too bad for seventeen-year-old, even."

I stretched and yawned where I lay, rubbing my back against her belly and breasts. "You sure got well in a hurry," I commented.

She didn't answer, just nuzzled my neck with her nose. There is a sort of radar that cannot be seen or heard that tells me true. I lay there for a moment, then disengaged myself and sat up. "Dearest Essie," I said, "what aren't you telling me?"

She lay within my arm, face against my ribs. "About what?" she asked innocently.

"Come on, Essie." When she didn't answer, I said, "Do I have to get Wilma out of bed to tell me?"

She yawned and sat up. It was a false yawn; when she looked at me her eyes were wide awake. "Wilma is most conservative," she said, shrugging. "There are some medicines to promote healing, corticosteroids and such, which she did not wish to give me. With them there is some slight risk of consequences many years from now—but by then, no doubt, Full Medical will be able to cope, I am sure. So I insisted. It made her angry."

"Consequence! You mean leukemia!"

"Yes, perhaps. But most likely not. Certainly not soon."

I got out of the bed and sat naked on the edge so that I could see her better. "Essie, *why*?"

She slipped her thumbs under her long hair and pushed it back away from her face to return my stare. "Because I was in a hurry," she said. "Because you are, after all, entitled to a well wife. Because it is uncomfortable to pee through a catheter, not to say unesthetic. Because was my decision to make and I made it." She threw the covers off her and lay back. "Study me, Robin," she invited. "Not even scars! And inside, under skin, am fully functional. Can eat, digest, excrete, make love, conceive your child if we should wish. Not next spring or maybe next year. Now."

And it was all true. I could see it for myself. Her long pale body was unmarked—no, not entirely; down her left side was an irregular paler patch of new skin. But you had to look to see it, and there was nothing else at all to show that a few weeks earlier she had been gouged, and mutilated, and in fact dead.

I was getting cold. I stood up to find Essie's robe for her and put my own on. There was still some coffee on the sideboard, and still hot. "For me too," Essie said as I poured.

"Shouldn't you be resting?"

"When I am tired," she said practically, "you will know, because I will roll over and go to sleep. Has been very long time since you and I were like this, Robin. Am enjoying it."

She accepted a cup from me and looked at me over the rim as she sipped it. "But you are not," she observed.

"Yes I am!" And I was; but honesty made me add, "I puzzle myself sometimes, Essie. Why is it that when you show me love it comes out in my head feeling like guilt?"

She put down her cup and lay back. "Do you wish to tell me about it, dear Robin?"

"I just have." Then I added, "I suppose, if anybody, I should call up old Sigfrid von Shrink and tell him."

"He is always available," she said.

"Hum. If I start with him God knows when I'd ever finish. Anyway, he's not the program I want to talk to. There's so much going on, Essie! And it's all happening without me. I feel left out."

"Yes," she said, "am aware this is how you feel. Is something you wish to do, so will not feel left out any more?"

"Well—maybe," I said. "About Peter Herter, for instance. I've been fooling around with a kind of an idea that I'd like to talk over with Albert Einstein."

She nodded. "Very well, why not?" She sat up on the edge of the bed. "Hand me my slippers, please. Let us do this now."

"Now? But it's late. You shouldn't be—"

"Robin," she said kindly, "I too have talked with Sigfrid von Shrink. Is good program, even if not written by me. Says you are good man, Robin, well adjusted, generous, and to all of this I also can testify, not to add excellent lover and much fun to be with. Come into study." She took my hand as we walked into the big room looking over the Tappan Sea and sat before my console in the comfortable loveseat. "However," she went on, "Sigfrid says you have great talent for inventing reasons not to do things. So I will help you get off dime. *Daite gorod Polymat.*" She was not talking to me, but to the console, which sprang at once into light. "Display both Albert and Sigfrid programs," she ordered. "Access both files in interactive mode. Now, Robin! Let us pursue questions you have raised. After all, I am quite interested too."

This wife of so many years, this S. Ya. Lavorovna I married, she surprises me most when I least expect it. She sat quite comfortably beside me, holding my hand, while I talked quite openly about doing the things that I had most wanted not to want. It was not just a matter of going to Heechee Heaven and the Food Factory and stopping old Peter Herter from messing up the world. It was where I might go after that.

But at first it did not look as though I were going anywhere. "Albert," I said, "you told me that you had worked out a course setting for Heechee Heaven from Gateway records. Can you do that for the Food Factory too?"

The two of them were sitting side by side in the PV tank, Albert puffing on his pipe, Sigfrid, hands clasped and silent, attentively listening. He would not speak until I spoke to him, and I was not doing that. " 'Fraid not," Albert said apologetically. "We have only one known setting for the Food Factory, Trish Bover's, and that's not enough to be sure. Maybe point-six probable that it would get a ship there. But then what, Robin? It couldn't come back. Or at least Trish Bover's didn't." He settled himself comfortably, and went on, "There are, of course, certain alternatives." He glanced at Sigfrid von Shrink beside him. "One might so manipulate Herter's mind by suggestion that he would change his plans."

"Would that work?" I was still talking to Albert Einstein. He shrugged, and Sigfrid stirred but did not speak.

"Oh, do not be such a baby," Essie scolded. "Answer, Sigfrid."

"Gospozha Lavorovna," he said, glancing at me, "I think not. I believe my colleague has raised this possibility only so that I might dismiss it. I have studied the records of Peter Herter's transmissions. The symbolism is quite obvious. The angelic women with the raptor beaks—what is a 'hooked nose', gospozha? Think of Payter's childhood, and what he heard of the 'cleansing' of the world of the evil Jews. There is also the violence, the punitive emotions. He is quite ill, has in fact already suffered one coronary attack, and is no longer rational; he has, in fact, regressed to quite a childish state. Neither suggestion nor appeals to reason will work, gospozha. The only possibility would be perhaps long-term analysis. He would not likely agree, the shipboard computer could not well handle it and, in any case, there is not time. I cannot help you, gospozha, not with any real chance of success."

Long and long ago I spent a couple of hundred mostly very unpleasant hours listening to Sigfrid's reasonable, maddening voice, and I had not wanted ever to hear it again. But, you know, it wasn't all that bad.

Beside me, Essie stirred, "Polymath," she called, "have fresh coffee prepared." To me she said, "I think will be here for some time."

"I don't know for what," I objected. "I seem to be stymied."

"And if you are," she said comfortably, "we need not drink the coffee but can go back to bed. Meanwhile am quite enjoying this, Robin."

Well, why not? I was strangely no more sleepy than Essie appeared to be. In fact, I was both alert and relaxed, and my mind had never been clearer. "Albert," I said, "is there any progress on reading the Heechee books?"

"Not much, Robin," he apologized. "There are other mathematical volumes such as the one you saw, but as yet no language— Yes, Robin?"

I snapped my fingers. The vagrant thought that had been in the back of my mind had come to the fore. "Gosh numbers," I said. "Those numbers the book showed us. They're the same as the ones the Dead Men call 'gosh numbers.' "

"Sure thing, Robin," he nodded. "They are basic dimensionless constants of the universe, or at least of this universe. However, there is the question of Mach's Principle, which suggests—"

"Not now, Albert! Where do you suppose the Dead Men got them?"

He paused, frowning. Tapping out his pipe, he glanced at Sigfrid before he said, "I would conjecture that the Dead Men interfaced with the Heechee machine intelligence. No doubt there was some transmission both ways."

"My very thought! What *else* do you conjecture the Dead Men might know?"

"That is very difficult to say. They are very incompletely stored, you know. Communication was extremely difficult at best and has now been interrupted entirely."

I sat up straight. "And what if we got back in communication? What if somebody went to Heechee Heaven to talk to them?"

He coughed. Trying not to be patronizing, he said, "Robin, several members of the Herter-Hall party, plus the boy, Wan, have failed to get clear answers from them on these questions. Even our machine intelligence has succeeded only poorly—though," he said politely enough, "that is primarily because of the necessity to interface with the shipboard computer, Vera. They are poorly stored, Robin. They are obsessive, irrational and often incoherent."

Behind me Essie was standing with the tray of coffee and cups—I had hardly heard the bell from the kitchen to say it was ready. "Ask him, Robin," she commanded.

I did not pretend to misunderstand. "Hell," I said, "all right, Sigfrid. That's your line of work. How do we trick them into talking to us?"

Sigfrid smiled and unlaced his hands. "It is good to speak to you again, Robin," he said. "I would like to compliment you on your very considerable progress since we spoke last—"

"Get on with it!"

"Of course, Robin. There *is* one possibility. The storage of the female prospector, Henrietta, seems rather complete, except for her one obsession, that is, with the unfaithfulness of her husband. I think that if a machine program were written from what we know of her husband's personality and interfaced with her—"

"Make a fake husband for her?"

"Essentially, yes, Robin," he nodded. "It wouldn't have to be exact. Because the Dead Men in general are so poorly stored, any responses that were inappropriate might be overlooked. Of course, the program would be quite—"

"Stow it, Sigfrid. Can you write a program like that?"

"Yes. With help from your wife, yes."

"And then how do we get it in contact with Henrietta?"

He looked sidewise at Albert. "I believe my colleague can help there."

"Sure thing, Sigfrid," Albert said cheerily, scratching one foot with the toe of the other. "One. Write the program, with ancillaries. Two. Read it into a PMAL-2 flip processor, with a gigabit fast-access memory and necessary slave units. Three. Put it in a Five and fire it off to Heechee Heaven. Then interface it with Henrietta and start the interrogation. I'd give that, oh, maybe a point-nine probability of working."

I frowned. "Why ship all that machinery around?"

Patiently he said, "It's c, Robin. The speed of light. Lacking an FTL radio, we have to ship the machine to where the job is."

"The Herter-Hall computer has an FTL radio."

"Too dumb, Robin. Too slow. And I haven't told you the worst part. All that hardware is pretty big, you know. It would just about fill a Five. Which means it arrives naked and undefended at Heechee Heaven. And we don't know who is going to meet it at the dock."

Essie was sitting beside me again, looking beautiful and concerned, holding a cup of coffee. I took it automatically and swallowed a gulp. "You said 'just about'," I pointed out. "Does that mean a pilot could go along?"

" 'Fraid not, Robin. There's only room for about another hundred and fifty kilos."

"I only weigh half that!" I felt Essie tense beside me. We were getting right down to it, now. I felt more clearheaded and sure of myself than in weeks. The paralysis of inaction was loosening every minute. I was aware of what I was saying, and very conscious of what it meant to Essie—and unwilling to stop.

"That's true, Robin," Albert conceded, "but do you want to get there dead? There's food, water, air. Your round-trip standard allowance, with all provision for regeneration, comes to more than three hundred kilos, and there simply is not—"

"Cut it out, Albert," I said. "You know as well as I

do that we're not talking about a round trip. We're talking about, what was it? Twenty-two days. That was flight time for Henrietta. That's all I need. Enough for twenty-two days. Then I'll be on Heechee Heaven and it won't matter."

Sigfrid was looking very interested, but silent. Albert was looking concerned. He admitted, "Well, that's true, Robin. But it's quite a risk. There's no margin for error at all."

I shook my head. I was way ahead of him—way ahead, at any rate, of where he was willing to go by himself. "You said there's a Five on the Moon that will accept that destination. Is there a what-do-you-call-it PMAL there too?"

"No, Robin," he said, but added sadly, "However, there is one at Kourou, ready for shipment to Venus."

"Thank you, Albert," I said, half a snarl because it was like pulling teeth to get it out of him. And then I sat back and contemplated what had just been said.

I was not the only one who had been listening intently. Beside me Essie set down her coffee cup. "Polymath," she commanded, "access and display Morton program, in interactive mode. Go ahead, Robin. Do what you must do."

There was the sound of a door opening from the tank, and Morton walked in, shaking hands with Sigfrid and Albert as he glanced over his shoulder at me. He was accessing information as he stepped, and I could tell by his expression that he didn't like what he was finding out. I didn't care. I said, "Morton! There's a PMAL-2 information processor at the launch base in Guiana. Buy it for me."

He turned and confronted me. "Robin," he said stubbornly, "I don't think you realize how rapidly you're eating into capital! This program is costing you over a thousand dollars a minute alone. I'll have to sell stock—"

"Sell it!"

"Not only that. If you're planning to ship yourself and that computer to Heechee Heaven— Don't! Don't even think of it! First place, Bover's injunction still prevents it. Second place, if you should manage to get around that, you'd be liable to a contempt citation and damages that—"

"I didn't ask you about that, Morton. Suppose I got Bover to lift his injunction. Could they stop me then?"

"Yes! But," he added, softening, "although they could, there is some chance they would not. At least not in time. Nevertheless, as your legal advisor, I have to say—"

"You don't have to say anything. Buy the computer. Albert and Sigfrid, program it the way we discussed. You three get out of the tank; I want Harriet. Harriet? Get me a flight, Kourou to the Moon, same ship as the computer Morton's buying for me, soon as you can. And while you're doing that see if you can locate Hanson Bover for me. I want to talk to him." When she nodded and winked away I turned to look at Essie. Her eyes were damp, but she was smiling.

"You know something?" I said. "Sigfrid never called me 'Rob' or 'Bobby' once."

She put her arms around me and hugged me close. "Maybe he thinks you are not to be treated like an infant now," she said. "And neither am I, Robin. Do you think I wanted to get well only so we could make love quickly? No. It was also so you would not be held prisoner here by a wife you thought it wicked to leave. And so that I would be well able to deal with it," she added, "when you left anyway."

We landed at Cayenne in pitch dark and pouring rain. Bover was waiting for me as I cleared Customs, half asleep in a foam armchair by the baggage terminal. I thanked him several times for meeting me, but he shrugged it off. "We have only two hours," he said. "Let us get on with it."

Harriet had chartered a chopper for us. We took off over the palms just as the sun was coming up from the Atlantic. By the time we reached Kourou it was full daylight, and the lunar module was erect beside its support tower. It was tiny compared to the giants that climb up from Kennedy or California, but the Centre

Spatial Guyanais gets one-sixth better performance out of its rockets, being almost on the equator, so they don't have to be as big. The computer was already loaded and stowed, and Bover and I got aboard at once. Slam. Shove. Retching taste of the breakfast I shouldn't have eaten on the airplane rising in my throat, and then we were under way.

It takes three days for the lunar flight. I spent as much of it as I could sleeping, the rest talking to Bover. It was the longest time I had spent out of reach of my comm facilities in at least a dozen years, and I thought it would hang heavy on my hands. It went like lightning. I woke up when the acceleration warnings went off, and watched the brassy Moon rise up toward us, and then there we were.

Considering how far I had been, it was surprising that I had never been on the Moon before. I didn't know what to expect. It all took me by surprise: the dancy, prancy feeling of weighing no more than an inflated rubber doll, the sound of the reedy tenor that came out of my mouth in the twenty-percent helium atmosphere. They weren't breathing Heechee mixture any more, not on the Moon. Heechee digging machines went like a bomb in the lunar rock, and with all the sunlight anybody could want to drive them it cost nothing to keep them going. The only problem was filling them with air, which was why they supplemented with helium—cheaper and easier to get than N_2.

The Heechee lunar spindle is near the shuttle base—or, to put it the right way around, the shuttle base was located where it is, near Fra Mauro, because that was where the Heechee had dug most a million years before. It was all underground, even the docking ports concealed under the lee of a rille. A couple of American astronauts named Shepard and Mitchell had spent a weekend roaming around within two hundred kilometers of it once, and never noticed it was there. Now a community of more than a thousand people lived in the spindle, and the digs and the new tunnels were branching off in all directions, and the lunar surface was a rash of microwave dishes and solar collectors and plumbing. "Hi, you," I said to the first able-bodied man who seemed to have nothing to do. "What's your name?"

He loped leisurely toward me, chewing on an unlighted cigar. "What's it to you?" he asked.

"There's cargo coming off the shuttle. I want it loaded onto the Five that's in the dock now. You'll need half a dozen helpers and probably cargo-handling equipment, and it's a rush job."

"Um," he said. "You got authority for this?"

"I'll show it to you when I pay you off," I said. "And the pay's a thousand dollars a man, with a ten thousand dollar bonus to you personally if you do it within three hours."

"Um. Let's see the cargo." It was just coming off the rocket. He looked it over carefully, scratched for a while, thought for a while. He wasn't entirely without conversation. A couple of words at a time it developed that his name was A. T. Walthers, Jr., and that he had been born in the tunnels on Venus. By his bangle I could tell that he had tried his luck on Gateway, and by the fact that he was doing odd jobs on the Moon I could tell that his luck hadn't been good. Well, mine hadn't been either, the first couple of times; and then it changed. In which direction is hard to say. "Can do it, Broadhead," he said at last, "but we don't have three hours. That joker Herter is due to perform again in about ninety minutes. We'll have to wrap this up before that."

"All the better," I said. "Now, which way is the Gateway Corp office?"

"North end of the spindle," he said. "They close in about half an hour."

All the better, I thought again, but didn't say it. Dragging Bover after me I prancy-danced back along the tunnel to the big spindle-shaped cavern that was headquarters for the area and argued our way into the Launch Director's room. "You'll want an open circuit to Earth for ID," I told her. "I'm Robin Broadhead, and here's my thumbprint. This is Hanson Bover—if you'll oblige, Bover—" He pressed his thumb on the plate next to mine. "Now say your bit," I invited him.

"I, Allen Bover," he said by rote, "hereby withdraw my injunction against Robin Broadhead, the Gateway Corp et al."

"Thank you," I said. "Now, Director, while you're verifying that, here's a signed copy of what Bover has just said for your records, plus a mission plan. Under my contract with Gateway Corp, which your machines can retrieve for you, I have the right to make use of Gateway facilities in connection with the Herter-Hall expedition. I am going to do so, for which purpose I need the Five at present parked in your landing docks. You will see by the mission plan that I intend to go to Heechee Heaven, and from there to the Food Factory, where I will prevent Peter Herter from inflicting any more damage to the Earth, also rescuing the Herter-Hall party and returning valuable Gateway information for processing and use. And I'd like to leave within the next hour," I finished strongly.

Well, for a minute there it looked like it was going to work. The Launch Director looked at the thumbprints on the register plate, picked up the spool of mission plan and weighed it in her hand, and then stared at me in silence for a moment, her mouth open. I could hear the whine of whatever volatile gas they were using in the heat engines, Carnot-cycling from under the Fresnel lenses to the shaded artichoke-shaped reflectors just above us. I didn't hear anything else at all. Then she sighed and said, "Senator Praggler, have you been getting all that?"

And from the air behind her desk came Praggler's growl. "You bet your ass I have, Milly. Tell Broadhead it won't work. He can't have the ship."

It was the three days in transit that had done me in. Automatically the passport identities of all passengers were radioed ahead, and the officials had known I was coming before the shuttle left French Guiana. It was just chance that it was Praggler who was there to meet me; even if he hadn't been, they had plenty of time to get orders from the headquarters in Brasilia. I thought for a while that because it was Praggler I could talk him out of it. I couldn't. I yelled at him for thirty minutes and begged for thirty more. No good. "There's nothing wrong with your mission plan," he admitted. "What's wrong is you. You're not entitled to use Gateway facilities, because Gateway Corp preempted you yesterday, while you were in orbit. Even if it hadn't, Robin, I wouldn't let you go. You're too personally involved. Not to mention too old for this kind of thing."

"I'm an experienced Gateway pilot!—"

"You're an experienced pain in the ass, Robin. And maybe a little bit crazy, too. What do you think one man could do on Heechee Heaven? No. We'll use your plan. We'll even pay you royalties on it—if it works. But we'll do it the right way, from Gateway itself, with at least three ships going, two of them full of young, healthy, well armed daredevils."

"Senator," I pleaded, "let me go! If you ship this computer to Gateway it'll take months—years!"

"Not if we send it right up there in the Five," he said. "Six days. Then it can take right off again, in convoy. But not with you. However," he said reasonably, "we'll certainly pay you for the computer *and* for the program. Leave it at that, Robin. Let somebody else take the risks. I'm speaking as your friend."

Well, he was my friend and we both knew it, but maybe not as much of a friend as he had been, after I told him what he could do with his friendship. Finally Bover pulled me away. The last I saw of the Senator he was sitting on the edge of the desk staring after me, face still purple with rage, eyes looking as though they were getting ready to weep.

"That's tough luck, Mr. Broadhead," said Bover sympathetically.

I took a breath to straighten him out, too, and stopped myself just in time. There was no point in it. "I'll get you a ticket back to Kourou," I said.

He smiled, showing perfectly chiseled Chiclets—he had been spending some of that money on himself.

"You have made me a rich man, Mr. Broadhead. I can pay for my own ticket. Also, I've never been here before and will not likely come again, so I think I'll stay a while."

"Suit yourself."

"And you, Mr. Broadhead? What are your plans?"

"I don't have any." Nor could I think of any. I had run out of programming. I cannot tell you how empty that feels. I had nerved myself up for another Heechee mystery-ship ride—well, not as much a mystery as when I was prospecting out of Gateway. But still a pretty scary prospect. I had taken a step with Essie that I had feared taking for a long time. And all for nothing.

I stared wistfully down the long, empty tunnel toward the docks. "I might shoot my way through," I said.

"Mr. Broadhead! That's—that's—"

"Oh, don't worry. I'm not going to, mostly because all the guns I know anything about are already loaded onto that Five. And I doubt they'll let me in to get one."

He peered into my face. "Well," he said doubtfully, "perhaps you, too, might enjoy just spending a few days—"

And then his expression changed.

I hardly saw it; I was feeling what he felt, and that was enough to demand all my attention. Old Peter was in the couch again. Worse than ever. It was not just his dreams and fantasies that I was experiencing—that everyone alive was feeling. It was pain. Despair. Madness. There was a terrible sense of pressure around the temples, a flaming ache from arms and chest. My throat was dry, then raw with sour clots as I vomited.

Nothing like that had ever come from the Food Factory before.

But then no one had ever died in the couch before. It did not stop in a minute, or in ten. My lungs heaved in great starving gasps. So did Bover's. So did everyone else's, wherever they were in range of his transmission. The pain kept on, and every time it seemed to reach a plateau there was an explosion of new pain; and all the

time there was the terror, the rage, the awful misery of
a man who knew he was dying, and hated it.

But I knew what it was.

I knew what it was, and I knew what I could do—
what at least my body could do, if I could only hold my
mind together enough to make it. I forced myself to
take a step, and then another. I made myself trot down
that wide, weary corridor, when Bover was writhing on
the ground behind me and the guards were staggering,
completely helpless, ahead. I blundered past them and
doubt they even saw me, into the narrow hatch of the
lander, tumbling all bruised and shaken, forcing myself
to dog it closed over my head.

And there I was, in the disastrously familiar tiny
cubbyhole, surrounded by shapes of molded tan plastic.
Walthers had done his part of the job, at least. I had no
way of paying him for it, but if he had put his hand in
the port as I was closing it I would have given him a
million.

At some point old Peter Herter died. His death did
not end the misery. It only began to slow it down. I
could not have guessed what it would be like to be in
the mind of a man who has died, while he feels his heart
stop and his bowels loosen and the certainty of death
stab into his brain. It goes on much longer than I would
have believed possible. It was going on all the time I
cut the lander loose and sent it up on its little hydrogen
jets to where the Heechee drive could work. I jammed
and heaved the course-guidance wheels about until they
showed that well-learned pattern Albert had taught me.

And then I squeezed the launch teat, and I was on
my way. The ship began its lurchy, queasy acceleration.
The star patterns I could see, barely see, by craning
past a memory-storage unit, began to drift together. No
one could stop me now. I could not even stop myself.

By all the data Albert had been able to collect the trip
would be twenty-two days exactly. Not very long—not
unless you are squeezed into a ship that is already filled
to capacity. There was room for me—more or less. I
could stretch out. I could stand up. I could even lie

down, if the vagrant motion of the ship let me know where "down" was, and if I did not mind being folded over between pieces of metal. What I could not do, for those twenty-two days, was move more than half a meter in any direction—not to eat, not to sleep, not to bathe or excrete; not for anything.

There was plenty of time on my hands for the purpose of remembering how terrifying Heechee flight was, and to feel all of it.

There was plenty of time, too, to learn. Albert had been careful to record for me all the data I had not had the wit to ask him for, and those tapes were available for me to play. They were not very interesting or sophisticated in delivery. The PMAL-2 was all memory: plenty of brain, not much display. There was no three-dimensional tank, only a stereo flat-plate goggle system when my eyes would bear watching it, or a screen the size of the palm of my hand when they would not.

At first I did not use it. I just lay there, sleeping as much as I could. Partly I was recovering from the trauma of Peter's death, so terrifyingly like my own. Partly I was experimenting with the inside of my head —allowing myself to feel fear (when I had every reason for it!), encouraging myself to feel guilt. There are kinds of guilt that I know I cherish, the contemplation of obligations unmet and commitments undone. I had plenty of those to think about, beginning with Peter (who would almost surely have been still alive, if I had not accepted him for that expedition) and ending, or rather not ending, with Klara in her frozen black hole —not ending because I could always think of others. That amusement staled before long. To my surprise I found that the guilt was not very overpowering after all, once I let myself feel it; and that took care of the first day.

Then I turned to the tapes. I let the semi-Albert, the rigid, half-animated caricature of the program I knew and loved, lecture me on Mach's Principle and gosh numbers and more curious forms of astrophysical speculation than I had ever dreamed of. I didn't really listen, but I let the voice roll over me, and that was the second day.

Then, from the same source, I poured into myself all that was stored about the Dead Men. I had heard almost all of it before. I heard it all again. I had nothing better to do, and that was the third day.

Then there were miscellaneous lectures on Heechee Heaven and the provenance of the Old Ones and possible strategies for dealing with Henrietta and possible risks to be guarded against from the Old Ones, and that was the third day, and the fourth, and the fifth.

I began to wonder how I would fill twenty-two of them, so I went back and did those tapes all over again, and that was the sixth day, and the eighth, and the tenth; and on the eleventh—

On the eleventh I cut off the computer entirely, grinning to myself with anticipated pleasure.

It was halfway day. I hung there in my restraining straps, waiting for the satisfaction of the one event this cramped and cussed trip could produce for me: the twinkling eruption of golden sparks of light in the crystal spiral that would signify turnover time. I didn't know exactly when it would happen. Probably not in the first hour of the day (and it didn't). Probably not, either, in the second or third . . . and it didn't. Not in those hours, nor in the fourth, or fifth, or the ones after that. It did not happen at all on the eleventh day.

Or on the twelfth.

Or on the thirteenth.

Or on the fourteenth; and when at last I punched in the data to check out the arithmetic I did not care to do in my head, the computer told me what I did not want to know.

It was too late.

Even if the halfway point occurred any time now —even in the next minute—there would not be water, food and air enough to carry me through to the end.

There are economies one can make. I made them. I moistened my lips instead of drinking, slept all I could, breathed as shallowly as I knew how. And turnover at last did occur—on day nineteen. Eight days late.

When I played the figures into the computer they came back cold and clear.

The halfway point had come too late. Nineteen days from now the ship might well arrive at Heechee Heaven, but not with a living pilot aboard. By then I would have been dead for at least six.

14

The Long Night of the Dreams

As she began to be able to speak to the Old Ones they began to seem more like individuals to her. They were not really old, either. Or at least the three that most often guarded her and fed her and led her to her sessions in the long night of the dreams were not. They learned to call her Janine, or at least something close enough. Their own names were complicated, but each name had a short form—Tar, or Tor, or Hooay—and they responded to them, at need or just for play. They were as playful as puppies, and as solicitous. When she came out of the bright blue cocoon, racked and sweating from another life and another death—from another lesson, in this course that the Oldest One had prescribed for her—one of them was always there to coo and murmur and stroke.

But it was not enough! There was no consolation enough to make up for what happened in the dreams, over and over.

Every day was the same. A few hours of uneasy and unrestful sleep. A chance to eat. Maybe a game of tag or touch-tickle with Hooay or Tor. Perhaps a chance to wander about the Heaven, always guarded. Then Tar or Hooay or one of the others would tug her gently back to the cocoon and put her inside and then, for hours, sometimes for what seemed like the entire span of a life, Janine would be someone else. And such strange someones! Male. Female. Young. Old. Mad. Crippled —they were all different. None of them were quite human. Most were not human at all, especially the earliest, oldest someones.

The lives she "dreamed" that were the closest in time were the nearest to her own. At least, they were the lives of creatures not unlike Tor or Tar or Hooay. They were not usually frightening, though all of them ended in death. In them she lived random and chaotic snatches of their stored memories of the short and chancy, or dull and driven, lives they had known. As she came to understand the language of her captors she found out that the lives she lived were those which had been specially selected (by what criteria?) to be stored. So each had some special lesson. All of the dreams were learning experiences for her, of course, and of course she learned. She learned how to speak to the living ones; to understand their overshadowed existences; to comprehend their obsessed need to obey. They were slaves! Or pets? When they did what the Oldest One told them they were obedient, and therefore good. When, rarely, they did not, they were punished.

Between times she saw Wan sometimes, and sometimes her sister. They were kept apart from her as a matter of policy. At first she did not understand why; then she did, and laughed inside herself at the joke too secret to share with even jokey Tor. Lurvy and Wan were learning too, and taking it no better than she.

By the end of the first six "dreams" she could speak to the Old Ones. Her lips and throat would not quite form their chirping, murmuring vowels, but she could make herself understood. More urgently, she could follow their orders. That saved trouble. When she was meant to return to her private cell they did not need to push her, and when she was supposed to bathe they did not have to strip her of her clothes. By the tenth lesson they were almost friendly. By the fifteenth she (and Lurvy and Wan as well) knew all they ever would about Heechee Heaven, including the fact that the Old Ones were not, and never had been, Heechee.

Not even the Oldest One.

And who was the Oldest One? Her lessons had not taught her that. Tar and Hooay explained, as best they could, that the Oldest One was God. That was not a satisfying answer. He was a god too much like his worshipers to have built Heechee Heaven or any part of it, including his own body. No. The Heaven was Heechee-built, for what purpose only the Heechee knew, and the Oldest One was not a Heechee.

Through all this the great machine was immobile again, motionless, almost dead, conserving its dwindling remnant of life. When Janine crossed the central spindle she saw it there, still as a statue. Occasionally there was a sluggish flicker of pale color around its external sensors, as though it were on the verge of awakening, perhaps following them through half-closed eyes. When that happened, Hooay and Tar would quicken their step. There was no touch-tickle or joking then. Mostly it was absolutely still. She passed Wan in its very shadow one day, she going to the cocoon, he coming away, and Hooay dared to let them talk for a moment. "It looks scary," Janine said.

"I could destroy it for you, if you like," Wan boasted, glancing nervously over his shoulder at the machine. But he had said it in English, and had the wisdom not to translate it for their guards. But even the tone of his voice made Hooay uneasy, and he hustled Janine away.

Janine was becoming almost fond of her captors, as one might be of a great, gentle Malemute that could talk. It took her a long time to think of a young female like Tar as either young or female. They all had the same scraggly facial hair and the heavy supraorbital lobes characteristic of the mature male primate. But they began to become individuals, rather than specimens of the class "jailer". The heavier and darker of the two males was called "Tor", but that was only one syllable out of a long and subtle name from which Janine could only understand the word "dark". It did not refer to his coloring. If anything, he was fairer than his fellows. It had something to do with an adventure of his childhood, in a part of the Heaven so strange and so seldom visited that there was little light from even the eternal Heechee-metal walls. Tor trimmed his beard so that it jutted down from his jaw in two inverted horns. Tor made the most jokes, and tried to share them with his prisoner. Tor was the one who jested with Janine, saying that if her male, Wan, was as infertile as he seemed to be while penned with Lurvy, he would ask the Oldest One for permission to impregnate her himself. Janine, cherishing her secret joke about their infertility, was not frightened. She was not repelled, either, because Tor was a kindly sort of satyr, and she believed she could recognize the jest. All the same, she began to think of herself as no longer a snotty kid. Each long dream aged her. In them she experienced the sexual intercourse she had never known in life—sometimes as a woman, sometimes not—and often pain, and always, at the end, death. The records could not be made from a living person, Hooay explained in a nonplayful moment; and his manner was not playful at all as he described the way in which the brain was opened and fed into the machine that made the records. She grew a little older while he was telling her.

As the dreams went on, they became stranger and more remote. "You are going to very old times," Tor told her. "This one now—" he was leading her toward the cocoon "—is the very oldest, and therefore the last. Perhaps."

She paused beside the gleaming couch. "Is this another joke, Tor, or a riddle?"

"No." He tugged soberly at the forks of his beard with both hands. "You will not like this one, Danine."

"Thanks."

He grinned, to crinkle the corners of his sad, soft eyes. "But it is the last I can give you. Perhaps—

perhaps the Oldest One will then give you a dream out of his own. It is said that he has sometimes done that, but I do not know when. Not in any person's memory."

Janine swallowed. "It sounds scary," she said.

He said kindly, "It frightened me very much when I had it, Danine, but remember that it is only a dream, for you." And he closed the cocoon over her, and Janine fought for a moment against the sleep, and failed as always . . . and was someone else.

Once there was a creature. It was female; but it was not an "it", if Descartes is to be believed, because it was aware of its own existence, and therefore it was a "she".

She had no name. But she was marked among her fellows by a great scar from ear to nose, where the hoof of a dying prey-beast had nearly killed her. Her eye on that side had healed with the lid pulled out of shape, and so she might be called "Squint".

Squint had a home. It was not elaborate. It was no more than a trampled-out nest in a clump of something like papyrus, partly sheltered by a hummock of earth. But Squint and her relatives returned to those nests every day and in this they were unlike any of the other living things that resembled them. In one other respect they were quite unlike anything else they grew up with, and that was that they used objects that were not parts of their bodies to do work for them. Squint was not beautiful. She stood not much over a meter tall. She had no eyebrows—the hair on her scalp merged with them, and only her nose and cheekbones were bare— and she had no chin to speak of. Her hands had fingers, but they were usually clenched so that the backs of them were scarred and calloused, and the fingers did not separate well—not much better than the fingers of her feet, which were almost as good at grasping things, and better at gouging out the vulnerable parts of a creature unfortunate enough to find her arms wrapped around its neck as it tried to run away. Squint was pregnant, although she did not know that this was so. Squint was full grown and fully fertile by her fifth rainy season. In the thirteen years she had been alive she had been pregnant nine or ten times, and had never known it until she was forced to note that she could no longer run quite as fast, that the bulge in her belly made it more difficult to rake the guts out of a prey-animal and that her dugs began to swell again with milk. Of the fifty members of her community at least four were her children. More than a dozen of the males were, or might have been, the children's fathers. Squint was aware of the former relationship, but not of the latter. At least one of the young males she knew to be a child of hers might well have been the father of another—a notion which would not have disturbed Squint, even if she had been capable of entertaining it. The thing she did with the males when the flesh beneath her skinny buttocks swelled and reddened was not in her mind related to childbirth. It was not related to pleasure, either. It was an itch that she suffered to be scratched whenever it happened. Squint had no way of defining "pleasure", except perhaps as the absence of pain. Even in those terms, she knew little of it throughout her life.

When the Heechee lander bellowed and flamed above the clouds, Squint and all her community ran to hide. None of them saw it come to earth.

If a trawl scoops a starfish from the bottom of a sea, a spade lifts it from the bucket of ooze and dumps it in a tank, a biologist pins it down and dissects out its nervous system—does the starfish know what is happening to it?

Squint had more self-awareness than a starfish. But she had little more background of experience to inform her. Nothing that happened to her from the moment she saw a bright light shining in her eyes made sense. She did not feel the point of the anesthetic lance that put her to sleep. She did not know she was carried into the lander and dumped into a pen of twelve of her fellows. She did not feel the crushing acceleration when she took off, or the weightlessness for the long time they floated in transit. She did not know anything at all until

she was allowed to waken again, and did not understand what she then experienced.

Nothing was familiar!

Water. The water Squint drank did not any longer
come from the muddy brink of the river. It came in a
shiny, hard trough. When she bent to lap it up nothing
lurked beneath its surface to lunge at her.

Sun and sky. There was no sun! There were no
clouds, and there was no rain. There were hard, blue-
gleaming walls, and a blue-gleaming roof overhead.

Food. There was no live thing to catch and dismem-
ber. There were flat, tough, tasteless clods of chewy
matter. They filled her stomach, and they were always
available. No matter how much she and her fellows ate,
there was always more.

Sights and sounds and smells—these were terrifying!
There was a stink she had never smelled before, sharp
in her nose and scary. It was the smell of something
alive, but she never saw the creature that owned it.
There was an absence of normal smells almost as bad.
No smell of deer. No smell of antelope. No smell of cat
(that one a blessing). No smell even of their own dung,
or not very much, because they had no rushes to tramp
into a home, and the places where they huddled together to sleep were sluiced clean every time they left
them. Her baby was born there, while the rest of the
tribe complained at her grunts because they wanted to
sleep. When she woke to lift it to her, to relieve the hot
pressure in her teats, it was gone. She never saw it
again.

Squint's newborn was the first to disappear immediately after birth. It was not the last. For fifteen years
the little australopithecine family continued to eat and
copulate and bear and grow old, its numbers dwindling
because the infants were taken away as soon as born.
One of the females would squat and strain and whimper
and give birth. Then they would all go to sleep, and
awaken with the little one gone. From time to time an
adult would die, or come close enough to it to lie curled
and moaning so that they knew it would not rise again.
Then too they would all go to sleep; and that adult, or

that adult's body, would be gone when they woke. There were thirty of them, then twenty, then ten—then only one. Squint was the last, a very, very old female at twenty-nine. She knew she was old. She did not know she was dying, only that there was a terrible crushing pain in her belly that made her gasp and sob. She did not know when she was dead. She only knew that that particular pain stopped, and then she was conscious of another sort of pain. Not really pain. Strangeness. Numbness. She saw, but she saw queerly flatly, queerly flickeringly, in a queerly distorted range of colors. She was not used to her new vision, and did not recognize what she saw. She tried to move her eyes and they did not move. She tried to move head, or arms, or legs, and could not because she did not have any. She remained in that condition for some considerable time.

Squint was not a preparation, in the sense that the live but exposed nervous system of a biologist's brittle star is a preparation. She was an experiment.

She was not a very great success. The attempt to preserve her identity in machine storage did not fail for the reasons that had terminated the earlier trials, with the other members of her tribe: poor match of chemistry to receptors; incomplete transfer of information; wrong coding. One by one the Heechee experimenters had met all of those problems and solved them. Her experiment failed, or succeeded only in part, for a different reason. There was not enough of an identity in the being that could be recognized as "Squint" to preserve. She was not a biography, not even a journal. She was something like a census datum, punctuated by pain and illustrated with fear.

But that was not the only experiment the Heechee had in progress.

In another section of the immense machine that orbited Earth's sun from half a light-year out, the stolen babies were beginning to thrive. They were leading lives quite different from Squint's—lives marked by automatic care, heuristic tests and programmed challenges. The Heechee recognized that, although these australopithecines were a long way from intelligent, they contained the seeds of wiser descendants. They decided to hurry the process along.

Not much development occurred in the fifteen years between the removal of the colony from its prehistoric African home and Squint's death. The Heechee were not discouraged. In fifteen years, they did not expect much. They had much longer-range plans than that.

As their plans also called for them, all of them, to be somewhere else long before any true intelligence could look out of the eyes of one of Squint's descendants, they built accordingly. They so constructed and programmed the artifact that it would last indefinitely. They arranged for it to be supplied with CHON-food from a convenient processor of cometary material, which they had already set operating to serve other of their installations, and which was potentially equally long-lived. They constructed machines to sample the skills of the descendants of the newborns from time to time, and to repeat, as often as necessary, the attempt to file their identities in machine storage for later review—if any of them ever came back to see how the experiment had gone. They would have estimated this as very improbable, in view of their other plans.

Still, their plans encompassed very many alternatives, all going simultaneously; because the object of their plans was of great concern to them. None of them might ever come back. But perhaps *someone* would.

Since Squint could not communicate, or act, in any useful way, the Heechee experimenters thriftily wiped the affective sections of her storage and kept her on the shelves only as a sort of library book, for consultation by later individuals of whatever kind they might be. (It was this that Janine was forced to consult, by reliving what Squint had lived all those hundreds of millennia before.) They left certain clues and data for use by whatever generations might be able to understand them. They tidied up behind them, as they always did. Then they went away and allowed the rest of that particular experiment, among all their experiments, to run.

For eight hundred thousand years.

* * *

"Danine," Hooay was moaning, "Danine, are you dead?"

She looked up at his face, unable at first to focus, so that he looked like a blurred, broad-faced moon with a double comet's tail wagging below. "Help me up, Hooay," she sobbed. "Take me back." Of them all, this had been the worst. She felt raped, violated, expanded, changed. Her world would never be the same again. Janine did not know the word "australopithecine," but she knew that the life she had just shared had been an animal's. Worse than an animal's, because somewhere in Squint had been the spark of the invention of thinking, and thus the unwanted capacity to fear.

Janine was exhausted and she felt older than the Oldest One. At just-turned fifteen, she was not a child any more. That account had been overdrawn. There was no more childhood left for her. At the slope-walled chamber that was her personal pen she stopped. Hooay said apprehensively, "Danine? What's wrong?"

"There is a joke to tell you," she said.

"You do not look like joking," he said.

"It is a funny joke, though. Listen. The Oldest One has penned Wan with my sister to breed them. But my sister cannot breed. She has had an operation so that she can never again bear a child."

"That is not a good joke," he protested. "No one would do a thing like that!"

"She did it, Hooay." She added quickly, "Do not be frightened. You will not be punished. Only now bring the boy to me."

His soft eyes were brimming with tears. "How can I not be frightened? Perhaps I should awaken the Oldest One to tell him—" Then the tears spilled over; he was terrified.

She comforted him and coaxed him, until other Old Ones came and he spilled his terrible joke to them. Janine lay down on her pad, closing her ears to their excited, woeful chatter. She did not sleep, but she was lying with her eyes closed when she heard Wan and Tor come to the door. When the boy was pushed inside she stood up to meet him.

"Wan," she said, "I want you to put your arms around me."

He looked at her grumpily. No one had told him what this was about, and Wan, too, had had his hour in the couch with Squint. He looked terrible. He had never really had a chance to recover from the flu, had not rested, had not accustomed himself to the great changes in his life since he had met the Herter-Halls. There were circles under his eyes and cracks at the corners of his mouth. His feet were dirty, and so were his frayed clothes. "Are you afraid you will fall down?" he shrilled.

"I am not afraid of falling, and I want you to talk to me properly. Don't squeak."

He looked startled, but his voice settled into the lower register she had tried to teach him. "Then why?"

"Oh, Wan." She shook her head impatiently and stepped forward into his personal space. It had not been necessary for her to tell him what to do. His arms went around her automatically—both at the same height, as though she were a barrel to lift, the palms pressing against her shoulderblades. She pressed her lips against his, hard, dry and closed, then pulled away. "Do you remember what this is, Wan?"

"Of course! It is 'kissing'."

"But we are doing it wrong, Wan. Wait. Do it again while I do this." She protruded the tip of her tongue between almost closed lips and ran it back and forth across his closed ones. "I think," she said, moving her head away, "that that is a better way, don't you? It makes me feel—it makes me feel—I feel a little bit as though I were going to throw up."

Alarmed, he tried to step back, but she followed him closely. "Not really throw up, just real funny."

He stayed tensely near her, face held away, but his expression was troubled. Carefully keeping the pitch of his voice down, he said, "Tiny Jim says people do this before copulating. Or one person does it sometimes to see if the other person is in heat."

"In heat, Wan! That *stinks*. Say 'in love'."

"I think that 'in love' is different," he said stubbornly, "but anyway to kiss is related to copulating. Tiny Jim says—"

She put her hands on his shoulders. "Tiny Jim isn't here."

"No, but Paul doesn't want us to—"

"Paul isn't here," she said, stroking his slim neck with the tips of her fingers to see what that felt like. "Lurvy isn't here either. Anyway, none of what they think matters." The way it felt, she decided, was quite strange. It wasn't really as though she were going to throw up, but as though some sort of liquid readjustment were going on inside her belly, a sensation like nothing she had ever known before. It was not at all unpleasant. "Let me take your clothes off, Wan, and then you can take off mine."

After they had practiced kissing again she said, "I think we should not be standing up now." And some time later, when they were lying down, she opened her eyes to stare into his wide-open ones.

As he raised himself for better leverage he hesitated. "If I do *that*," he said, "perhaps you will get pregnant."

"If you don't do *that*," she said, "I think I will die."

When Janine woke up, hours later, Wan was already awake and dressed, sitting at the side of the room, leaning against the gold-skeined wall. Janine's heart went out to him. He looked like himself fifty years later. The youthful face seemed to have lines graven by decades of trouble and pain.

"I love you, Wan," she said.

He stirred and shrilled, "Oh, yes—" Then he caught himself and dropped his voice to a grumble, "Oh, yes, Janine. And I love you. But I do not know what they will do."

"Probably they won't hurt you, Wan."

Scornfully, "Me? It is you I worry about, Janine. This is where I have lived all my life and sooner or later this would have happened. But you—I am worried about you." He added gloomily, "They are very noisy out there, too. Something is happening."

"I don't think they will hurt us—any more, I mean," Janine corrected herself, thinking about the dreaming

couch. The distant chirping cries were coming closer.
She dressed quickly and looked around, as Tor's voice
hailed Hooay outside the door.

There was nothing to show what had happened. Not
even a drop of blood. But when Tor opened the door,
fussed and worried, he stopped to squint at them suspiciously, then sniffed the air. "Perhaps I will not have
to breed you, Danine, after all," he said, kind but
frightened. "But Danine! Oowan! There is a terrible
thing! Tar has fallen asleep and the old female has run
away!"

Wan and Janine were dragged to the spindle, filled
with nearly all of the Old Ones. They were milling
around in panic. Three of them lay sprawled and snoring where they had been dumped—Tar and two others
of Lurvy's guards, failures in their missions, found
sound asleep and brought back in fear and disgrace for
the judgment of the Oldest One. Who lay motionless
but alert on his pedestal, cascades of color rippling
around his perimeter.

To the flesh-and-blood creatures the Oldest One
showed nothing of his thoughts. He was metal. He was
formidable. He could be neither understood nor chal-
lenged. Neither Wan nor Janine, nor any of his near
hundred quaking children, could perceive the fear and
anger that raced through his circulating memories. Fear
that his plans were in jeopardy. Rage that his children
had failed to carry out their orders.

The three that had failed would have to be punished,
to set an example. The hundred-odd others would also
have to be punished—somewhat more lightly, so that
the race would not become extinct—for failing to keep
the three to their duty. As for the intruders—there was
no punishment grave enough for them! Perhaps they
should be abolished, like any other challenging organism that threatened to damage its host. Perhaps worse
than that. Perhaps nothing within his powers was quite
severe enough.

But what was still in his power? He forced himself to
stand. Janine saw the ripple of lights flicker and freeze
into a pattern as the Oldest One rose to his extended

height and spoke. "The female is to be recaptured and preserved," he said. "This is to be done at once."

He stood there, wobbling uneasily; the effectors for his limbs were performing erratically. He allowed himself to kneel once more while he pondered his options. The exertion of going to the control room to set course —the turmoil in his mind that had led him to do it— half a million years of existence, all had taken their toll. He needed time to "rest"—time, that is, for his autonomic systems to retrace and repair what damage they could, and perhaps time no longer would be enough. "Do not wake me again till this is done," he said, and the lights resumed their random flicker, and slowly dwindled to darkness.

Janine, circled in Wan's arm—his body half toward the Oldest One, half sheltering her, trembling with fear —knew without being told that "preserved" meant killed. She was frightened, too.

But she was also puzzled.

The Old Ones who lay snoring through their trial and judgment had not fallen asleep by chance. Janine recognized the results of a sleep-gun. Janine knew also that none of her party had had one.

For that reason, Janine was not entirely surprised when, an hour later and back in their pen, they heard a stifled grunt from outside.

She was not surprised to see her sister run in, waving a gun and calling to them; not surprised that behind Lurvy a tattered Paul stepped over the sleeping form of Tor. She was not even surprised, or not very much surprised, to see that with them was another armed man she almost recognized. She was not sure. She had met him only when she was a child. But he looked like the person she had seen on the relayed PV broadcasts from Earth, and in jolly messages that came from him on anniversaries and holidays: Robin Broadhead.

15

Older Than the Oldest One

Not at his worst—not even when he was feeling older than the Oldest One himself and as dead as dead Payter—had Paul looked as bad as the pitiful creature waving a gun at him from the hatch of his own ship. Under the skungy, month-old beard the man's face looked like a mummy's. He stank.

"You'd better take a bath!" Paul snapped. "And put that silly gun away."

The mummy slumped against the hatch of the ship. "You're Paul Hall," it said, squinting at him. "For God's sake, do you have anything to eat?"

Paul stared past him. "Isn't there plenty still left in there?" He pushed into the ship and found that, of course, there were stacks of CHON-food packets exactly as they had been left. The mummy had been into the water bags, had ripped at least three of them open; the floor of the ship was puddled and muddied. Paul offered a ration. "Keep your voice down," he ordered. "And by the way, who are you?"

"I'm Robin Broadhead. What do you do with this?"

"Bite into it," snapped Paul, exasperated—less because of the man himself, or even because of the way he smelled, than because he was still shaking. He had been terrified that it would be an Old One he had come across so unexpectedly. But—Robin Broadhead! What was he doing here?

But he could not put the question just then. Broadhead was almost literally starving. He turned the flat pillow of food over in his hands, frowning and shaking, and then bit into a corner of it. As soon as he found it could be chewed he wolfed it down, crumbs spilling from his mouth. He stared up at Paul while he jammed his mouth full faster than his teeth could deal with it. "Take it easy," Paul said, alarmed. But he was too late. The unfamiliar food, after so long deprivation, did what could have been expected of it. Broadhead choked, gagged and vomited it up. "Damn you!" Paul snarled. "They'll smell you all the way to the spindle!"

Broadhead leaned back, gasping. "Sorry," he mumbled. "I—thought I was going to die. I pretty near did. Can you give me some water?"

Paul did, a couple of sips at a time, and then allowed the man just a corner of one of the brown and yellow packets, the blandest there was. "Slowly!" he ordered. "I'll give you more later." But he was beginning to realize how good it was to have another human being there after—what was it?—it must have been two months, at least, of his solitary skulking and hiding and plotting. "I don't know what you're doing here," he said at last, "but I'm glad to see you."

Broadhead licked the last crumbs off his lips and managed to grin. "Why, that's simple," he said, eyes avidly on the rest of the food in Paul's hands. "I came here to rescue you."

Broadhead had been dehydrated and almost asphyxiated, but not really starved. He kept down the crumbs Paul let him have and demanded more; kept that down too, and was even able to help Paul clean up the mess he had made. Paul found him clean clothes from Wan's sparse store in the ship—the garments were too long and too slim by far, but the waistband of the kilt did not really need to close all the way—and led him to the largest of the water troughs to get himself clean. It wasn't daintiness. It was fear. The Old Ones did not hear any better than human beings, nor see even quite as well. But their noses were astonishingly acute. After two weeks of the narrowest of escapes, in his first terrified blundering around Heechee Heaven after Wan and Lurvy had been captured, Paul had learned to bathe three times a day.

And much more.

He took post at a juncture of three corridors, mounting guard while Broadhead got the worst of his thirty days in a Heechee ship off his skin. Rescue them! In the first place, it wasn't true—Broadhead's intentions were more subtle and complicated than that. In the second place, Broadhead's plans were not the same as those Paul had been maturing for two months. He had some notion of tricking information out of the Dead Men and only the haziest notion of what to do with the information when he got it. And he expected Paul to help him carry two or three metric tons of machinery around Heechee Heaven, never mind the risk, never mind that Paul might have ideas of his own. The trouble with being rescued was that the rescuers expected to be in charge of the operation. And expected Paul to be grateful!

Well, he admitted to himself, turning slowly to keep each corridor in view—though the Old Ones were less diligent in patrolling than they had been at first—he would have been grateful enough if Broadhead had showed up at first, in those days of panic when he ran and hid and did not dare either stay or leave; or again, a couple of weeks later, when he had begun to work out a plan, had dared to go to the Dead Men's room and make contact with the Food Factory—and learned that Peter Herter was dead. The shipboard computer was no use to him, too stupid and too overburdened even to relay his messages to Earth. The Dead Men were maddeningly— Were maddening. He was entirely on his own. And slowly his nerve came back and he began to plan. Even to act. When he found that he could dare coming quite near the Old Ones provided he bathed enough to leave no odor trace, he began his plan. Spying. Scheming. Studying. Recording—that was one of the hardest parts. It is very difficult to keep records of how your enemy behaves, what paths are frequented and on what occasions none of them are likely to be about, when you have nothing to write with. Or a watch. Or even the change of day and night, unheard of in the steady blue glow from the Heechee-metal walls. It had finally occurred to him to use the habits of the Old Ones themselves as his chronometer of their behavior. When he saw a party of them going back toward the spindle where the Oldest One lay motionless, they were getting ready to sleep. When he saw a party moving away, it meant the beginning of a new day. They all slept at once, or almost all, out of some imperative he could not imagine; and so there were times when he dared come nearer and nearer to the place where Wan, Janine and Lurvy were kept. Had even seen them once or twice, daring to hide behind a berryfruit bush as the Old Ones were beginning to stir, peering between the branches and then racing breathless away. He knew. He had it all worked out. There were no more than a hundred or so of the Old Ones, and they traveled usually in parties of only two or three.

Remained the question of how to deal with, even, a party of two or three.

Paul Hall, leaner and angrier than he had ever been in his life, thought he knew how to do that. In his first panicked days of flight and hiding, after the others had been captured, he had blundered far and far into the green and red corridors of Heechee Heaven. In some of them even the lights were fading and sparse. In some of them the air had a sour and unhealthful tang, and when he slept there he awoke with his head pounding and thick. In all of them there were objects, machines, gadgets—things; some of them still purring or ticking quietly to themselves, some flickering with a ceaseless rainbow of lights.

He could not stay in those places, because there was no food or water, and he could not find what he most sought. There were no real weapons. Perhaps the Heechee had not needed them. But there was one machine that had a gate of metal strips at one side and, when he wrenched them away, it did not blow up or electrocute him, as he had half thought it would. And he had a spear. And half a dozen times he encountered what looked like smaller, more complicated versions of the Heechee tunnelers.

And some of them still worked. When the Heechee built they built forever.

It took Paul three frightened, thirsty, baffling days of experiment to make any of them function, stopping to creep back to the gold corridors or the ship for food and water, always sure that the thundering noise of the machine would draw the Old Ones down on him before he was ready. But it did not. He learned to squeeze the nipple that hung down from the steering yoke to make the ready lights spring into life, to shove the ponderous knurled wheel forward or back to make it advance or retreat, to tread on the oval floorplate that caused the blue-violet glow to lance out before the machine, softening even the Heechee metal it touched. That was the noisy part. Paul feared greatly that he would destroy something that would wreck Heechee Heaven itself, if he did not bring down a search party. When he came to move the machine to the place he had picked out it was almost quiet, oozing forward on its rollogons. And he stopped to consider.

He knew where the Old Ones went, and when.

He had a spear that could kill a single Old One, maybe could let him defeat even two or three if he came on them by surprise.

He possessed a machine that could annihilate any number of Old Ones, if he could only get them to mass in front of it.

It all added up to a strategy that might even work. It

was chancy—oh, God, it was chancy! It depended on at least half a dozen trials by combat. Even though the Old Ones did not seem to seek him armed, who was to say that they might not learn? And what arms might they have? It meant killing some of them, one by one, so expertly and carefully that he did not attract the attention of the whole tribe until he was ready for it—and then attracting them all at once, or so large a majority of them that he could handle the rest with his spear. (Was that really a good gambling bet?) And, above all, it meant that the Oldest One, the great machine Paul had only glimpsed once or twice at long range and about whose powers he knew nothing, must not intervene, and how likely was that?

He had no sure answers. He did have hopes. The Oldest One was too large to move easily through any of the corridors but the gold-skeined ones. Nor did it seem to move frequently at all. And perhaps he could somehow trick it, too, before the devouring haze of the tunneling machine—which could not, in this place, really be a tunneling machine, but seemed to work in about the same way. At every step the odds were against him, true.

But at every step there was at least a slim chance for success. And it was not the risk that stopped him at the last.

The Paul Hall who stole about and schemed in the tunnels of Heechee Heaven, half crazed with anger and fear and worry for his wife and the others, was not entirely crazy. He was the same Paul Hall whose gentleness and patience had made Dorema Herter marry him, who had accepted her saucy, sometimes bratty little sister and abrasive father as part of the bargain. He wanted very much to save them and bring them to freedom. Even at risk. There was always a way out of the risk for him, if only to crawl aboard Wan's ship and return to the Food Factory and thus—slowly, alone and mournful, but safe—ultimately to Earth and wealth.

But, apart from risk, what was the cost?

The cost was wiping out perhaps an entire population of living and intelligent creatures. They had taken his wife from him, but they had not really harmed her. And, try as he would, Paul could not convince himself he had the right to exterminate them.

And now here was this "rescuer," this nearly dead castaway named Robin Broadhead, who listened sketchily to Paul's plan and smiled loftily and said, politely enough, "You're still working for me, Hall. We'll do it my way."

"The hell we will!"

Broadhead stayed polite enough, and even reasonable—it was amazing what a bath and a little food had done for him. "The key," he said, "is to find out what we're up against. Help me lug this information-processing stuff to where the Dead Men are, and we'll take care of that. That's the first thing."

"The first thing is rescuing my wife!"

"But why, Hall? She's all right where she is—you said so yourself. I'm not talking about forever. One day, maybe. We find out what we can from the Dead Men. We tape it all, pump them dry if we can. Then we take the tapes and stick them in my ship, and then—"

"No."

"Yes!"

"No, and keep your God-damned voice down!" They squared off like kids in a schoolyard, both flushed and furious, their eyes locked. Until Robin Broadhead grimaced and shook his head and said, "Oh, hell. Paul? Are you thinking what I'm thinking?"

Paul Hall let himself relax. After a second he said, "Actually, I'm thinking the two of us would do better to figure out what is the best thing to do, instead of arguing about who makes the decision."

Broadhead grinned. "That was what I was thinking, all right. You know what my trouble is? I'm so surprised to be still alive that I don't know how to adjust to it."

It only took them six hours to haul and set up the PMAL-2 processor where they wanted it, but it was six hours of hard work. They were both near the frayed end of exhaustion and it would have made sense to sleep, but they were itching with impatience, both of them. Once they had the main power source connected to the program banks Albert's prerecorded voice instructed them, step by step, on how to do the rest—the processor itself sprawled across the corridor, the voice terminals inside the Dead Men's chamber, next to the radio link. Robin looked at Paul, Paul shrugged to Robin, Robin started the program. From just outside the door they could hear the flat, wheedling voice from the terminal: "Henrietta? Henrietta, dear, can you answer me?"

Pause. No answer. The program Albert had written with Sigfrid von Shrink's help tried again: "Henrietta, it's Tom. Please speak to me." It would have been faster to punch out Henrietta's code to attract her attention, but harder to square with the pretense that her long-lost husband had reached her from some far-off outpost by radio.

The voice tried again, and once more. Paul scowled and whispered, "It isn't working."

"Give it a chance," Robin said, but not confidently. They stood there nervously, while the dead computer voice pleaded. And then at last, a hesitant voice whispered, "Tom? Tomasino, is that you?"

Paul Hall was a normal human being, squashed a little out of shape, perhaps, from four years of imprisonment and a hundred days of flight and fright. Normal enough, though, to share the normal prurience; but what he heard was more than he wanted to hear. He grinned in embarrassment at Robin Broadhead, who shrugged uneasily back. The hurt tenderness and spiteful jealousy of other people is humiliating to hear and can only be eased by laughter; the divorce detective passes around his bootleg tape of a wired bed for comic relief on a slow day at the office. But this was not comic! Henrietta, any Henrietta, even the machine revenant called Henrietta was not funny in her moment of heart's-desire, when she was being gulled and betrayed. The program that wooed her was skillfully done. It apologized and begged, and it even sobbed, in rustly tape-hissing sobs, when Henrietta's own flat tape voice broke with sobs of spent sadness and hopeless joy. And then, as it had been programmed to do, it settled in for the kill. Would you— Dear Henrietta, could you— Is it possible for you to tell me how to operate a Heechee ship?

Pause. Hesitation. Then the voice of the dead woman said: "Why—yes, Tomasino." Another pause. It lengthened itself, until the programmed deceiver moved in to fill the gap:

"Because if you could, dear, I think I might be able to join you. I'm in a sort of a ship. It has a control room. If I knew how to work it—"

It was incredible to Paul that even a poorly stored machine intelligence could succumb to such transparent blandishments. Succumb Henrietta did. It was repellent to him to take part in the fraud, but take part he did, and once started Henrietta could not be stopped. The secret of controlling the Heechee ships? Of course, dear Tomasino! And the dead woman warned her fake lover to stand by for burst transmission and hurled out a whistling crackle of machine talk of which Paul could not understand a sound and in which he could not find a word; but Robin Broadhead, listening to the private status-report voice of the computer on his headset, grinned and nodded and held up thumb and forefinger in a circle of success. Paul signed silence and pulled him down the corridor. "If you've got it," he whispered, "let's get out of here!"

"Oh, I've got it!" chortled Robin. "She's got it all! She was in open circuit with whatever kind of machine runs this thing, it picked her brains and she picked its, and she's telling the whole thing."

"Great. Now let's find Lurvy!"

Broadhead looked at him, not angry but pleading. "Just a few more minutes. Who knows what else she's got?"

"No!"

"Yes!"—and then they looked at each other, and shook their heads. "Compromise," said Robin Broad-

head. "Fifteen minutes, all right? And then we go rescue your wife."

They edged back along the corridor with smiles of
rueful satisfaction on their faces; but the satisfaction
drained. The voices were not embarrassingly intimate
now. They were worse. They were almost quarreling.
There was somehow a snap and a snarl in the flat metallic voice that said, "You're being a pig, Tom."

The program was cloyingly reasonable: "But, Henrietta, dear, I'm only trying to find out—"

"What you try to find out," grated the voice, "depends on what your capacities to learn are. I'm trying to
tell you something more important! I tried to tell you
before. I tried to tell you all the while we were coming out here, but, no, you didn't want to hear, all you
wanted was to get off in the lander with that fat
bitch—"

The program knew when to be placatory. "I'm sorry,
Henrietta, dear. If you want me to learn some astrophysics I will."

"Damn right you will!" Pause. "It's terribly important, Tom!" Pause. And then: "We go back to the Big
Bang. Are you listening, Tom?"

"Of course I am, dear," said the program in its hum-
blest and most endearing way.

"All right! It goes back to how the universe got
started, and we know that pretty well—with one little
hazy transition point that's a little obscure. Call it Point
X."

"Are you going to tell me what 'Point X' is, dear?"

"Shut up, Tom! Listen! Before Point X, essentially
the whole universe was packed into a tiny glob, no
more than a matter of kilometers through, super-dense,
super hot, so squeezed it had no structure. Then it exploded. It began to expand—up to Point X, and that
part is pretty clear. Do you follow me so far, Tom?"

"Yes, dear. That's basically simple cosmology, isn't
it?"

Pause. "Just pay attention," Henrietta's voice said at
last. "Then, after Point X, it continued to expand. As it
expanded, little bits of 'matter' began to condense out

of it. First came nuclear particles, hadrons and pions, electrons and protons, neutrons and quarks. Then 'real' matter. Real hydrogen atoms, then even helium atoms. The exploding volume of gas began to slow. Turbulence broke it into immense clouds. Gravity pulled the clouds into clumps. As they shrank the heat of contraction set nuclear reactions going. They glowed. The first stars were born. The rest," she finished, "is what we can see going on now."

The program picked up its cue. "I see that, Henrietta, yes. How long are we talking about, now?"

"Ah, good question," she said, in a voice not at all complimentary. "From the beginning of the Big Bang to Point X, three seconds. From Point X to right now, about eighteen billion years. And there we have it."

The program was not written to deal with sarcasm, but even in the flat metal voice sarcasm hung. It did its best. "Thank you, dear," it said, "and now will you tell me what is special about Point X?"

"I would tell you in a thick minute, my darling Tomasino," she said sunnily, "except that you are not my darling Tomasino. That ass-head would not have understood one word of what I just said, and I don't like being lied to."

And no matter what the program tried, not even when Robin Broadhead dropped the pretense and spoke to her direct, Henrietta would say no more. "Hell with it," said Broadhead at last. "We've got enough to worry about in the next couple of hours. We don't have to go back eighteen billion years for it."

He hit a pressure release on the side of the processor and caught what came out: the thick, soft rag-flop tape that had caught everything Henrietta had said. He waved it aloft. "That's what I came for," he said, grinning. "And now, Paul, let's take care of your little problem—and then go home and spend our millions!"

In the deep, restless sleep of the Oldest One there were no dreams, but there were irritations.

The irritations came faster and faster, more and more urgent. From the time the first Gateway prospectors had terrifyingly come until he had written (he thought) the last of them off, only the wink of an eye— not more than a few years, really. And until the strangers and the boy were caught, hardly a heartbeat; and until he was awakened again to be told the female had escaped no time at all—none! Hardly even time for him to decouple sensors and effectors and settle down; and now there was still no peace. The children were panicked and quarrelsome. It was not their noise alone that disturbed him. Noise could not awaken the Oldest One; only physical attack, or being addressed directly. What was most irritating about this racket was that it was not quite addressed to him, but not quite not, either. It was a debate—an argument; a few frightened voices demanding he be told something at once, a few even more frightened ones pleading against it.

And that was incorrect. For half a million years the Oldest One had trained his children in manners. If he was needed, he was to be addressed. He was not to be awakened for trivial causes, and certainly not by accident. Especially now. Especially when each effort of waking was more of a drain on his ancient fabric and the time was in sight when he might not wake at all.

The fretful rumpus did not stop.

The Oldest One called on his external sensors and gazed upon his children. Why were so few of them there? Why were nearly half of them sprawled on the floor, evidently asleep?

Painfully he activated his communications system and spoke: "What is happening?"

When, quailing, they tried to answer and the Oldest One understood what they were saying, the bands of color on his shell raced and blurred. The female not recaptured. The younger female and the boy gone too. Twenty more of the children found hopelessly asleep, and scores of others, gone to search the artifact, not reporting back.

Something was terribly wrong.

Even at the very end of its useful life the Oldest One was a superb machine. There were resources seldom used, powers not tapped for hundreds of thousands of years. He rose on his rollogons to tower over the quaking children and reached down into his deepest and least-used memories for guidance and knowledge. On his foreplate, between the external vision receptors, two polished blue knobs began a faint drone, and atop his carapace a shallow dish glowed with faint violet light. It had been thousands of years since the Oldest One had used any of his more punitive effectors, but as information from the great stores of memories gathered he began to believe that it was time to use them again. He reached into the stored personalities, even, and Henrietta was open to him; he knew what she had said, and what the new interlopers had asked. He understood (what Henrietta had not) the meaning of the hand weapons Robin Broadhead had been waving around; in the deepest of all memories, the ones that went back even before his own flesh-and-blood life, there was the lance that made his own ancestors go to sleep, and this was clearly much the same.

Here was trouble on a scale he had never known before, of a kind he could not readily cope with. If he could get at them— But he could not. His great bulk could not travel through the artifact's passages, except the gold-skeined ones; the weapons that were ready to destroy would have no targets. The children? Yes, perhaps. Perhaps they could hunt out and overcome the others; certainly it was worth the effort to order them to do so, the few survivors, and he did. But in the rational, mechanical mind of the Oldest One the capacity for computation was unimpaired. He could read the odds well. They were not good.

The question was, was his great plan endangered?

The answer was yes. But there, at least, there was something he could do. The heart of the plan was the place where the artifact was controlled. It was the nerve center of the entire construct; it was where he had dared to set in motion the final stages of his plan.

Before he had finished framing the decision he was acting it out. The great metal bulk shifted and turned, and then rolled out across the spindle, into the wide-mouthed tunnel that led to the controls. Once there, he

was secure. Let them come if they chose! The weap-
onry was ready. Its great drain on his dwindling powers
was making him slow and unsteady to move, but there
was power enough. He could blockade himself and let
the flesh-and-blood things settle things however they
might, and then—

He stopped. Ahead of him one of the wall-aligning
machines was out of place. It sat squarely in the center
of the corridor, and behind it—

If he had been just a trifle less drained, the fraction
of a second faster. . . . But he was not. The glow from
the wall aligner washed over him. He was blind. He was
deaf. He felt the external protuberances burn off his
shell, felt the great soft cylinders he rolled on melt and
stick.

The Oldest One did not know how to feel pain. He
did know how to feel anguish of the soul. He had failed.

The flesh-and-blood things had control of his artifacts, and his plans were at an end forever.

16

The Richest Person There Is

My name is Robin Broadhead, and I am the richest person there is in the whole solar system. The only one who comes close is old Bover, and he would come a lot closer if he hadn't thrown half of his money into slum clearance and urban rehabilitation and a lot of what was left into an inch-by-inch scan of trans-Plutonian space, looking for the ship with what was left of his wife, Trish. (What he is going to do with her if he finds her I can't imagine.) The surviving Herter-Halls are also filthy with money. That's a good thing, especially for Wan and Janine, who have a complicated relationship to sort out, in a complicatedly unwelcoming world. My wife, Essie, is in the best of health. I love her. When I die, that is, when even Full Medical can't patch me up any more, I have a little plan about how to deal with someone else I love, and that satisfies me. Almost everything satisfies me. The only exception is my science advisor, Albert, who keeps trying to explain Mach's Principle to me.

When we took over Heechee Heaven, we got it all. The way to control Heechee ships. The way to *build* Heechee ships, including the theory that makes it possible to go faster than light. No, it doesn't involve "hyperspace" or the "fourth dimension". It is very simple. Acceleration multiplies mass, so says Einstein—the real one, not Albert. But if the rest mass is zero it does not matter how many times you multiply it. It remains zero. Albert says that mass can be created, and proves it by basic logical principles: it exists, therefore it can be created. Therefore it can be eliminated, since what can be made to be can also be made to stop being. That is the Heechee secret, and with Albert's help to set up the experiment, and Morton's help to coerce the Gateway Corp into making ships available, we tried it out. It didn't cost me a cent; one of the advantages of great wealth is that you don't have to spend it. All you have to do is get other people to spend it for you, and that's what law programs are for.

So we sent two Fives out at once from Gateway. One was on lander power only, and it contained two people and a cylinder of solid aluminum with strain detectors attached. The other held a full crew, ready for an actual mission. The instrument ship had a live camera pickup with an image split three ways: one on the gravity meter, one on the second ship, one on a cesium-atom digital clock.

To my eyes the experiment didn't show a thing. The second ship began to disappear, and the gravity meter recorded its disappearance. Big deal! But Albert was elated. "Its mass began to disappear before it did, Robin! My God. Anyone could have tried that experiment any time in the last dozen years! There's going to be at least a ten-million-dollar science bonus for this!"

"Put it in petty cash," I said, and stretched, and rolled over to kiss Essie, because we happened to be in bed at the time.

"Is very interesting, dear Robin," she said drowsily, and kissed me back. Albert grinned and averted his eyes, partly because Essie has been tinkering with his program and partly because he knew as well as I did that what she said was politely untrue. Astrophysics did not much interest my Essie. What interested her was the chance to play with working Heechee machine intelligences, and that interested her very much. Eighteen hours a day much, until she had tracked down all the major systems in what was left of the Oldest One, and the Dead Men, and the Dead Non-Men whose memories went back to an African savannah the better part of a million years ago. Not that she cared a lot about what was in the memories; but *how* it was there was her very business, at which she was very good. Reshuffling my Albert program was the least of what Essie got out of Heechee Heaven. What we all got was a very great deal indeed. The grand charts of the Galaxy, showing everywhere the Heechee had been. The grand charts of black holes, showing where they are now. Even where Klara is. As one tiny fringe benefit, I even got the answer to one question that on a purely subjective level had been interesting me very much: why was I still alive? The ship that carried me to Heechee Heaven had flipped over into deceleration mode after nineteen days. By all the laws of parity and common sense, that meant it would not arrive for another nineteen, by which time I should have been surely dead; but in fact it docked in five. And I wasn't dead at all, or not quite; but why?

Albert gave me the answer. Every flight ever successfully completed in a Heechee ship had been between two bodies that, relatively, were more or less at rest—a few tens or at most a few hundreds of kilometers a second difference in their relative velocities. No more. Not enough to make a difference. But my flight had been pursuing an object itself in very rapid motion. It had been almost all acceleration. The slowdown had taken only a tiny fraction of the speedup. And so I lived.

And all that was very satisfying, and yet—

And yet there is always a price.

There always has been. Every big jump forward has

carried a hidden cost, all through history. Man invented agriculture. That meant someone had to plant de cotton and someone had to hoe de corn. And dat's how slavery was born. Man invented the automobile, and got a dividend of pollution and highway death. Man got curious about the way the sun shines, and out of his curiosity came the H-bomb. Man found the Heechee artifacts and tracked down some of their secrets. And what did we get? For one thing, we got Payter, almost killing a world, with a power no one had ever had before him. For another we got some brand-new questions, the answers to which I have not yet quite nerved myself up to face. Questions that Albert wants to try to answer, about Mach's Principle; and that Henrietta raised, with her talk about Point X and the "missing mass". And a very big question in my own mind. When the Oldest One broke Heechee Heaven out of its orbit and sent it flying through space toward the core of the Galaxy what, exactly, was he heading toward?

The scariest, I guess, and also the most satisfying, I know, moment of my life was when we had burned the feelers off the Oldest One and, armed with Henrietta's instructions, sat down before the control board of Heechee Heaven. It took two to make it move. Lurvy Herter-Hall and I were the two most experienced pilots present—if you didn't count Wan, who was off with Janine, rounding up the waking Old Ones to tell them there had been a change in government. Lurvy took the right-hand seat and I took the left (wondering a lot just what strange-shaped butt had first sat in it). And there we went. It took more than a month to get back to orbiting the Moon, which was the point I had picked out. It wasn't a wasted month, there was plenty to do on Heechee Heaven; but it went pretty slowly, because I was in a very big hurry to get home.

It took all the nerve I had to squeeze that teat, but, you know, it wasn't all that hard. Once we understood that the main bank of controls carried the codes for all the preset objectives—there are more than fifteen thousand of them, all over the Galaxy and some outside—it was just a matter of knowing which code was which. Then, all of us really delighted with ourselves, we decided to show off. We got a squawk from the radio-astronomers on the far side because our circumlunar orbit was getting in the way of their dishes every time we came around. So we moved. You do that with the secondary boards, the ones no one has ever dared to touch in midflight and that don't seem to do much on the original launch. Main boards, preprogrammed objectives; secondary boards, any point you want, provided you can spell out its galactic coordinates. But the joker is that you can't use the secondary boards until you've nulled the primaries by setting them all down to zero—that translates to a clear deep red color on each —and if any prospector ever happened to do that on his own, he lost his programming to get back to Gateway. How simple everything is once you know. And so we put that big son-of-a-bitching artifact, half a million metric tons of it, in close Earth orbit, and invited company.

The company I wanted most was my wife. What I wanted next was my science program, Albert Einstein —that's not really a reflection on Essie, you know, because she wrote him. It was a tossup whether I went down to her or she came up to me, but not in her mind. She wanted to get her hands on the machine intelligences in Heechee Heaven, I would judge, at least as much as I wanted to get mine on her. In a 100-minute Earth orbit the transmission time isn't bad, anyway. As soon as we were in range the machine Albert had programmed for me was talking to him, pumping everything it had learned into him, and by the time I was ready to talk to him he was ready to talk back.

Of course it wasn't the same. Albert in full three-dimensional color in the tank at home was a lot more fun to chat with than black-and-white Albert on a flat plate in Heechee Heaven. But until some new equipment came up from Earth that was all I had, and anyway it was the same Albert. "Good to see you again, Robin," he said benevolently, poking the stem of his pipe toward me. "I guess you know you have about a million messages waiting for you?"

"They'll wait." Anyway, I had already had about a million, or it seemed that way. What they mostly said was that everybody was annoyed but, in the long run, delighted; and I was once again very rich. "What I want to hear first," I said, "is what you want to tell me."

"Sure thing, Robin." He tapped out his pipe, regarding me. "Well," he said, "technology first. We know the general theory of the Heechee drive, and we're getting a handle on the faster-than-light radio. As to the information-handling circuits in the Dead Men and so on— as I am sure you know," he twinkled, "Gospozha Lavorovna-Broadhead is on her way to join you. I think we may confidently expect considerable progress there, very quickly. In a few days a volunteer crew will go to the Food Factory. We are pretty sure it, too, can be controlled, and if so it will be brought into some nearby orbit for study and, I think I can promise, duplication. I don't suppose you want to hear about minor technology in detail just now?"

"Not really," I said. "Or not right at this minute."

"Then," he said, nodding as he filled the pipe again, "let me get to some theoretical considerations. First there is the question of black holes. We have unequivocally located the one your friend, Gelle-Klara Moynlin, is in. I believe it would be possible to send a ship there with reasonable assurance that it would arrive without serious damage. Return, however, is another question. There appears to be nothing in the Heechee stores that gives us a cookbook recipe for getting anything out of a black hole. Theory, yes. But if one should desire to convert the theory into practice that will require R&D. A lot of it. I would hesitate to promise results in less than, say, a matter of years. More likely decades. I know," he said, leaning forward earnestly, "that this is a matter of personal importance to you, Robin. It also may be a matter of grave importance to all of us, by which I mean not only the human race but machine intelligences as well." I had never seen him look so serious. "You see," he said, "the destination of the artifact, Heechee Heaven, has also been unequivocally identified. May I show you a picture?"

That was rhetoric, of course. I didn't reply, and he didn't wait. He shrank down into a corner of the flat-plate screen while the main picture appeared. It was a wash of white, shaped like a very amateurishly drawn Turkish crescent. It was not symmetrical. The crescent was off to one side, and the rest of the picture was black except for an irregular sprinkle of light that completed the horns of the crescent and protracted them into a hazy ellipse.

"It is too bad you cannot see this in color, Robin," said Albert, squinting up from his corner of the screen. "It is blue rather than white. Shall I tell you what you are seeing? It is orbiting matter around some very large object. The matter to your left, which is coming toward us, travels fast enough to emit light. The matter to the right, which is going away, travels more slowly relative to us. What we are seeing is matter turning into radiation as it is drawn into an extremely large black hole, which is located at the center of our Galaxy."

"I thought the speed of light was not relative!" I snapped.

He expanded to fill the screen again. "It is not, Robin, but the orbit velocity of the matter which produces it is. That picture is from the Gateway file, and until just recently it was not located in space. But now it is clear that it is at, indeed that in a sense it forms, the galactic core."

He paused while he lit his pipe, looking at me steadily. Well, that's not quite true. There was the split-second lag, and even Albert's circuits couldn't do anything about it; if I moved his gaze lingered where I had been for just long enough to be disconcerting. I didn't rush him, and when he had finished puffing the pipe alight he said:

"Robin, I am often unsure of what information to volunteer to you. If you ask me a question, that's different. About any subject you suggest, I will tell you as much of what I know as you will listen to. I will also tell you what *may* be so, if you ask for a hypothesis;

and I will volunteer hypotheses when, according to the constraints written into my program, that seems appropriate. Gospozha Lavorovna-Broadhead has written quite complex normative instructions for this sort of decision-making, but, to simplify, they come down to an equation. Let V represent the 'value' of a hypothesis. Let P represent its probability of being true. If I can complete the sum of VP so that it equals at least one, then I should, and do, volunteer the hypothesis. But, oh, Robin, how hard it is to assign the correct numerical values to P and V! In the specific case now at issue I cannot be in any way sure of any value I can give its probability. But its importance is very high. To all intents, it might as well be regarded as infinite."

By then he had me sweating. What I know for sure about Albert's programming is that the longer he takes to tell me something, the less he thinks I am going to like hearing it. "Albert," I said, "get the hell on with it."

"Sure thing, Robin," he said, nodding, but unwilling to be rushed, "but let me first say that this conjecture satisfies not only known astrophysics, although on a rather complex level, but also some other questions, e.g., where Heechee Heaven was going when you turned it around and why the Heechee themselves disappeared. Before I can give you the conjecture I must review four main points, as follows.

"One. The quantities Tiny Jim referred to as 'gosh numbers'. These are numerical quantities, mostly of the sort called 'dimensionless' because they are the same in any units you measure. The mass ratio between the electron and the proton. The Dirac number to express the difference between electromagnetic and gravitational force. The Eddington fine-structure constant. And so forth. We know these numbers to great precision. What we do not know is *why* they are what they are. Why shouldn't the fine-structure constant be, say, 150 instead of 137-plus? If we understood astrophysics —if we had a complete theory—we should be able to deduce these numbers from the theory. We do have a good theory, but we can't deduce the gosh numbers from it. Why? Is it possible," he asked gravely, "that these numbers are in some way *accidental?*"

He paused, puffing on his pipe, and then held up two fingers. "Two. Mach's Principle. This also turns out to be a question, but perhaps a somewhat easier one. My late predecessor," he said, twinkling a little—I think to reassure me that this was, indeed, easier to handle— "my late predecessor gave us the theory of relativity, which is commonly understood to mean that everything is relative to something else excepting only the velocity of light. When you are at home on Tappan Sea, Robin, you weigh about eighty-five kilograms. That is to say, that is a measure of how much you and the planet Earth attract each other; it is your weight, in a sense, relative to the Earth. We also have a quality called 'mass'. The best measure of 'mass' is the force necessary to accelerate an object, say you, from a state of rest. We usually consider 'mass' and 'weight' to be about the same, and on the surface of the Earth they are, but mass is supposed to be an *intrinsic* quality of matter, while weight is always relative to something else. But," he twinkled again, "let's do a gedanke-experiment, Robin. Let's suppose that you're the only thing in the universe. There's no other matter. What would you weigh? Nothing. What would your mass be? Ah, that's the question. Let's suppose you have a little rocket-belt and you decided to accelerate yourself. You then measure the acceleration and compute the force to move you, and you come out with your mass—do you? No, Robin, you do not. Because there is nothing to measure movement against! 'Moving', as a concept, is meaningless. So mass itself—according to Mach's Principle—depends on *some* external system, Mach thought it might be what he called 'the entire background of the universe', to be meaningful. And according to Mach's Principle, as my predecessor and others extended it, so do all the other 'intrinsic' characteristics of matter, energy and space . . . including the 'gosh numbers'. Robin, am I wearying you?"

"You bet your ass you are, Albert," I snarled, "but go ahead!"

He smiled and held up three fingers. "Three. What Henrietta called 'Point X'. As you remember, Henrietta failed her doctoral defense, but I have made a study of her dissertation and I am able to say what she meant by it. For the first three seconds after the Big Bang, which is to say the beginning of the universe as we now know it, the entire universe was relatively compact, exceedingly hot, and entirely symmetrical. Henrietta's dissertation quoted at length from an old Cambridge mathematician named Tong B. Tang and others; the point they made was that *after* that time, after what Henrietta called 'Point X', the symmetry became 'frozen'. All the constants we now observe became fixed at that point. All the gosh numbers. They did not exist before 'Point X'. They have existed, and are unchangeable, ever since.

"So at Point X in time, three seconds after the beginning of the Big Bang, something happened. It may have been some quite random event—some turbulence in the exploding cloud.

"Or it may have been deliberate."

He stopped and smoked for a while, watching me. When I did not react he sighed and held up four fingers. "Four, Robin, and the last. I do apologize for this long preamble. The final point in Henrietta's conjecture had to do with 'missing mass'. There simply does not appear to be enough mass in the universe to fit the otherwise very successful theories of the Big Bang. Here Henrietta made an immense leap in her doctoral dissertation. She suggested that the Heechee had learned how to create mass and destroy it—and in this, as we now know, she was correct, although it was only a guess on her part, and the seniors before whom she conducted the defense of her dissertation were very quick to challenge it. She then made a further leap. She suggested that the Heechee had, in fact, caused some mass to disappear. Not on a ship, although if she had guessed that she would have been correct. On a very large scale. On a universe-wide scale, in fact. She conjectured that they had studied the 'gosh numbers' as we have, and come to certain conclusions which seem to be true. Here, Robin, it gets a little tricky, so pay close attention—but we are almost home.

"You see, these fundamental constants like the 'gosh numbers' determine whether or not life can exist in the universe. Among very many other things, to be sure. But if some of them were a little higher or a little lower, life could not exist. Do you see the logical consequence of that statement? Yes, I think you do. It is a simple syllogism. Major premise, the 'gosh numbers' are not fixed by natural law but could have been different if certain different events had taken place at 'Point X'. Minor premise, if they were different in certain directions, the universe would be less hospitable to life. Conclusion? Ah, that's the heart of it. Conclusion: If they were different in certain *other* directions, the universe might be *more* hospitable to life."

And he stopped talking, and sat regarding me, reaching down into a carpet slipper with one hand to scratch the sole of his foot.

I don't know which of us would have outwaited the other then. I was trying to digest a lot of very indigestible ideas, and old Albert, he was determined to give me time to digest them. Before either of those could happen Paul Hall came trotting into the cubicle I had made my own yelling, "Company! Hey, Robin! We've got visitors!"

Well, my first thought was Essie, of course; we'd talked; I knew she was on her way to the Kennedy launchport at least, even if not actually waiting there for our orbit to settle down and get off. I stared at Paul and then at my watch. "There hasn't been time," I said, because there hadn't.

He was grinning. "Come and see the poor bastards," he chortled.

And that's what they were, all right. Six of them, crammed into a Five. Launched from Gateway less than twenty-four hours after I had taken off from the Moon, carrying enough armament to wipe out a whole division of Oldest Ones, ready to save and profit. They had flown all the way out after Heechee Heaven, reversed course and flown all the way back. Somewhere en route we must have passed them without knowing it. Poor bastards! But they were pretty decent guys, volunteers, taking off on a mission that must have seemed insecure even by Gateway standards. I promised them that they would get a share of the profits—there was plenty to go around. It wasn't their fault that we didn't need them, especially considering how much we might have needed them if we had.

So we made them welcome. Janine proudly showed them around. Wan, grinning and waving his sleep-gun around, introduced them to the gentle Old Ones, placid in the face of this new invasion. And by the time all that settled down I realized that what I needed most was food and sleep, and I took both.

When I woke up the first news I got was that Essie was on her way, but not due for a while yet. I fidgeted around for a while, trying to remember everything Albert had said, trying to make a mental picture of the Big Bang and that critical third-second instant when everything got frozen . . . and not really succeeding. So I called Albert again and said, "More hospitable how?"

"Ah, Robin," he said—nothing ever takes him by surprise—"that's a question I can't answer. We don't even know what all the Machian features of the universe are, but maybe— Maybe," he said, showing by the crinkle at the corners of his eyes that he was only guessing to humor me, "maybe immortality? Maybe a faster synaptic speed of an organic brain, *i.e.*, higher intelligence? Maybe only more planets that are suitable for life to evolve? Any of the above. Or all of them. The important thing is that we can theorize that such 'more hospitable' features could exist, and that it should be possible to deduce them from a proper theoretical basis. Henrietta went that far. Then she went a little further. Suppose the Heechee (she suggested) learned a little more astrophysics than we, decided what the right features would be—and set out to produce them! How would they go about it? Well, one way would be to shrink the universe back to the primordial state, and start over again with a new Big Bang! How could that happen? If you can create and destroy mass—easy! Juggle it around. Stop the expansion. Start it contracting again. Then somehow stay outside of the point concentration, wait for it to explode again—and then, from *outside* the monobloc, do whatever had to be done to *change* the fundamental dimensionless numbers of the universe, so that a new one was born that would be—well, call it heaven."

My eyes were popping. "Is that *possible*?"

"To you or me? Now? No. Absolutely impossible. Wouldn't have a clue where to begin."

"Not to you or me, dummy! To the Heechee!"

"Ah, Robin," he said mournfully, "who can say? I don't see how, but that doesn't mean they wouldn't. I can't even guess how to manipulate the universe to make it come out right. But that might not be necessary. You have to assume they would have some way of existing, essentially, forever. That's necessary even to do it once. And if forever, why, then you could simply make random changes and see what happened, until you got the universe you wanted."

He took time to look at his cold pipe thoughtfully for a moment, and then put it in his sweatshirt pocket unlit. "That's as far as Henrietta got with her dissertation before they really fell in on her. Because then she said that the 'missing mass' might in fact prove that the Heechee had really begun to interfere with the orderly development of the universe—she said they were removing mass from the outer galaxies to make them fall back more rapidly. Perhaps, she thought, they were also adding mass at the center—if there is one. And she said that that might explain why the Heechee had run away. They started the process, she guessed, and then went off to hide somewhere, in some sort of timeless stasis, maybe like a big black hole, until it ran its course and they were ready to come out and start things over again. That's when it really hit the fan! No wonder. Can you imagine a bunch of physics professors trying to cope with something like that? They said she should try for a degree in Heechee psychology instead of astrophysics. They said she had nothing to offer but conjecture and assumption—no way to test the theory, just a guess. And they thought it was a bad one. So they refused her dissertation, and she didn't get her doctorate, and so she went off to Gateway to be a prospector and wound up where she is. Dead. And," he said thoughtfully, pulling the pipe out again, "I do actually, Robin, think she was wrong, or at least sloppy. We have very little evidence that the Heechee had any possible way of affecting matters in any galaxy but our own, and she was talking about *the entire universe*."

"But you're not sure?"

"Not a bit sure, Robin."

I yelled, "Don't you at least have a fucking *guess?*"

"Sure thing, Robin," he said gloomily, "but no more than that. Please calm yourself. See, the scale is wrong. The universe is too big, from anything we know. And the time is too short. The Heechee were here less than a million years ago, and the expansion time of the universe to date is something like twenty thousand times that long—recoil time could hardly be less. It's mathematically bad odds that they would have picked that particular time to show up."

"Show up?"

He coughed. "I left out a step, Robin. There's another guess in there, and I'm afraid it's my own. Suppose this *is* the universe the Heechee built. Suppose they somehow evolved in a less hospitable one, but didn't like it, and caused it to contract to make a new one, which is the one we're in. That doesn't fit badly, you know. They could have come out to look around, maybe found it just the way they wanted it. And now maybe the ones who did the exploring have gone back to get the rest of them."

"Albert! For Christ's sake!"

He said gently, "Robin, I wouldn't be saying these things if I could help it. It's only a conjecture. I don't think you have any idea how difficult it is for me to conjecture in this way, and I wouldn't be able to do it except for—well, here's the thing. There is one *possible* way for something to survive a contraction and a new Big Bang, and that is to be in a place where time effec-

tively stops. What kind of place is that? Why, a black
hole. A big one. One big enough so that it is not losing
mass by quantum tunneling, and therefore can survive
indefinitely. I know where there's a black hole like that,
Robin. Mass, about fifteen thousand times the sun. Location, the center of our Galaxy." He glanced at his
watch and changed expression. "If my calculations are
close, Robin," he said, "your wife should be arriving
about now."

"Einstein! The first damn thing she's going to do is
rewrite *you*!"

He twinkled. "She already has, Robin," he pointed
out, "and one of the things she has taught me to do is
to relieve tension, when appropriate, by some comical
or personally rewarding comment."

"You're telling me I ought to be all tensed up?"

"Well, not really, Robin," he said. "All this is quite
theoretical—if that much. And in terms of human life,
perhaps a long way off. But perhaps not. That black
hole in the center of our Galaxy is at least one possibility for the place where the Heechee went, and, in terms
of flight time in a Heechee ship, not all that distant.
And—I said that we had determined the objective of
the Oldest One's course? That was it, Robin. It was
heading straight for that black hole when you turned it
around."

I was tired of being on Heechee Heaven weeks before Essie was. She was having the time of her life with
the machine intelligences. But I wasn't tired of Essie, so
I stayed around until she at last admitted she had
everything she could use on rag-flop tape, and forty-
eight hours later we were back at the Tappan Sea. And
ninety minutes after that Wilma Liederman was there
with all the tools of her trade, checking Essie out to the
last crumb under her toenail. I wasn't worried. I could
see that Essie was all right, and when Wilma agreed to
stay on for a drink she admitted it. Then she wanted to
talk about the medical machine the Dead Men had used
to keep Wan in shape, all the time he was growing up,
and before she left we had set up a million-dollar re-

search and development company—with Wilma as president—to see what could be done with it, and that's how easy it was. That's how easy it all is, when everything's going your way.

Or almost everything. There was still that sort of uneasy feeling when I thought about the Heechee (if it was the Heechee) at that place at the middle of the Galaxy (if that's where they were). That is very unsettling, you know. If Albert had suggested that the Heechee were going to come out breathing fire and destruction (or just come out at all) within the next year, why, sure, I could have worried the hell out of that. If he'd said ten years or even a hundred I could have worked up pensiveness as a minimum, and probably full-scale fright. But when you come to astronomical times—well, hell! How easy is it to worry about something that might not happen for another billion years?

And yet the notion just would not go away.

It made me fidgety through dinner, after Wilma left, and when I brought in the coffee Essie was curled in front of the fireplace, very trim in her stretch pants, brushing her long hair, and she looked up at me and said, "Will probably not happen, you know, Robin."

"How can you be so sure? There are fifteen thousand Heechee targets programmed into those ships. We've checked out, what? Fewer than a hundred and fifty of them, and one of those was Heechee Heaven. Law of averages says there are a hundred others like that somewhere, and who's to say one of them isn't racing in to tell the Heechee what we're doing right now?"

"Dear Robin," she said, turning to rub her nose against my knee in a friendly way, "drink your coffee. You know nothing about statistical mathematics and, anyway, who's to say they would mean to do us harm?"

"They wouldn't have to mean to! I know what would happen, for God's sake. It's obvious. It's what happened to the Tahitians, the Tasmanians, the Eskimos, the American Indians—it's what has always happened, all through history. A people that comes up against a superior culture is destroyed. Nobody means it. They just can't survive!"

"Always, Robin?"

"Oh, come on!"

"No, mean it," she insisted. "Counterexample: What happened when Romans discovered Gauls?"

"They conquered the shit out of them, that's what!"

"True. No, nearly true. But then, a couple of hundred years later, who conquered who, Robin? The barbarians conquered Rome, Robin."

"I'm not talking about conquest! I'm talking about a racial inferiority complex. What happens to any race that lives in contact with a race smarter than they are?"

"Why, different things under different circumstances, Robin. Greeks were smarter than Romans, Robin. Romans never had a new idea in their lives, except to build with or kill people with. Romans didn't mind. They even took Greeks right into their homes, teach them all about poetry and history and science. As slaves. Dear Robin," she said, putting down her coffee cup and coming up to sit next to me, "wisdom is a kind of resource. Tell me. When you want information, who do you ask?"

I thought it over for a minute. "Well, Albert, mostly," I admitted. "I see what you're saying, but that's different. It's a computer's *job* to know more and think faster than I do, in certain ways. That's what they're for."

"Exactly, dear Robin. As far as can tell, you have not been destroyed." She rubbed her cheek against mine and then sat up straight. "You are restless," she decided. "What would you like to do?"

"What are my options?" I asked, reaching for her, but she shook her head.

"Don't mean that, anyway not this minute. Want to watch PV? I have a taped section from tonight's news, when you and Wilma were scheming, which shows your good friends visiting their ancestral home."

"The Old Ones in Africa? Saw it this afternoon." Some local promoter had thought it would be good publicity to show Olduvai Gorge to the Old Ones. He was right. The Old Ones didn't like it a lot—hated the heat, chirped grumpily at each other about the shots they had had to take, didn't care much for the air flight. But they were news. So were Paul and Lurvy, at the moment in Dortmund to arrange for a mausoleum for Lurvy's father as soon as his remains got back from the Food Factory. So was Wan, getting rich on PV appearances as The Boy from Heechee Heaven; so was Janine, having a marvelous time meeting her singing-star pen-pals at last in the flesh. So was I. We were all rich in money and fame. What they would make of it, after all, I could not guess. But what I wanted at last became clear. "Get a sweater, Essie," I said. "Let's go for a walk."

We strolled down to the edge of the icy water, holding hands. "Why, is snowing," Essie announced, peering up at the bubble seven hundred meters over our heads. Usually you can't see it very clearly, but tonight, edge-lighted from the heaters that keep snow or ice from crumbling it, it was a milky dome, broken with reflections from lights on the ground, stretching from horizon to horizon.

"Is it too cold for you?"

"Perhaps just here, near the water," she acknowledged. We climbed back up the slope to the little palm grove by the fountain and sat on a bench to watch the lights on Tappan Sea. It was comfortable there. The air never gets really cold under the bubble, but the water is the Hudson, running naked through seven or eight hundred kilometers before it hits the Palisades Dam, and every once in a while in winter chunks of sheet ice bob under the barriers and wind up rubbing against our boat dock.

"Essie," I said, "I've been thinking."

"Know that, dear Robin," she said.

"About the Oldest One. The machine."

"Oh, really?" She pulled her feet up to get them off the grass, damp from vagrant drifts from the fountain. "Very fine machine," she said. "Quite tame, since you pulled its teeth. Provided is not given external effectors, or mobility, or access to control circuits of any kind— yes, quite tame."

"What I want to know," I said, "is whether you could build one like it for a human being."

"Ah!" she said. "Hum. Yes, I think so. Would take some time and, of course, large sums of money, but yes."

"And you could store a human personality in it—after the person died, I mean? As well as the Dead Men were stored?"

"Quite a good bit better, would say. Some difficulties. Mostly biochemical, not my department." She leaned back, looking upward at the iridescent bubble overhead and said consideringly: "When I write computer program, Robin, I speak to computer, in some language or other. I tell it what it is and what it is to do. Heechee programming is not the same. Rests on direct chemical readout of brain. Old Ones brain is not chemically quite identical with yours and mine, therefore Dead Man storage is very far from perfect. But Old Ones must be much farther from actual Heechee, for whom process was first developed. Heechee managed to convert process without any apparent difficulty, therefore it can be done. Yes. When you die, dear Robin, is possible to read your brain into a machine, then put machine in Heechee ship and fly it off to Sagittarius YY black hole, where it can say hello to Gelle-Klara Moynlin and explain episode was not your fault. For this you have my guarantee, only you must not die for, say, five to eight years yet, to allow for necessary research. Will you promise that for me, please?"

There are times when something catches me so by surprise that I don't know whether to cry, or get angry, or laugh. In this case I stood up quickly and stared down at my dear wife. And then I decided which to do, and laughed. "Sometimes you startle me, Essie," I said.

"But why, Robin?" She reached out and took my hand. "Suppose it was the other way around, hey? Suppose it was I who, many years ago, had been through a very great personal tragedy. Exactly like yours, Robin. In which someone I loved very much was harmed very severely, in such a way that I could never see that person or explain to her what happened. Do you not think I would want very much to at least speak to her again, in some way, to tell her how I felt?"

I started to answer, but she stood up and put her finger on my lips. "Was rhetorical question, Robin. We both know answer. If your Klara is still alive, she will want very much to hear from you. This is beyond doubt. So," she said, "here is plan. You will die—not soon, I hope. Brain will go into machine. Maybe will make extra copy for me, you permit? But one copy flies off to black hole to look for Klara, and finds her, and says to her, 'Klara, dear, what happened could not be helped, but wish you to know I would have given life itself to save you.' And then, Robin, do you know what Klara will answer to this strange machine that appears out of nowhere, perhaps only a few hours, her time, after incident itself?"

I didn't! The whole point was that I didn't! But I didn't say so, because Essie didn't give me a chance. She said, "Then Klara will answer, 'Why, Robin dear, I know you would. Because of all men ever born you are the one whom I most trust and respect and love.' I know she would say this, Robin, because for her it would be true. As it is for me."

17

The Place Where the Heechee Went

At six o'clock on Robin Broadhead's tenth birthday, he had a party. The woman next door gave him socks, a board game and, as a sort of joke present, a book entitled *Everything We Know About the Heechee*. Their tunnels had only recently been discovered on Venus, and there was much conjecture about the location of the place where the Heechee went, their physical appearance and their purposes. The joke part of the book was that, although it contained a hundred and sixty pages, all of them were blank.

At that same time on that same day—or at any rate, at its equivalent in local time, which was a great deal different—a person was taking a turn under the stars before retiring for sleep. He was also anticipating an anniversary of a sort, but not a party. He was a long way from Robin Broadhead's birthday cake and candles, more than forty thousand light-years; and a long way from the appearance of a human being. He had a

302

name, but out of respect and because of the work he had done, he was usually called something which translates as "Captain". Over his squared-off, finely furred head the stars were extremely bright and close. When he squinted up at them they hurt his eyes, in spite of the carefully designed glass-like shell that covered the place he lived and much of his entire planet. Sullen red type-Ms, brighter than the Moon as seen from Earth. Three golden Gs. A single hot, straw-colored F, painful to look at. There were no Os or Bs in his sky. There were also no faint stars at all. Captain could identify every star he saw, because there were only ten thousand or so of them, nearly all cool and old ones, and even the dimmest clearly visible to the naked eye. And beyond those familiar thousands—well, he could not see beyond them, not from where he strolled, but he knew from his many spaceflights that past them all was the turbulent, almost invisible, blue-tinged shell that surrounded everything he and his people owned of the universe. It was a sky that would have terrified a human being. On this night, rehearsing in his mind what would happen after he woke, it almost frightened the captain.

Wide of shoulder and hip, narrow front to back, the captain waddled as he walked back to the belt that would bring him to his sleeping cocoon. It was a short trip. By his perceptions, only a few minutes. (Forty thousand light-years away Robin Broadhead ate, slept, entered junior high, smoked his first dope, broke a bone in his wrist and had it knit, and put on nearly ten kilos before the captain got off the belt.) The captain said good-night to his drowsy roommates (two of whom were, from time to time, his sexual mates as well), removed the necklaces of rank from his shoulders, unstrapped the life-support and communications unit from between his wide-spaced legs, raised the lid of his cocoon, and slipped inside. He turned over eight or ten times, covering himself with the soft, spongy, dense sleeping litter. The captain's people had come from burrowers rather than scamperers across a plain. They slept best as their prehistoric ancestors had slept. When the captain had made himself comfortable, he reached one skinny hand up through the litter to pull the top of the cocoon closed. As he had done all of his life. As all of his people had done to sleep well. As they had pulled the stars themselves over to cover them when they decided on the necessity for a very long and worrisome sleep for all of them.

The joke of Robin's birthday book was a little spoiled, because it was not quite true. Some things *were* known about the Heechee. In some ways it was evident that they were very unlike human beings, but in very significant ways—the same! In curiosity. Only curiosity could have led them to visit so many strange places, so very far apart. In technology. Heechee science was not the same as human, but it rested on the same thermodynamics, the same laws of motion, the same stretch of the mind into tininess and immensity, the nuclear particle and the universe itself. In basic chemistry of the body. They breathed quite similar air. They ate quite compatible food.

What was central to what everyone knew about the Heechee—or hoped, or guessed—was that they were not really, when you came right down to it, all that different from human beings. A few thousand years ahead, maybe, in civilization and science. Maybe not even that much. And in that what everyone guessed (or hoped) was not wrong. Less than eight hundred years passed between the time the first crude Heechee ship ventured to try mass-cancellation as a means of transport and the time when their expeditions had washed over most of the Galaxy. (In Olduvai Gorge, one of Squint's ancestors puzzled over what to do with the antelope bone his mother had given him.)

Eight hundred years—but what years!

The Heechee exploded. There were a billion of them. Then ten. Then a hundred. They built wheeled and rollered vehicles to conquer the unfamiliar surface of their planet, and in no more than a couple of generations were off into space on rockets; a few generations more, and they were searching the planets of nearby stars. They learned as they went. They deployed instruments of immense size and great subtlety—a neutron star for a gravity detector; an interferometer a light-year across to catch and measure the radio waves from galaxies whose red-shifts approached the limit. The stars they visited and the galaxies they gazed at were almost identical with those seen from Earth—astronomical time does not trouble with a few hundred thousand years—but they saw more keenly and understood more thoroughly.

And what they saw and understood was, at the end, of surpassing importance to them. For Albert's conjecture was true—nearly true—true in every detail up to the point at which it became terribly false.

As a result of their understanding, the Heechee did what seemed to them best.

They recalled all their farflung expeditions, tidying behind them to carry away everything that might be useful and could be moved.

They studied some million stars and from them chose a few thousand—some to cast away, because they were dangerous, some to bring together. It was not hard for them to do. The ability to cancel mass or create meant that the forces of gravity were their servants. They selected a population of stable stars and long-lived, winnowed out the dangerous ones, and brought them together, or near enough together to do what they wanted off them. Black holes come in all sizes. A certain concentration of matter in a certain volume of space and gravity wraps it closed. A black hole can be as big as a galaxy, with its component stars hardly closer than in our own. The Heechee's plans were not so grand. They sought a volume of space a few dozen light-years across, filled it with stars, entered it in their ships. . . .

And watched it close around them.

From that time on the Heechee were sealed off from the rest of the universe, burrowed into their nest of stars. Time changed for them. Within a black hole the flow of time slows—slows greatly. In the universe outside more than three-quarters of a million years went by. Within, what seemed to Captain no more than a couple of decades. While they were stamping out comfortable nests for themselves in their captured planets (long since hewn into livability; they had had nearly a century in which to work), the mild, gentle Pliocene epoch gave place to the storms and siroccos of the Pleistocene. The Günz ice crept down from the north, and retreated; then the Mindel, the Riss, the Würm. The Australopithecines Captain had kidnaped—to help along, perhaps, or at least to study in the hope of finding hope in them—disappeared, a failed experiment. Pithecanthropus appeared, and was gone; Heidelberg man; the Neanderthalers. They crept north and south as the ice directed, inventing tools, learning to bury their dead and ring them with a circle of ibex horns, learning—beginning to learn—to speak. Land bridges sprouted between the continents, and were washed away. Over some of them scared, starving primitive tribes crept, a wave from Asia that ultimately flowed down from Alaska to Cape Horn, another wave that stayed where it was, growing pads of fat around the sinuses to shield its lungs against the stinging Arctic cold. The children that Captain fathered in the warrens of Venus, and kept with him while he and his teams surveyed the Earth and selected the most promising of its primates for acquisition, were not yet fully grown when homo sapiens learned the uses of fire and the wheel.

And time passed.

Each beat of Captain's twin hearts took half a day in the universe outside. When the Sumerians came down from their mountains to invent the city on the Persian plateau, Captain was invited to participate in the forthcoming anniversary talk. As he prepared his guest list, Sargon built an empire. While he instructed his machines with the program for the meeting small, shivering men hewed blue stone into menhirs to form Stonehenge. Columbus discovered America while Captain was fretful over last-minute cancellations and changes; he finished his evening meal while the first human rockets tottered into orbit and decided to stretch his legs before retiring as a human explorer, wild with surprise, broke into the first Heechee tunnel on Venus. He slept through the time of Robin Broadhead's growth, puberty, voyage to Gateway and voyages from it, the discovery of the Food Factory, the decision to explore it. He half woke just as the Herter-Hall party was starting its four-year climb to orbit, and went back to sleep—to him it was the equivalent of less than an hour—through all their wearying trip. Captain, after all that, was still relatively young. He had the equivalent of a good ten years of active, energetic life ahead of him—or what the outside universe would see as a quarter of a million years.

The purpose of the anniversary meeting was to review the Heechee decision to retreat to a black hole, and to contemplate what else might need be done.

It was a short meeting. All Heechee meetings were short, when they were not social and prolonged purely for the pleasure they gave; machine-mediated discussions eliminated so much waste that the fate of a world could be settled in minutes.

Settled many things were. There was disquieting news. The F-type star they had, somewhat hesitantly, included in their nest was showing some signs which might indicate ultimate instability. Not soon. But it might be well to consider expelling it from their neighborhood. Some of the news was unhappy but expected. The most recent messenger ship from outside revealed no trace of another spacefaring civilization coming to life. Some of it was expected and discounted in advance. The most rigorous theoretical tests had shown that the theory of oscillating universes was correct; and that, indeed, the Mach's-Principle hypothesis (they did not call it by that name) which suggested that at an early point in the Big Bang the dimensionless numbers could be changed was valid. Finally, the decision to so situate themselves that time outside passed forty thousand times faster than in their closed-up sphere was reopened for discussion. Was 40,000 to 1 enough of a gain? It could be made more—as much more as anyone could wish—simply by contracting the size of the hole, and perhaps, at the same time, excluding that troublesome F. Studies were ordered. Congratulations were exchanged. The meeting was over.

Captain, his work for the time through, went once again to the surface for a stroll.

It was daylight now. The transparent screens had darkened themselves accordingly. Even so, fifteen or twenty bright stars shone in the blue-green sky, defying their sun. The captain yawned widely, thought of breakfast, decided instead to relax. He sat drowsily in the tawny sunshine, thinking of the meeting and all that surrounded it. Heechee-human similarities were great enough for the captain to be a little disappointed, on the personal level, that those creatures he himself had chosen and established in the artifact had not come to anything much. Of course, they might yet. The messenger rockets came in only every year or two, as they might have estimated it—more like every fifty thousand years by the standards of human beings on Earth—and a star-going civilization might slip between the cracks. Even if his own project failed, there were still fifteen or sixteen others, all around the Galaxy, where they had seen at least hopeful traces of some-day intelligent life. But most were not even as advanced as the Australopithecines.

The captain sat back in his forked bench, his life-support capsule comfortably resting in the angle beneath him, and squinted up at the sky. *If* they came, he wondered, how would they know *when* they came? Would the sky split open? (Silly, he chided himself.) Would the thin Schwarzschild shell of their black hole simply evaporate, and a universe of stars shine in? Not much more likely.

But, if and when it happened, they would know. He was sure of that.

The evidence was sure.

It was not the sort of evidence that only the Heechee could read. If any of their experiments did attain civilization and science, they would see it too. The anisotropic nature of the 3K cosmic background radiation, showing an inexplicable "drift". (Human beings had learned to read that, if not to understand it.) The physical theory that suggested such fundamental numbers as made life possible in the first place could be changed. (Human beings had learned to understand that, but not to be sure it was true.) The subtle clues from distant galaxies that showed their rate of expansion was slowing down, had already for some of them begun to reverse. This was past the point of human capability for observation—yet; but only, perhaps, by a matter of years or decades.

When it became clear to the Heechee not only that the universe might be destroyed in order to rebuild it—but that Someone, somewhere was actually doing it—they were appalled. Try as they would, they could get no fix on Who was doing it, or where They might be. All that was sure was that, with Them, the Heechee wanted no confrontation.

So Captain, and all the other Heechee, wished their experiments great wisdom and prosperity. Out of charity and kindness. Out of curiosity. And out of something else. The experiments were more than experiments. They were a sort of buffer state.

If any of the experimental races the Heechee had started truly had flourished, they might by now be truly technological. They might by now be finding traces of the Heechee themselves, and how awed they might be, the captain thought, by those evidences the Heechee had left behind. He tried to smile as he formed the equation in his mind: "Experiments" (are to) "Heechee" (as) "Heechee" (are to) ... "Them."

Whoever "They" were.

At least, Captain thought grayly to himself, when They do come back to reoccupy this universe that They are reshaping to suit Their whims, They'll have to get through those others before They get to us.

Frederik Pohl has been about everything one man can be in the world of science fiction: fan (a founder of the fabled Futurions), book and magazine editor, agent, and, above all, writer. As editor of *Galaxy* in the 1950s, he helped set the tone for a decade of SF—including his own memorable story such as *The Space Merchants* (in collaboration with Cyril Kornbluth). His recent works include *Man Plus, Gateway, Jem* and his memoirs, *The Way the Future Was*. Pohl travels extensively during the year on the lecture circuit; he lives with his family in New Jersey.